The Familists

V.E.H. Masters

Books by VEH Masters

The Seton Chronicles:

The Castilians
The Conversos
The Apostates
The Familists

First Published in Scotland in 2023 by Nydie Books

A CIP catalogue record for this book is available from the British Library

Paperback ISBN 978-1-8382515-7-4

Also available as an ebook, ISBN 978-1-8382515-8-1

Cover Design: Mike Masters

Maps and images reproduced with kind permission of the National Library of Scotland, Deutsche National Bibliothek and Bibliothèque de Genève

www.vehmasters.com

For Mike

And our wonderful grandchildren; Aliya, Oban, Ash, Maia, Hannah, Ayla and Kyle.

STEL *nouo dou sta*
fero del gran Turcho

SLea

S.Andrea

LAVVLACA

ARSENALE

Porta leuas de
le Reui

S.Lucas
Eraimophia

Family, in the 1500s, referred to a collective group forming one household which included parents, children, servants and anyone else living permanently within the household.

The Players

Bethia, a Scottish Catholic who is married to Mainard and has fled with him across Europe to Ancona, Italy.

Mainard de Lange, Bethia's husband, whose family are Conversos originally from Portugal; that is, his parents converted from Judaism under threat of the Inquisition.

Will Seton, Bethia's younger brother, a Protestant and assistant to the reformer John Calvin and with links to John Knox.

John Seton, Bethia's wild youngest brother who lives in a currently Catholic Scotland.

Grissel, Bethia's faithful Scottish servant who ay applies good sense.

Samuel-Thomas, Jacopo and Abram, Bethia and Mainard's children.

Dona Gracia Mendes (1510–69), a Conversa so wealthy she lends money to kings. A great philanthropist, she provides extensive funds to help Jews flee the Inquisition. Through Dona Gracia's influence and support, Bethia sets up her own business.

Don Joseph Nasi (1524–79), a Converso who was also known as Don Juan Micas but changes his name when he reaches Constantinople and reverts to Judaism. He's Dona Gracia's nephew and is also married to her daughter. Mainard is in debt to him and relies on the Mendes family for much of his business.

John Calvin (1509–64), French pastor and reformer who lived in Geneva. The Protestant theology advanced by him, and his followers, is known as Calvinism.

John Knox (1514–72), a leader of the Protestant Reformation in Scotland who lived in Geneva for a time and was influenced by Calvin.

Part One

Will

Winter 1553 to Spring 1554

Chapter One

Ferrara

Will saw the city walls of Ferrara rising above the plain long before he reached them. He'd heard of the Italian engineers, in demand across Europe for their skill in building impregnable fortifications and, as he drew nearer, knew he was seeing a remarkable example of their work. Massive walls and mighty bastions of immense thickness which, unlike the perpendicular walls of the castle in St Andrews, Scotland where he hailed from, were angled so they commanded a much wider field of fire as well as easily deflecting shot. No enemy could attack here without being hit from multiple vantage points and, should they by some miracle manage to reach the wall, the sparkling water of the broad moat surrounding it provided a further barrier.

The barge he'd travelled on from Venice came in to moor amid a plethora of other small vessels. Will said farewell and stepped ashore. The captain raised his hand in salute while shouting at his crew to take care not to damage the cargo of cabinets they'd started to offload.

Will could see guards on the high parapet above watching. He gripped the pommel of his sword with one hand and patted his jacket with the other, hearing the comforting rustle of paper. The letter was safe.

He crossed the bridge over the moat and the captain of

the guards was called to peruse Will's credentials at the gate. The fellow read slowly, lips moving, then passed the papers back, stained by his greasy fingers. Will relaxed his shoulders as he was waved through. He made his way along the broad street, eyes fixed on the castle dominating the city and built of the same warm red brick as its walls. Although small, the Duchy of Ferrara was widely known as a centre where artists and thinkers gathered under the, generally benevolent, gaze of its dukes.

In front of him a packman led his horse, the animal so heavily laden it sagged in the middle, while a woman equally laden by the bale of cloth on her back trudged next to him. The air was warmer within the city walls after the chill of the river but the drifting smoke from cooking fires soon had Will coughing.

He reached the castle forecourt and stood in the shadow of a nearby house, pausing to listen to the music floating out from the windows above.

The castle, like the walls, had a moat around it with more than one drawbridge by which to gain entry, and all heavily guarded. He had a letter of introduction but was uncertain about the propriety of approaching the Duchess of Ferrara, whom it was addressed to. He decided to reconnoitre the town first.

Skirting the space around the castle, he wove through the worshippers emerging from the imposing doors of the nearby cathedral and turned into a broad piazza. Shops lined it, their sagging roofs propped against the long side wall of the cathedral. The market traders were packing up for the day in a great bustle, children and dogs waiting to scavenge what they could. Will tightened his hold on the satchel swung over his shoulder; it contained all he owned. A child, thin-faced, barefoot and dressed in a dirty tunic which was too small for her, glanced up at him and gaped. Will relaxed his grip. He was acting as fearful as a wee lassie, for he towered head and shoulders above the crowd, much like the castle of this town rose above its streets. He tossed her a coin and moved on.

Beyond the marketplace he ventured into a maze of narrow twisting alleys, cool and dim. A group of men with long beards and bright eyes emerged from a doorway; they conversed with great animation, pointing and gesticulating, fingers wagging, faces thrust close to one another in passionate debate as they walked away. He peered inside the dark tiled entrance hall. A fellow appeared from the gloom, head inclined inquiringly. He said something.

Will shook his head. 'I've little Italian.'

The fellow smiled and spoke again in French, pink tongue visible mid the grey beard. 'This is a synagogue.'

Will flushed and retreated.

'An Englishman?' said the man, coming to stand in the doorway. 'With the red hair like your King Henry.'

'Scottish,' said Will abruptly. He didn't care to be compared with the now dead Henry VIII. If it hadn't been for him and his machinations Will most likely wouldn't have ended up a galley slave.

He bowed and strode away. Still, it was of note that Jews lived freely within Ferrara and without the yellow hat they were required to don in Venice. Perhaps similar tolerance was accorded to Protestants, especially with the rumours its duchess was showing a marked inclination towards that religion. The knot of fear loosened.

Will found an inn opposite the cathedral and close by the castle. It was crowded with men in the rough grey woollen tunics of workers drinking fast and talking loud. He was directed to a quieter section where the customers, by the quality and colours of their clothing and the feathers in their caps, clearly had more to spend. He was pleased to be accorded a space among them and grateful to his brother-in-law for gifting him a doublet which, although worn, was made of silk and dark-coloured – the most difficult dyes to achieve – and thus signifying the wearer was a man of substance.

He was glad to sit down and rest his elbows on the board but could feel the edge of one of the few gold coins sewn in the lining of his waistband digging into his skin. He shifted, trying to reposition it and not wanting to think of what he'd do once the coins were all spent – but the fear rose up again tight as a noose around his neck.

The innkeeper came with a plate of fish, the head flattened with milky glazed eye. Will swallowed. 'Have you nothing else?'

'It's Friday,' said the man dourly.

'Bring me some bread and cheese.'

'You don't want the fish? It's fresh caught from the river.'

Will thought of the men he'd seen releasing their stream into the grey waters of the river. 'Just the bread and cheese,' he said, grateful the fellow understood French.

'Where do you hail from, traveller?' said a hearty voice, and Will swung round to see a ruddy smiling face. The man's tunic was strained tight across the belly and he was so large his buttocks overspilled the stool they rested upon.

'Venice.'

The man pursed his large lips – was there no part of him not fleshy as an over-ripe peach – and winked. 'You're no Venetian. More a giant of the north.' He narrowed his eyes and inclined his head, all the while staring at Will. 'One of those dark, cold countries where they take life seriously and where the frivolities of Venice would be frowned upon.'

Will stared at this fat fellow wondering whether to take offence, indeed would likely have risen to his feet and departed were it not he'd nowhere to go. The man's lips spread almost as wide as his broad face and he let out a laugh, which travelled down his whole body so that his belly jiggled.

The innkeeper returned with Will's repast, and the fat fellow slid his stool over and joined him, saying, 'Let's break bread as two travellers together.'

'Where are you from?' said Will, and the fellow pushed himself to his feet and bowed with a flourish of his bonnet.

'Giscard Ory of France at your service.'

Will stood up and bowed in return. 'William Seton of Scotland at yours.'

'Ah. And what brings you to the fine city state of Ferrara?'

Will stretched out one leg and then the other, realising he should've had an answer ready for such a question, but best to stay as close to the truth as possible. 'I have a letter to deliver.' He paused and stared into Ory's eyes, which gleamed out amid the puffy face and froth of beard. He looked benign enough but spies were everywhere.

'This is your first visit?'

Will nodded.

Ory lifted his chin and stretched his neck like a baby bird seeking food. 'Scotland you say, home of the young Queen Mary currently residing in France.'

Will opened his mouth to tell of how he once met, even spoke to the wee queen, and closed it as quickly. It would require an explanation of how he happened to be on the galley transporting her to France.

'A good Catholic country, although like everywhere these days the so-called reformers cause trouble.' Ory squeezed his eyes shut then opened them wide. 'There was a siege in that Scottish town where the pilgrims went. What was its name?' He paused but Will said nothing. 'St Andrews, that was it. We French saved the day and sorted those Protestant bastards out.'

Will went still as the sea in the eye of a storm. If he was a true follower of right-thinking then he should call this fat Catholic out, should not be hiding his beliefs, should stand tall as Christ once did. He wondered what John Calvin or John Knox would do in this situation. Yet he knew both Protestant leaders chose their moments of challenge with care. It would benefit the true religion little if he got into a fight now.

Ory leaned in confidentially. 'You're here for the hanging?'

Will near fell off his stool. 'I know nothing of a hanging.'

'It's tomorrow. Fantini, the duchess's confidant, is to be executed and his body burned not ten steps from where we sit. He is one of those reformers. The duke is a patient man where his duchess is concerned but she pushed him too far.' He leant in confidentially. 'I hear she's naught but a heretic herself.'

'Will she be here?' said Will, disregarding the invective sprayed at him and calculating what his chances might be of approaching her with Calvin's letter if she were.

'That's a fair point, my friend. Would've been better if she were forced to watch the hanging, for a duke must rule in his own castle, even if his wife is a princess of France.'

Will looked away, the sight of the soggy lump of bread moving around Ory's open mouth making him nauseous.

Ory was speaking again and Will realised he'd missed what the fat man was saying.

'…have recently gone to Consandolo.'

Will ran his tongue around the inside of his dry mouth. 'And what is at Consandolo?' he said hoarsely.

'Consandolo is where the Duchess of Ferrara, Renée of France, lives in the large house presented to her by her most generous and forbearing husband.'

Will swallowed. All he need do was quietly slip away from one Giscard Ory and find his way to Consandolo, wherever that was.

Chapter Two

Renée of France

The Duchess of Ferrara's home at Consandolo was a gracious villa bounded by gardens and with a range of buildings to house the French court which surrounded her. It sat amid marshland, and Will considered it would be a most unwelcoming place in the summer – likely plagued by all manner of biting insects. Fortunately it was winter now.

He was curious to meet this erstwhile princess. As a child, so the stories went, she'd shared her lessons with a former queen of England, Anne Boleyn – to have been one of Henry's wives was as dangerous as being Protestant in a Catholic country, he thought.

He'd wondered at Duke Ercole gifting his duchess a villa fifty miles from the castle at Ferrara, but overhearing a group of gossiping men at the inn last night he now understood.

'Sons must marry where their fathers direct and do their duty by the wife however little she may be to their taste.' The speaker leant back in his seat and his audience had nodded at the words of wisdom.

'Very true, very true,' said another. 'And most unfortunate for the duke that his duchess could not be described as a pretty woman. Still, he got her with child five times. She did well producing the son first, but then three daughters followed and a duke must have a spare. Ercole kept to his duty until the second son was finally birthed.'

'Better than many wives manage,' said another. And Will, gazing at his face, pitied any wife living with such bitterness.

'The old duke should never have made the match with the king of France in the first place. Treachery and trickery from the beginning: no sooner was the treaty signed and the marriage consummated than that duplicitous king reneged on their agreement and aligned himself with the Hapsburgs, who, greedy as pigs, gobble up duchies.' He turned and spat on the rushes strewn across the floor, narrowly missing Will's leg.

'Ah well, the duke was fortunate to have had a place to which his ugly wife could remove herself.'

The first speaker sniffed. 'It wasn't only her face he wanted removed but her heretical practices.'

Will straightened up, eager to hear more, but the speaker, alerted by his sudden movement, buried his face in his tankard and turned the subject to the paucity of the grape harvest.

A fly danced in front of his face as Will waited at the gates; not cold enough to keep them away after all. He shifted from one foot to the other as the guards gazed impassively past him. Just when he feared he'd be relieved of Calvin's letter and turned away, a woman came. She was attended by a servant and, for a moment, Will thought it might be the duchess herself, for she was richly dressed in a flowing gown of pale green satin, the front panel embroidered with flowers and a high ruff around her neck; obviously French, as no Venetian woman would so conceal their décolletage. But looking down into her face he realised she was much too young, and pretty if his informants of last night were to be believed, to be the duchess.

'Duchess Renée would like to speak with you,' said the young woman in a clear, light voice. Will felt a shiver run down his spine. It was a most peculiar sensation, as though his future were foretold. He shifted his gaze past her. Those green eyes were a deep enough pool for a man to drown in, if he didn't take care. He expected her to lead the way but it seemed she was in no hurry.

'You were recently in Geneva.'

Will inclined his head.

'What were you doing there?'

Will considered his answer but then shrugged. By all accounts Renée's court had staunch Protestant leanings. It was not a time for dissembling.

'I was assistant to Calvin and taking instruction to become a pastor.'

The young woman's eyes narrowed, and Will, forgetting himself, gazed into them. He blinked, batted at a fly before his own eyes, although truth be told he was by no means certain there was one, while this composed young woman led him to her duchess.

Renée of France was small, made more so encased as she was in the great folds of a red satin dress with high neck ruff and an elaborate headdress. He couldn't help but notice the smooth hair drawn beneath it was of a similar colour to his own red mop. He made his obeisance, bowing low, and she held out her hand for him to kiss.

'You're a man of Scotland,' she said in a soft, quick voice.

'I am, my lady.'

She held Calvin's letter up. 'Monsieur Calvin commends you… high praise indeed.'

Will bowed once more but not so low. 'I am grateful to him.' He glanced up. 'Calvin says you are most learned.' Then wondered at his own temerity to offer an opinion uninvited.

Fortunately she smiled. 'Then we both have cause to

be grateful to him. I'm glad he has sent you. Right-thinking people are always welcome at my court.'

'I thank you most humbly for your graciousness,' he said, bowing yet again.

And she smiled, a smile of such warmth Will wondered why he'd thought this small woman ordinary to look upon.

The duchess waved her hand and the audience was at an end.

'I'll speak with the housekeeper,' the young woman said once the door was closed behind them, 'and she'll attend to your needs.'

Will let out the breath he hadn't realised he'd been holding. He had sanctuary again, at least for the time being.

They crossed a courtyard skirting a group of men at their sword work and he was left with the housekeeper. As soon as the young woman had gone, leaving a delicate scent of rose petals floating behind her, he inquired who she was.

'For in meeting the duchess, such courtesy was forgot and she has the advantage of me, being already in possession of my name.' He stuttered to a halt knowing he was over-explaining a simple request.

'She is Cecile Beranjon, most faithful attendant to our duchess.'

Cecile, Will repeated to himself as he followed the housekeeper.

She showed him to a small chamber high up in the villa, but not so high it was in the attics. He was delighted to discover he was to have the room and bed to himself. He was even more surprised, the next morning, to be called to the duchess's presence and introduced to her daughters and the great flurry of women and men surrounding her. He realised his first meeting with her had been unusual, for Renée barely moved without her French court clustered close. One of the men he'd seen yesterday came and spoke, saying his name was Dauvet, and Will asked to join their swordplay, 'for I am sadly out of practice.'

'You would be most welcome, since our group is small we are all too familiar with one another's feints and dashes,' Dauvet responded.

Will found himself enjoying his time in Consandolo and soon fell into a pattern. He joined the group of men each day for sword work and was provided with the use of a fine horse when they hunted across the flatlands, even receiving some tuition in how to fly a hawk.

He had some new clothes fashioned more in keeping with the style of the court, which were constrained in comparison to what was worn in Venice but still more lavish than he'd ever owned before. The doublet he was especially delighted with and could not help spreading it out across his bed and stroking the soft nap when was alone in his chamber.

Yet he was made uneasy by his self-indulgence and hoped some levity, in what up to now had been a most God-fearing life, was not too much of a sin. When he was no more than sixteen years old he'd been among the group who took St Andrews Castle, at seventeen he was imprisoned as a galley slave and since then he'd most earnestly followed first John Knox and then John Calvin. And when would he, a merchant's son, ever again get to play amid the aristocracy.

Although it was winter there was a picnic one day in the woods. A lavish affair with many servants in attendance and a great bonfire in the centre which the young, and some not so young, prodded with long sticks. He learned to play *jeu de paume*, a game where players hit the ball with the palm of their hand instead of with a racquet. Musical soirees were held most evenings – Will now could tell the difference in sound between a harp and a mandolin – and sometimes there was dancing, which he watched from a window embrasure, his eyes invariably drawn to Cecile Beranjon.

He was surprised the Protestant-leaning duchess encouraged dancing, since it was forbidden in Geneva. But then the religious practices of Consandolo were an odd mix of Catholic and Protestant, from what he could ascertain. He did wonder that the duke tolerated such religious separation within his household but, when he discreetly inquired as to why, his question was greeted with wry amusement.

'You've seen the duchess. What is that word you Scottish people are so fond of to describe the prettiness or otherwise of a woman?'

Will rolled his eyes, couldn't think for a moment. 'You mean bonny.'

Dauvet had licked his finger then run it across one eyebrow, licked it again and smoothed the second eyebrow, then confirmed what Will had already overheard at the inn. 'She would not have been the duke's choice. You'll have noticed that besides verging on ugly, she was born with a twisted spine, giving a most peculiar shape to her back.'

Will had observed the way the duchess's back humped at one side, although it was mostly well concealed by the capes she wore. Yet he didn't agree she was an unattractive woman – there was something very attractive to him about any woman continually in search of learning, and who endeavoured to follow her conscience.

'And,' said Dauvet, 'the duke must tread warily. The duchess has no compunction about seeking assistance from her powerful relatives should her husband bring any pressure to bear. There have been several times when Ercole has been left twisting and turning in the wind as both the king of France and the Pope have risen to her defence.'

'But I don't understand. From what I've observed, and indeed heard from her own lips, she is a Protestant.'

'Hush, we don't say that aloud.' Dauvet paused. They'd strolled to the stables and were looking over the new stallion which Renée's younger son had ridden in from Ferrara. He bent and smoothed its hocks. 'Looks to have over-slender legs for such a big beast. Young Luigi best take care not to ride it too hard else he may find himself landing on the ground with unexpected suddenness.' He straightened up and gazed at Will. 'It's all about power and alliances. The king of France will not tolerate a princess of his realm to be accorded any less than her full rights. He's determined that the duke will show her due deference and exerts his influence accordingly. That's she permitted to command her court as she sees fit is all that is needful to the king – that she's determined to follow the Protestant faith is a lesser matter.'

Will was quiet as he absorbed these words. 'So it's likely she'll be left to pursue the true faith.'

Dauvet raised his eyebrows. 'She must tread warily for all that she has powerful relatives. It's fortunate she has her priest, Richardot, to guide her.'

Will heard voices as some other fellows came to admire the stallion and no more was said. Yet he wondered how far the Catholic Duke of Ferrara would let a Protestant court go before he intervened.

Chapter Three

The Nicodemite

Days passed, each one of pleasure and ease. The duchess seemed to approve of Will's new garments and awarded him a small pension as one of her courtiers.

He ordered new boots from the cordwainers and the duchess heaped praise upon him. 'It is a delight to look upon a man of your height and breadth of shoulder. Are all the men of your country of such size and strength?'

Will, never having received such approbation from anyone, and especially not the daughter of a king, basked in her words like the sun breaking through the dense fog which pressed against the windows and blanketed the fields beyond the villa.

'Your royal highness is too kind.'

'You must not call me highness now. I've been a duchess these twenty years.'

He bowed. 'Your royal duchess.'

There was a tinkle of laughter. 'The men of Scotland are most charming,' she said to the ladies surrounding her.

Will was grinning in response when he caught Cecile's eye. She was not smiling, indeed was looking gravely at him. Will shifted his gaze away. She was only one of several young women in the duchess's court, and not the prettiest either. His eyes flicked to the girl standing next to her with the yellow hair and blue eyes – much more attractive and with a becoming softness of manner. He looked back at Cecile but she was gazing over his shoulder. Will became aware his sparring partner was watching. Dauvet winked at him, and Will raised his eyebrows in return, but really felt as irritated as though he'd an infestation of fleas.

Dauvet came and tugged on the back of his jerkin. 'Time for today's practice,' he murmured.

Renée gave a wave of her hand, and the two men, taking it as a signal they were dismissed, made their bows and retreated. 'You need to watch that one,' said Dauvet once they were outside. 'You wouldn't be the first fool to be caught by those wildcat eyes.'

Will chewed on his lower lip. 'No, I prefer the blue-eyed one. She has a gentler spirit.'

'You are correct, gentle to the point of sending any man to sleep, which green eyes will never do. Yet who wants a woman who can argue as well as a man.'

'Indeed,' said Will, shutting down the memory of the absorbing debates he used to have with Mainard's sister, Katheline. But he wasn't about to allow himself to be dangled like some marionette on strings by another woman. First Marjorie, who choose John Knox over him, and then Katheline had toyed with him. Women were best avoided.

They ran through a series of exercises with the swords then began to fence in earnest, but Will made a poor show of it. Dauvet chided him for his absent-mindedness and Will decided he'd better pay attention, either that or be thoroughly bested by the older man.

He was aware he'd been adopted by these nobles as a kind of pet. And one day they took him to the nearby town. Will thought it was a singer they were going to hear, which sounded a harmless entertainment. It was only when he'd been herded inside, caught in the middle of this group of so-called friends, he realised he was within a bordello. The young women came swarming over them showing more feminine flesh than Will had glimpsed in all his twenty-three years. Dauvet whispered to one and she went to Will and tugged on his arm, insisting he rise and follow her. He pulled away but she held on most determinedly while his companions urged him on, shouting he was man enough and could manage her. Men at other tables joined in and soon everyone in the place was hammering on the board and calling *Allez-y*.

Mortified, Will rose slowly to his feet and allowed himself to be led from the room. He was both reluctant and yet curious. Once in the chamber the young woman slid her wrapper off and encouraged him to touch her. Her skin was wondrous soft and suddenly he was eager. She guided him and he did the necessary. When he returned red-faced to his seat soon after, he was loudly cheered. Already he felt shamed by his urgency, and shamed he could not now say to his future wife, whoever she may be, that he came to the marriage bed as pure as she. He knew that neither his old mentor Knox nor his new one Calvin would have approved of his actions.

His fellows chaffed him mercilessly and were surprised when he steadfastly refused to accompany them again. Soon they were characterising him as dour, or the French *bute*. And Will didn't care whether he was dour or *bute*, it was not his intent to become the entertainment for a group of bored aristocrats. He began to spend time riding out alone, casting his mind over his days as a pastor in Geneva. It was a relief to leave matters of the flesh behind and return to matters of the soul.

One day in February he was called to attend the duchess and found both Cecile and Richardot, the duchess's priest, sitting with her, but, unusually, no one else from the court.

'Master Calvin tells me you're a most learned young man, wise beyond your years, especially in the tenets of the faith,' Renée began.

Will looked from her to Cecile to Richardot. The priest was a thin man, almost as tall as Will, with a permanent stoop. He stood behind the seated Renée, rising over her like a crow in his black gown. Will had heard tell she referred to him as her kindly spectre.

'Although I've yet to see much evidence of any attention to doctrine. Since you arrived here, you seem to place far more emphasis on physical activity than anything cerebral. Yet Calvin assures me I'll find a knowledgeable advisor in you, if I dig deep.' She paused, clearly awaiting a response.

'I am glad to serve your royal highness in whatever way may be most useful, and thank you for your great kindness to me.' He knew he was babbling but couldn't think what to say.

'In Consandolo we work to follow the principles Calvin espouses, but this must be tempered by maintaining the goodwill of my husband. My faithful Richardot,' she turned and glanced up at the priest, 'has been astute in the guidance he's offered so I may balance my spiritual practice along with the duke's desire that I follow certain Catholic rituals. However, Cecile here, in her greater wisdom, has determined Richardot's views to be unsound.'

Will watched as Cecile opened her mouth to speak, but Renée held up her hand and continued.

'I do not have wise Calvin near, and he has suggested you may be an appropriate substitute.'

Will swallowed, his throat dry, wondering what Calvin wanted of him.

'As you're no doubt aware, we celebrate Mass here.'

Will was fully aware and had avoided attending.

'Richardot and I have discussed it many times, and he's of the opinion, with which I have concurred, that attending Mass is not only permissible for a Protestant but may even be advisable when refusal to attend could be offensive or upsetting to weaker Christians.'

The priest leant forward so that the sleeves of his gown came close to brushing the top of the duchess's head. 'God looks at the heart and sees who is true and who is not,' he said, his voice raspy and nasal. He tugged a handkerchief from his pocket and blew his nose loudly, making the duchess jump. She turned, glaring at him, and he stepped back.

Will waited, wondering what he was meant to say. The silence stretched. 'I'm sure your highness will have considered Calvin's view on this subject,' he said eventually.

Renée sighed; the sharp point of her shoe was visible beneath her dress, tapping. Will realised she wanted his perspective and, most probably, did not want to discuss Calvin's thoughts and, no doubt, instructions. He suspected that she would prefer he agreed with Richardot.

'Forgive me.' He bowed. 'This is a matter of import which I must think and pray on, so I may give a considered response.'

Richardot's face flushed and he bent to whisper in the duchess's ear. She flapped her hand for him to move away. 'I know he's young, but Calvin speaks most highly of him and Calvin is not a man to bestow praise where it hasn't been earned.'

It was Will's turn to flush.

'I look forward to hearing your cogitations, let us say within two days?'

Will thought he needed more time, but it was an order and not a request. 'I am for the library then and will put my thinking cap on.'

His forced jocularity did not raise a smile, and the duchess flicked her fingers in dismissal. He was surprised to find Cecile beside him as he left the chamber.

'Thank you,' she said as they walked along the wood-panelled passageway. It was lined with portraits, and

Will could never feel entirely easy at being observed with such severity by the many deceased members of the Ercole dynasty.

He frowned. 'What are you thanking me for?'

'Richardot is prevaricating. We cannot straddle faiths. We are either Protestants or Catholics... unless we're to set up a third religion which essentially is about saving our skins depending on the prevailing mores of the time and where we happen to live.'

They stopped outside the library and she touched him lightly on the arm. 'Calvin did write most favourably of you.'

She moved away before Will could formulate a reply and he stood gazing at her retreating figure. Her skirts were so wide they brushed the sides of the passageway and yet she moved light as a small bird.

The range and quantity of material Renée held within her library was remarkable. She had at least as many books as Calvin and the contents of this room alone must be worth a small ransom. He should've entered this treasure trove sooner and was again ashamed he'd wasted time on inconsequential matters. He pulled a tome at random from the shelves, and a smile crept across his face when he read the title, *De revolutionibus orbium coelestium*, the work of Copernicus. A first edition too, which was said to be the last thing he'd looked upon before his death. Will's smile grew broader as he remembered younger brother John's absorption in the book, which had been smuggled into their home, his arguments with their father and their mother's shouted plea that she cared not whether the sun rotated around the earth as long as she could have some peace. His smile faded when he thought on Calvin's view of Copernicus's work and he went in search of Calvin's *Commentary on Genesis*, which he was sure the library would contain. Finding it, he sat on the solid carved chair which dominated the chamber, aware it was most likely for the duchess's use, but really he was weary of perching on stools with his knees knocking his chest. He spread the open book on the board knowing he was allowing himself to get distracted, but this was one way of easing back into the quiet introspection which had formerly been his way of life. He followed the words with his finger looking for the text he remembered.

The circuit of the heavens is finite, and the earth, like a little globe, is placed in its centre.

Well that was clear enough. He turned next to Calvin's commentary on the psalms.

The heavens revolve daily and immense as is their fabric and inconceivable the rapidity of their revolutions yet we experience no concussion. How could the earth hang suspended in the air were it not upheld by God's hand?

How indeed! Reading these confidently written words, Will again felt the rightness of Calvin's thinking. And yet there was still the matter of Servetus, which was why Will had left Geneva in the first place. He leant forward and rested his face in his hands. He sat like that for a long time, only lifting his head when a servant came to tend the fire.

Chapter Four

Cecile

Will was not even given the permitted two days to consider his response to the duchess but was summoned the following morning. Richardot was there, rising up behind her as ever.

'Well, Master Seton. What do you have to tell me of the task I set you? How does your thinking progress?'

Will gulped. He felt like a fly piniened between the duchess's stubby fingers. 'I would not want to give an ill-considered response and am in the midst of organising my thoughts and writing them down.' This was not entirely a lie, for he did *intend* to write them down.

'You have until tomorrow. No more.'

Will bowed his way out. He went to sit in the library, head between his hands hoping inspiration would come. The door opened and he looked up to see Richardot, black gown flapping around his skinny legs and in his hands a pile of correspondence.

'I've brought Calvin's recent letters to the duchess and am happy to talk you through them and give my counter-arguments.'

Will felt the weight pressing down on him lighten. It was a beginning.

'Perhaps I might peruse the letters and then speak with you once I've absorbed the contents?'

Richardot hesitated, crushing the papers in his hand. 'This is complex doctrine and it would be better if a young man such as yourself received support rather than be left to read without guidance.'

Will stiffened. 'I was assistant to Calvin, as well as pastor to a small community in Geneva.'

Richardot's eyes narrowed. 'One has to wonder why you left then.'

Will sat back. 'Master Calvin sent me here.' He knew he was dissembling.

'Then I am at a loss as to why you would have need to peruse his letters if you're already an expert on Calvin's doctrine.'

'I assume the duchess wishes me to read the letters?'

Richardot tutted, dropped them on the board and left the room slamming the door behind him, the effect somewhat marred when his gown caught in it.

Will laid the letters out, smoothing the paper and ordering them by date. Calvin, it appeared, communicated with Renée more frequently than Will had realised, but then he wrote many letters outwith the awareness of his erstwhile assistant. Indeed, the first Will had known of the frequency of Calvin's correspondence with the duchess was when he went to Calvin to say he was leaving. Will frowned, struggling to remember their conversation. He'd been in such an agony of mind after witnessing the terrible end of Michael Servetus all was blurred.

'I know you think me wrong,' Calvin had said, 'but I would remind you again, I never sought such a death for the man.'

Will had stared at Calvin. 'Where in the words of Jesus Christ does he advocate the burning of another human being?' He'd stood up, towering over the old man who had, up until then, been his much-loved spiritual leader. 'Where did Jesus ever say a disagreement with him should be met by cruel death? Where did he say that his enemies should suffer as he had done? He said we must love our enemies, not burn them.'

Will had stopped then for he was trembling; they passed through his body in great shuddering waves.

Calvin had taken his arm and tugged on it. 'Sit down, my son.'

Will sank down; his legs could barely have held him up much longer.

'When you find yourself in a position of moral authority over others, which I have no doubt you will do, as you grow in age and wisdom – although hopefully no more in height,' Calvin had allowed himself a small smile but Will didn't return it, 'you will have to make difficult decisions. Decisions you would rather not have anything to do with. Whether I have erred where Servetus is concerned history will be my judge.' He passed his hand over his face, but Will caught sight of the anguish before Calvin composed himself.

'You are leaving Geneva.'

Will had nodded.

'Where will you go – to your sister in Venice?'

'Most probably.'

Calvin had sighed. 'Venice is much in need of Protestant pastors, but it will be dangerous for you.' He paused, smoothing his cap down over his head. 'Would you be willing to go to Ferrara? It's not far from Venice you know and the duchess is a great friend to the cause. I think she is in need of sound doctrine.'

And Will had agreed, eager to find a place again where he belonged.

He picked up Calvin's letters. His former mentor had made a wrong step but it was the only one. Jesus preached forgiveness; Jesus recognised we all have weaknesses. Calvin had been weak with regard to Servetus; he should have stood up to the synod. And he, Will, had shown naught but weakness since he arrived in Consandolo, but that time was over.

He shuffled through the letters. Richardot had only brought the last few months of a correspondence that had gone on regularly for the past fifteen years at least, if what Cecile had told him was to be believed. There was much here that was fascinating but he should not allow himself to become distracted. It was Calvin's thoughts on the practice of Mass which were the most crucial.

He scanned the letters quickly. Calvin wrote with great affection and, at times, approval.

I have observed in you such fear of God and faithful disposition to obey him.

Will remembered Calvin once saying something of a similar nature to him and how uplifted he'd felt. He brushed the back of his hand across his eyes and bent to the letters once more. And here it was unequivocally…

Mass is a sacrilege and a blasphemy. Mass is the worse kind of idolatry because it is the worshipping of idols in the name of Christ. It makes use of a trust in physical objects for the forgiving of sins rather than in Christ's sacrifice on the Cross.

Calvin had a final word of loving care.

Our good God is always ready to receive us in his grace and, when we fall, holds out his hand that our falls may not be fatal.

Will should remember that himself. Whatever he might do, God would always be there to catch him. But what did Renée want him to say? Calvin's view was unequivocal. They should most certainly not be celebrating Mass in this Protestant court.

He stood up and walked around the chamber swinging his arms. It was as though a heavy weight had slid off his back. Even if he had a father who might support it, he was not for a life of leisure and play. Calvin must be forgiven his one transgression – not that Calvin would care to hear it so worded – but that was how Will thought of it. Forgiveness was the right and true way. But before he could fully gather his thoughts to speak to the duchess, a most upsetting situation arose.

Will had gone riding to clear his head, when Dauvet shouted the news to him. He couldn't believe what he was hearing. 'By whose order has Cecile been arrested?' he called back.

But Dauvet had galloped ahead and his words were left floating on the still air. Will spurred his horse to catch up, knowing he should've obeyed his first impulse and refused to join the ride. The mist was rising off the plain and the horses' legs were half hidden beneath it so the riders in front looked as though they were floating on a ghostly sea, with a yellow-red sun hanging in the sky above. Yet there was a restful stillness about the scene after days of biting wind whipping around the villa, backing down the chimneys and filling the chambers with sooty smoke.

He galloped after Dauvet desperate to discover why Cecile was being held under guard. And where was she being held? Was she locked in her chamber, had they placed her in one of the cells adjoining the guardhouse at the entrance to the villa, or even worse, had they sent her to Ferrara?

He could see Dauvet spurring his own horse and glancing over his shoulder as though inviting Will to race. Will frowned with frustration then deliberately slowed his horse. He wasn't going to play this game. One of the other fellows came abreast and Will called out, 'I hear tell there's been an arrest.'

'Ah, la belle Beranjon. The duchess is very angry with her.' The fellow, Will couldn't remember his name, reined his horse, eyes glinting and eager to tell the tale. 'Come to think of it, I haven't seen you at Mass. Strange that you're permitted not to show and yet Beranjon is arrested for a similar transgression.'

'She refused to attend?'

'Not so much, more she was in attendance and refused to take the sacrament. Declared she could not, in all conscience, take something that is very wrongly called the blood and flesh of our Lord Jesus Christ.'

Will felt as though his eyes were about to burst from his head.

'The duchess commanded her to take the bread and wine and still Beranjon refused. 'Tis a shame you missed it. What a scene there was. Renée was absolutely spitting with rage to have her authority challenged, and before her entire court too.'

'I must return,' Will said with a calmness he most certainly did not feel. 'The duchess has work for me. I've been neglectful of my duties.'

Chapter Five

A Proposal

Cecile had not been imprisoned so much as confined to her chamber and the women she normally shared it with moved elsewhere. There wasn't even a guard in the hallway.

'I don't know who holds the key,' she whispered from behind the locked oak-panelled door.

Will touched the golden wood lightly, running his finger along the grain. 'I'll find out,' he whispered in return. He was fearful it might be the duchess, but, of course, she hadn't engaged in the detail of the incarceration, only ordered it.

He discovered that it was Richardot who had custody of the key. When applied to, Richardot delved deep into the pocket of his black robes and then stood turning the key over and over in his fingers. 'What are you going to say to the duchess?' he asked bluntly.

'I need to speak with Cecile Beranjon so I am clear on all the issues before I go before her royal highness.'

Richardot stood, blinking – then extended his hand with the key lying in his palm. Will was surprised he gave it up so easily.

He'd not considered the impropriety or otherwise of entering the bedchamber where a young woman sat alone. He left the door ajar and stood near it, arms folded.

He felt a stirring as he glanced at the bed and quickly shifted his eyes to gaze at the solemn face before him. God's bones she was pretty, and those strange slanting green eyes would pierce any warm-blooded man's heart.

'You know Calvin would call us all Nicodemites,' Cecile said.

Will drew back at such an impassioned opening, any stirrings quickly subsiding.

'Nicodemus was a rabbi who would visit Jesus only at night for fear of the Jews discovering his Christian leanings,' Cecile continued.

'I know who Nicodemus was.'

'Then you will no doubt also know Calvin said we should not conceal our faith. The way in which we serve Christ and worship God is of great import. The confession of the heart cannot be separated from the confession of the mouth. How can we then, in all conscience, take Mass?'

'We cannot,' said Will, with an equal firmness. 'However, what has given me pause for thought was Calvin's own concealment. I recently learned he came to Ferrara, admittedly nigh on twenty years ago, calling himself Charles d'Espeville. He concealed who he was, may even himself have attended Mass while in Ferrara, and certainly did not openly refuse to do so. And I cannot help question his right to direct, from the safety of Protestant Geneva, the actions of any Protestant living in a most Catholic Italy.'

'Who told you Calvin came here secretly?'

'Richardot.'

'And you believe him.'

'I do. He only confirmed what I'd heard elsewhere.'

Cecile rose and walked to the window. She stood, with her back to Will gazing out on the gardens which Renée had so lovingly created. 'You are correct,' she said, still with her back to him. 'Calvin should not so direct from his place of safety.' She turned suddenly, brows

30

lowered. 'But I believe he is directing from his heart, from true doctrine, from sound thinking.' She tapped her finger on the soft curve of her lower lip.

Will shook his head to clear it of the distracting image.

'And I will remain true to what I believe is right. I will not attend Mass.'

Will nodded. 'And nor will I. But that is a different matter from what I should advise the duchess, a most public and highly visible figure, who is hanging on by the thinnest of threads to the right to direct her life here in Consandolo. The duke, I understand, is coming under increasing pressure to curtail her activities, and he had her adviser Fantini hung. It's only his determination not to allow the Pope to intervene in the internal affairs of his duchy that has prevented the Inquisitor coming here.'

'I know, I know.'

'And that is no doubt why the duchess considered it necessary to confine you.'

'I'm not a fool. You've said nothing I don't already know.'

'You should leave here.'

'So should you.'

'I've already determined to go, once I've spoken with the duchess.'

'Take me with you.' The words burst from her.

Will stared at her. 'Is that what you want?'

'I do.'

I am going to ask you a question and leave you to ponder what your answer might be.'

She stared at him in turn.

'Are you willing to hear my question?'

'I am waiting.'

'I will take you, but only as my wife.'

He hurried out the door before she could answer, but as he locked it, he heard her call out.

'That wasn't a question.'

He strode along the passageway, certain the line of

portraits were winking at him as he passed. He smiled and the smile widened to a grin, couldn't believe he'd had such temerity. And she hadn't immediately said no. He felt his back straighten, was sure his head was near to brushing the ceiling.

He went in search of the duchess, asked to speak with her, and was led almost immediately into her presence. She was, as nearly always, surrounded by her court. Some of the ladies bent over their needlework, one stringing idly on the small harp resting in her lap, Dauvet at the board in the corner with two others, playing cards in their hands, a dog licking its splayed parts with great thoroughness. It was like a painting which had once hung in his brother-in-law's home in Antwerp.

Renée clapped her hands suddenly and demanded that all except Will should leave. 'Well, Master Seton,' she said when the chamber had emptied, the departing court casting curious glances at Will as they passed.

Will didn't prevaricate. 'I agree with John Calvin. The confession of the heart cannot be separated from the confession of the head.' He paused, could see her waiting for further elaboration. 'However, I also consider it all very well for Calvin to direct from the safe haven of Geneva. You have a fine line to tread, my lady, and, although I do not agree with Richardot, I cannot fault him for finding a way for you to follow the faith which also keeps peril at bay.'

She was silent for so long Will feared he'd offended by speaking so plainly.

'I thank you for those considered words. You've reassured me and I will write to Calvin of what you've said.'

Will inclined his head. He was surprised how unconcerned he felt that Calvin would learn that he, a lad from Scotland, had dared to contradict him.

'You're planning to leave us soon?' the duchess said.

Will nodded, surprised by her perspicacity. 'May I

make a request before I go?'

She inclined her head in turn. 'You may.'

'I would like to marry Cecile Beranjon, if she's in agreement, and take her with me.'

The duchess raised both hands and pushed at the headpiece which covered her hair. Her forehead wrinkled and he suspected the weight was paining her. 'That is an excellent solution to a difficulty. I will order it so.'

Will bowed deeply. He'd no intention of marrying without Cecile's agreement but was not unhopeful of her acquiescing. As he left the chamber he could feel a power coursing through him the like of which he'd never experienced before. God willing, he would soon have a wife who shared his beliefs and was as bold as she was beautiful. He could never have imagined such felicity, and God was most assuredly watching over him when his attachment first to Marjorie Bowes and then to Mainard's sister Katheline had come to naught. But he was getting ahead of himself; he should go immediately and discover what the lady's answer was.

Will and Cecile were married three days later. He'd had a moment of doubt beforehand – it wasn't wise to take a wife as he'd little to give. He could apply to his father, and his brother-in-law too would no doubt advance him funds. Yet he couldn't be so dishonest as to borrow monies which he'd no means of repaying. But he spoke with her and Cecile was adamant their faith would see them through whatever difficulties, financial or otherwise, that life might throw at them.

Will had expected it to be a quick, discreet wedding ceremony – only his bride, him and the priest. But Renée entered into the spirit of the occasion, insisting she would hold a wedding breakfast and sending her dresser, along with the headdress she'd worn a few days earlier as a gift to adorn the bride. Will suspected she was seeking distraction, for there was word a Jesuit priest was on his way, sent by the duke.

Richardot had drawn closer to Will recently and showed him a letter from Duke Ercole to his duchess.

'*Et sub viri potestate eris,*' Will read. He looked up at Richardot. '*You shall be under the rule of man?*'

Richardot nodded. And the duchess in turn responded, '*My lord, you are lord over my body but not over my soul.*'

'She's a brave woman.'

'I fear for her.'

Privately, Will thought Richardot should fear more for himself. The duke was unlikely to consign the duchess to the flames but would have fewer qualms about her priest.

Richardot conducted the marriage ceremony the next day.

'He's the nearest thing we can get to a priest of the true religion,' Cecile said when Will asked if she had any objection.

He was relieved, had feared Cecile might insist on travelling with him unwed, until they could be married in Geneva. And, apart from being injurious to both their reputations, the waiting would be interminable. He was eager to make her his own.

They made their vows before the whole court, Renée smiling on. Then Richardot hand-fasted them – tying the ribbon around their wrists to join them together in a most clumsy fashion – but then he was unused to such a procedure, even referring to it as pagan. Will had insisted. It was a tradition in Scotland and he wouldn't feel he and Cecile were truly bound together without it.

The wedding breakfast seemed interminable and yet all too short. Cecile was led away to the bed chamber while Will pressed his hands firmly down on his knees to stop them from jumping. He could see he was being watched. Dauvet was leaning in and saying something to his fellows, who all stared at Will and roared with laughter. Dauvet rose and, grinning broadly, came over and sat down in the chair Cecile had vacated.

'It is as well I introduced you to a woman of the night so you have some idea of where to put it.'

Will scowled at him.

Dauvet's face softened and he patted Will on the arm, leaning in to murmur in his ear. 'Cecile is a fine woman and I know you will be gentle with her. Having had some small practice should mean you can keep the terrible urgency under control.'

Will swallowed. But when, in his nightshirt, he was pushed into the chamber on a wave of laughter and a plethora of lewd comments to find Cecile, in the flickering candlelit, sitting up in bed holding the sheet tight under her chin, he forgot the noise. He strode to the bedside with a confidence he certainly didn't feel and sat down, taking her hand in his. Her eyes were downcast and she was shaking. It was the first time he'd ever seen Cecile not in command of the situation and somehow that steadied him.

'I won't do anything you do not wish me to,' he said.

She looked at him. 'And what of the hordes awaiting the evidence outside the door?'

He rolled his eyes. 'It won't be difficult to provide.' He paused. 'Although I left my clothes, along with my dagger, in another chamber. Perhaps you have a small knife and I can cut my thumb,' he waggled it before her, 'and sprinkle the sheet with my blood.'

She looked at him again from under lowered brows and ran her tongue along her lower lip. He shifted, uncomfortably aware of his response. It was clear she hadn't meant to be provocative; her arms were tightly folded clutching the bedcovers to her.

Will shifted so his lower body was half turned away, tugging on his nightgown to hide the protuberance. A smile crept across her face, although she kept her eyes lowered, but Will was too intent on covering his own embarrassment to care.

There was a sudden banging on the door which made them both jump, followed by a battery of catcalls. Some fellow started singing in a remarkably shrill and tuneless voice.

> *Summer is i-cumin in*
> *Loud sing, cuckoo!*
> *Groweth seed and bloweth med*
> *And springeth the wood anew.*
> *Sing, cuckoo!*

Cecile and he looked at one another and burst out laughing. A shout from outside the door informed them where their attention should be, and it wasn't on laughing. This made them laugh even more, and Will, finding the tumescence had mostly dissipated, was able to move without embarrassment. He stood up, flicked the covers back, and Cecile slid across the bed allowing him entry.

What followed was a night of joy such as Will could never have imagined. He took it slow, as Dauvet had advised, until he could no longer hold the charger back. There was no doubt a moment of pain for Cecile but she bore it with fortitude, and then, he was certain it wasn't his imagination, she seemed as eager as he to take up further exploration and even showed him a few moves, although shortly after dawn, when he was intent on making his third entry of the night, she complained of a great soreness. At once he desisted, all concern. He sat up and could see the white of her face in the grey light creeping through the shutters.

She was looking at him most tenderly. 'I'm sure I will have recovered by this evening.'

He lay down again, drawing her close. 'It is enough, my love. You've been most generous,' He buried his face in her hair, which smelt of the lavender that grew so abundantly in the gardens around the villa. 'I had not known such bliss could exist between man and wife.'

'And more to come,' she whispered.

'More to come,' he repeated, feeling a most unhelpful rise in excitement but great wonder in knowing he had a loving wife who, it seemed, would not only tolerate, but welcome, his attentions.

Chapter Six

Departure

The duchess was no longer attending Mass every day, instead making an appearance every few days. Neither Cecile nor Will went at all – and no demand was made that they should.

They had made no firm plans for departure. Will knew it was unwise to linger, but their nuptials were so recent, surely they could enjoy the comforts of Consandolo for a few weeks. It was spring now and they walked daily in the gardens enjoying the fresh green growth, the call of nesting birds and the sense of renewal.

'I always find it remarkable,' said Cecile, as they strolled arm in arm one day, 'the rose stems look dead then suddenly life pushes through.'

They drew close to the stable yard and Will could see, between the twisted branches of an ancient plane tree, a flurry of activity there. Cecile sought to move closer but Will was wary and insisted they keep to the shade of the tree. A large man was being helped down from a cart and Will gasped when he caught sight of the florid face. He gripped Cecile's arm and hurried away, hushing her when she tried to speak. They found a bench at the back of the walled garden.

'What is it, my love?' she said.

It was the first time she'd so addressed him and Will

38

allowed himself a moment to savour it.

'Will, who was that?'

'A man called Ory, who I met in Ferrara. He seems jovial enough, but behind the corpulent body and wide smiles sits a most calculating mind. I suspect he's a spy for France.'

'That need not affect us.'

'I pray you're correct. In any case, it's the impetus needed for us to make plans to depart.'

Before he could say more, Richardot came striding along the path, black cloak flapping behind like the wings of a corbie.

'I've been ordered to leave,' he called loudly before he reached them. 'Ory and that snake Peltier have devised a seven-point plan which the duchess must abide by or else be confined without books or companions.'

'But they only just arrived?'

'They were in haste to lay all before our duchess.'

Will raised the palm of his hand outwards to slow Richardot down. 'I know of one of the men, Ory, and he's not to be trusted – but who is this Peltier?'

Richardot tutted. 'He also comes by order of the king of France, and is a priest of the Inquisition. How else could he issue orders to our beloved duchess as though she was nothing more than a servant? She'd only returned from playing *jeu de paume* and they insisted, nay demanded, she meet with them immediately.' He rubbed his hands over his eyes. 'She'll never stand it. And her daughters are to be sent away. She is to be kept here without her children, companions or books.' Richardot shuddered. 'It is a most unchristian way to treat the daughter of a king.'

Will and Cecile looked at one another. He could see her beautiful green eyes grow wide. 'And yet the king of France has ordered this, if I understand you correctly.'

'Peltier orders... orders I ask you... who is he to command?' Richardot turned a full circle in his agitation.

After a moment he went on making an obvious attempt to speak with less passion and more gravitas as befitted his holy orders. 'The duchess is to get rid of all her women, the duke will provide more suitable companions.' He paused. 'The king and the duke must be in agreement on this else the duke would not dare to hold a princess of France under what amounts to arrest. Ory says, if she resists, he will report her obstinacy and the king will seize the land she owns in France.'

Will half rose but Cecile gave a light tug on his arm and he dropped back onto the bench again. He glanced at her and she inclined her head towards Richardot, who was still talking, his thin face looking more pinched than ever.

'She's to say Mass every day, although that was not unexpected, recite the rosary and give customary prayers to the Virgin too.'

Will took Cecile's hand under cover of her spreading skirts and squeezed it.

'Can the duchess not return to France?'

'She's begged the king for permission to return. He says she may, but he'll confiscate the property she owns there so she'll be left destitute.'

'And has the duke truly sanctioned what Ory and Peltier, and indeed the king, are commanding?'

Richardot opened his mouth wide to answer, a dark hole in a papery white face, but before he could speak two servants were seen running across the lawn. They arrived breathless, and no wonder, for it transpired Duke Ercole himself had arrived.

Will saw him only in passing: a stocky man with unnaturally large ears and a determined expression on his face. Then he and Cecile were packing their belongings, which were few on his part, but Cecile had a large chest to hold her second and third dresses, three shawls, two headdresses, stockings, four pairs of shoes – how could anyone need four pairs he wondered – a pot of perfume, pots of unguents and sundry other items.

'We must go to Ancona,' he said. 'You know, where my sister is.'

'Surely we are for Geneva, husband?'

Will didn't want to admit he must beg his brother-in-law for the funds to travel. It was a poor kind of husband who couldn't support his own wife.

'And Ancona is in the opposite direction to Geneva, is it not?'

'We can take a ship from Ravenna's seaport.'

Cecile cast her eyes down and Will felt a moment of panic. She regretted marrying him, no doubt. It'd all been done in such a hurry to protect her and he'd never made plain how lacking in substance he was: no home, no visible means of support. He should not have taken a wife – at least not without fully revealing his situation.

'Of course, we must go to Ancona if you wish, husband. Please forgive me, I've been with the duchess since I was a child. 'Tis a big wrench to leave her is all, especially when her situation is so fraught.'

Will was about to point out that Cecile could only make matters more difficult for the duchess if she stayed, but Cecile, his wise wife, was before him.

'Though all things considered, it's probably better for my poor duchess if I go, and go quickly.'

Will smiled, a smile as bright as the shaft of sunlight which was currently reaching between them. His wife was like to an angel and no man could be more blessed than he.

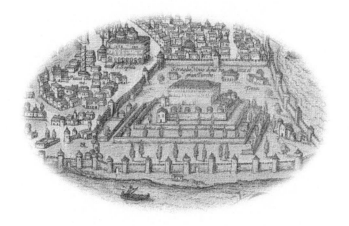

Part Two

Bethia and Mainard

1554 to 1555

Chapter Seven

Ancona

Bethia reached the top of the hill and stood under a cloudless sky with the pale half-circle of last night's moon hanging above. She gazed out at the deep inlet of the bay with the expanse of rich blue sea beyond. In the port, three small ships were being unloaded, a large galleass was coming in and half a dozen more boats swinging at anchor. It felt good to have that long perspective once more, almost as though she was standing on the cliff by the castle in her home town of St Andrews and gazing out upon the German Ocean.

'That's some hill,' panted Grissel, as she struggled up the steep incline to stand beside Bethia. She lowered Abram to the ground and Bethia reached out to grab her youngest child's hand while Grissel wiped the sweat from her forehead with the back of her hand.

'Stay beside us,' said Bethia as Abram tugged to escape. She allowed him to pull her around and he giggled as they circled. 'Where are Samuel-Thomas and Jacopo?' she said to Grissel.

'They were right ahint me,' said Grissel, turning a full circle herself.

'Well they're not there now. Stop, Abram. We must find your brothers.' She looked towards the neighbouring hill, its summit enclosed by the massive ramparts of the Cittadella. The building work had only finished a few years ago and the huge blocks of stone, still looking freshly hewed and unstained, gave off a mellow glow which belied the fierceness of their purpose.

'You should've kept a better watch on them, Grissel.' Bethia set off down the hill with Abram.

She could hear Grissel muttering behind, 'Only if I had eyes in the back of ma heid,' but chose to ignore it. She'd long since given up any attempt to control her unruly servant or any hope that Grissel would ever behave as a servant should. But then, she reflected, Grissel was fiercely loyal and that counted for a lot.

'Nae almond cakes for them tonight,' Grissel was saying. 'It'll be early tae bed without ony supper.'

Bethia caught sight of the reprobates halfway up the side of the hill opposite, climbing fast towards the castle with Jacopo in the lead. She'd no doubt it was the younger boy who had determined the route and Samuel-Thomas was the unwilling follower, anxious his brother came to no harm. She understood all too well; there was forever a knot of fear in the pit of her stomach about Will. She prayed he was safe, for it was some months since she'd last heard from her younger brother.

She set off down the hill and Grissel overtook her, moving at speed. Bethia was chasing after Abram who was birling down the path as fast as his fat wee legs would carry him, when she heard a shout of laughter. Grissel could never stay angry for long, and no doubt Jacopo had managed to charm her. Born in Venice, the joy of that city seemed to have been imbibed into him with her milk. Bethia rubbed her temples. She missed Venice but it'd been wise to leave. Conversos were no longer welcomed there as they'd once been and word had got out that brother Will was a Protestant, so their family were doubly at risk – although how they could be accused simultaneously of being secret Judaisers *and* Protestants escaped her. But anything was possible where the Inquisition was concerned.

Bethia caught up with Grissel and the boys close to the narrow alleyway which led into the maze of small streets around the harbour. She took a last breath of fresh air before the stench of privies, slaughtered beasts, smoke of many fires and the smells wafting from cooking pots assailed her.

Ysabeau was lingering in the entrance hall when Bethia came into the house. Bethia frowned; surely there was work she could be about rather than dithering. The lass stood stroking her rounded belly and gazing vacantly at the floor. Bethia was sure Ysabeau must have conceived on the first night of her marriage. As Grissel said, Johannes was clearly no laggard – most surprising given how diffident and tongue-tied he normally was.

Bethia tapped Ysabeau lightly on the arm and she jumped. She hoped the baby would not be a deaf-mute too, and would pray to the Virgin that Ysabeau's child be whole. But Ysabeau was pulling on Bethia's arm. She went rigid, fearful something had happened to Mainard. Yet Ysabeau didn't look distressed, only eager.

'Grissel, let the children play in the garden. Johannes will keep an eye on them,' Bethia said, divesting herself of her bonnet and light cloak and handing them to Ysabeau. She opened the door to the salon where Ysabeau had pointed, and gasped.

Will rose to his feet and the young woman sitting next to him rose too. Her hair was dark and sleek beneath her headdress, her skin white and smooth, and she had the most curious almond-shaped green eyes.

'Bethia, this is Cecile,' Will said in French. He stood tall, his shoulders broad, chest thrust out and a smile on his face as wide at the Scheldt river which she'd sailed up to Antwerp so long ago now. If a man could be said to burst with pride, then Will looked on the verge of explosion.

'My wife,' he added, quite unnecessarily in Bethia's view.

Cecile lowered her eyes to the gloves she was twisting in her hands and a blush tinged her cheeks. Bethia liked her modesty. With her eyes lowered, Cecile became a demure young bride, but, as Bethia stepped forward to hug her new sister, those green eyes fixed on her like a cat stalking its prey, and Bethia faltered. Instead, she smoothed her own skirt, saying, 'I am most happy to make your acquaintance. Welcome to our home.'

Cecile dipped a curtsy and Bethia one in return.

'Mainard too will be delighted for you both,' said Bethia with a forced gaiety, turning as though Mainard might somehow have magically appeared by her side. She waved her hand at Grissel, who was standing, arms hanging, face turning from one player to the next. 'Some refreshments... and take Ysabeau with you, she looks in need of a rest.'

She gestured to the chairs but Will led his wife to the settle, keeping hold of her hand as they sat down.

Will raised his eyebrows as Ysabeau walked awkwardly from the chamber and Bethia inclined her head.

'Ysabeau is with child?' he said, his voice much deeper than Bethia remembered. Perhaps it was a consequence of becoming a husband, for certainly the small glances, the squeeze of the fingers, the blush which still suffused Cecile's cheeks all pointed towards a most active marriage bed. Bethia shook her head to clear it of thoughts of her brother in blissful congress.

'Ysabeau was recently married.'

Will smiled. Clearly the prospect of any newly married couple made him happy.

'Who is the fortunate groom?' He frowned. 'Is he a deaf-mute too?'

'No, no. It's Johannes. You remember, he was once our potboy in Antwerp but, thanks to Grissel's care, has grown into a fine young man.'

Grissel, manoeuvring her way around the door with

a heavy tray and hearing her name spoke amid the French, glanced at Bethia.

'I was only saying how well you had done by Johannes.'

'Aye, he's no turned oot bad. Although now he's to be a father he's fair awa' wi' himself.'

Will snorted.

'And you can get up and gie me a hand, if you're nae too big for yer breeches.'

'Grissel!' Bethia looked to Will, fearful in his new-found state as a married man he might take umbrage at such familiarity. But he laughed, rose as commanded, and cleared the big account book from the board so that Grissel was able to lay the tray down.

'I see you're still busy about your figures,' he said, smiling at Bethia, and she nodded ruefully in response.

Grissel served the malmsey, taking her own sweet time about it, no doubt hoping to be party to some conversation – but the small group fell silent, watching her as she moved about her duties. Bethia was surprisingly grateful to Grissel for her snail-like demeanour, and didn't understand why she felt so awkward before the married couple. Grissel, of course, felt no such discomfort, and, once she'd finished offering the sweet biscuits, stood with her hands on her hips grinning at Will.

'Ye are married?'

'I am.'

'Aye, I thocht so. I can see it has done ye the power o' good. You look like a new man althegether.'

'That will be all, Grissel,' said Bethia firmly.

'Yes, mistress.' Grissel turned to face Bethia, her back to the married couple, dipped a curtsy and widened her eyes so much Bethia had to bite down on her lip to prevent the laughter escaping.

The door opened and the boys rushed in. Samuel-Thomas stopped suddenly and his smallest brother bumped up against him and sat down with a thud. Abram opened his mouth to howl but Grissel picked him up and whispered in his ear.

'Boys, greet your uncle properly, please,' said Bethia. 'And this is your new aunt. Show her how well you make your obeisance.'

Samuel-Thomas bowed with a serious face, but Jacopo, ever the performer, made his bow with a flourish and a grin. A squirming Abram was released and stepped forward to imitate his brothers. Will stood and bowed back. Cecile's eyes skimmed over the boys and rested on Jacopo. She held out her hand and, without prompting, he bent to kiss it.

'This one will charm all,' she said to Will.

Bethia gazed at her lap, as much to give herself time to think as anything. She wanted to ask what brought them to Ancona, tactfully.

'I am so happy to meet you,' she said to Cecile. She waited and, as the pause lengthened, shifted in her seat. Still Cecile said nothing, indeed behaved as though Bethia hadn't spoken, instead reaching out and pulling Jacopo towards her.

After a moment Bethia rose. 'Excuse me, I will go and speak with the servants about your chamber.'

Neither Will nor Cecile responded, Will because he had his eyes fixed on his bride, and Cecile – Bethia knew not why.

The house was smaller than their previous home in Venice. She would move the older two boys in with her and Mainard, and Abram could sleep with Grissel in her small attic room. She wondered how long the young couple would stay and why they'd left the Duchy of Ferrara. She sighed. No doubt there was disagreement about doctrine involved somewhere. But Ancona was not a safe place for Protestants either.

She gave directions to the servants to prepare the chamber then sat down and scribbled a note to Mainard telling of their visitors and begging that he return home. Once she'd given Johannes the note to deliver she'd no reason not to return to her brother and his wife – although little attention was paid when she did. She wondered if Will had taken his eyes from Cecile at all during her absence. And as for Cecile, she was teaching Jacopo French while Samuel-Thomas stood by frowning, unused to being eclipsed by his younger brother.

Chapter Eight

Family Visit

'I will speak with Will as a matter of urgency,' Mainard promised Bethia when she came rushing into the garden to greet him the moment he passed through the gate. 'But let us at least enjoy this one evening as a family together and celebrate their nuptials before I do.'

When he saw his brother-in-law so happy, Mainard was glad he'd not immediately questioned Will about his plans. Bethia was less sanguine – indeed he'd rarely seen his usually tranquil wife so consumed by anxiety and... decidedly irritable.

'We had to leave Venice because Will turned up unexpectedly, and now he does the same again here. Italy's not some benevolent state he can drift through as it suits him,' she said as soon as Will and Cecile had retired after their evening meal. She walked up and down restlessly, while Mainard sat patiently watching her. He'd spent too long standing today while inspecting a shipment of perfumes, cloth and wax bound for Constantinople. He disregarded the throbbing in his damaged foot as best he could, knew if he evinced the slightest sign of pain then Bethia would be all concern. He'd no patience for being fussed over and must turn his attention to hastening his brother-in-law on his way.

He reached out and caught her by the hand. 'Do you

remember what we were like when we discovered the wonders of the marriage bed?'

He could see her face softening, and the restlessness drained from her like water when the bung is pulled from a bucket.

She squeezed his hand in return and smiled. 'I do, very well.' The faraway look was quickly replaced by her more usual workaday expression. 'It is simple enough. I will tell Will we are likely leaving here so he cannot expect to stay with us for long...' she hesitated, '...and I do not think it will much suit him, as a devout Protestant, to come with us to the land of Islam, if we end up there.'

'There are worse places he could go. I've been told many times of how the Turks tolerate Jew and Christian alike, allowing us all to follow our faith without fear of retribution.'

She flicked her fingers at him. 'I know this, else I'd never consider going there, but I doubt there are many Protestants among the Christian Orthodox. Indeed, I'm concerned I may not find a Catholic church to worship in.'

'Of course you will, in a city the size of Constantinople where so many faiths and cultures come together. But I promise to write to Joao, or more correctly Don Joseph as he's now styling himself, to make certain there is a suitable place for us to worship.'

She raised her eyebrows at him then. 'So you do not intend to follow your sister?'

Mainard smoothed the twin furrows between his eyebrows then looked up at his wife. 'I do not. You and I will remain united in the faith we follow. But speaking of Catarina, I must tell you she recently wrote to me...'

'And?'

'She wants me to exhume Papa and bring his remains with us.'

'What? Why on earth does she want that?'

'She doesn't want him left in Venice, with no family there.'

'I don't understand. Gracia Mendes herself left her husband in the great tomb she built for him in Venice.'

A smile drifted across Mainard's face. 'I think, my dear, were you to investigate Francesco Mendes's sarcophagus you'd find it empty.'

'But why would taking her husband's remains to Constantinople be any better than leaving them undisturbed in Venice?'

'Francesco has journeyed a long way. He died in Portugal, then rested temporarily in Antwerp before his bones were brought to Venice and thence onwards to Turkey. I should imagine Gracia will soon take him to his final resting place in the Holy Land.' Mainard leaned back and stretched his leg out, flexing his aching foot, but Bethia was so caught up in the story she didn't seem to notice. Instead she waited, brow wrinkling, for him to continue.

'It is prophesied that Tiberias is the place where the Messiah will appear and those buried nearby will then be the first to be resurrected,' he said.

She chewed on her lower lip. 'Then we must take Papa there.'

Her reaction surprised him, and it was in such moments he was reminded why Bethia was his beloved and how fortunate he was to have such a wife.

'But,' she added, 'must it be you who disinters him? Surely we could pay someone to bring his remains here to us in Ancona?'

'I would not so dishonour my father. And the only way to be certain it's his bones we carry is to do it myself, else who knows what remains could be foisted upon us.'

A giggle escaped her and he stared.

'Sorry. I was imagining us carrying animal bones all the way to Tiberias and burying them reverentially.'

He smiled wearily, although he was not amused. 'And Dona Gracia sought permission from the Pope to disinter Francesco. It is not so simple.' He leaned back in his chair, 'But, in the meantime the more pressing problem is our newly wedded couple.'

'I'm not sure about her.'

Now Mainard's smile was genuine. 'She'll be a challenging wife for Will, I suspect. She certainly doesn't hold back.' He thought of Cecile at the board that evening correcting Will on some small fact when he told the story of the seven-point plan the Duchess of Ferrara must now abide by.

Bethia reached down and took his hand. Mainard let her haul him to his feet.

'Come, let's to bed and get your foot elevated. Although I doubt we'll be overly comfortable with the boys sharing it.'

Mainard groaned.

He was groaning even louder early the next morning when he was awoken by a small stubby finger poking his closed eyelid.

It was not easy to detach the newly married couple from one another. When Mainard suggested Will come with him to the docks, Cecile stood up saying, 'I'll fetch our cloaks.'

Bethia stepped in then. 'I'd hoped to show you my garden. The blossom on the trees is most beautiful and there is a pretty walk over the hills behind us.'

Will turned to Cecile, saying, 'Yes, my dear, spend some time with Bethia.'

Cecile paused but then bent her head in acceptance.

Mainard and Will set out through the maze of narrow streets that led to the harbour. It was too busy to speak there, especially of such confidential matters. Ancona was no longer the safe haven it'd once been, and for him, a Converso, to be seen in the company of a Protestant was perilous. He could but trust that no one there would know who Will was. He conducted his business quickly and they returned to an empty house.

'You've been fortunate in your wife, I think,' Mainard said as an opening preamble.

'She is an angel and I am the most blessed of men. And especially to find a woman as right-thinking as my Cecile,' said Will fervently. He rubbed his face with both hands, making his fair skin flush even further. 'I had not understood before, you see, the state of bliss that can exist between man and wife.'

Mainard looked down at his feet to hide the smile.

Will's face grew sombre. 'But you will want to know when we are leaving.'

Mainard decided against prevaricating; it would dishonour them both. 'I am sorry it's this way, but life here grows ever more perilous. Were it not for the Mendes family and the duties I'm required to carry out as one of their agents, we'd already have removed to Constantinople or Salonika where my sister resides.'

'Ah, Katheline, how is she?'

'Perhaps you were unaware, but she's known as Catarina now.'

'Yes, yes, excuse me, I forgot.' Will hesitated, then added, eyes downcast, 'I will always think of her as Katheline.'

Mainard decided it was best to ignore that comment. Surely Will no longer thought of Catarina now he had the perfect wife in Cecile. 'I gather Cecile shares the same views as you?'

'Of course. I could not have contemplated matrimony without it.' Will paused. 'I have little in the way to offer a wife. Indeed, if she hadn't been in a most precarious position I wouldn't have had the temerity to marry her.'

'She has no family?'

'No. She came as a child with her father to the court of Renée but he died some time ago. She's no one in the world but me.'

'Grandparents, uncles, brothers or sisters?'

'None.'

'You are in need of funds?'

Will held up his hand. 'I wouldn't ask again, were it not for my wife.'

Mainard contained a sigh. He was not surprised, but he would've been pleased to be proved wrong.

'I've written to my father and hope, if he is generous, I may soon repay you.'

Mainard thought it unlikely. Even if Will's father would overlook the trouble Will's determined espousal of Protestantism had caused the family, Will would need whatever monies he could lay his hands on to support his wife and no doubt growing family.

'I can advance you some funds, enough at least to get you to Geneva. I assume that's where you are headed?'

Will nodded. Mainard could see him swallowing, no doubt disappointed Mainard wasn't offering more.

'I'm sorry, Will, but I have unpaid debts. The de Lange family wealth took a sore hit when we left Antwerp, and with the move from Venice things have again become fraught.'

'I had hoped...' said Will.

But Mainard interrupted him, determined not to weaken. 'I have a family and I must get them safely out of here and settled in Constantinople. I advanced you funds when we parted in Bern and then when you arrived in Venice.' He was about to add, *and I paid for your journey from Antwerp to Geneva,* but contained himself. There was no need to press Will's face further in the dirt.

Will flushed and Mainard felt embarrassed he'd been so emphatic. 'I am sorry. I've many worries at the moment.'

'I thank you, my good brother. If you could help me to discover a ship bound for the south of France then we will be quickly gone.'

'I will make inquiries.' He rubbed the back of his neck then brushed at his breeches to wipe the sweat off his hand. He was relieved to hear the chatter of children in the passageway, a call from Bethia for Samuel-Thomas to take care, Jacopo's giggle – that child was ever finding things to be amused by – the rattle of the latch and then, thank God, his family were among them. Cecile slipped across the room to take her place at Will's side and immediately took his hand in hers. Mainard watched as she looked inquiringly at him and saw Will give the slightest of nods.

Jacopo climbed into Mainard's lap. 'Did you have a good walk?' he said, lifting Abram onto the other knee. Jacopo sprawled out trying to push his smaller brother off. 'Be nice,' Mainard said repositioning him.

'We saw an eagle,' said Samuel-Thomas. 'It was big as this.' He held his arms wide and ran around in a circle to demonstrate.

Jacopo slipped off Mainard's knee. 'No, it was big as this.' He ran in a wider circle.

'We walked up to the cathedral,' said Bethia, coming into the salon while the boys ran in ever wider circles, adding a curious buzzing sound to their interpretation, and Abram watched from the safety of Mainard's lap.

'It was hot,' said Cecile, fanning herself.

'Boys, boys,' called Mainard. 'Since when did birds sound like bees?'

The noise changed to one of loud chirping and the boys ran faster until the inevitable happened and they crashed into one another and went rolling across the floor. Mainard could see Will watching their antics in astonishment.

'Can you imagine,' Will said to Bethia, 'ever conducting ourselves thus in the presence of our father?'

She shook her head.

'A good thrashing would've ensued,' Will added.

Mainard didn't know if this was meant as a criticism of his ability as a parent but didn't care. 'I will never whip my children. Although the rod was applied constantly during my schooldays, my own father never administered such punishment and I had nothing but love and respect for him.'

'Then I salute you. I respected my father but I can't ever say I was eager to be in his company – I feared him too much.'

Bethia shepherded the children out and Mainard excused himself to go to the workroom.

'How was it?' he asked Bethia when she appeared at his side later.

'The walk you mean? Long. Cecile's not an easy woman to speak to. She has a most serious disposition and I don't think she approves of me because I told her I will never become a Protestant. Although...' Bethia giggled, 'she did share some matters of a fairly private nature with me.'

'And?'

'She wanted to know if it was always so vigorous.'

'What?'

'You know... remember when we were first married.'

'Ah.' He reached out and pulled her towards him. 'I have a vague memory.'

'I told her to enjoy it while she may, before children and the burden of responsibilities weigh upon them.'

Mainard gave another tug and Bethia dropped onto his knee. He wrapped his arms around her and nuzzled into her neck.

'Cecile said that Will is like a dog at a bitch in heat.'

Mainard drew back and gazed at her. 'That sounds most inappropriate language from a respectable young woman.'

'I don't think Cecile cares. You know she refused to attend Mass while she was in Ferrara and the duchess had her held prisoner. She was only released when Will said he would marry her.'

'He's a brave man to take on such a determined woman.'

'Will seems to like his women that way. Remember

how he hung after your sister.'

'I do. And am happy for them both that they realised it was unsuitable.' He pressed his lips into Bethia's neck, whispering, 'I take it you're warming to Cecile now?'

Bethia slid off his lap. 'Cecile doesn't overmuch care what I or anyone else thinks of her. It's hard to warm to a woman who exudes such coolness. But watching them together, and after hearing her story, I cannot help but feel glad she makes my brother happy.'

'It is better to like one's relations, if one can.'

'You are becoming very wise, my husband the sage.'

'It matters not greatly though, my love. They'll be gone as soon as I can find a ship to carry them away.'

And although Bethia wept when barely a week later Will and his bride left, he knew she was as relieved as he to see them safely gone.

Chapter Nine

Jews of Ancona

Mainard, reading a note sent by a fellow merchant, considered the ways of the world strange. The current Pope, Julius III, another inevitably crusty old man, had had copies of the Talmud seized and burned in Rome, Bologna and, as Mainard well-remembered, Venice, declaring the sacred book an attack on the Christian faith. Yet he'd recently confirmed that the Jewish residents of Ancona might continue to be treated almost as the equals of their Christian neighbours, might worship and practise their faith without hindrance and – most peculiar of all – had decreed reverting Conversos would have the same freedom of worship as other Jewish residents without fear of punishment. Over and above that, Catholic residents of Ancona were urged to treat Conversos kindly and be accepting of their Jewish origins. It was most puzzling, for apostasy was usually considered a far graver crime than being Jewish. It could be the old man was becoming confused, and his attack on Jewry in most Italian cities, yet protection of them in Ancona, a sign he was indeed in his dotage – or more likely the gifts from the Jews and Conversos of Ancona were greater than from elsewhere.

Bethia came into the workroom, her arms full of these strange flowers come from Turkey called tulips, her step light and face unclouded. He gazed at her and gave thanks again that God should honour him with such a wife. Yet the knot in his gut tightened when he thought of all they had to lose should there be a change of Pope and, inevitably, policy.

Bethia faltered in the doorway. 'What troubles you, my love?'

'You like Ancona?'

'I've grown to like it. Ancona is not the equal of Venice but I prefer the smaller city, more like St Andrews in size. We've a garden for the first time ever,' she indicated the flowers, 'and I've made a few friends, although I could do without the curiosity of our Christian neighbour as to how I, an Old Christian, came to marry a Converso – and whether you are somehow made differently than her husband.'

Mainard, who'd become distracted by the great roll of cloth come from Bombay to be made into turbans which was lying on top of the chest in the corner – he must get Johannes to take it to the seamstress – swung back to his wife. 'Made differently?'

She let out a gurgle of laughter. 'You know, down there.'

'And how have you responded?'

'I have knowledge of no man but you so I couldn't say. I was tempted to ask the details of her own husband's parts and what she imagined the difference to be but did not want to encourage such coarse talk.'

'Very wise.'

'Instead I said you were baptised as a baby, as were we all, and indeed she sees us in church regularly.' She placed the flowers on the board and shouted over her shoulder for Grissel to bring a jug of water.

Mainard gazed at them thoughtfully. 'I'm sure there must be a market for such blooms. They grow from bulbs, do they not?'

Bethia nodded as Grissel marched into the room.

'They laddies will be the death of me,' she said, plonking the jug down so heavily that water splashed out.

'Take care,' said Bethia.

Grissel grunted. 'I made *biscotti* and Jacopo crept into the kitchen and stole half when they were laying on the tray to cool. Then he crushed them in his hand and scattered the crumbs in the garden. He telt me the birds needed them to feed their bairns.'

'That was very naughty,' said Bethia, smothering a smile.

'Send him to me and I will make certain he never does such a wicked thing again,' said Mainard fiercely.

'Aye, no. I can deal with the lad,' said Grissel. 'I maun get on, for the potage willna mak itself.'

Bethia, glancing at Mainard, could see he was holding in the laughter until the door closed behind Grissel. He did laugh but then grew sombre. 'It is funny, I know, but how am I ever to exert any discipline on these wild sons of ours when Grissel rises like a daimona to protect them?'

'Was your papa never stern?'

Mainard smiled ruefully. 'Not nearly enough. He indulged me far too much. I would've been a better son had he not.'

Bethia came to him and, reaching up, tugged on his beard. Drawing his face down to hers she kissed him, saying, 'Papa did an excellent job, for there's not a better man in this world than you.'

He wrapped his arms around her pulling her to his heart.

They'd been living in Ancona near on a year now, and it was many months since Will and his bride had departed. Trade was booming and the Mendes family seemed satisfied with the work Mainard was doing as their agent. Mainard felt himself beginning to relax and Bethia said he was no longer grinding his teeth in his sleep, or at least not quite so relentlessly. He pressed his fingers into the hollows beneath his ears where the jawbone slid into the skull – it didn't feel it quite as painful as usual. But he should have known better than to let his guard down, ever.

In the late spring of 1555 word came that Pope Julius had died. The most likely successor was a man who was a great admirer of the Inquisition in Spain, indeed had been an advisor to Ferdinand and Isabella in their determined extermination of Jews, and who had roundly criticised the Inquisition in Italy for its lack of vigour. Mainard didn't wait for the cardinals to meet and any appointment to be made, be it this evil man or another. All his senses told him it mattered not who the next Pope was, for no Pope could disregard this continued turning from the Catholic Church by Protestants, nor show any further liberality towards Jews and Conversos. Several years ago he'd lingered in Antwerp to secure the family wealth and had been made a cripple, indeed was fortunate to escape with his life. This time he would act quickly. They would leave Ancona as soon as he could secure passage on a ship for Constantinople.

He had all the arrangements made within three days, grateful Bethia trusted his instincts and supported him to be ready for departure in such a short time. But he reckoned without Joseph Nasi. Don Joseph's instincts were as finally honed as Mainard's and he knew Mainard would wish to take his family to safety. The instructions in his message were unequivocal and bore no other interpretation. Mainard was not to leave Italy, was needed in Ancona, for now. If he chose to send his family on ahead, which Don Joseph advised him to do, then Mainard could be assured most excellent care would be taken of them, as if they were Don Joseph's own wife and children.

'I will not go. Not without you,' shouted Bethia when he told her. 'You promised, Mainard, after Antwerp, we would never be parted again. You promised!'

But she knew. He didn't even need to say the words – *and what of the safety of our sons* – before she bowed her head and wept. He was close to weeping himself, especially since the journey to Constantinople was not straightforward, despite the regular trade between there and the eastern Italian sea ports, and there was always the risk of attack by corsairs.

'You could disregard Don Juan, or Joseph, or whatever he's styling himself now,' she said when she could speak again.

'I could,' he said slowly. 'But we have to live, and although I've some store of goods here, the proceeds from their sale won't last long. And if I disobey Joseph Nasi's instructions then I'll be at odds not only with him, but also Dona Gracia. We'll be little better than beggars in Constantinople without their patronage.' He turned to gaze out of the open window where he could see all three sons engaged in a most exciting game of catch the ball with Grissel and Ysabeau. It was unwise for Ysabeau to be running, with her belly so swollen with child. The shouts and shrieks of laughter rose and he swallowed. He held all these people's future in his hands.

He went to his wife then and held her.

In the event, Malachi Montorro – another of Dona Gracia's many agents – was travelling to Constantinople and Mainard was able to consign the care of his family to him. Montorro was a decent man, Dona Gracia would not make use of him otherwise, and he felt a degree of confidence as he stood on the docks and waved farewell with Johannes at his side. He had thought Johannes should accompany the party, especially since his child was, judging by the size of Ysabeau, due very soon, but Bethia had been adamant. She would not leave him alone as she'd done in Antwerp. Either Johannes stayed or they all stayed.

They were barely gone before the new Pope pounced

like a cat on a small bird, his loathing of Jews evident in every word of the diktat he issued. The special privileges enjoyed by Italian Jews were to be revoked. The insolence of a people whose ancestors had betrayed our Lord Jesus Christ must be punished. Not only did they have the audacity to live amidst Christian communities, some even had houses sited next to churches. These Jews must learn their place and be restrained in the many acts of contempt they committed.

Mainard stood among a small crowd reading the long list of requirements which had been pinned to the door of the synagogue. Word had already come that the Jews of Rome had been expelled from their properties and forced to move to a *Jews Only* area. He assumed it would be as cramped as the place known as the Ghetto in Venice where Jews had lived apart for the past thirty years. It was actually surprising the Jews of Rome had been permitted to live where they chose, some within sight of the walls of the Vatican, for so long.

He read on, aware of the muttered disquiet around him as people shifted and whispered to their neighbours who couldn't see, or were unable to read, the notice. There must be a clear distinction in dress between Jews and Christians. Jews must wear the yellow badges denoting their status at all times and must never appear in the black hat of a Christian. The employment of Christian servants by Jews was henceforth strictly forbidden and a Jew should never be addressed as 'sir' by a Christian.

Mainard took a deep breath and read on. But then the list of constraints got truly to the heart of the matter, attacking the very survival of Jewry.

Jews who were physicians could no longer treat Christian patients. Jews could no longer own property. All trading privileges for Jewish merchants were revoked, except the trade in second-hand goods. Mainard covered his mouth to contain the gasp of shock.

He moved back, treading on the toes of the man behind him, and left the environs of the synagogue. As he walked swiftly away, he bumped into a fellow merchant, an Old Christian, one Francesco Foscari, with whom he'd done business and who he respected as an astute, but honest, fellow.

'Difficult times,' said Foscari, gazing at him with narrowed eyes. The fellow leaned forward and gripped Mainard's arm. Mainard could see the flesh of the man's belly wobbling as he reached out. He wanted to sink to his knees, rest his head upon it and plead with Foscari to protect him... but he said nothing.

'Yes, you're wise to be wary. This has the stink of greed about it. I swear this decree has little to do with faith and is all about what the Pope and that scheming nephew of his can acquire.'

Foscari paused again, clearly expecting Mainard to agree, but Mainard would not be forced into speaking incautiously.

'If you decide to leave in a hurry then I'll give you a fair price for your goods.'

Mainard nodded. He could see Johannes out of the corner of his eye waiting for him, rocking back and forth from heel to toe in that peculiar way he had. He was a skinny lad still and easily overlooked but, Mainard had realised, was nobody's fool.

Mainard hurried home with Johannes following behind. He wondered if the stipulation about not employing Christian servants applied to Conversos as well as Jews. If so, Johannes would have to go, either that or suddenly discover Converso ancestry.

'It's not so bad as it seems. My friend tells me the Jews of Ancona are to keep their trading rights,' said Johannes as soon as they were safely inside the house. 'His master says it's too inconvenient to the Pope, and the Old Christian merchants, if they do not.'

'I hope your friend's correct,' said Mainard, but he felt

some of his burden lessen. If the Jews of Ancona could keep their trading rights then he'd a chance of recovering the debts he was owed by Jewish merchants.

While Mainard awaited a delivery of sheepskin and attempted to collect at least some of the funds owed to Dona Gracia, as well as to himself, he went to work on rechecking his inventory and tallying it against the household goods which there hadn't been space on ship for Bethia to take with her. It was an unnecessary task, for Bethia had left everything carefully recorded in her neat copperplate, but Mainard found it a welcome distraction from the rising fear. The only items missing were two bone spoons from the set of six. Mainard suspected they were likely in the pockets of two small boys, for Samuel-Thomas and Jacopo had considered them most effective weapons for duelling.

The Jews of Ancona might have retained their trading privileges, but they were not exempt from being forced from their comfortable homes and moved into the few narrow streets of cramped housing designated for them. Mainard, on his way to the harbour one day, watched as Felipe Navarro, a Converso merchant who'd openly reconverted to Judaism, argued with the Pope's men come to remove him and escort him to the Jewish quarter.

'I am a Christian,' he shouted over and over as they dragged him from his home, his wife following with their four children huddled about her and a babe in her arms. In the end they shackled him around the wrists and ankles. He fell to the ground, but the guards showed no mercy and hauled him away over the rough cobblestones.

'My wife, please help my wife,' he called out to Mainard.

Mainard had never felt so helpless. What kind of man was he to stand by while his people were taken? Yet he knew there was nothing he could do but join Navarro in prison. The Pope's man entered the house, ledger under his arm to take an inventory of all Navarro's possessions, which were now the property of the Papal State. Mainard limped over to Navarro's wife, who was weeping freely.

'Do you have somewhere to go?'

She nodded. 'My brother will take us.'

'Then let me escort you there.'

Prisoners being marched in chains through the streets of Ancona became a daily sight, and stories of their torture were whispered everywhere. Foscari came to Mainard's door complaining bitterly about the increasing numbers of Conversos being arrested who owed him money.

'How are we to trade when we have not the funds to do so, I ask you? I spoke to the Inquisitor, who claims all will be quickly resolved. He insisted any monies owed to the original Jewish community of Ancona will be honoured.'

'And the Conversos who've been imprisoned?'

Foscari shook his head. 'It seems the new Pope and his grasping nephew have a particular grudge against the Converso community.'

Foscari paused and rubbed his bald pate, which was shiny as though it had a slick of oil upon it. Probably does, thought Mainard, from being constantly touched by stubby greasy fingers. And yet he respected Foscari for disdaining to hide his baldness beneath a wig.

'Of course, in his greed, it was probably inevitable the Pope would turn his eye on Conversos.' He rubbed his head again. 'You're no fool so I may say this… you Conversos are wealthier than most Jews because of the trading privileges you've been permitted, and are thus a much richer prize for his coffers.' He looked at Mainard, small, clever eyes narrowing. 'That you have an Old Christian for a wife may protect you up to a point but I understand she has gone among the Turks, which will not be looked upon favourably.'

Mainard rubbed his own head with his hand.

'If I were you I'd remove to Pesaro.'

Mainard nodded. 'Yes, best I go there.'

'Ah, well. Sad days, sad days.'

Mainard held the front door wide and Foscari paused on the doorstep. 'Go, my friend. Go soon and with all possible haste.'

Mainard nodded. He packed a small bag. Dusk fell and still he lingered. He'd been promised repayment of a particularly large debt this evening. As soon as he received it he would slip from the city. He wished Don Joseph would come and collect his debts himself, had expected to see him back in Europe for just that reason. But Don Joseph had taken umbrage at his treatment by the Venetians and vowed he would not set foot on Italian soil until the death sentence for his abduction of Dona Gracia's niece was revoked and an apology given.

He reminded himself, yet again, that the Mendes were powerful people; that Dona Gracia had often given funds to previous Popes who dare not risk offending her. But this new Pope didn't seem to care, for he could simply seize all that belonged to those he was arresting and swell his coffers that way – regardless of how short term it was as a means of acquisition.

He waited. The silence in the house was oppressive. Where was Johannes? It was dark outside now, a moonless night. Yet again it seemed the debtor had reneged. He went down the stairs, not bothering to light a candle – instinct telling him it was better the house remained in darkness. The kitchen was lit by the soft glow of the embers in the fire, the corners in shadow, no sign of the servant girl who was supposed to prepare his food – and no meal.

Mainard shivered. He moved to bar the back door, already had the key to the front door weighing heavy in his pocket. He was lifting the bar, about to slot it in place, when the door burst open. He leapt back, dropping the length of wood and raising his fists. He blinked, could see the thin, startled face of Johannes in the gloom.

'Where have you been?'

'Sorry, master. I was with a servant who works in the Inquisitor's house.'

Mainard realised he was still clenching his fists ready to swing and let his arms fall to his side. He bent to pick up the bar and slotted it in place, locking out the night. 'How do you know this servant?'

'I didn't, until today. But, for a price, he gave me information.'

'And what did you discover?'

Johannes pressed his hands together as though in prayer. 'We must leave. The Inquisitor has ordered you to be seized tomorrow.'

'Not unexpected.' Mainard paced the length of the kitchen, head down. 'Johannes, gather your things.'

The skinny lad raced past Mainard towards the stairs and the attic room he'd shared with Ysabeau. But it was too late. There was a sudden thunderous banging on the front door. They froze.

The banging came again, spurring Mainard into action. He would escape out the back. He lifted the bar from the back door and came face to face with two armed men on his doorstep. Like a fool he'd tarried too long.

Chapter Ten

Constantinople

Bethia had been in Constantinople for sixty-one days now, not including the time it'd taken to reach there. She counted each one off. Nine days since she last saw Mainard, twelve days since she last saw Mainard, fourteen days, twenty days, forty days. She wanted to stop; she wanted to believe she'd received no letter because he was on his way, following close behind her, nearly here. But there was a clenching, knotting sensation within, a thick heaviness, a dark cloud of foreboding that pervaded her dreams, clotting them with overly vivid colours and strange storms. Why was she dreaming about the weather? She'd never done so before, at least not in this dense obsessive way. During the day there were at least some distractions: the children; adjusting to another new home; the servants required direction – although Grissel, robust as ever, did her best – and her limited funds needed careful husbandry. This should be what peppered her dreams, not a great turbulence of the air.

A letter from Mainard had awaited her arrival in this great city, for the trip had taken longer than expected. Bethia swallowed, remembering the rough seas. She had hoped they would put in to Salonika where Mainard's sister was, but in the event the storms made it impossible.

Instead they stopped at Kavala while repairs were made, and a number of islands of varying sizes to take on food – and especially water, which was presumably why Mainard's letter reached Constantinople before she did.

Joseph Nasi had sent a man to bring it to her. He didn't come himself, which was as well, for Bethia was by no means certain she could contain her anger. And Mainard had counselled many times, as Don Joseph sent him hither and thither like an errand boy across Italy, they must keep him on side.

'How did we become so dependent on the Mendes for our living?' she'd said. 'It wasn't so when we lived in Antwerp.'

'We lost a lot when we had to flee Antwerp. The house itself represented a sizeable chunk of our capital and, as you well know, is impounded still.'

'Will we ever be able to sell it?'

Mainard had shrugged. 'Who knows. But the Mendes have not yet realised the funds from their much grander mansion there despite Don Joseph risking returning to Antwerp to do just that – and despite his manoeuvrings with kings and sultans to place pressure on the Hapsburgs to permit him to sell the house.'

She'd gripped his arm, staring up into his face. 'Promise me you'll never return to Antwerp.'

'I cannot go back. I escaped from prison there, or have you forgot?'

She gave a forced laugh. 'I wish I could.'

But it hadn't only been the house, it was the loss of business they'd conducted mostly with English merchants, selling cloth. And, arriving in Venice, where the Mendes were already well connected, even the Doge coming to visit them rather than they him, it'd been unavoidable – they became agents of the Mendes, rather than having agents of their own.

The sixty-second day, and Bethia, as usual, knelt before the image of the Virgin, which she'd brought from

Venice, and pressed the small gold crucifix to her lips, beseeching the Lord and Saint Christopher to carry her husband safely to her. Tomorrow she'd again venture out of the crowded Jewish area, to the small Orthodox church she'd discovered close to the high wall encircling the city, where the priest had welcomed her, and light another candle. She'd pay for a prayer from her dwindling funds, pleading to Christ Jesus to watch over Mainard. Then she was determined, despite the added expense of paying a boatman, to cross the Golden Horn to Galata where Gracia Mendes apparently resided in yet another spacious palazzo and demand – well perhaps not demand but firmly and unapologetically ask – for assistance both to find him and for funds to be advanced. She would have gone before but Malachi Montorro, to whose care Mainard had entrusted his family, had advised against it. 'Don Joseph is away,' he'd said, 'and Dona Gracia has been most unwell. Now is not the time.'

Well Bethia had decided now was the time. Surely the Mendes must owe Mainard some payment for dallying in Ancona on their behalf. Tomorrow she would visit them.

She gazed down at the crucifix lying in her hand; it might fetch some money. At least the gold would be worth something melted down. And suddenly she couldn't breathe.

She bent low, touching her forehead to the floor like she had learned the men of Islam did while at prayer. It felt rough, knobbly and uneven, unlike the polished floors of their home in Antwerp, and certainly a far distance from the marble floors of Venice. It was all the lodgings she could afford until Mainard arrived. She had hoped for better when Montorro had brought them here. But at least they weren't beggars on the street. The only thing of any importance, and urgency, was to have her husband restored to her. She crawled into bed next to her sleeping sons and lay in the dark gazing upwards, cross in hand, whispering to the Virgin to keep him safe, but the sense of foreboding grew.

The next day Bethia rose, dried out with tiredness, and dressed slowly as an old woman, covering her bright Venetian dress with the dark robes she was required to wear in the streets. At least she didn't have to cover her face like the Turkish women, but it left her feeling exposed when she ventured out of the Jewish quarter. The men did stare so.

Samuel-Thomas came and placed his thin arms around her waist, pressing his head against her belly. 'Don't be sad, Mama,' he whispered. She stroked the dark curly head. He grew more like his father every day and considered that the burden of responsibility for the family rested on his small shoulders in his father's absence.

'He's only seven, too young to be the man of the family,' Bethia had said when Mainard laid the task upon his eldest child.

'It's never too young to learn how to do your duty as a man,' said Mainard, patting his son's head.

And wee Samuel-Thomas had looked up and solemnly said, like he was taking an oath, 'I will be the man of the family for you, Papa.'

'Come,' Bethia said briskly, 'let's see what food Grissel has prepared.'

They moved through to the only other chamber in this small wooden house dominated by Papa's chair, which Mainard had insisted she bring. Ysabeau was sitting on a stool in the corner feeding her daughter. The child had been born early on their voyage on the deck of the ship, and Bethia considered the Virgin must've taken a special interest in watching over the baby that she'd survived thus far. Through the open door she could see Grissel at work in the shared outdoor cooking area. There was a stone-built fireplace with a cunning rest for the pot, beneath which the fire crackled, the heat hazing in the air. Grissel wiped the sweat from her face with the back of her hand, ignoring the neighbour waiting impatiently behind for their turn, and shouted to Samuel-Thomas to stop dithering and bring the plates.

They sat in the dark room on low stools with bowls of barley porridge on their laps. There was none of the flat bread on offer today but Bethia said nothing. Grissel was doing her best with limited resources. She would send her to the market later to purchase a small piece of lamb. The fish market in Galata was said to be exceptional; perhaps she could pick up some cheap fish at the end of the day, after her visit to Dona Gracia. She watched Abram swallow with difficulty, for he struggled with the lumpiness of the barley however well soaked and cooked. But there was no alternative and he was hungry enough to make the best of it. They finished their meal and Grissel took the younger two children to market with her, in the company of a neighbour who spoke some Italian. They were living among the Greek Jews of Constantinople, who spoke, unsurprisingly, a Judeo-Greek which bore little relation to the Judeo-Spanish Bethia had learned from her mother-in-law, all adding to her sense of isolation.

Ysabeau went to sleep in her corner, the baby laid beside her untroubled by the noise of the streets, for they were surrounded by craftsmen beating copper and fashioning tin, not to mention the dyers, pearl stringers, bakers, razor and mirror makers, enamellists and tailors, who all created their own unique noise – and smells. Bethia got out one of her few precious books, sat down at the board and Samuel-Thomas slid in next to her. She tried to give the lad her full attention but couldn't stop her foot from tapping. Time was moving at the pace of a slug. Perhaps she would just set out now; she curled her fingers inwards. It would not help her petition to be calling on Dona Gracia before the lady had broken fast, which she no doubt did in a leisurely manner – and with an abundance of food before her.

'Mama, what's this word here? I cannot make it out,' said Samuel-Thomas.

She bent her head to the book and together they read the page.

'Now we'll do some Latin,' said Bethia.

Samuel-Thomas screwed up his face. 'Papa said I should learn Turkish and Arabic when we were in Constantinople, and Latin didn't matter.'

'Little pitchers have big ears,' she said, tugging gently on his ear. 'You shouldn't listen to Mama and Papa's private conversations.'

Samuel-Thomas looked earnestly at her. 'But how can I know things if I don't?'

Bethia put her head back and let out a peal of laughter. Her son looked at her in astonishment and she covered her mouth with her hand, surprised by the immoderate sound.

'We'll work on your Latin, and when Papa joins us he can find you a teacher for Turkish and Arabic. And we must do some counting, if you're to be a merchant too.'

He nodded his little head, an expression of great solemnity on his face, and she wanted to gather him into her arms as she'd done when he was a small child but knew he would resist.

'I'm a big boy now, Mama,' he'd said the last time she'd attempted. She must respect his wishes even though it broke her heart that he should feel so weighed down by responsibility at such a young age.

Eventually she heard the noon call to prayers. The boys returned with Grissel scolding as they came in the door because they'd run too far ahead and got lost in the crowd.

'I'll put a rope on you like twa wee dogs,' she was threatening. She looked at Bethia. 'They nearly knocked an old woman ower wi' their nonsense. And I dinna ken how to apologise to her. I canna make heid nor tail of the language they all gabble awa' in.'

'I am sure you did your best,' said Bethia. 'And you know you did learn to speak Dutch and Italian.'

The baby was crying and Bethia shook Ysabeau gently awake. Ysabeau had perfected a way of always having a hand resting on her sleeping child so if she fell asleep herself she could feel when the baby stirred, but, exhausted by broken nights, it didn't always work.

'Dutch wasnae so different frae Scots, but I micht as weel be as deaf as Ysabeau for all the sense I can make of thae Greeks all aroond. But I will learn some o' that Turkish,' said Grissel with a glint in her eye. 'There's a bonny Turkish lad who can speak some Italian. I met him in the market. He'll teach me.'

'Take care, Grissel.'

Grissel humphed. 'I'm aywis careful.'

Bethia heard a clap of thunder and looked outside in time to see the rain descend so heavily it was bouncing off the earth.

'I dinna think yer going anywhere the day,' said Grissel peering over Bethia's shoulder.

'I fear you may be right.'

The next day and the pile of coins had grown smaller, however much Bethia stared at them. The factor appeared seeking rent and Bethia felt very foolish. She'd assumed Don Joseph would cover it, especially since Mainard was away at his behest.

'Need tae sell some o' yer jewellery,' said Grissel when the man left, saying he would return in a few days and expected to receive payment.

Bethia sighed. 'I'd hoped to hold out longer. Once it's gone we've nothing to fall back on.'

'Ye could always sell one of these rascals,' said Grissel as the boys charged past riding their wooden horse sticks which Mainard had had made for them in Ancona, intent on a very exciting game of capture the robber.

'Whoah, look out,' shouted Grissel as they nearly

overturned Ysabeau coming through the doorway carrying her baby. Startled, the child, who was for once not crying, set up a great roaring.

'Aye well, at least there's naething wrong with that one's voice,' said Grissel.

Bethia nodded her agreement and moved into the next room to spread her jewellery out on a kist and decide what she could bear to part with. There wasn't much, yet each piece had a special significance. The emerald ring given to her when Samuel-Thomas was born and the matching earrings after Jacopo. And, when Bethia said she needed nothing further after Abram's birth and Mama intervened saying a woman could never have too much jewellery, for it was her safeguard in times of great need, the large lapis lazuli on a gold chain Mainard had surprised her with. How wise, and prescient, her mother-in-law had been, and how she wished Mama's gentle counsel was here with her.

She picked up each piece in turn, running her fingers over it and swallowing hard. Then she thought of her children going hungry and knew it was the right thing to do. If he was here, Mainard would agree. She'd begin with the earrings. She wrapped them in soft cloth and slid them back into their pouch. Now was as good a time as any to set about this business. She could go to the Grand Bazaar but the long passageways, secret corners, numbers of people and especially the noise frightened her. There were stalls in the Jewish quarter where gold and precious stones were sold. She would go there.

She shouted to Grissel to come and help her with her clothes.

'Why are you putting on them fancy things?' said Grissel. 'You'll get them all mucky in the market.'

'The finer I look, the less desperate they'll think me and so I'll get a better price,' said Bethia with a firmness she didn't feel. 'I'll have the dark robes over all, but the traders will glimpse what's beneath.'

Bethia sallied forth, with Grissel following as a servant should. The boys were under strict instructions not to venture out and Samuel-Thomas insisted on standing guard with his stick by the door. She returned several hours later with a purse of gold coin and a sense she'd driven a stout bargain, achieved by arousing the acquisitive instincts of more than one buyer. These stallholders were nothing if not competitive, and each determined to outdo their fellows. Somehow it made the loss of her precious earrings more bearable.

They could eat for a while longer. She wouldn't allow herself to think of what would happen once her jewellery was gone.

Chapter Eleven

Galata

Bethia went to dress for her visit, for she was determined to meet with Dona Gracia today. The kists containing their clothes were piled one on top of the other and she called Grissel to help lift them down. Of course, the clothes she sought were in the bottom one. Between them, she and Grissel extracted the skirt and shook it out. It was of a rich green satin, worn regularly when she was a fine Venetian lady but which hadn't seen the light of day since she came to live in the back streets of Constantinople. Grissel went to heat an iron to smooth the creases from the skirt and Bethia turned her attention to her hair. Lifting her arm to brush out the tangles, she caught a whiff of sweat and dropped her arm as quickly. It would not do. She went to fetch water from the bucket and some squares of linen. She washed, lifted her arms and sniffed again. There were bathing houses in this city but she didn't understand how they worked, had no one to show her and her funds were needed for more important things than cleaning her body. She would carry a pomander.

Grissel returned and helped her into the skirt, lacing the bodice tight. She braided Bethia's hair into a long loose pleat at the back and pinned on the headdress.

'Yon lad that speaks Italian, I've telt him to gane wi' ye.'

Bethia burst out laughing. 'You can't just ask any man you meet in the market to act as an attendant to me.'

'He's no ony man. He's a fine-looking one.' Grissel looked at her feet and then at Bethia. 'Ye canna go all alone. It's no proper.'

'Thank you, Grissel. I'm sure he'll do very well.'

'T'would look better if I came wi' ye too, but…'

Bethia inclined her head. 'You're needed here with the boys – I can't leave them alone when I've no idea how long I'll be.'

She had to take a boat across the Golden Horn to reach Galata. The water danced and sparkled, the air felt fresh and there was a gentle breeze. She was briefly afraid as the boat rocked when she stepped down into it but that quickly passed. It was good to get away from the narrow, dark streets and feel the sun on her face, albeit briefly.

Galata, the area where Dona Gracia and many other wealthy Conversos and merchants lived, was dominated by its tower, which grew ever more impressive the closer they got. A huge circular stone structure, the few small windows placed high up below a colonnade of decorative arches and atop them a conical hat of a spire, drawing the eyes skywards.

'Genoa built it,' said Grissel's man, Kadri, when she pointed towards it. 'Long, long time ago when Galata belong to them.'

They bumped up against the quayside and Kadri leapt from the boat onto the stone steps and extended a hand to help Bethia out. She took it gratefully. Standing on the busy pier she looked back over the waterway dense with small boats moving back and forth, skirting around the larger vessels moored there. The hills on which Constantinople was built rose before her enclosed behind the high city wall which stretched as far as the eye could see in each direction. To her left, where the Golden Horn met the Bosphorus, were the silhouettes of domes and chimneys within the Topkapi Palace, Suleiman's primary home. To her right the enormous dome of the sultan's new mosque dominated the skyline, its four minarets rising higher and the antlike figures of the swarm of men still working on the complex visible even from this distance. Instinctively she hunched her shoulders. This city was of a size and scale she'd not encountered before in her long journey from her homeland. It would be all too easy for her and the children to disappear, never to be found again. And if Mainard didn't come, who would ever look for them?

She turned and walked quickly through the gate in the high wall which surrounded Galata, then breathlessly up the street into a piazza in the centre of a group of homes which clung to the hillside. She didn't know where Dona Gracia lived but was certain if she looked for the grandest house in Galata she'd find her. Kadri asked the way and they were indeed directed to a four-storeyed palazzo with a colonnaded entranceway.

The servant narrowed his eyes when he opened the door, but she'd been wise to dress in her beautiful Venetian clothes, even if the sweat was pooling beneath her breasts and under her arms. He stood aside and ushered her in, waving Kadri back to wait outside. The door closed behind her and Bethia stood in the cool darkness of the square hallway with a mosaic of tiles bright beneath her feet.

She waited while the servant made inquiries as to whether the grande dame was available. Of course, he didn't actually say *grande dame*, but it was how Bethia always thought of Dona Gracia – as near to royalty as she was ever likely to encounter. A woman as rich as kings... probably richer, for they borrowed from her.

Dona Gracia was seated on a low couch with her daughter Reyna next to her and a coterie of women hovering around. She'd aged in the few years since Bethia last saw her in Venice, the once smooth skin of her face a network of fine lines. Bethia was surprised to see

Reyna there, for she'd recently married her cousin, Joseph Nasi – although, she reminded herself, marriage should be no barrier to visiting your mother.

'Bethia! How delightful to see you. I didn't know you'd already reached Constantinople. It's as well you're here with this new Pope asserting himself. When did you arrive?'

Bethia curtsied, hiding her confusion that Dona Gracia had not been informed of her arrival.

'I've been here...' she hesitated, there was no benefit in wrong-footing Joseph Nasi, 'for a few weeks.' Speaking Ladino again felt awkward after so long. It was the language Dona Gracia spoke, never having learnt French even during the years she'd lived in Antwerp.

Dona Gracia frowned. 'I'm surprised your husband didn't let me know of his arrival. I've been waiting to hear from him.'

'As have I,' said Bethia.

Dona Gracia blinked. 'He isn't with you?'

'Don Joseph wanted him to stay in Ancona. There were some debts Mainard was to recover.'

The frown left Dona Gracia's face. 'In that case I can understand. Don Joseph takes care of many things for me and I don't always remember the details.'

This Bethia doubted. She'd never met a woman with a better grasp of what transpired in her trading empire, and the small matters were attended to with the same attention as the large ones.

'I've not heard from my husband since I reached Constantinople, apart from one letter waiting when I arrived. But it was written near four months ago. And nothing has come since.'

Dona Gracia turned to her daughter. 'Do you know anything of this, Reyna?'

Reyna, who'd been a silent child Bethia remembered, said nothing, giving only a slight shake of the head.

'I will make inquiries. Don't worry, my dear. 'Tis

probably nothing more than he has had to go to Venice or Rome or some other place to carry out Don Joseph's instructions.'

But that would not have prevented him from writing to me, Bethia wanted to say, but she bowed her head and nodded. It was enough that Dona Gracia promised to take action, for she was a woman who could be relied upon.

'Now, we'll have some refreshments... the delicious sherbet the Turks so cleverly make. I have in my employ a man whose sole job is to produce it.'

Dona Gracia gestured to a cushion and Bethia spread her skirts and lowered herself down. The hour passed in *blethers*, as Grissel would say, which meant it was inconsequential chatter and Bethia learnt nothing, although she was certain Dona Gracia, that skilful extractor of information, learned plenty. She did notice her eyes narrow when, in response to a question, Bethia said where she was living.

'It won't be what you're accustomed to.'

'No, it's not,' Bethia replied, refusing to dissemble. She could barely keep still, and every moment she wanted to leap up, rush from the chamber, locate Joseph Nasi and demand of him what was going on.

Eventually Bethia determined she'd stayed long enough not to cause offence and short enough not to cause irritation. She rose to give her obeisance and leave.

Much to her surprise, Dona Gracia rose too and took her arm. 'I remember you enjoy books. Let me show you the new ones we had printed recently in Ferrara.'

Bethia didn't know how Dona Gracia would know about her passion for reading, but then nothing should surprise her about the woman. Yet she clearly *hadn't* known about Mainard and, Bethia suspected, would not be pleased with Don Joseph.

Dona Gracia guided Bethia into a smaller more private room behind her audience chamber where several volumes lay on a highly polished board. 'This is a revised translation of the Bible into Judeo-Spanish. She picked up the heavy volume and looked at Bethia. 'Can you read Ladino?'

'A little.'

Gracia patted her arm. 'You do well to speak it.' She picked up another volume. 'Here we have Samuel Usque's *Consolation for the Tribulations of Israel*, which you'll likely find of interest since it's your husband's and sons' heritage. In it he asks us to consider if suffering has any purpose. A most pertinent question for Jews.' She hesitated then looked Bethia full in the face. 'I am aware you too have your tribulations, on a minor level of course, and I will speak with Don Joseph as soon as he returns. I'll send word when I have any information.' She waved to a servant and instructed her to wrap up the book, which she insisted Bethia take. Bethia was ushered from the room, stumbling out her thanks.

The next day several men appeared with carts at Bethia's door. She was handed a note from Dona Gracia's factor saying her family were to remove to a house in Galata and these men were here to help. They were packed and on the move between one call to prayer and the next.

The new house, for it was a proper house and not two small rooms, had a garden, their own cooking facilities – and privy. The boys ran through it and then out into the garden shouting. She'd not realised how constrained they'd been in the previous hovel, surrounded as they were by people whose language they didn't speak and who treated them with suspicion because it soon became known their mother was not a Jew. Galata felt a healthier place to be generally with homes more widely spaced and behind its tower a gate in the wall led to open countryside.

The house even came with furniture. Yet another sign of the care Dona Gracia showed those who served her faithfully. Bethia, who'd never entirely warmed to Dona Gracia on their previous meetings, was ready to throw herself at the woman's feet and weep with gratitude. That night she crawled into a bed without her children, and slept the restful sleep of the righteously weary.

But the next day all was in turmoil once more, for Johannes was delivered to them by one of Joseph Nasi's agents and could tell them little of what had happened to Mainard, beyond he was likely taken.

Part Three

Will

1555 to 1556

Chapter Twelve

Geneva

Will wanted to travel to Frankfurt and join John Knox. Truth be told he'd not parted from either of his teachers on the best of terms, but now he cared not that Knox had won the fragrant Marjorie, for no woman could compare to his Cecile. But Cecile was equally determined that they should go to Geneva and Calvin. Will, still unbelieving of the great blessing God had bestowed by giving him such a wife, could refuse her nothing.

He hadn't corresponded with Calvin since he'd left the duchess's court and even before then had written fitfully. On their first day in Geneva he went, with some trepidation, to Calvin's chambers, where he found Calvin preoccupied by events unfolding in Frankfurt. He spoke to Will as though Will had just stepped outside for a moment rather than been absent for nigh on nine months.

'It's unconscionable the way they're treating poor Master Knox,' Calvin said within a few minutes of Will's arrival.' He sat hunched, his hands pressed into his belly – but then it had always caused him pain – his skin dull and grey.

Will leant forward from where he'd been waved to a seat opposite. 'I've heard the rumours and our landlady could speak of little else last eve. Is it true that Knox called the Book of Common Prayer superstitious, impure and unclean?'

Calvin pressed on his belly harder and winced. 'That has been exaggerated. Master Knox's main issue was that the congregation wanted to repeat the prayer book responses aloud, which...' he peered over the top of his eye glasses at Will, 'gives a most inappropriately Roman feel to a devout service. It seems they were seeking a more *English* face to their church.' He snorted. 'But if that is so, then they should be returning to the Catholic Church, for, as you will well know, Queen Mary of England has been most cruelly determined that her country once again comes under the sway of the Pope. I wrote to Knox telling him he should remind his congregation *the gospel of Christ be not disturbed on account of the ceremonies dreamed up by men.*' He stopped abruptly and glared at Will as though Will had disagreed.

Will said nothing. He was remembering how Knox forbad his congregation in Berwick to kneel at prayer. The man always pushed further and faster than people were ready to go, but then Knox considered that suffering led the sufferer to a true understanding of personal salvation.

There was silence in the chamber apart from the crackling of the logs in the fire. Will could hear a vendor calling from outside the opaque window behind Calvin. He raised his head from where he'd been studying his hands as he reflected on Knox and realised Calvin was looking at him expectantly. 'Perhaps it was not wise of Knox to call the Holy Roman Emperor a greater enemy to Christ than Nero.'

Calvin's eyes widened. 'You heard of this, even in faraway Ferrara?'

Will nodded.

'It's unfortunate the story's so widely known. Not that Knox was entirely wrong in his summation.'

Will shifted in his seat. The stool was low to the ground and he couldn't find a comfortable position for his long legs. 'I understand the emperor was nearby in Augsburg at the time. There's a saying in Scotland, *keep your breath to cool your porridge,* and I think there are weightier matters Knox could risk arrest for than some dismissive comment about Charles of Hapsburg.'

Calvin stared at him and Will swallowed.

'Marriage has changed you, Seton. I never heard you so assured before.'

Will sat as upright as his ever paining back would permit. 'My wife is a most remarkable and God-fearing woman. Did you know she was imprisoned in Ferrara for her refusal to attend Mass?'

'I did not.' The lines on Calvin's brow deepened. 'Renée was led astray by that fool Richardot. She was certainly not following my counsel when she permitted the Catholic service to continue. But of more pressing concern is John Knox and his troubles. I shall write to the English congregation in Frankfurt and prevail on them to follow good Knox's guidance.'

He paused and looked expectantly at Will, who, after a moment, reached across the table for paper, quill and ink.

'The usual greetings, please, Seton. Then I would say *Master Knox, you are, in my judgement, being neither godly nor brotherly dealt with by all...'*

Will wrote steadily as Calvin dictated. He was both touched and surprised his former teacher had so quickly, eagerly even, reinstated him as a scribe, and he hoped the position would come with some remuneration. There were many French Protestants sheltering in Geneva now, indeed some said they outnumbered the Genevans themselves, and he and Cecile had accommodation with one such family, but he didn't know how long they'd be welcome to stay, and in any case, as a married man, it was time he set up his own household.

'Finish by saying that I write *with a troubled heart,'* said Calvin, and Will did so with a flourish of the *h* and *t.*

It was remarkable with what ease Will slipped back into being Calvin's assistant. 'It's as though I'd never left,' he told Cecile, as they sat over their midday meal. 'And as though I never dared to reprimand him about Servetus.'

She gazed upon him and he basked in the warmth of her smile.

'Of course, he has other secretaries, but Farni is no longer there.'

'I thought you said Calvin relied on Farni?'

He was pleased she'd remembered. 'Farni has done something odd. He's an elderly man, must be near on seventy, and has become engaged to a girl of no more than eighteen – and is imploring Calvin to attend his wedding. Calvin says he blushes for Farni's weakness, especially as Farni said not six months ago that any old man who married a young woman was a naught but a madman.'

'I wonder what the young woman is thinking. She's most probably poor and hopes he'll not live long.'

Will stared at her, surprised she should speak so cynically. 'You don't think she can love him?'

Cecile shrugged. 'Who knows. Women have to make pragmatic choices.'

'Is that what you did?'

She tapped him lightly on the arm. 'I was fortunate my pragmatic choice involved a man who is young, and not unattractive.'

Will smiled uneasily in return, conscious he was distinctly lacking in substance – unlike Farni, who could promise his young wife a secure living and a sufficient estate when he died. 'Calvin *is* going to pay me. It isn't much but we can at least afford rent and food.'

Cecile smiled. 'That is good tidings, husband.'

They finished the sparse repast, Will swallowing down the charred meat, which Cecile had prepared, somehow without it sticking in his throat. She'd lived as a lady in the court of a duchess and knew nothing of housewifery but was doing her best to learn. He held out his hand and she took it. They bowed their heads and gave thanks to God.

'I met a Madame Bernier today,' Cecile said as she rose to clear away. 'She says she knows you well and you're a godly young man.'

Will, who'd started at the mention of Madame Bernier, was surprised to hear himself spoken of in such glowing terms.

'She told me you'd fallen in with a bad woman?'

Will gave a great bellow of laughter. 'I would hardly describe Mainard's sister as a bad woman. Indeed it would be difficult to find a more devoted follower of God. The problem was she cleaved to the religion of her ancestors.'

'She is an apostate?'

'She's a Jew whose family were forced to convert and, despite the peril, she would not relinquish Judaism.'

'You admire her?'

'I do. As someone who has chosen to follow a faith I most fervently believe is the right path to God and Christ Jesus, how can I despise another with equal strength of belief, however wrong-thinking the path she has chosen may be.'

Cecile's lips narrowed in a way he was becoming unfortunately familiar with; a clear sign of her displeasure. ''Tis better we discuss this no further since we're unlikely to agree.'

She took the bucket and went to fetch water. Will sat with his head in his hands. He didn't know how to make her understand. He could never follow Catarina, nor could he ever return to Rome, but, having witnessed first Wishart in St Andrews and then Servetus in Geneva burn at the stake for their beliefs, he could never condone persecuting those who thought differently – but with an equal passion. The anathema for him were people like his sister, who drifted along accepting prevailing wisdom without any effort to examine their conscience or the doctrine. The first he'd ever seen of Bethia exhibiting a true sense of faith was when she rejected Calvin and all his works because Calvin derided the veneration of the Virgin. But, having done so, she slipped back into unquestioning obedience, as far as Will had observed. Of course, she was a busy wife and mother, but it should not preclude a true and constant examination of faith.

Cecile heralded her return with a slammed door. Will went to her and, placing his hands on her shoulders, turned her around to face him. She came unresistingly but kept her eyes on the floor.

'Look at me, my sweet one.'

She raised her eyes slowly and the angry flush on her face subsided. He kissed her. 'We will always be united in the one truth faith. Let others look to themselves.'

She nodded slowly.

'Now I must return to Master Calvin. He has a pile of correspondence to be sifted through.'

'And I am for the Good Wives Group. Madame Bernier invited me.'

Will sniffed, and Cecile looked at him in surprise.

'I thought you'd be happy I'm making friends.'

'I am – but whatever you do, don't dance. Bethia nearly got us thrown out of Geneva for so doing.'

'I can safely promise you I will not dance.'

When Will arrived back at Calvin's offices he found him pondering a letter from John Knox. Calvin shook his head slowly. 'Is it not enough Knox should be at near war with his English congregation without this?' He flapped the letter in his hand. 'He's now produced a tract on the fitness of Queen Mary of England to rule, attacking the bishops who brought her to the throne. And this letter asks me four questions.'

Will could see Calvin was not as exasperated as he'd first appeared, for there was nothing he enjoyed more than a knotty problem to untangle.

'What think you, young Seton: *can a minor rule by divine right; can a female rule; should people obey ungodly or idolatrous rulers; and what path should godly persons follow to resist an idolatrous ruler?*'

Together they composed a reply. Will felt a great satisfaction when the letter was sealed and ready for collection. This was work he loved. He reminded himself to remain humble in the face of good fortune and be mindful of the Book of Proverbs and how *pride goeth before a fall*. And almost inevitably soon discovered his brief time of tranquillity was over.

Chapter Thirteen

John Knox

Cecile returned from a recent meeting of Good Wives in high spirits. Her cheeks rosy red, she blethered on telling Will of what the women spoke and how they were committed to supporting Calvin in making Geneva the most godly city in Europe.

'And Will, there is this poor woman. She's from France, like me.' The enthusiasm faded briefly from her face. 'I've heard whispers in the street and when I'm at the market. The Genevan's complain the city is overrun by French and they do not like us.'

'And yet Calvin is a Frenchman and when once he left Geneva its council begged him to return.'

'Very true, and I am as faithful a follower of Calvin as any Genevan.'

'Which you more than demonstrated when you were imprisoned in Ferrara.'

Her face lightened and the passion returned. 'But I wanted to speak to you of this poor woman. Her husband is wicked, he beats her. She told me only because her sleeve fell away and I inquired as to the cause of the bruising which was revealed. She grew flustered and gave a garbled story. I pressed her gently but she begged me not to speak of it to the group.' Cecile shook her head. 'She is so very ashamed.'

Will frowned. 'It's not her who should be ashamed but her husband.' He paused, saying slowly, 'There's a tribunal which Calvin set up to deal with precisely these kind of issues. He thinks it very wrong neighbours should condone any beating a man may give his wife by turning a blind eye.'

'I told her but she's afraid, indeed considers it may result in even worse beatings should she publicly accuse him.'

'What can we do to help her then? If she refuses to raise a complaint I can see no way forward.'

Cecile grabbed Will by the arm and gazed earnestly up into his face. 'I must find a way.'

Will smoothed his beard. 'I'll speak to Calvin and see what he advises.'

'Thank you,' Cecile said, and tugged on his beard. He bent his head most willingly to kiss her and, for a time, they both forgot the poor woman of France.

When Will arrived at Calvin's home the next day he was still suffused by the warm glow of love which permeated his dealings with Cecile. Calvin greeted him, and before Will could speak, said, 'There's news from Frankfurt and I'm sad to say it's not good. The English congregation have disregarded my plea on behalf of Knox. He has been expelled.'

'That's most concerning.' Will paused. 'Do you think he'll be asked to return there, as you once were to Geneva?'

'I think it most unlikely. I didn't have a charge of treason hanging over my head.'

'So Knox *has* been charged with treason – presumably for the comment about Charles of Hapsburg and Nero.'

Calvin nodded.

Will walked up and down in front of the board where Calvin sat hunched over, gripping his belly.

'The pain is bad today?'

Calvin waved his hand at Will dismissively and Will

felt annoyed at himself. Calvin didn't like attention drawn to his suffering any more than Will did to his painful back, the legacy of his time on the galleys.

'Do you think Knox will come to Geneva?'

'Most probably. It's certainly not safe for him to return to England. Queen Mary is having a great conflagration. Almost every week I hear of another poor soul's suffering.' Calvin stopped speaking abruptly and gazed down at his hands. Will wondered if he was thinking of the blood on them after his part in Servetus's demise.

Calvin looked up again. 'There's plenty of work for Knox here, as well as an increasing demand for ministering in France. Not that I would suggest Knox go there. He'd likely be discovered immediately.'

Calvin inclined his head and gazed at Will thoughtfully. He said nothing, for which Will was grateful. Both visits to France he'd made, first as a prisoner and then as Bethia's escort to safety, had been perilous, and he'd no desire to ever return.

'Anyway, we must to St Pierre, where I have a service to take, and afterwards there's plenty transcribing to do. People are already inquiring when the book of my sermons will be published.'

Will found time to ask Calvin about the poor beaten Frenchwoman as they walked towards the cathedral. Calvin repeated what Will had already told Cecile, and when Will countered with the same thoughts Cecile had expressed, Calvin grew silent. A passerby stopped Calvin to commend him on his most recent discourse and clarify a point of doctrine. Will stood aside waiting for Calvin and watched a crowd of small boys kick an inflated sheep's bladder around. He remembered as a laddie, playing golf in the streets of St Andrews, and how the householders would come shouting when the golf balls whacked off their doors and occasionally broke a window. The ball the Genevan laddies were using looked to be on the verge of bursting. They should have the bladder encased in leather to protect it. He'd seek one out from the leather workers – he swallowed at the prospect of going near the tannery by the lake, for a most eye-watering, rancid stink hung over the place – but this was a wholesome activity the boys were engaged upon which should be encouraged.

He became aware Calvin's parishioner had moved on to discussing staging a play about the Apostles. 'I know there was recently objection to a proposed performance of the *Labours of Hercules* but surely there could be none to such a holy subject as the Acts of the Apostles?' he said.

Calvin promised to give it due consideration and, satisfied, the man went on his way. To Will's surprise Calvin said nothing about the morals or otherwise of play-acting, returning instead to the misused wife. 'There is one other thing this beleaguered woman might do. She could divorce her husband.'

Will's mouth dropped open. 'But... but... 'tis only men who can divorce.'

'Why?' said Calvin briskly. 'I see no reason why a woman may not divest herself of a wicked partner in life.'

It seemed a most peculiar idea to Will, but the more he pondered it the more he considered that Calvin had made a valid point. As soon as he'd finished his duties for the day he hurried home to share Calvin's words with Cecile.

She was waiting for him, sitting by the fire, hands resting in her lap. He hesitated in the doorway – it was so unusual to find her unoccupied. Cecile was forever busy at something, and if not, she was reading her Bible.

He knelt by her side. 'Is all well?'

'I've some news.'

He looked at her curiously.

'Actually, I have the best news. I think there is to be a child.'

At first he didn't understand.

'A baby,' she said touching her belly.

He stood up and walked around the chamber barely

101

aware of what he was doing. And then to know his secret hope was likely to be met, the sense of joy came so swift. He stopped, and pulling her gently up, he enfolded her in his arms. It was as he held her the fear came, dropping on him like a stone. He wanted a child with the greatest of longing but it was such a perilous journey for any woman. If he could but hold her close all would be well. Which was why, when John Knox arrived in Geneva a few days later and Will was told by Calvin he must accompany Knox to Scotland, he absolutely refused.

Cecile intervened. She planned to invite the poor beaten French woman, whose name Will learned was Marie Beauchamp, to take refuge with her. Marie would keep her company during Will's absence; she would not be alone. Will resisted even more strongly. There was no safety to be found in leaving Cecile with a woman whose husband might turn up at any moment and attack them both. But wise Calvin acted – the man was swiftly called before the council and banished from Geneva, much as Catarina had once been.

Now he had no reason, Cecile said, not to join Knox. She was in the early stages of her pregnancy and he would be back in Geneva comfortably before her time of travail. There was nothing to worry about and she was better off without a husband fussing over her. He was not leaving her alone, for Marie would be with her. Eventually she wore him down and, reluctantly, he agreed.

It was strange to be in Knox's company again. Will had not seen John Knox since he'd left Berwick six years previously and found Knox even more declamatory than formerly. He had the same huge energy, firing off in all directions, and little was safe from his pronouncements. But Will had forgotten Knox's frequent use of humour, often at his own expense.

'You're married and to become a father, I hear,' said Knox at their first meeting.

Will bowed his head in acknowledgement.

Knox reached up to clap him on the shoulder. 'Quick work, my lad. You've sped ahead of me. I shall have a task to do to catch you up on the family front.'

Both pleased and proud, Will couldn't help smiling.

'I will bring Marjorie back with me on my return and finally we can begin our married life together,' Knox added.

'To have a wife who is your true companion is one of God's great blessings, I have learned.'

'Very true. Very true. And I am to be blessed with not one but two women.'

Will stared at him and Knox laughed.

'Marjorie's mother will join us in Geneva.'

Will remembered Elizabeth Bowes and her constant whining in Knox's ear about her immortal soul and her never-ending questions on doctrinal matters. He didn't envy Knox his future household.

'Richard Bowes has died?'

Knox thrust his chin out. 'No, he's still alive, and a most disagreeable and ungodly fellow he is too. He resisted my marriage to Marjorie and calls Elizabeth a *runaway* wife.'

'It must be difficult for a man to forgive his wife when she fails to show the obedience a husband would expect.'

Knox, Will was surprised to see, cast his eyes downward and didn't respond. Will thought to add that Elizabeth's actions didn't set a good example to Knox's future women parishioners, but Knox would no doubt justify Elizabeth's intransigence, to himself if not to others, as entirely appropriate in the eyes of Jesus Christ, since she had left her husband to follow the true faith.

The subject was dropped and they turned their attention to planning their trip.

'Calvin has advised we skirt around the edge of France. It's most unsettled at the moment and who knows where the next push against French Protestants will be,' said Will.

'And we want to avoid Philip of Spain's domains at all costs. He's committing terrible acts in Flanders – more Nero-like than even his father.'

Will sighed, wishing Knox realised it was sometimes prudent to hold his tongue. And no safe haven at the end either, he thought, between an England gripped by a Marian terror and Marie of Guise, as regent of Scotland, most determinedly holding to Rome too.

They left a few days later. Calvin, preoccupied by the riot which had ensued because of the staging of the play about the Apostles – for it seemed no play-acting, however holy the subject, would be tolerated by upstanding Genevan citizens – bade them an absent-minded farewell. They made for Marseilles, making use of the waterways whenever they could. There, tidings came that England had declared war on France, determined to wrest Calais from its grip once and for all. Thence a most cramped journey by cargo boat to the Bay of Biscay, another jump by sea to Brest, where both the broad city ramparts and large numbers of ships and galleys in its harbour indicated a military presence of great strength, and which had both Will and Knox preferring to stay safely on board until the captain arranged their next passage. They were now in the heartland of Scotland's long-term ally, and a ship on the point of sailing to their homeland was quickly found.

So it was, after a journey completed with remarkable speed, Will found himself stepping onto an Ayrshire shore. It was the time of year he'd always loved best in Scotland. The freshness of late autumn, the light on the hills, the call of the gulls swooping and diving over Ailsa Craig, that great lump of rock in the bay in front of Ayr, from which the stone for curling was quarried – a game his father was fond of. Will swallowed the lump in his throat which felt not much smaller than a curling stone. He was home, back in his ane country.

Chapter Fourteen

Scotland

Will had expected John Knox to make immediately for Northumberland to collect his bride, but it transpired it was of greater importance he make contact with the Lords who'd written urging his visit to Scotland. Knox sent a quick note to Elizabeth Bowes saying he'd made the journey to be with her but was certain she would understand his first priority must always be God's work. Will, scribing the letter at Knox's direction, was aghast. Not that Knox would say the Lord's work came before aught else, which was right and true, but that he should write thus to his future mother-in-law and not his wife-to-be. Even if it was inferred the letter was meant for both mother and daughter, it was directed to Elizabeth. Could Knox not see how inappropriate this was? Knox could not and was most annoyed to have it pointed out to him.

'Your task is to write as directed and not suggest corrections to my correspondence,' Knox said, glaring at Will. He hesitated, gazed at the floor, smoothed his beard and then spoke in a softer tone. 'Forgive me, Seton. Of course you should always challenge my thinking – how else can I be certain I'm on the correct path without constant debate and discourse. But where it's the most sacred bond between a man and his soon-to-be wife then this debate is inappropriate. It was unwise of me to have you scribe a personal communication and I won't do so again.'

It was Will's turn to bow and offer his heartfelt apologies. However, he was left wondering at the strangeness of it all. Surely Knox could've married Marjorie before now? It would've been no more difficult to join him in Frankfurt as the pastor's wife than in Geneva. There was the issue of extracting her from a hostile England, and perhaps this visit to Scotland was now more tenable since there were many who'd appealed for him to come. Yet Knox was still incurring considerable personal risk in being here and perhaps this was what was, understandably, making him more short-tempered than usual. Will, fully aware he, too, could be quick to anger, vowed to remain calm whatever peevishness Knox might display.

There was a knock at the door of this comfortable chamber in the tower house where they were biding and a servant requested they come to the great hall where their host was waiting. Will watched as Knox relaxed, surrounded as he was by well-wishers and those who hung on his every word. A prayer giving thanks for God's bounty was said with appropriate solemnity but soon Knox was leaning back in his seat laughing. Will too felt greatly valued when he was listened to with almost the same respect as Knox. There was a sense of safety in being surrounded by right-thinking people who cherished visitors bringing the Word from Geneva.

There had been much discussion between Knox and Calvin about Mass, its centrality to worshippers, and what should replace it in the Protestant service.

'Mass has been esteemed in great holiness and honouring of God but is the foundation of our former religion,' Knox said, many times. 'Our challenge is that, in the opinion of many, there is no true worshipping nor honouring of God on earth without it. The holy supper, held as Jesus Christ ordained it, is our singular and inestimable treasure.'

However frequently Knox spoke of this, there was always a pause before he continued. He would shift in his seat or stroke his beard and then the next words would explode from him, almost as though he was still convincing himself. 'But Mass is, and always will be, idolatry before God and blasphemous to the death and passion of Christ.'

It was exciting to Will to watch how Knox developed the Lord's Supper. 'The Table of the Lord is most rightly ministered when it approaches nigh to Christ's own actions,' said Knox as he blessed the silver goblet of wine and passed it among the faithful.

'I need to make more of it,' he said to Will privately. 'God will guide me.'

They were in Ayrshire for six weeks before moving north to Finlayston Castle. It was the seat of the powerful Lord Glencairn, who was part of the regency which was governing Scotland until Mary, Queen of Scots reached her majority. Although who knows if she would ever return to take up her sceptre since she was to marry the dauphin of France. Having spent time in both countries, Will considered Mary would not find it easy to return to the darker and bleaker Scotland, especially since the French court was rumoured to be the most magnificent in all of Europe. The dauphin would presumably become king of Scotland once they married – a king in permanent absentia. But Mary's half-brother James, the eldest of her father's many bastards, was waiting to seize his chance. Indeed, he might already be regent were it not for the power of the Guise family and the funds they made sure came from France to resist the perpetual threat from England. James would be good for Scotland too for he was sympathetic to the Protestant cause. Then Will, as well as Knox, could return home permanently. He wondered what Cecile might have to say about living here, but no point in thinking of what might never come to pass.

At Finlayston, Knox began holding the Communion of the Lord's Supper beneath an ancient yew tree in the castle grounds. It meant more people could attend and, even though it was now winter, only the strongest of winds, chilliest of frosty days or unrelenting rainfall deterred this connection with Christ and each other.

Will thought of George Wishart, whose burning was where Will's exile from Scotland began. Wishart had travelled in this part of the country ten years ago preaching in the open to ever greater numbers. It was this which had, in part, provoked Cardinal Beaton into retaliating by bringing an end to Wishart once and for all. Knox, with Wishart's fate no doubt ever-present in his mind, did not follow this path.

'It's not wise to bring together ever larger groups and to roam around the countryside thus,' he said when Will inquired. 'We must be canny, and a move to holding hedge sermons will not advance the cause as much as time spent discreetly with the nobles who have expressed support for a reformed Scotland.'

Will had nodded his agreement at the time but reflecting on what Knox had said he was made uncomfortable. He thought of Wishart – humble and kindly. Knox had quite a different temperament. And then there was Calvin ensconced safely in Geneva writing out to all his supporters in Catholic Europe that they must hold firm against Mass whatever the consequences. Knox *had* stepped into danger by visiting Scotland but he was not rubbing the authorities' faces in it. But then George Wishart sought a martyr's death, bravely and single-mindedly while Knox was fearful of capture, and the further they moved from the safety of enfolding Ayrshire the more anxious he became. And Will too was anxious, but for a different reason – Knox showed no signs of being ready to leave.

They crept ever closer to Edinburgh but one day Knox halted. He instructed Will to go on to the capital without him and arrange lodgings, and turned his face south for Northumberland, Marjorie and, of course, Elizabeth Bowes. Will was relieved. Now that Knox was finally to be married they'd soon return to Geneva, for surely he wouldn't expose his new wife to the perils of travelling with him.

Will had only been in Edinburgh once before. His Aunt Jennet lived there, but Father had not overly cared for his sister's husband – *a prancing ninny* had been his summation when Jennet introduced him to the family. The husband had died leaving Jennet well-off, but with no children. On the family's one visit to her comfortable land in the High Street, close by the castle, brother and sister had argued, for Father had found Aunt Jennet a new husband, a trading partnership most useful to him, and she had absolutely refused to countenance a second marriage.

'I admit he's not unattractive, but why would I give up my single state to have a man, however bonny, direct me?'

'It's no natural,' Father had responded. 'Yer a young woman still. Dae ye no want a family?'

'Not enough to relinquish my freedom. There's no point in importuning me. I've not been without offers – this property,' she'd lifted her arms and gazed above her at the high painted ceiling, 'is most enticing to any fortune hunter regardless of how they might personally feel about me.' She narrowed her eyes and stared at her brother. 'In any case, as you've no doubt considered, if I die without issue then my property will pass to your sons.'

'Aye, I'm well aware of that,' said Father drily. 'But it's of more immediate use to me to consolidate this partnership with Gilchrist than any distant claim my heirs will have on your estate.' Father had drawn himself up to his not inconsiderable height and glared at his sister, who was also tall, for a woman, while Will had stayed silent in his corner, hardly daring to move in case he came to Father's attention.

'I am sorry to disappoint but I must refuse your kind proposal,' Jennet had said, gathering her skirts ready to beat a dignified retreat.

Father's eyes had bulged and Will could see he was trying to contain his rage.

'Think on it, Jennet. It must be a lonely life here with no husband, and especially no children. And the Gilchrist family are well connected, they attend court. Ye'd often be in company of the king and queen.'

But Jennet remained unmoved by the splendour of such opportunities, which, Will reflected, was as well, for not long after the king had died and the court was then constantly on the move to evade the capture of wee Queen Mary by her malevolent uncle, King Henry VIII of England.

Fortunately, Jennet's house was in a prominent position and Will easily recognised it. He wondered if he'd be permitted entry when he knocked, since his father and Jennet had not parted on good terms. But she came smiling into the salon where he'd been left kicking his heels by the dour retainer.

'William,' she said, holding her hands out to clasp his. 'What an unexpected pleasure. I doubted I'd ever see you again.' She waved him to sit, and Will lowered himself onto a settle which was covered in cushions stuffed so thick with filling he felt as though he was balancing on a ship's bollard, while that strange bird the parrot – which he remembered from his previous visit – shifted on its perch in the corner repeatedly uncurling one claw followed by the other.

'Bring us some wine, Thomas,' she said to the servant lingering in the doorway.

'You call your servant Thomas?' Will gulped, hadn't meant the words to burst so loudly from his lips.

Aunt Jennet's eyes twinkled. 'That is his name.'

'His surname?'

'I prefer the Christian name, in this case.'

Will couldn't help but smile. Thomas was also Father's name.

'I am sure my father would be honoured to be so remembered.'

'And I am equally certain he would not, which is after all the point.'

Will let out a peal of laughter. 'You're still estranged?'

'We've reconciled recently. And you?'

'We correspond occasionally. He has John, who'll be his heir, and must be of an age now where he can be useful.'

Will detected a twinkle in his aunt's eye at the mention of John but she said nothing more and he let it pass.

They ate together and chatted. Jennet insisted Will should take up residence with her while he was in Edinburgh.

'I'm travelling with John Knox,' he said, unwilling to deceive her.

'I'd assumed so. Word of Knox's visit is creeping out. So long as you're circumspect then I'd like to have you with me, nephew. I assume your visit is to be of short duration?'

Will nodded while surreptitiously brushing away the tear that had sprung into his eyes at these kind words.

Jennet reached out and squeezed his hand. 'But where is Master Knox? I understood the two of you to be quite inseparable?'

'You are well informed.'

'Clearly not entirely so, since I don't know his current location.'

'He's gone to fetch his wife, but please keep the information to yourself.'

Jennet leant back in her chair and laughed. 'John Knox with a wife? This I have to see.' Her smile faded.

111

'Poor woman.'

Will was about to defend his mentor but there was a great clatter and the door crashed open. Will leapt from the board fumbling for the dirk in his waistband, his sword had been left behind in Geneva at Calvin's suggestion.

'Sorry I'm late, Aunt.'

Will absolutely stared, then he let out a great shout and leapt forward. 'John!'

John's mouth dropped open and he stood arms dangling.

'Shut yer mouth or you'll catch flies,' said Will.

John blinked. 'What are you doing here?' He looked past Will. 'Is Bethia with you?'

Chapter Fifteen

John Seton

Will gave John an affectionate thump on the shoulder. 'Am I not enough for you?'

John grinned and thumped him back in return.

Will took a step back and looked John up and down. 'Almost a man,' he said.

John pushed hard and sent Will staggering.

'Boys, boys,' called Aunt Jennet. 'Take care. You don't want the first intimation of Will's visit to be when I send your father the bill for damages to my expensive furniture come from Flanders.'

'Sorry, Aunt,' said John, and patted her on the head.

Aunt Jennet giggled, and Will could see John had her wrapped around his little finger.

'And where have you sprung from, Will?'

'Ayrshire,'

'You've been here a wee while?'

'Aye, longer than I planned, near on four months.'

'So this is just a visit?'

Will nodded. 'Scotland is still not ower friendly to Protestants.'

'That's changing, and I have a presentiment t'will not be long before they're welcomed, especially now Knox is come among us.'

Will gazed at brother John's open, fresh face and felt a

shiver ripple down his spine. At present, reform might only be a tussle between the Lords but it wouldn't take much for it to erupt into slaughter and burnings as was happening in France. John wasn't much older than Will had been when he got drawn into the siege and that had not ended well.

'Are you a follower of the true faith then?'

John tossed his head. 'I'm a supporter of whichever cause lets me cut a caper and cuddle a pretty wench.'

'John!'

'Sorry, Aunt.'

'Sit down, boys,' said Aunt Jennet in a tone which brooked no disobedience. She leant forward, eyes so fierce they were near popping out her head. 'This is not some laddie's game, John. And I promised your father I'd make sure you didn't get into mischief.'

'I think you need have no fears for John at the moment, beyond him getting picked up by the watch. I don't expect Knox to arrive for several weeks.'

She pulled out her handkerchief and patted her chest gently. 'Then John may show you his Edinburgh and especially the work he is engaged upon, which your father is most pleased with.'

Will reached out, took Aunt Jennet's hand and bent to kiss it. Now her smile lingered.

'Do you plan to visit your parents while you're in Scotland?'

'I think it unwise, much as I'd like to see them. I'm well kent in St Andrews and people will remember my part in the siege. It's different in Edinburgh – no one knows me here, apart from you.'

John, who'd been shovelling collops of bacon, beef stew, bannocks, roasted egg and anything else left over from their meal, all washed down with ale, into his mouth as fast as he could, wiped it with the back of his hand, belched, stood up and said, 'Let us away, brother.'

Will was surprised to see Aunt Jennet looking fondly

upon John still, for behaviour which would have earned John a reprimand if Father had been there.

It was a cold dark March night, the wind birling sleet around and whimsically changing direction so one moment they were being hurried down the High Street and the next they were propelled back, mouth, nose and eyes whipped by wet snow. They didn't speak as they walked, too intent on pushing against the weather and holding their cloaks tight. John stopped before a door with faint yellow light leaking from the gaps in the wood. Both men had to bend low to avoid dunting their heads on the door frame but were given an effusive welcome by the innkeeper, clearly delighted to have customers on such a wild night.

A serving lass was by their side immediately, cloth in hand, which she reached high to wipe dry John's face before she relieved him of his wet cloak, spreading it before the fire to dry. The girl was quickly back and two pots of ale were placed on the board before them. She hung around, tousling John's hair, touching his shoulder and leaning in with great familiarity to ask if they wanted aught else.

Will raised his eyebrows and looked pointedly at John, who grinned back. Eventually he said, 'My brother and I have much to catch up with.'

'Och, I kent ye were brothers what wi' the yellow-red hair and they great shoulders, ye could be naething else.'

'Cousins, perhaps,' said John, and nudged her.

She let out a roar of laughter, far more than the quip warranted in Will's opinion. Then she thrust out her not immoderate bosom, wiggled her hips, looked at Will and said, 'Has he telt ye we're tae be married?'

Will stared at John, who had the grace to blush. Will's eyes shifted to the lassie, who stuck her chin out. He felt sorry for her then and said gently, 'John and I haven't seen one another for a long time. I was just about to learn all his tidings.'

115

'I can tell you,' she said, pulling over a stool to join them. 'We have no secrets frae one anither.'

Will glanced at his brother again, but John was finding the pitted surface of the board absorbing. He had a strong suspicion John had brought him here because he needed rescuing.

'I'm sure you can,' Will said firmly. 'But I'd very much like to speak with my brother, alone.' The last word came out louder than he meant, but it was enough to startle the lass, who dropped her stool and retreated.

Will waited for John to speak. John buried his face in the tankard and took a long drink of his ale, thumped it back on the board and wiped his mouth with the back of his hand.

'It's a bonny city, Edinburgh,' he said with great heartiness. He stretched his legs out then sat, knees wide apart, elbows resting on the board, eyes on Will.

'I'm surprised Father let you out of his sight.'

'He sent me here to the university with instructions to charm our aunt.'

'Didn't think Father had the word *charm* in his vocabulary.'

John snorted. 'That was the gist.'

'Are you at the university still?'

'No, finished with all that. God's blood, it was dreary stuff. And hard when I didn't have Bethia to help with the Latin.' He looked wistful then leaned forward eagerly. 'I know you've seen her.'

'I have, in Italy and before that in Antwerp, but now I believe she is gone to Constantinople. Far beyond our reach.'

'How is she?'

'Surrounded by bairns who're almost as wild as you were.'

John leant back and Will could see him swallowing. 'Her husband is a good man, John. He's helped me several times.'

John nodded slowly. 'And I hear you're to be congratulated on your marriage,' he said with unnatural brightness.

'Aye,' said Will, trying, unsuccessfully, to contain his pride.

'A Frenchwoman too. And you always sae sober and correct.'

Will frowned. His wee brother was getting uppity here. 'My wife's name is Cecile and she's the most beautiful creature who ever walked God's earth. But more importantly she follows the true faith.'

'Aye, aye,' said John, hands raised, palms outwards.

Will took a deep breath and let his shoulders drop. 'She is most precious to me. And,' he said, lightening, 'I am to be a father.'

John smiled broadly. 'That is the best news, brother. We must celebrate.' He turned and shouted to the innkeeper. 'A bottle of brandy, Colp. My brother has good tidings.'

Colp came to the table immediately, bottle in one hand and two small quaichs pinioned between his thick fingers. Before Will could remonstrate either about the bottle or the smudged pewter, the brandy was poured and John was holding up his glass to toast the father-to-be.

Some hours later they staggered out into the dank streets. The snow hadn't lain and the cobbles were wet and slimy underfoot. Will staggered into a doorway and slipped down the wall. His head was spinning like a street performer's plate on a stick. If this was what it felt like to be inebriated, he was glad he'd avoided it up till now and would take pains to make sure it never happened again. John, who seemed more in command of himself, leant down and hauled him up. Through blurry eyes Will could see a dark figure creeping up behind John, arm raised. Will gave a shout and John turned so the blow fell on his shoulder rather than head. Will charged at their attacker, sent him staggering and then was flailing his arms to stop landing face first in the muck. He regained his balance in time to see John swinging his fist at a second rogue. The punch landed and the villain sat down hard. Before he could act, the fellow rolled onto his hands and knees, scrambled to his feet and took to his heels.

'That was a mighty blow, brother,' said Will. 'You've clearly had practice.'

He could see the smile as John's teeth gleamed in the dark. 'I am better with the fist than the sword.'

'And next time I'll be better prepared and have my dagger ready in my hand.'

They set off on a wavering path to the top of the High Street and Aunt Jennet's home.

But neither were laughing the next day. Will sat, head in his hands, vowing he'd never again touch brandy except for medicinal purposes, while Aunt Jennet looked on with pinched lips.

'Here for barely a day and already a drunkard.'

'Hardly,' said Will, wishing his aunt's voice didn't hit quite such a shrill note.

'Your brother's leading you astray.'

'Where is he, by the way?'

'Gone to work with a sair heid. Can't have any idlers here. Your father is determined John shall become essential to my business and he must toil if he's to have it. Nothing is handed out on a plate.' Jennet leant forward suddenly and tapped him on the knee. 'There is a place for you here, and John can go home to St Andrews.'

Will looked up at her. 'I wouldn't be comfortable usurping my brother.'

'Your sentiment does you credit, but John will already inherit a wealthy living from your father. He doesn't need both. And to tell the truth, despite his charm, I am become weary of his wild ways and suspect he'd be better away from Edinburgh.'

Will, remembering the claim made by the servant lass, thought she was probably right.

'He can go home, and your father will soon have him back on the leash.'

But Will, thinking of the thrashings John was constantly subjected to as a lad, which did little to dampen his fierce spirit, doubted even Father could rope him in. He became aware his aunt was awaiting a response.

'That is a most generous offer, Aunt. Let me think on it.'

'Please don't take too long. I'm no longer a young woman and am almost as eager as your father to have my property settled.'

Chapter Sixteen

Edinburgh

Will did indeed ponder Aunt Jennet's offer. He'd missed Cecile and her loving companionship but now he desperately needed her. No one better to help him think this dilemma through than his practical wife. He thought on how she would approach the decision, realising there were similarities between her and his aunt, and suspected Jennet would like Cecile. Somehow that made the decision more, rather than less, difficult.

He knew the prudent course was to accept his aunt's generous offer. He had a family to support with little means to do so. They would live in comfort and security in his aunt's fine home, Cecile would want for nothing and, when the time came, he would have a good living to pass onto his son in turn. But he doubted Cecile would be swayed by these arguments, for faith was more important to her than security. But if Knox prevailed and Scotland did turn Protestant then it wouldn't matter. And yet… and yet…

John took him about and Will quickly realised how well kent his young brother was on these city streets. Street sellers, street performers, pedlars, even beggars, all hailed him, and he had many friends among the wealthy sons of local merchants and lairds. Indeed, from the lordly affability he exuded anyone would've thought

John was the son of nobility himself. His brother had no serious side, as far as Will could ascertain. All was about pleasure and indulgence. In the old days Will would've mightily disapproved of John, but his brief time in Ferrara had exposed him to another way of living for which he could see the temptation all too clearly, and because of these experiences Will was less stern, less dour and more willing to allow some levity to enter his life. And all this was greatly assisted by John's admiration, openly expressed, towards him.

'This is my brave brother who has endured much and has the strength of Atlas,' he said more than once when introducing Will to yet another acquaintance.

'You must be careful what you say of me,' Will warned. 'I've no desire to see the inside of Edinburgh's tolbooth.'

John gave a casual wave of the hand. 'Dinna fash yerself, brother. Everyone is saying the queen will remain in France and never return. Her mother is growing old and when she dies James Stewart will take up the reins. Already the tide is turning and our country will cleave to the reformed faith.'

Will raised his eyebrows. 'You truly believe that?'

'I do,' said John with a most solemn face. 'And I am a Protestant myself.'

Will stared at him. 'But you go to Mass.'

'Aye,' said John slowly. 'Awbody goes to Mass.'

They were heading down one of the narrow streets which dropped steeply from the High Street to Nor' Loch. From a doorway a woman threw a bucket of slops onto the cobbles, narrowly missing them.

'Hey, watch out,' shouted John.

Speech became impossible, all attention on avoiding landing on their arses in the sewage which ran down the close and drained into the loch.

Once they reached the bottom Will stopped by the stained stone of Trinity College Kirk, built, he remembered from his schooldays, in memory of King James II. He wondered what possessed James's queen to raise a church where the stink from the loch would be right under the noses of the worshippers. Perhaps she'd not been so fond of her husband after all.

'John, you cannot claim to be a Protestant while following Catholic rituals.'

John drew his head back. 'Why not?'

Will didn't know quite where to begin, but begin he did. Soon he was fairly sure, by the speed with which John was walking, that he was saying a lot more than John wanted to hear... but Will would not be gainsaid.

'Christ's wounds, Will, you don't have to persuade me. Just tell me what to do and I'll do it.'

'Even if *you* might end up in the tolbooth?'

'Well,' said John slowly, 'I wouldn't go as far as that...'

'So you're a fair day follower.'

John grinned. 'I think *you* have martyred yourself sufficiently that I need not do so.'

'It doesn't work like that,' said Will, but the heat had gone out of him and the words were spoken with a gentleness which surprised even the speaker. He could not be a pastor without more fire in his belly and an unrelenting determination to guide people along the true path. Perhaps it was a sign he should take up Aunt Jennet's offer.

He skirted around a line of carts carrying all manner of luxury goods which would have arrived from France, Flanders, Poland and Denmark and were being brought into Edinburgh from Leith, enjoying the walk in the clear air with the Fife coast before him and the view of the contours of the land rising steadily to the twin paps of the Lomond Hills.

But once he reached the warehouse by the docks at Leith and sat down with Aunt Jennet's small, earnest factor and the day book spread before him, the feeling of well-being dissipated like thistle seed blown on the breeze. The factor, whose name Will had not retained, kept turning to him anxiously. John, of course, had escaped out to the docks on some pretext or another and Will was left with this droning fellow. The sibilance of his whispering voice soon meant he was fighting sleep to add to his general discomfort. But then he and John had been out late again last night. And what of the serving lass – John had got himself in too deep there. His eyes drooped and he could feel himself pitching forward.

Will stood up with a suddenness which had the factor leaping to his feet, still talking.

'Please excuse me. I must find my brother,' Will said abruptly.

'Aye, but if ye'd let me finish, young master, then we'll have done with the hides and can go on to the fish.'

'I must relieve myself,' countered Will. He rushed out the door and down the flight of wooden stairs. Conscious the factor was likely watching from a window, he stood at the edge of the dock and let his stream arc out over the water. He gazed down on the scum floating on the surface, which was barely moving on this unusually calm day. Out past the many ships swinging at anchor he could see two being towed into the quayside, the rowers in the small boats straining and heaving. He felt ashamed of his self-indulgence. Here he was given the opportunity to learn about Jennet's business and he couldn't sit still while an earnest man explained it to him. Then John was at his elbow, an anxious look upon his face.

'There is this man... I see him everywhere we go. I think we're being followed.'

He looked worried, brow furrowing and eyes darting. Will tried to keep his own composure, but the fear was there.

'I came to fetch you for I thought we could go on to the salt pans today. It's a most interesting trade and one I think Father would do well to invest in, and, turning quickly, I banged right into him. He wasn't expecting it, I think.' John's laugh sounded forced. 'He has a most sinister demeanour.'

Will glanced around.

'There's no point in looking for him. It's only when you seem preoccupied, or change direction suddenly, he will appear out of the corner of your eye. He's like a ghost shadow. And these last two days I swear he's been everywhere we've gone.'

'Are you sure? I've not been aware of anyone following us.'

John looked at him wide-eyed.

'Come, let's walk. We've stood here like two feart old women for long enough.'

Back up the hill they went resisting the temptation to keep glancing over their shoulders. They strode faster and faster so they were quite breathless by the time they again reached the loch lying stinking and putrid. High above it sat the castle, its great walls clinging to the edge of the crags. Will chided himself. He shouldn't have come to Edinburgh and wandered about as though he was a reputable citizen. There was no safety here with this castle, like the eye of the Devil – all-seeing and all-knowing.

He was aware of John looking to him. 'I could get a group of my fellows and we could capture this evil creature and make him tell us what he's about.'

'And what if he's a government spy? No, John, I wouldn't place you in such danger, nor your friends. 'Tis bad enough you're my brother and have been seen with me. I think I must disappear.' He contained a sigh, and now when it might be snatched away, the secure living Aunt Jennet had offered was tempting. He rubbed his brow hard, didn't want to consider the perilous position he'd placed his aunt in. He shouldn't have been walking around this country as though he'd a right, especially when he'd left here as a prisoner. He would tie up loose ends and leave.

'John, what of this servant lass who thinks you're to be wed?'

John flushed, his eyes flicking all around as though searching for inspiration.

'Have you got her with child?'

John shook his head vehemently. 'She told me I had, but I've since discovered she was mistaken... or lied.'

'Then she has no hold on you. Stay away from her and keep your pizzle in your breeches.'

John nodded, looking relieved.

He was back at Aunt Jennet's, packing his meagre possessions, determined to find a ship and get away as quick as he could and feeling his heart lift at the prospect of soon being reunited with his beloved wife, when the servant brought him a note. He recognised the bold, thick strokes immediately. It was from John Knox saying he'd arrived in Edinburgh with his new family and seeking Will's immediate presence.

Chapter Seventeen

A Festival of Preaching

When Will congratulated him on his nuptials, Knox simply nodded without even a glance at Marjorie sitting by the fire plying her needle on some plain sewing.

Despite his recent marriage, the great sin of apostasy was absorbing all Knox's attention. 'We must rid the country of this confessional struggle and spread the knowledge of Protestant sacraments and prayers widely,' he said.

'Yes, ministering to the Lord's table should be our priority.' Will rubbed at the back of his neck, almost surprised to hear the words issue from his own lips. But from the moment he was back in Knox's forceful presence all thoughts of taking up Jennet's offer had vanished. It was a relief to have the muddle in his head washed away and replaced once more by clear thinking. His path was as a servant of God.

'Like Christ in the wilderness, if I can have but forty successful days here I'll die feeling my life has not been in vain.' Knox took a turn around the chamber, clearly uplifted by his own rhetoric and determined his mission to Scotland would bring more converts into the fold. The bishops had tried to issue a summons for Knox to appear before them but Knox's powerful *assured men* had challenged it and the bishops had backed down leaving him confident to pursue his vision of a festival of preaching.

'It's a wonder there has been no underground church here such as in France. Perhaps it's because there have been no burnings since Wishart. Mary of Guise, whatever we may think of her religious views, takes a more tolerant approach than the French monarchy,' Will said, hoping to temper Knox's confidence and remind him he should not seek to deliberately antagonise the regent.

But Knox did not consider this evidence of the regent's tolerance sufficient and penned her a letter. 'I will only give her counselling,' he said when Will asked if it was wise to write – and especially to thrust further in the regent's face that he was in Scotland.

When Will was invited to peruse the letter he considered it started well enough. Knox was suitably, if unusually, humble, as would be expected of any man writing to the queen mother, even describing himself as *a most wretched worm*. However, this was followed almost immediately by a suggestion, indeed almost a promise, that Mary was drinking from a cup of poison if she did not *stop idolatry and the persecution of the poor members of Christ's body*. He went on to say she was to immediately *promote true worshipping by allowing me the span of forty days without arrest so I may have liberty of tongue to preach unhindered. In thus obeying God's will, God shall crown your battle with double benediction and reward you with wisdom, riches, glory, honour, and life everlasting.*

'I wonder if saying *Your Grace's power is not so free as a public reformation would require and I know you may not do all things that you would prefer,* is perhaps too provoking? You do not want to be the first person burnt for heresy in Scotland for ten years.'

But Knox was not to be swayed and off the letter went. And he indeed followed up with the preaching festival in a large home not many houses further down the High Street from Aunt Jennet's. Will could barely contain his own joy at the numbers who attended, and more coming each day. They crowded into the large chamber, its small antechamber, and soon were clustered on the winding staircase both above and below. Knox's voice thundered out so all could hear and people gathered to listen on the street outside. Elizabeth Bowes stood as close to Knox as she could inveigle, chin lifted, arms folded and as puffed with pride as though Knox were her own son. Marjorie was scarce noticed, small, slender and insipid next to her large-bosomed mother. Will could scarce believe he'd once near broke his heart over her.

He was delighted to see brother John's freckled face frequently in attendance, and his aunt too. She was well kent by the owners of the house, and wealthy enough to be accorded a seat close to Knox rather than crushed amongst the standing congregation. Will saw her frequently nodding in agreement, John less so. He had a suspicion John was there more for the excitement of being amid normally respectable citizens who were acting against the law.

The first day Knox spoke for barely an hour and all held their breath wondering if they would be dispersed – or worse arrested. But when the gathering wasn't broken up, Knox let the time he spoke each day lengthen, till, by day four, it was near on four hours. The heat and smell within the chamber was overpowering, but, even when several ladies swooned, Knox barely faltered as they were carried out through the crowd.

Knox prepared each day. No standing before his congregation and hoping the Lord would fill his mouth with words. First he prayed long and alone. Then more prayers with Will, Elizabeth Bowes and sundry others in attendance. Will found the community of the small group more uplifting than being one among the multitude. Then Knox would have private discourse with Will and the two of them would together examine Knox's ideas. Often they paused, seeking an apt passage from the Bible on which the sermon would be based or support an argument or find a reading. Will savoured this time together above all else, for Knox, not the most forgiving of men, seemed to value Will's contribution despite his departure from Berwick.

Frustratingly for Will, as each day passed, Elizabeth Bowes increasingly inserted herself into their time together. First it was only to oversee the refreshments brought to them, but then she would linger to listen. Soon she was adding her comments to their discussion, and by day five made no pretence she was come for any other reason than to participate as an equal member. Will thought of the many times he and Cecile debated points of doctrine and wondered what it was that he found so tiresome about Elizabeth's contribution – beyond the whining note upon which every one of the many questions she posed to Knox ended. Marjorie, on occasion, would slip into the room but more usually to inquire if Knox required anything. She leant over him, whispering so close in Knox's ear that sometimes he would put his hand up to rub it. Again, Will thought of Cecile and how very different his own reaction was to any whispers she might make in his ear. Knox didn't appear to be consumed by the wonders of newly married life in the way Will had been. Most probably, and rightly, all Knox's passion was directed into his preaching. And it seemed Elizabeth was the spiritual companion and Marjorie was to be the brood mare. Will shook his head at such mundane thoughts and sat up straight, determined to attend to each word Knox spoke and not allow his mind to wander.

And then one day he found Knox's mind most degraded – the man was in the grip of a white-hot fury and could speak of nothing but his outrage.

'But how do you know this?' Will asked once he'd finally understood what was angering Knox. He shook his head as Knox explained. It was astonishing what gossips the nobility were, even worse than the fishwives of St Andrews. If you wanted a rumour spread fast then they were the place to set it off. It would seem Mary of Guise, far from anger and indignation that Knox should write to her in such forceful terms, had treated his letter as little more than a joke. Extracts had been read aloud by her secretary imitating Knox's gruff and impassioned tones and those present had fallen about with mirth. And now much of what he'd written was circling around the court, increasingly misrepresented.

'She'll soon feel the hot displeasure of God,' Knox shouted. 'She's little better than her namesake and daughter's cousin, Bloody Mary of England. The crown which adorns her is a mere frippery and no more than a saddle upon the back of an unruly cow.'

'Hush, dearest husband. Do not allow this story to consume you. Best not speak about the regent when she's nearby in Stirling and may be told of it.'

There was silence in the chamber and all eyes turned to Marjorie. Will closed his mouth, which had fallen open to hear her caution Knox – indeed reprimand him.

Elizabeth half rose in her seat, face flushed and eyes bright. 'Marjorie, I do not think it at all appropriate you should speak to your husband thus, especially when his anger is both reasonable and justified.'

Will wanted to laugh at Elizabeth's righteous indignation, which he suspected was mostly that she should be so outdone by her daughter.

Knox held up his hand. 'No, no. There is some wisdom in what Marjorie advises. She is correct to chide me when I have her to consider now.'

'I'm not thinking of myself so much as you, my dear. T'would be the greatest tragedy for God's work were you to be silenced, and only over one letter.'

'Pah,' said Elizabeth.

'Enough,' said Knox, staring at her.

The redness flowed up her neck, suffusing her face.

'Marjorie gives wise counsel and I'll take heed.'

Now it was Marjorie's turn to blush bright as a beet. She shuffled her feet and gazed at the finely polished floorboards in this comfortable home clearly overcome by her husband's loving words. Will rose, thinking he wouldn't intrude further on this moment of marital harmony. He glanced at Elizabeth Bowes. She looked almost tearful to have been reprimanded. Will tried to think of a reason to invite her to leave the chamber with him but none came to mind.

He bowed to Knox. 'I'll return later. I've some small errands to undertake for my aunt.'

Knox frowned. 'You'll not be long. There's correspondence you can assist me with.'

'Perhaps I might help,' said Elizabeth eagerly.

'No, it's more a matter for Seton here.'

Elizabeth glared at Will, most unfairly, he thought. He headed for the door, glad to escape.

Returning a few hours later, he found the earlier altercation was all forgot, for a letter had come from Knox's English-speaking congregation in Geneva entreating him to return.

'They've made great efforts to come together, for you know they've only recently formed as a congregation in Geneva,' said Knox. 'They write that as their elected minister they've need of me and these are good people who rendered their support during my *troubles* in Frankfurt, uprooting themselves from their comfortable lives and following me to Geneva because they understood the vital need to take the path of justification by the faith and personal salvation.' He paused to draw breath, and said more calmly, 'However, I won't go till I've completed my forty days of preaching here.'

'I am most eager to go to Geneva, my dear,' said Marjorie. 'And we will have our own home for the first time…' her face clouded over '…will we not?'

'Yes, yes.' Knox paused. 'I should expect so.'

There was a banging on the front door below which

made them all start. Will leapt to his feet and opened the door of the chamber. He, Knox and Marjorie all crowded around the doorway to listen. Will recognised the voice and hurried down the stairs.

'It's my brother,' he said to the servant who was looking doubtful about permitting young John entry.

John's freckled face was solemn, no twinkle in his eye for once. 'Aunt sent me,' he said quietly as Will and he stood close together in the entrance hall, the others having returned to the salon when they realised it was only Will's brother.

John leaned in to whisper urgently. 'She had a visitor after you left, a most distinguished visitor who brought disquieting information and advised her to immediately cease attending Knox's services. The bishops are, unsurprisingly, furious about the daily preaching. They insist Master Knox must be reined in and cannot be allowed to continue these great gatherings unchallenged and the regent has agreed. There is no doubt he is to be called before them to answer a charge of heresy.'

Chapter Eighteen

Heretic

Will soon established the information brought by John was accurate. The bishops had petitioned the regent demanding action be taken against Knox. He could not be permitted to travel from one end of the country to the other, preaching sedition and setting up privy kirks so that his work continued whether he was there or not. Furthermore, the audacity of the man running his daily preaching within spitting distance of both Queen Mary's castle on one side and home at Holyrood on the other, was beyond belief. He was not the only man in Scotland setting himself up as a leader of the Protestant faith and, they insisted, if Knox was not stopped then others would likely become equally audacious. A fire would be set burning across the land that would become impossible to stamp out.

Will watched and waited, wondering what Mary of Guise and her bishops would do... but most of all what action Knox himself would take: stay as George Wishart had, or flee.

Will also knew he himself must come to a decision, and quickly. They'd already tarried in Scotland for far longer than planned. He wanted to be safely back in Geneva before his child's birth. He should leave, even if Knox chose to remain, but however often he wrestled over what might be the right choice, however many sleepless nights tossing and turning on a wool-filled mattress which had once seemed sumptuous and now felt lumpy as rock, however much he thumped the oily smelling pillow filled with seabird feathers, he could not come to a decision. Then Cecile wrote in response to Will's letter explaining why he'd not yet left, saying he need not return to Geneva without Master Knox, for she would close the door against him if he did. Will burst out laughing when he read these words, so like his Cecile. But still it was a source of constant anxiety for him, working away in his belly like a rat gnawing at the wainscoting.

Knox may have decided he would not be seen to flee but he also determined to wind down the preaching festival which was consuming all of Protestant Edinburgh, and providing an orgy of gossip for everyone else. Instead of the forty days Knox had aspired to, it ended after only ten – but what a great and glorious ten days.

They didn't immediately depart Edinburgh once the festival was over, although Will noticed Knox was on edge every time there was a bang on the front door. Poor Wishart had been taken away and held in the pit prison in Hailes Castle for far less and Will was surprised the bishops hadn't acted.

Aunt Jennet soon apprised him. It seemed there was nothing much went on in Edinburgh without her knowing. It transpired that the restraint on the bishops had been placed by the woman who Knox had called a Jezebel, a French whore, the Devil's daughter: his most recent arch enemy, Regent Mary of Guise.

'No, it's true,' said Jennet when she came to tell them.

'Hah!' said Knox. 'That wily, cunning weasel of a woman is up to something.'

Will stroked his beard. 'There are some who don't want a Scotland consumed by burning and murderous slaughter. I believe the regent is among them.'

'She's a snake,' spat Knox, 'and cannot be trusted.'

'No man nor woman among the nobility can be trusted,' said Jennet. 'And I think all the regent seeks is to keep Scotland as a faithful ally to France against the English.'

Knox looked so surprised to be interrupted when he was moving into full flow that Will had to cover his mouth to prevent the laughter escaping.

'You've done God's work here most faithfully,' Jennet continued. 'We need your strength and purpose to continue. Save your breath for another day when we'll overcome the resistance of all.'

Knox leapt to his feet, head nodding. 'You are correct. I'll leave now but not for long. And when I come back I'll sweep all before me.' He went to the high window and opened the mottled pane to lean out and gaze at the street below. 'God is with me. God wants me to succeed. I will go back to Geneva, but when I return it will be to drive reform throughout Scotland, once and for all.'

Marjorie, who'd lingered after showing Jennet in, slipped out.

'She's gone to pack,' said Knox, turning from the window. 'I need not even direct her to do so for we are of one mind. Seton, you must accompany them to France while I do a few last visits in Haddington and Ayrshire before I leave the country. I'll join you in Dieppe.'

Will was so relieved to know he could go, even the prospect of being in close company with Elizabeth Bowes didn't trouble him.

He escorted Aunt Jennet the short distance home. 'I understand,' she said as she removed her bonnet in the hallway and handed it to the waiting servant. 'A merchant's life is not for you.' She inclined her head and gazed on him. 'Your path is with this new religion and in supporting Knox to spread it far and wide. My thoughts and prayers go with you.'

Knox was gone the next day, swift to act having made his decision. What he hadn't done before setting off on his final tour was make any arrangements for his wife and mother-in-law's journey. This, it appeared, was up to Will – including funding it.

Marjorie was all about the practical – a kist needing its metal clasp repaired, some small purchases and a few comforts for the ship. 'We can be ready the moment you say we are to leave,' she said to Will.

Elizabeth Bowes was full of nervous energy, fluttering around behind Marjorie breathlessly muttering, 'There is so much to do, and how will it all be arranged, and surely it would've been better for our good Knox to accompany us.' She narrowed her eyes and stared at Will as though he was some callow youth and not a man of five and twenty.

'Ma,' said Marjorie more sharply than Will had ever heard her speak to anyone before, never mind her own mother, 'I'm certain Master Seton knows what he's about and will see to our comfort as best he can.'

Will bowed and departed for the docks at Leith eager to escape both the fussing woman and the stench of the High Street and take the walk down the hill in the fresh air. But the air was surprisingly chill for an April morn and he tugged his cloak close around him, walking faster and faster until he was near running as he dodged the multitude trudging up the hill. Many were carrying heavy baskets of goods strapped to their backs, others pushing handcarts with crates of chickens and even a couple of pigs, off to the market in Edinburgh.

He went to Aunt Jennet's warehouse seeking the factor's assistance in locating a ship for passage to Dieppe.

'Not so easy,' said the factor shaking his head. 'Most are bound for Antwerp or Gdansk. There's one going to Newcastle, for we do more trade with England since

King Edward died and a Catholic queen took the throne.'

'Do you think I'd have a better chance of finding a ship bound for Dieppe there?'

'I'm sorry, Master Seton,' the factor said in his earnest voice. 'I'm no expert on Newcastle and can tell you only of what goes on in this port.'

John appeared as Will walked the piers seeking a ship at least going to France, for that would be a start. Eventually he found one bound for La Rochelle with a cargo of cured herring.

'This ship has a most powerful odour about it,' said John, but Will didn't care. The captain, for a price, was willing to put in at Dieppe.

'We sail in two days and you must be on board tomorrow evening as we leave with the tide at first light,' he said.

Will nodded agreement while privately quailing both at the prospect of marshalling his charges in time and of being shut up with them for near on a week. Mayhap they would be so sick from the motion of the sea they'd keep to their bunks. Then he felt ashamed of himself for such unchristian thoughts.

But when John echoed them, saying, 'Likely they'll be too sick to give you much trouble,' Will burst out laughing.

The brothers hurried back up the hill and parted company on the side of Nor' Loch. Elizabeth Bowes shrieked when told they were to be on the ship by the next evening. Marjorie said calmly that she could be ready to go by the next bell if necessary, so tomorrow gave ample time. As Will left them to return to his aunt's home for the final night, he could hear Elizabeth saying, 'I do not think we should go. Much better to wait for good Knox and we'll travel together.'

Will hesitated on the doorstep then reluctantly re-entered the house calling out to the women.

'You may wait for Knox if you choose but I'm leaving

on this ship. I would strongly advise you to travel with me, for I think it likely Knox will take ship from the Ayrshire coast and not come back here.'

Marjorie, disentangling herself from her mother's restraining hand, stepped forward, touching Will lightly on the arm. 'I thank you for your assistance. We'll be ready tomorrow.'

Will inclined his head. 'If you need me for any reason in the meantime, send a message to my aunt's house.'

Aunt Jennet had offered to cover the costs of the journey unbidden and Will was most grateful. He organised a cart to carry their possessions down to the docks and, after some thought, reluctantly arranged another to transport the two women. He'd been tempted to have them walk, it was downhill after all, but the prospect of listening to Elizabeth Bowes' complaints, or demanding his arm to support her, had him rethink.

They managed the short journey without mishap, and Will was encouraging the women on board, Elizabeth silent for once as she concentrated on negotiating the narrow plank, when John appeared.

'What's wrong?' Will said, leaping back onto dry land. They'd already said their farewells in Edinburgh and John's offer to accompany them to Leith had been given with such reluctance Will had smilingly refused. 'I thought you were for the tavern?'

'I was, but there are rumours I thought you should be aware of.'

Will pulled John away from the ship side and the listening women. 'What?'

'Knox is to be burned in effigy tomorrow.'

'Huh! So the bishops did prevail.'

'The story is he was tried in absentia and found guilty of the crime of heresy.'

'Then I'm very glad we're leaving and thank you for bringing this information.' He held out his hand and John shook it. After a moment Will pulled his brother towards him and gave him a brief hug. He could feel John tense and, when he gazed briefly in John's face before his brother turned and strode away, he knew they were both trying to contain their emotions.

The ship headed out to sea as the sun rose the next morning. Gazing back at land, Will could see the great castle perched on its plug of rock through the twists of smoke from hundreds of cooking fires rising against a brilliant blue sky. He should be sad to leave but wished only that he could fly like a bird back to Geneva.

Chapter Nineteen

Dieppe

The journey was completed with greater ease and speed than Will had dared hope. The two women were surprisingly stoic travellers, especially given they'd never been on board a ship before and had only a narrow cabin barely wide enough for them to lie down side by side. As for Will, he slept on deck along with the crew, and considered himself most fortunate for at least he could stretch out and move freely around the ship, unlike the rowers, who'd to keep to their benches. These were, in the main, free men who worked for pay rather than under threat of the whip. Will often stopped to speak to them during their rest period and became aware he was being treated with some deference because of his understanding of what they had to endure.

It was a joy to breath sea air. Edinburgh had attained a level of putridness above any other town Will had visited, which now amounted to a fair number. He felt no fondness for the city and was glad to be done with it. If he'd taken up Aunt Jennet's offer he would've made a most crabbit merchant, miserable in himself and curmudgeonly to any who came near. There was the matter of how he was to comfortably support a wife and child, but he was confident Calvin would find more work for him, and Knox already behaved as though Will was again his assistant. Will weighed the coin purse in his hand. It would be a poorer living were he to align himself with Knox. It was not deliberate, it was simply that, rightly, Knox was preoccupied with spreading the true word and leaving Scotland in a fit state to carry on.

Somehow the realisation he was supporting Knox by taking up the burden of the women leaving Knox free from family obligation, lightened Will's own load and made him deal more pleasantly with his charges. He even sought them out once a day and inquired into their well-being. And then, with remarkable ease, they were being off-loaded at Dieppe and now he had nowhere to hide from them – and no knowledge of how long he would be lingering in the town until Knox arrived.

Within a couple of days, Will suggested they continue their journey. 'Knox can join us as easily in Geneva,' he said, 'as here.'

'No, that cannot be,' said Elizabeth, before Marjorie could speak. 'John told us to wait in Dieppe for him and here we will wait.'

'Until the funds run out,' muttered Will, but Elizabeth ignored him and Marjorie remained silent. Will desisted; he would give Knox a wee while longer before he insisted they depart.

The next day Marjorie approached him as he sat slumped on the settle idly twisting a tankard of ale between his palms and gazing vacantly into a fire, the only thought in his mind a curiosity as to why it had been lit on a warm morn.

'I have good tidings,' she said in her soft voice. Will looked beyond her, but she was, unusually, unencumbered by her mother. He wondered how Marjorie could stand the constancy of that querulous presence and no hope of escaping it, ever.

'The innkeeper's wife has approached us. She's become aware of who my husband is.'

The tankard slipped from Will's fingers, slewing its

contents across the floor. He sat up. 'That does not sound like good tidings at all.'

'No, no,' Marjorie waved her hand. 'She's one of us and has suggested we can take refuge with another member of the local congregation until my husband comes. Indeed, they're excited to hear what good Knox has to say.'

Will stood up and looked down at this slight woman. There was a determined line to her lip which he'd not seen before, but then she had defied her father to marry. 'I will meet with these people,' he said. It was a statement, not question.

'It's unnecessary. I've been among many such groups in England and know their hearts to be true.'

Marjorie's French was at best passable and he thought it unlikely she'd reached a clear understanding. 'I am answerable to your husband for your safety.' He wondered if she was going to be another one like Bethia, forever challenging his authority as the man of the party, but Marjorie remained silent.

Elizabeth Bowes came bustling into the chamber pulling on her gloves. 'Come, Marjorie. We must away.'

'Seton is coming with us,' she said softly.

Elizabeth continued buttoning her gloves. 'As he wishes.'

He followed his charges reluctantly, sidestepping a man rolling a barrel along the street and then was near overturned by the fellow following behind him, also barrel rolling. By the time he'd righted himself the ladies had whisked around the corner. Will went to run after them then slowed to tighten his belt. He would not be hurried.

The gathering was in a large house on the outskirts of town. Family groups, appearing as though they were simply out for a stroll, followed by their servants, moved at a leisurely pace towards the house then vanished amid the cluster of tall sycamores to the rear of the property.

The path was circuitous and now they were in the orchards, the blossom lying in great swathes atop the detritus of last year's fallen leaves. Eventually he found himself at the back of the house and was guided in through the kitchen with its fireplace large enough to spit-roast a side of beef. The great hall was already pungent with the crowd and thankfully no fire lit in its equally large fireplace. Seats were found for the ladies and Will squeezed in to lean against the wooden panelling which lined the lower half of the walls.

He enjoyed the service – readings from Matthew, earnest prayers and then a psalm sung gently but which still filled the vaulted ceiling with the purity of voices in true commune with the Father, the Son and the Holy Spirit. The preacher, who looked to be around Will's age, didn't have Knox's loud passion but inclined more towards Calvin's gentler spirit. Will found opportunity to draw him aside once the service was over.

'You speak French very well,' said Monsieur Virel, after they'd exchanged pleasantries. 'And I understand have spent time with Master Calvin.'

Will inclined his head. He could see Marjorie in conversation with a well-dressed woman, most probably the chatelaine of the house from the way she was directing the servants. Elizabeth Bowes stood by, for once silent, and from the way she was gazing around her, probably not following what was being said.

'Calvin is a great man.' Virel narrowed his eyes. 'William Seton, you said your name was? I think I may have heard of you.' He leant in and gripped Will's arm. 'You should come to France. We have great need of pastors to minister to the many communities following Calvin's word.'

Will's eyes widened.

Virel held up his hand. 'No need to say anything now. Talk it over with Calvin when you reach Geneva, but remember God's word cannot be spread by remaining safely within its walls.'

He turned away before Will could respond, his attention demanded by another of his flock.

Will walked slowly back to the inn, again trailing the two women.

'We've been invited to stay in the house until my husband arrives,' said Marjorie as soon as they were inside. She touched his arm lightly. 'And I know you're most anxious to return to your wife.'

Will felt a great weight roll off his back. If they'd been offered accommodation, and the protection it afforded, then he could leave with a clear conscience. And the longer they remained in the inn the more concerned he was becoming about the funds at his disposal. Now all was resolved.

The very next day Marjorie and Elizabeth removed to the large house. Of course, there was a risk in them staying there, for every so often the French authorities had a purge against these home churches and rumour had it the Pope was demanding the French king set up an Inquisition to root out Protestants. But Dieppe, although not so far from Paris, was not part of the Duchy of Lorraine, and had thus far escaped the depredations – or slaughter – initiated by the Guise family. It was probably at greater risk of attack by England, although conflict with France had lessened since Catholic Mary had taken the throne, except inevitably over Calais.

Will headed for the docks as soon as the women had gone, fortuitously finding a ship bound for Bordeaux. The passage was not entirely comfortable once they entered the Bay of Biscay but at least was swift. A terrible sense of urgency had come over him and he stayed not even one night in the city but immediately found a barge which would take him into the heartland of France. It was pretty enough scenery – fields, trees and people working under bright sunshine – but he barely noticed, for every part of him was straining to reach Cecile.

Within four days he was again in Lyon but made no inquiries as to his old adversary Monsieur de Vaudemont. Instead, he set out on horseback in company with three other men quietly bound for Geneva. The sense of urgency increased the closer he came and it was with great relief he found himself entering the walled city state just before the gates were shut for the night. But when he finally rid himself of his horse and reached his home all was in darkness. He banged on the door but could feel the hollowness of an empty house. Cecile was gone.

Part Four

Bethia

1556

Chapter Twenty

Sultanate of Women

'Pope Paul the fourth is a fool but a vindictive one,' said Don Joseph in his high fluting voice. The voice of a young girl really, thought Bethia, but anyone who dismissed him as such was making a huge mistake, for this man was ruthless in pursuit of his Aunt Dona Gracia's interests – as long as they were aligned to his own. 'The city fathers of Ancona sent one of their own to Rome to plead for clemency, saying the new edict is causing suffering to Christian merchants and is hurting trade greatly.' Don Joseph paused. 'If Jesus Christ was here, he would, I'm certain, from all I was taught of his doctrine, have roundly condemned the actions of his representative on earth.' He gave a bark of laughter. 'Indeed would likely cast him from the fold. Imagine that, a Pope excommunicated by Christ!'

Bethia was not entertained. She opened her mouth to plead for Joseph Nasi to turn all his attention to finding her husband but he was off again before she could speak.

'The Pope has now declared he wants no Conversos in Ancona and has issued an instruction to the Inquisition to arrest all still there and seize their property.' Don Joseph sniffed. 'But our people had fled to Pesaro, and when the Pope, furious they'd evaded capture, demanded of its duke that he return them, he refused.'

He smiled. 'Duke Ercole has of course seen an opportunity and is offering refuge for Conversos in Ferrara as well.'

Bethia remembered the Duke of Ferrara. He'd seemed kindly enough, but not so much when it came to his wife's espousal of Calvinism, at least according to Will. Perhaps Will might help her now if she wrote to him in Geneva. But what could he do really? Go to Italy, search for Mainard – and likely end up imprisoned and tortured, as a Protestant. Weary already from the strain of the months without her husband, Bethia wasn't sure how much longer she could sit listening without leaping to her feet and screaming or, almost as bad, falling to her knees and weeping.

Dona Gracia leant forward. Her chair had a higher back than the one Don Joseph rested in. 'And what of the Jews of Ancona?'

'That was the Pope's one concession. He's given permission for the Jews in Ancona, as opposed to either Conversos or what he refers to as apostate Jews... those Conversos who've recently returned to Judaism...' he added in response to Bethia's obvious bewilderment, 'to trade as before.'

Bethia could stay silent no more. 'But where is Mainard?' It came out as a shout and both stared at her.

Joseph Nasi looked to Dona Gracia, who nodded at him. 'Your husband, as you may be aware, has an outstanding debt to us which amounts to more than a thousand ducats.'

Bethia swallowed. She knew they were in debt but hadn't realised the full extent.

'Understandably, we were eager to recover the funds and he was equally eager to find a means of repayment.'

Don Joseph paused and Bethia spoke before she could stop herself. 'What did you have him do?'

'A simple enough commission which involved travel to Germany. He was in the company of a Christian who

150

serves us, Foscari. I was surprised to receive no word from Foscari but now I learn he was murdered.' He rubbed his nose. 'But there's no mention of de Lange and I've been unable to find out what happened to him.' He again paused. 'I will be blunt, for you seem a woman who would rather the truth than any dissembling. Your husband may well be lying in a ditch somewhere with his throat cut but he could equally be in Germany carrying out his commission, or even in Pesaro.'

'Could he be in prison in Ancona?' said Bethia.

'He could, but I had communication only today updating me on the situation.' He picked up the letter lying in his lap. 'This includes a list of those Conversos being held in Ancona, which amounts to seventy in all, and Mainard de Lange's name is not among them.'

Bethia felt the room spinning and rolled forward on her chair letting her head hang. 'Blessed Virgin save and keep him. Blessed Virgin watch over him,' she mumbled, making the sign of the cross.

When she sat up she could see Don Joseph and Dona Gracia exchanging glances and knew it wasn't wise to remind them of her Old Christian origins. But in this moment she didn't care.

'It is of course possible his name is simply missing from the list,' said Dona Gracia softly. Her voice grew stronger. 'But as Joseph says, it's more likely he's on his way to Frankfurt or even already there, and that is what we must pray is the case. In the meantime I may have some work for you.'

'There are opportunities here which I would suggest you seize,' said Dona Gracia, as they crossed the Golden Horn to where the white walls of the sultan's palace rose. 'The concubines used to be housed in a different enclave some distance away, but Suleiman, even before he took the unusual step of marrying Roxelana, moved the women into the Topkapi Palace, which he's enlarged significantly over the past thirty-five years.'

Bethia, clutching onto the side of the boat, which was rocking uncomfortably in the steady breeze whipping the waves into white caps, wished Dona Gracia would save her familiarisation until they were safely on dry land. Dona Gracia, unperturbed by the glistening water all around, sat straight-backed beneath the canopy gazing ahead as she spoke.

'Roxelana is a woman of great power and charisma. If I'm to get the ear of Suleiman and his assistance in Ancona then she is the way in. She, of course, is not Turkish.'

Bethia blinked and, briefly forgetting the buffeting she was enduring, turned curiously to Dona Gracia. 'Which country did she come from? Is she the daughter of a king?'

Dona Gracia gave a tinkling laugh. 'No, no, my child. All the sultan's concubines come from slave markets. They are, I believe, in the main Greek or Hungarian, but Roxelana came from Rus' Land, or Ukraine as it's sometimes known. And she captured Suleiman's heart, for it's said he has taken no other for many years.' She turned to Bethia. 'I am telling you this so you may understand and not be deceived. Roxelana may appear gentle, even malleable, but behind her benign exterior beats a heart ruthless in pursuit of her own and her children's interests.'

Bethia thought this description could equally apply to Dona Gracia – actually to any mother.

She tapped Bethia's knee. 'I know you're no foolish girl and have navigated your way through great peril several times but I cannot emphasise enough how important it is to get, and keep, the *Hürrem Sultan* on side.'

Seeing Bethia's look of puzzlement, Dona Gracia said, '*Hürrem Sultan* is how she is known and what you should call her. Not that you are very likely to speak her name in her presence, but to others within the harem you must never refer to her as Roxelana for she would consider it an unpardonable familiarity.'

'I'll be careful,' said Bethia.

'She has red hair, you know, although it's shot with grey now. It could be a point of contact between you.'

Bethia looked curiously at her.

'I know your hair is dark but your brother's is red.'

Yet again Bethia was amazed at how no piece of information was too minor for Dona Gracia to attend to – she'd never met Will and yet she knew of his hair colour.

'Both my brothers, and my father too,' Bethia said, folding her arms tight beneath her chest.

There was silence within the boat, although outwith the noises of the Golden Horn intruded: slap of the water against the side; shouts of other boatmen; call of the gulls; cries of the porters and vendors as they neared the dock. Bethia closed her eyes momentarily, determined the tears that were forming were from the dazzle of the sun and nothing else.

'There is a good business to be had here, for the women of the harem cannot leave the palace. They use others to bring goods for their inspection and purchase. You're young like them and should endeavour to make connections.'

Bethia nodded. 'What happens to the concubines when they grow old?'

'They're given pensions and moved out once they reach thirty I believe. Not so bad a fate really.'

The boat slid up the side of the dock and one of the boatmen leapt out to tie it off while another offered them assistance to disembark.

Dona Gracia's serving men and women, transported by the boats in front, were waiting and cleared a path before them to the litter. They were carried up the hill by the side of the highest city walls Bethia had ever seen. Turrets intersected them every forty paces or so, the tall hats of the many guards visible above the parapet, which was bristling with the long snouts of cannon.

Then they were before the gates, which opened silently, and passed through the deep archway of the outer entrance. Before them was a long courtyard of grass and trees. To their left a building with clusters of people waiting quietly outside it and then what looked to be a church in the Orthodox Christian style. Bethia turned to Dona Gracia, eyebrows raised.

'Yes, yes it was a church but the Turks have used it as an arsenal since they took the city a hundred years ago.'

They stopped before a second gate, even more magnificent than the first and here they were made to dismount for only the sultan was permitted to ride through the gates to the second courtyard and everyone else must walk. Bethia resisted the temptation to gaze upwards at the stone pillars topped by conical spires which flanked it, for Dona Gracia had instructed she should keep her eyes humbly lowered. Past the stables they went, the warm musty smell of horses strong, past the kitchens and royal bakeries with their smoking chimneys, the sweet smell of baking bread reminding Bethia she hadn't eaten, and across the wide courtyard. They were bowed through by young pages with their heads shaved except for a long tail of hair. Tall janissaries lined their path, and dwarves, scimitars thrust in their waistbands, stood before them. It was difficult not to keeping looking with everywhere another wonder, and even the very pavement itself sparkled with inlaid gems.

Bethia grew more nervous the further they went. *The Hürrem Sultan* she muttered over and over, or was it the *Sultan Hürrem*. She would stay silent and hope she need not utter anything rather than risk the wrong name escaping. She jumped. There was an animal roaring and another roaring back – had never heard such a ferocious sound. It must be lions in the famous menagerie the sultan kept. The bear she saw in the pit when they were in Bern had been a marvel... but a lion! How the boys would love it.

'Here's the harem now,' said Dona Gracia softly. 'Be on your guard, Bethia.'

The passageway was long, narrow and dark. The eunuch who led the way was so large he filled it and anyone coming in the opposite direction would've had to press against the wall to allow him through – but of course no one was coming the other way. They came to a paved courtyard, small in comparison to the magnificence outside the harem but enough to give a glimpse of blue sky and white clouds above. The windows looking into the courtyard were covered in an ornamental fretwork allowing light into the small rooms but wooden shutters hung on the outside of them meaning they could be closed whether the occupants wished it or no.

The women were beautiful. All of them. There were no blemishes, no harelips, no gaping teeth, no birthmarks; their skin looked as though it had been polished, their hair loosely plaited hung thick and glossy down their backs with a tassel of small pearls binding the end and only a small cap of cloth of gold covering their heads. They wore breeches made of shimmering white cotton, shoes with small heels and satin short jackets each a different colour with long necklaces of pearls, long earrings bright with gems and gold bangles around their wrists and ankles. It was the sultan's menagerie of women, in which, rumour had it, he never played, so smitten was he by Roxelana.

The women staring silently at their visitors suddenly vanished, as though following an unspoken command. Finally, they were ushered into the presence of Roxelana. The cloying smell of perfumes everywhere, even stronger here, clogged her nostrils, and Bethia swayed, feeling near to fainting. She pinched the soft skin of her inner arm to steady herself. No one spoke, and Bethia, as instructed, kept her eyes fixed on the floor. The chamber, although exquisitely gilded and mosaicked was surprisingly compact – Roxelana sitting on a low divan – and the silence oppressive.

Dona Gracia had brought gifts of shawls of intricate patterns which were spread out for the *Hürrem Sultan* to gaze upon and a curious bracelet in gold fashioned like a twisted snake, the tail being clamped in its mouth. Roxelana curled her bejewelled fingers and the bracelet was brought to her. She turned it over in her hands then slid it on her arm, where other gold bracelets heavy with gems clinked together. Bethia could feel Dona Gracia next to her relax, ever so slightly. It must be strange for her to pay homage to another woman.

They were invited to sit and refreshments were brought. Bethia, her mouth dry as hot sand, sipped her cup of cold, sweet yet slightly bitter, sherbet with pleasure. There was a street seller who regularly passed their house carrying a large container of the drink on his bent back. The boys loved it and would come running to plead for a cup and a coin to buy some. She paused, trying to decide which had a better flavour, the palace one or that from the little old man. On balance she preferred the latter. She became aware the *Hürrem Sultan* was staring at her with those unusual pale green eyes, not dissimilar to Cecile's. Bethia dropped her own gaze, quickly swallowing the mouthful of sherbet she'd just taken and choked. Then she was coughing and spluttering while servants bustled around patting her back, which somehow made her cough more. The *Hürrem Sultan* dismissed her with a slight incline of the head and she was led from the chamber still coughing.

Nevertheless, Dona Gracia seemed well pleased when she appeared soon after, although she chided Bethia. 'The *Hürrem Sultan* asked a question of you. You must attend and not let your mind wander. It was very evident you were thinking of other things. Not good, Bethia.'

Bethia's eyes filled with tears, much to her own surprise as well as Dona Gracia's.

'Never mind. It gave me the chance to explain how great your fear is for your husband and she was not unsympathetic. She talked of her own agony when Suleiman is away, saying she pleads always to *be the sacrifice for his pain.* I'm hopeful she may mention your husband to Suleiman and press for aid for those in Ancona.'

'Thank you. Oh, thank you,' said Bethia, the tears running freely down her face.

'You must be calm, my dear. These big emotions only get in the way. But it was a good meeting. A very good meeting.'

Chapter Twenty-One

Hamam

A few days later and Bethia was again called to Dona Gracia's home.

'It seems Nurbanu is made curious by you, as well as having great sympathy for your situation. She's requested you attend her today, and of course you must go.'

Bethia wanted to ask which one Nurbanu was but managed to restrain herself from such a display of absent-mindedness. Her head felt so full of fear and worry it was as though it was stuffed with wool.

'Bethia, I need you fully aware of all that's happening around you while you're in the harem. A translator will accompany you so we're not reliant on the court translators.'

Bethia kept her face expressionless, knowing this translator was as much about Dona Gracia being kept informed of everything that transpired.

'And both you and she need to watch for the silent language of the hands which they employ in the palace.'

'Will you not come?'

Dona Gracia raised her eyebrows. 'My presence has not been requested.'

Bethia twisted her own hands in her lap. She did not want to go into that oppressive place by herself.

Dona Gracia pressed her lips together, a narrow line. 'This is a rare opportunity to build a relationship with the beloved of Suleiman's son and heir.'

Bethia nodded slowly, as though she knew who Nurbanu was before Dona Gracia reminded her.

'There's a business to be made here if Nurbanu, who's known as the *Haseki Sultan* – please remember – decides she likes you. You can become a supplier of goods to her and another pair of eyes, and ears, on the world outside the harem, which she only sees when being transported from one residence to another and that from behind thick curtains.' Dona Gracia paused. 'The lives of all women are constrained, but that of a royal concubine more than most.'

And so Bethia went to the Topkapi Palace, with Grissel in attendance. She'd been uncertain whether to take her, since Grissel rarely curbed her tongue. However, Bethia determined it was unlikely even the most skilled linguist in the palace would understand Scots, so Grissel trotted behind on the pavement of gems, through the courtyards where the pillared gate to each was unique, passed fountains and gardens until they came to the entrance to the harem with its fluted pillars, gold fretwork and stone carvings, which looked curiously more like a building of Antwerp than Constantinople, her eyes as big as platters and, for once, too overwhelmed by her surroundings to need restraining.

What Bethia hadn't counted on was that Grissel, despite being only a servant, was an object of curiosity herself. Like the Valkyrie of Norse mythology, her height, her yellow hair, her eyes as blue as the Bosphorus drew attention wherever she went. Bethia was so used to it she barely noticed. It was just Grissel, the daughter of her parents' servant, who'd followed Bethia everywhere from when she could first walk.

Led into Nurbanu's presence, Bethia laid down the

gift Dona Gracia had advised her to bring. A flick of the hand instructed one of the pretty serving girls to unwrap it and it was set before Nurbanu. *Affife Nurbanu* Dona Gracia said was how Roxelana referred to her daughter-in-law, meaning virtuous. She added that Nurbanu was, of course, a name given to the young girl when she arrived in the harem since her original would not suffice, and meant *queen who scatters the light of God*. Bethia, as ever, was left in awe of Dona Gracia's grasp of detail.

She spoke with Nurbanu, answering questions about how she came to be in Constantinople as best she could. She didn't want to reveal why they had to leave Antwerp, but it was common knowledge Conversos had been fleeing across Europe. The *Haseki Sultan* had a sweet face and a gentleness of manner and must be about the same age as her. The connection was made easier when it transpired Nurbanu had some Italian and they were able to get by without a translator.

Eventually she indicated by a wave of her hand that the audience was over. 'I am here for a few more days only before returning to the old palace, so perhaps you will come back tomorrow?'

It was posed as a question but Bethia understood it as a command.

'And if you can bring some of the silks I've heard Dona Gracia has recently sourced it would be appreciated.'

Bethia bowed and backed away. In the antechamber she looked for Grissel but couldn't see her. A eunuch waited at the door; other concubines too were staring at her. Where *was* Grissel? She moved out into a courtyard to find her servant in the corner engaged in a whispered conversation with another servant.

'Grissel,' she hissed. Grissel gave a slight wave of her hand and finished her conversation. Just as though I was the servant and she the mistress, thought Bethia. Fortunately, Grissel remained silent as they moved through the lines of slaves, dwarves and janissaries.

'Yon lassie can speak Dutch,' said Grissel as they passed through the final set of gates. 'She was telling me aw aboot whit goes on in the harem. You wouldna believe some o' the nonsense they get up tae. And whit's with they giant scary men with the squeaky voices?'

'You mean the eunuchs.'

'Aye, if you say so. Whit is a eunuch?'

'A man who has been castrated so he can serve within the harem.'

Grissel stopped and turned to Bethia, eyes huge. 'They cut off their pizzles?'

'No. Their testicles.'

Grissel nodded slowly. 'Aye, that would work.'

'The eunuchs hold great power. Be very wary of them.'

'Ye dinna hae to tell me that. I'm wary of awthing in yon harem.'

They clambered into the boat for the return trip and Bethia was too busy hanging onto the side with one hand and pressing her belly with the other to give Grissel the intended tongue lashing.

'You have a most lively servant,' said Nurbanu when Bethia appeared the next day, Grissel trailing behind, arms full of packages.

'We were children together and I can trust her like a sister.'

Nurbanu raised her eyebrows. 'Sisters are not necessarily any more trustworthy than brothers.'

Bethia gulped, remembering the fratricide practised here, and wondered if it extended beyond the sultan's family 'I have two brothers and they've always taken exceptional care of me.' She thought of John helping her to escape marriage to Fat Norman and then remembered Will's refusal to leave the siege in St Andrews Castle. 'In the main they have,' she amended.

Nurbanu laughed. 'As long as taking care of you aligned with their own interests.'

Bethia could not help but smile in return.

Nurbanu picked over the silks which her servants had spread before her. 'Can you get me more of this and this one. I'll have my servants all dressed in the pale green to match my darker green.'

'Yes, my lady.'

'And you will speak with the chief eunuch and he will arrange payment.'

Bethia bowed low to hide her relief she was to be reimbursed.

'And now I have an experience for you I think you will enjoy. We are for the *hamam*. Will you join us?'

Bethia bowed her acceptance without having the slightest idea what it might involve.

She was led down another long, narrow corridor most beautifully lined with mosaic tiles which covered the floors and rose high up the walls. The air grew warm and damp and she could see steam seeping through a door at the end but there was no smell of cooking nor food. She guessed it was a bathhouse with which this city seemed to abound and was in equal measure curious and fearful.

In an ante-chamber two serving women came to divest her of her clothes. She stood passively, for there was no point in resisting, allowing herself to be stripped and wrapped in a cloth fine as gossamer. When she turned her head, she could see Grissel watching mouth agape and back against the wall.

Then she was led into the hamam which consisted of a series of small interconnecting rooms with walls and floor of white marble, and deep marble basins affixed to the floor. The women, sitting in alcoves, scooped water from the basins with copper bowls pouring it over themselves while they chatted to one another. Bethia hunched with embarrassment didn't know where to look. She'd never seen another woman naked before, and here there were so many.

The serving woman pointed to a marble slab and indicated she should lay face down. Bethia did as directed, closing her eyes when the cloth was unwrapped exposing her naked body. She was washed most thoroughly and intimately, then flipped over like fish in a pan, and her other side done. They flipped her back again and began to knead her body as though she was bread. Bethia, whose muscles had felt as tightly knotted as a fishing net since she left Ancona, gradually felt the knots loosen. It was the strangest sensation. When she was eventually released from their ministrations, she could barely gather the momentum to stand up, for her bones felt turned to liquid. She staggered and the taller of her two angels stroked her back, staring into her face and saying soft words which Bethia couldn't understand but found soothing.

Mist floated in front of Bethia's eyes making her blink and sticking to her lashes, while water trickled down her face. It all felt like a kind of witchery as figures half emerged and then were again obscured in a fog as thick as any which regularly blanketed her home town in November. The serving woman took her by the hand like a small child and Bethia, fearful she might slip, was grateful. She was guided to where Nurbanu sat with several women around her. Nurbanu beckoned and the women made a space for her.

Carefully Bethia lowered herself down and leant against the wall. She gazed up at the ceiling, which was a cupola created of curved panes of opaque glass with a large candelabra of coloured glass balls hanging in the centre. Bethia watched mesmerised. Was it her imagination or were the glass balls spinning?

'Did you enjoy the massage?'

She came awake, embarrassed to have slept in the presence of this powerful woman. Just the sort of behaviour which would greatly displease Dona Gracia, and most unwise.

'I am so sorry. I didn't mean to drift away.'

'No matter. It has the same effect on us all. Have you known Dona Gracia long?'

'I met her several years ago when she was living in Ferrara but I wouldn't claim to know her. My husband's family have done business with the Mendes family since even before they were forced to leave Portugal. We've drawn close recently over our shared concerns about what's happening in Ancona.' Bethia brushed her cheek, damp from the steam anyway and all tearfulness disguised.

Nurbanu leant forward and murmured in Bethia's ear. 'I have need of eyes and ears outside the palace. Will you be those eyes and ears?'

Bethia paused for a moment, but there was little chance that, naked and vulnerable in the hamam, she was going to refuse. She inclined her head. 'I would be honoured, my lady.' Anyway, no doubt she'd be only one among many.

'You'll have been to the covered market which our wise sultan so cleverly had built.'

'I have indeed. It's the most magnificent market I've ever seen,' said Bethia, meaning it.

'There are slippers there, quite exquisite and embroidered with gold thread. You will know the ones I mean when you see them. I want you to purchase three pairs in different colours for me.' She put up a finger. 'But don't reveal who they're for, else the trader will charge twice as much.'

The woman next to Nurbanu, who clearly understood Italian, whispered to the woman next to her, and so the *Haseki Sultan's* words were passed along, evoking a tinkle of laughter.

By the time Bethia rose to follow Nurbanu from the hamam the skin on her hands was as wrinkled as an old crone's. A servant splashed her with water so cold it took her breath away, and she was released into Grissel's care.

'That was most peculiar,' said Bethia.

'It isna normal, all that rubbing o' oils all ower yer body.'

'Certainly it was... intimate.'

Grissel sniffed appreciatively. 'But I hae to say it smells something wonderful. You're like one great bottle o' perfume. But I'm fair melting wi' the heat.'

'Did you try the baths?'

Grissel shook her head. 'They're nae for the likes of me.'

'Were you offered the opportunity?'

'Aye, but I wisnae going to get water o'er ma hale body. It's no good for yer skin, as I can see by the state yours is in.'

'That's enough, Grissel,' said Bethia more sharply than she meant to. 'Next time try it. You can learn much where women are so relaxed they're near to melting.'

The next day and Bethia was back at the palace with Grissel following, carrying her purchases.

'I wasn't certain which colours you'd prefer, my lady,' she said as she unwrapped the slippers. 'And so I bought one of each.'

Nurbanu studied them and nodded slowly. 'He has expanded his range. I like this purple especially, and look...' She slipped it on one small foot. 'It fits perfectly. You are very clever.'

'We are about the same foot size, my lady, so it was not so difficult.'

Nurbanu hesitated in the process of putting her foot in the other slipper. 'You've had these on your feet?'

'Oh, no, my lady. I could see they were the right size just by looking at them.'

'Very good.' She put the other slipper on and wiggled her feet around while her women coo'd their approval.

She beckoned Bethia to come closer. 'I've spoken with Prince Selim. He's as concerned for the welfare of the men of Ancona as you, and most sympathetic to the plight of a woman without the guiding presence of her husband. He's promised to raise the matter with our most magnificent sultan.'

Bethia clasped her hands together and curtsied low. 'You are most generous and kind. Thank you, oh thank you.'

'Well, well,' said Nurbanu flicking her fingers. 'I can make no promises but it looks hopeful.'

Bethia hastened to the house of Dona Gracia as fast as was possible given the bumpy boat ride, to apprise her of the good news.

Chapter Twenty-Two

Suleiman

Bethia waited for word from the palace. She took to pacing her chamber for most of the day and, since she never slept well without Mainard by her side, for half the night as well. She could settle to nothing, attend to nothing, could not eat, could barely swallow for the fear sat like a plug in her throat choking her.

'Why do you have so many sticky-out bones, Mama?' Jacopo asked. 'I liked it better when you were soft.' She'd liked it better too but she had to be strong, could not risk relying on anyone but herself if her family was to be safe.

Grissel cooked foods Bethia especially liked and brought baklava from the market to tempt her, but nothing could. The baklava lay untouched with the children stealing small corners until only a few crumbs were left and soon they too were gone. Bethia suspected Abram had licked the plate when he knew Grissel's back was turned.

'Yer skin and bones. Dae ye want the master tae come back and find you've faded away tae nothing like one on yon wraiths of the other world? And whatever happens you have tae stay well for they laddies.'

Bethia knew Grissel was right. If Mainard did not return then she must be strong and she must eat, for she could not leave her boys all alone in the world. There was

Catarina but she had a family of her own now. No, she didn't want her sons to go to Catarina, who would no doubt have them circumcised and converted to Judaism. Their Scottish heritage would vanish altogether. Grissel would look after them, of course, but she herself would be adrift with no money and the boys would likely end up the servants of others and that was a hard life with little security unless you found a good family. She sat down on the edge of the kist in her chamber with her head in her hands and rocked back and forward trying to think what to do.

The solution came and she lowered her hands and slowly raised her head. What was she thinking! Of course Father would take them. He wouldn't leave his grandsons defenceless and alone. And she knew he'd move heaven and earth to get them to Scotland. She determined to find a notary here in Constantinople, or whatever form the legal profession took, and make a new will, for she'd not updated hers since she was awaiting Abram's birth. And it was possible to get a letter sent by ship which would eventually reach Scotland. She took pen and paper through to the kitchen and sat in the large chair which had once been Mainard's father's, and which he'd insisted she bring to Constantinople despite its unwieldiness.

It was peaceful for Grissel had taken the boys out. She must start their lessons again, had let things slide too much as despair overtook her. But now she had a plan she felt better. It took her a long time to compose the letter for she didn't want any hint of criticism of the choices Mainard had made, either overt or implied. And she also didn't want Father to think she was entirely unprotected. There was Dona Gracia, but she had so many other hangers-on, and she might leave Constantinople and move on, as she'd done from Venice, Antwerp and Portugal before.

Bethia finished her letter and set out for Dona

Gracia's home, for that lady had a spy network which reached as far as France and possibly into England too and would have some idea how to get a letter delivered with all possible speed to St Andrews, Scotland. She'd expected she'd have to leave it with a servant along with a plea for it to be sent urgently but was somewhat flustered to be ushered into the quasi-royal presence for she was still in her workaday dress.

'Suleiman has agreed to see me,' said Dona Gracia, waving the paper she held in her hand. 'Of course it is likely I will meet with the grand vizier but the sultan will be nearby, listening. Nothing passes within his domain without Suleiman knowing. I am told he even goes out in disguise into the streets so he may learn what is spoken of there.'

Bethia had never seen her so animated; the mask of impassivity for once had slipped. Dona Gracia rose from her chair with the carving of the wolves' heads on the arms. 'We must go, quickly as possible, while he's amenable.'

Bethia looked at her blankly.

Dona Gracia stared back then ran her eyes over what Bethia was wearing. Judging by her expression she was not overly pleased by what she was seeing. 'We must dress you.'

'But, but... neither the sultan nor grand vizier will want to see me.'

'I should imagine neither will have any objection. And who better to take before them than a pretty woman whose husband is missing in Ancona.' She looked to one of the serving women. 'Take her away and see what you can do to dress her suitably. And let her hair flow down her back. Men like long, thick hair,' she muttered.

Bethia glanced away, conscious that Dona Gracia, who when they first met near on ten years ago had had long thick hair herself, now wore a wig to cover her thinning grey locks. She was led away and submitted to being groomed and arranged without a murmur. A fine dress was found for her amongst Dona Gracia's serving maids, for it wouldn't do for her to be clothed in one of Dona Gracia's own garments, even though they were of similar height and size.

They set out with Dona Gracia's entourage accompanying them, including serving ladies and several fearsome men carrying cudgels, some leading the way and others bringing up the rear. Dona Gracia was robed even more magnificently than usual in a dress stitched with pearls and gold thread, a headdress of rich purple embroidered with more pearls and a large diamond set at its centre. As they descended the streets to the quayside, people came out of their houses to see such magnificence, watching in silence while they passed. Bethia, rather than enjoying the attention, grew embarrassed, and, for once, was glad when they embarked on the boats and could pull away, leaving the folk on the quayside gazing after them.

Litters were procured, men running to serve the *hanimefendi*. The *great lady* was transported into the Topkapi as far as the Imperial Gate, where she and Bethia as ever had to step out and walk.

'Do not underestimate Suleiman,' whispered Dona Gracia as they passed beneath its twin towers. He's known to be as ruthless as he is fair.'

Remembering the tale of how he'd had his eldest son garrotted, when he suspected him of fomenting a rebellion, Bethia thought it unlikely she'd ever drop her guard in his presence. She sent up a prayer to the Blessed Virgin not to let her fears for Mainard overcome her good sense during whatever audience they were granted.

They were led between the double turrets of yet another gate and met by a man with a dark clipped beard and dark watchful eyes wearing a high and intricately wrapped turban, the white cloth covering his head in smooth swathes.

'Rüstem Pasha, the vizier. Say nothing,' hissed Dona Gracia.

They passed along the walkway lined by even more janissaries than usual and what seemed like at least a hundred dwarves, hooded hawks resting on their gloved wrists. They were invited to wait in an anteroom where low couches covered in embroidered silk were positioned and refreshments had been left on an equally low table. Bethia perched uncomfortably on the edge of the couch, one hand clutched in the other to contain her anxiety and trying to remember what Dona Gracia had told of the vizier.

'We must convince Rüstem Pasha as much as Suleiman, for he will enact what the sultan commands,' she had said. 'He's the sultan's most trusted advisor. Suleiman even gave Rüstem Pasha his daughter as a bride. And he was the architect of a most advantageous treaty – for the Turks – with the Holy Roman Empire, which Charles has been attempting to overturn ever since it was made. Although it'll now fall to Philip since the rumours are that Charles's plans to abdicate in his favour finally seem to be coming to fruition.'

Bethia gripped her hands even more tightly, wishing they could've delayed coming until she was made better aware of all the politics and wily manoeuvring within the court. She could be no help to Mainard if any time she opened her mouth she might commit some solecism which would harm their case.

Two of Gracia's servants, who'd followed them in, stood in the corner straight-backed and impassive, holding the gifts Dona Gracia had brought for the sultan. The sultan's men took the gifts into the innermost chamber. Dona Gracia and Bethia were bid to follow, the vizier taking the lead. Bethia swallowed – it seemed they *were* to be taken before Suleiman.

The chamber was full to bursting with more courtiers, heads wrapped in white silk turbans, and janissaries, still as statutes, the plumes of their tall hats equally motionless, yet Bethia knew they were watching every move made by the guests. She looked around but could see no sign of anyone who might be the sultan. Then they were led through another doorway. It was more magnificent than the grandest palazzo in Venice: the soaring vaulted ceiling; the plethora of mosaic tiles forming both small repetitive patterns and then great curls; the crystal chandelier hanging in the centre sparkling with a myriad candles; gold used in abundance and precious stones inlaid within the designs. Bethia blinked. So bright was the scene that it hurt her eyes.

A man came on each side of Bethia and Dona Gracia and, gripping their arms, guided them forward. Bethia was most uneasy at being held so, but she observed that Dona Gracia remained impassive despite this affront to her person. Then they were before the sultan, who sat in the centre of his broad divan, his white silk turban, higher than anyone else's, decorated with a horse tail. She wondered at the weight of the turban upon his head – he must have a strong neck. She'd a sudden memory of a guest at their home in Venice claiming the sultan's turban was used as his shroud when he died, hence the great length of cloth necessary to form it.

Suleiman the Lawgiver, builder of mosques, covered markets, universities, aqueducts and bridges, who wrote poetry, studied history, astrology, science and the principles of good governance, as well as being skilled in working gold, looked upon them. Bethia, standing, along with everyone else in the chamber, her eyes cast down, longed to lift them and take a good look at the man whose turban was the only thing she'd glimpsed so far.

There was silence, a heavy silence which pressed down on them. Bethia gulped. Dona Gracia was led forward and bent to kiss the sultan's feet, and Bethia in turn did the same. His slippers were of green satin embroidered with gold thread, and a large emerald decorated the toe of each. She rose quickly and backed away, her arms still held. A sultan, she was guessing, must likely encounter the danger of attack everywhere, even in his heavily guarded audience room.

Head bowed, she was placed against the wall, as far from his eminence as the chamber would permit. The silence continued and she found it hard to breathe. She raised her head just enough to peep from under her brow. Suleiman was gazing at them; shrewd brown eyes in a long thin face dominated by a long narrow nose, neatly trimmed moustache and beard, slender but with broad shoulders across which a cape of ermine was laid in part covering the ornate pattern stitched in red on the white kaftan he wore, a scimitar at his waist, the scabbard encrusted in jewels; more dazzle to her eyes, which she quickly dropped.

A courtier, after a nod from Suleiman, spoke in French, much to Bethia's relief.

'Suleiman, Shadow of God, Commander of the Faithful, Lord of the Lords of the World, welcomes you.'

Two other courtiers stepped forward and spread the gifts Dona Gracia had brought before the sultan. He waved his hand towards a small bowl fashioned from gold and with its handles cunningly carved like dragons. It was brought for him to examine more closely. He gave a nod of approval and the courtier backed away.

Suleiman slid each hand inside the opposite sleeve of his kaftan and rested his eyes first on Dona Gracia and then on Bethia.

'You are seeking my intervention,' he said, and the words were translated into French.

His voice was well modulated and rather attractive.

He turned to the vizier. 'They may speak. Briefly.'

Bethia, turning to Dona Gracia, could see her swallow. 'We beg the support and influence of a mighty ruler.'

She opened her mouth to continue and the sultan

173

waved his hand again. Dona Gracia closed her mouth.

'I will write to my friend the king of France and see if together we may bring influence to bear on the Pope.'

The vizier nodded and came forward ready to lead them from the throne room, but Suleiman's hand came up once more. He flicked a lazy finger towards Bethia and she was brought forward again to kneel at his feet.

'You are from a country of the north,' he said softly.

'Yes, my sultan.'

'It is a land of red-haired people, or so I am given to understand.'

Bethia spoke, mouth so dry she could barely get the words out. 'My brothers and my father have red hair. It is very common in my country as you wisely say, my sultan.'

He nodded slowly and she backed from the throne room along with Dona Gracia.

'That was the most remarkable spectacle ever. More magnificent even than Emperor Charles and Philippe of Spain's royal entry to Antwerp,' said Bethia when they had finally emerged from the labyrinth of the palace and stood on its private dock.

She realised, from Dona Gracia's pursed lips, that she shouldn't have spoken first.

'What did he want of you?'

'To know if everyone in Scotland has red hair, why I do not.'

Dona Gracia's eyes widened and she burst out laughing.

Chapter Twenty-Three

A Visitor

Suleiman's message to the king of France had not borne fruit. And he was angry, for rulers do not expect to have their requests disregarded; it makes them look weak. The Jews of Ancona continued to be tortured and imprisoned. And still there was no word of Mainard. If Bethia hadn't had three sons, a household to run and her new work as *kira* to the harem then she would've taken to her bed and lain there frozen with fear. But each day she must get up, wash, dress, apply the perfumes which Dona Gracia insisted she drench herself in so she too smelt as overpoweringly of scent as the women of the harem, and wend her way through the vast covered market with Grissel and Johannes in attendance to fulfil their requests.

She quickly realised she herself exerted a certain power, for it was soon discovered, by means unknown to her, that *Kuzey'in kadını,* the woman of the north, had powerful connections beyond the reach, or imagination, of any trader. It became difficult, and tiresome, for her to conduct business without being endlessly importuned. She was one day pondering a solution as she walked down the hill, past the enormous dome of the Hagia Sofia mosque – which had been the Byzantines magnificent church for nine hundred years before the Turks took the city – to the quayside where her boat awaited, trailed by

Grissel, Johannes carrying the many packages and Grissel's Italian-speaking Turk equally laden down, when her usual boatman called out saying there was a stranger asking for her.

Bethia stopped with such abruptness her small troupe had to take evasive action. She put her hands to her heart, could feel it beating wildly, convinced it must be Mainard. 'Where is he?' she said, her head turning frantically.

'He was here a moment ago,' said the boatman. 'I said you'd likely soon return.'

'Which way did he go?'

'Ahmed,' he shouted, 'where did the giant go?'

But Bethia had seen the tall figure approaching. A sob escaped her; it wasn't Mainard. It looked like Will but the hair flowing out from beneath his cap and touching his shoulders was a lighter red.

'John?' she called.

It was him. John had come. Her wee brother grown into a man.

She heard a gasp from behind, and Grissel shot past her, scattering packages and, grasping John by the arms, shook him. 'John, you wee bugger, whit are you doing here?'

Bethia stood before her brother saying, 'Oh John, I'm so happy to see you,' for it was true now she'd squashed the disappointment it wasn't Mainard.

He gazed down upon her. John with a beard! But then he grinned and she could see again the impudent lad forever up to mischief.

Somehow they all got into the boat with their parcels and across the Golden Horn to Galata.

Grissel had much to say, asking of her mother, the journey and how long it had taken. 'It's an awfie thing, travel. I dinna think I wid ever hae set oot if I'd kent how uncomfortable, nasty and dangerous it is.'

Bethia let her speak and shook her head slightly at

176

John when he went to ask questions of her. Better to wait till they were in the privacy of her home.

'I do not understand,' John kept repeating when they were finally able to have a private conversation. 'How can it be that you've had no word of his whereabouts? If, as you say, this Gracia woman has a list of all Conversos imprisoned in Ancona, and Mainard is not among them, then in Ancona he cannot be.' He paused. 'Unless he's in hiding since that's where your servant last saw him.'

'It's a long time to hide and surely he would've gone to Pesaro since other Conversos who escaped did.' Bethia pressed her palms together. 'None of it makes any sense. How can my Mainard have vanished so completely? He was working with a man called Foscari and Joseph Nasi had word that Foscari was ambushed and killed but there was no mention of Mainard.'

John frowned. 'Who is Joseph Nasi?'

'Dona Gracia's nephew.'

'You've not much enlightened me.'

'They're powerful people to whom we are in debt. But Dona Gracia has been gracious towards me.'

'She lives up to her name then.'

'Yes. If not for her we would likely have been on the streets by now.'

John's face darkened. 'Did my brother-in-law really leave you so unprovided for?'

'No, no it wasn't like that. He sent us with funds but he was to follow soon after. The money all but ran out. But,' she said brightly, 'now I have a small business which is quite profitable.' She couldn't help the note of pride from creeping into her voice. of my capable sister.'

'Enough of me. Did father send you here? I wrote to him.'

She looked expectantly at John, who avoided her eyes.

'Not exactly.'

'So how do you come to be here?'

177

'I saw Will in Edinburgh.'

'Will was in Edinburgh!'

'Yes, following that fellow Knox about.'

'Was Cecile with him?'

'The wife, no. What's she like?'

'Very French, and opinionated.'

'You don't like her?'

Bethia tilted her head. 'I didn't dislike her, but she's not someone you'd warm to. Holds herself back and didn't approve of me being a Catholic.' She shook her head at him. 'But in any case we're getting distracted. How do *you* come to be here?'

John grinned and again she could see the wild freckle-faced devil that was her wee brother. 'You and Will have had adventures. I wanted to have some too. And you did promise when you left me all alone with our parents that you'd come back.'

She reached over and lightly touched his arm. 'And I would've done too, if only it was easily possible. But what of poor Father? He'll be so upset and worried. I hope you left him a note.'

'Well,' said John slowly. 'It was like this. I was in Leith, for Father has a warehouse there now, which I oversee, as well as helping Aunt Jennet.'

Bethia stared. John seemed barely old enough for such responsibility.

'And these fellows came in and they were talking about trading opportunities and I just thought about how I could set something up that was all mine instead of being under Father's thumb – which is not an easy place to be for there's little space left to wiggle – and then I went out onto the docks and there was a ship bound for Genoa, which is not a common thing. Not common at all. And I remembered what that fellow Horace had to say, *carpe diem, quam minimum credula postero,* and I knew if I didn't seize the day such a chance was unlikely to come again.'

Bethia's mouth dropped open. 'I don't know what I'm

more amazed by – that you got on the ship or that you actually can remember some of the Latin so painfully, and reluctantly, learned.'

John smiled at her fondly. 'You were ay a good and patient teacher.'

Bethia's answering smile faded. 'Oh John, Father will be so upset.'

'And angry. I know. At least he can't whip me.'

'Yes, you're way too tall for him to try. But I think he'll be very worried about you.' She chewed on her lip. 'In any case, how did you know I was here?'

'I got to Venice. Christ's wounds, what a place, and I was going to Ancona when I met a fellow who said you'd come to Constantinople.'

'What was his name?'

John shrugged. 'Can't remember – his eyebrows joined in the middle like a furry pelt.'

'That's not very helpful. The Virgin was certainly watching over you that you reached here at all. How *were* you planning to find us in Constantinople?'

'There was a fellow on the ship who said many Conversos lived in Galata, and I thought you'd likely be here and be known.'

Bethia laughed as she looked up at her brother, his face, burnt red from the sun, now near matching his hair colour.

'İskoçya,' I was told to say.

It was so good to have him here, and he was resourceful enough for anything. 'Yes,' she said, 'it could have worked, for some here call me *Iskoç bayan*. It means Scottish lady.'

'That's bonny.'

'Yes, I rather like it. But however you came, glad I am to have you,' she said, wrapping her arms around his waist and pressing her face into his waistcoat.

'Enough, enough,' said John, and she knew he was embarrassed by such a display of sisterly affection. The last time she'd hugged him was as a small boy when she left Scotland and even then he'd brushed her off and run away to hide his tears.

She stepped back and spoke, counting the points she was making off on her fingers. 'But just to be clear: you have reached here more by luck than good judgement; you've come without Father's permission; your funds are exhausted.'

'I wouldn't say exhausted exactly, more they are quite low.'

The door of the salon opened and a small boy's head appeared.

'Now who is this?' said John.

The head disappeared and there was a shout as he called to his brothers. 'There's another giant here like Uncle Will, but not him.'

The boys came piling into the chamber and stood in a line gazing up at John. 'Well now,' said John, 'you laddies will need to show me around. Do you think you can do that?'

The boys grinned at one another.

'Oh, yes,' said Jacopo.

John was soon established in the house. This new uncle was an even greater favourite than Uncle Will, who was fun but was solemn betimes, whereas Uncle John was always ready to enter into any prank, ploy or daring deed. Although when he took the bedclothes to make a rope from which the boys could be lowered from the upper casement, Bethia was inclined to agree with Grissel he'd gone too far.

'Whit are ye thinking, ye unholy terror? Dae you want they laddies to break their wee necks? And these are guid blankets we brung all the way from Antwerp.' Grissel stood hands on her hips glaring while John winked at the boys, who were backing away.

Bethia, standing on the sidelines, watched her brother

charm Grissel and thought what an unholy terror he must be with the lassies, as well as the lads.

'Now, Grissel, dinna fash yerself. What were we corsairs to do but make good our escape from the dreaded Barbarossa? You wouldna have yer boys captured, would you?' He reached out a long arm and tickled Grissel, who let out a giggle as she batted him away, and then, with a nod from John the boys piled in too and soon Bethia had to rescue her servant before she collapsed from laughter. But oh it was good to have some fun after the months of worry and fear.

'You dinna whip the laddies?' John asked one day when they had brief moment of privacy after Jacopo had left the room, head hanging, having been roundly scolded for chasing Abram with a dead mouse.

Bethia, about to broach the topic of what John's plans were, was happy to let it rest for a wee while longer.

She shook her head emphatically. 'Mainard was never beaten by his own father and doesn't consider it has much merit as a punishment.'

'Wise man.'

'I take it you wrote to Father when you were in Venice. It's not so difficult to send a letter from there.'

John gazed at his feet.

'Get thee to the board and I will supply the pens, ink and paper.'

He dropped down on the settle, picked up the quill and slowly sharpened it, placed a piece of paper in front of him and paused the pen above the inkwell. He looked expectantly at Bethia.

'What should I say?'

She sighed. 'Tell him you had a prescient sense I needed you.'

John rolled his eyes. 'I may as well tell him I went to an astrologer who warned me you were in trouble. Father will either not believe it or think I've gone mad.'

Bethia sniffed. 'Don't deride astrologers. Sometimes

181

they can make the most powerful of prophecies.' She walked up and down the small chamber. 'Suleiman himself dabbles in astrology and there's even been a chief astrologer at court, although I understand they must take care within the tenets of Islam how that's managed.'

'I could simply say I wanted to see my only sister.'

'That might suffice,' said Bethia slowly.

John threw down the pen. 'What are you going to do, Bethia?' He stood up and took her hands in his, gazing down upon her. 'What happens, pray to God it doesn't, if de Lange never returns? I think you must all come home with me.'

She shook her head, unable to speak as her eyes filled with tears.

'You know I'm right.'

'But what if he does return and I am gone?' she wept.

'Then, if his past actions are anything to go by, he'll come for you.'

'Give me another month.'

'Let us at least work out what funds we need for a journey of three adults and three children, for we cannot leave Grissel behind, and see how much that leaves – and from that how long we can stay here.'

'Five adults, three children and a baby,' said Bethia. 'I will not leave Johannes and his family behind.'

John huffed. 'I understand, but that gives even less capacity to linger.'

Bethia pressed her hands against her belly. It was like she was burning away deep inside at the prospect of a life without Mainard.

'Let me think on it,' she said slowly. 'But in the meantime, what about your fledgling business? I think there might be some work and connections I can put your way.'

John sat up straight. 'I'm all ears.'

Bethia, glancing at the rather large ears poking through his hair, bit her lip to hold in the smile.

Chapter Twenty-Four

Eid

Galata had many of the wealthier Conversos living in its neighbourhood but it was also the location of large homes of wealthy Turks. Ramadan was over and the celebration known as Eid, although some called it Ramadan Bayrami – which to Bethia was most strange for wasn't bayram a kind of sweet – was now underway. The streets were even more overfull of people than usual: Moslems dressed in their yellow slippers with white turbans, enjoying the end of their lengthy period of daily fasting, amid the Jews with their yellow hats and blue slippers, Greeks dressed in sky blue, and Armenians sporting violet slippers. Bethia's neighbours had even sent their children over to wish them *Happy Bayrami*, bringing a plate of sweet jellies so delicious she managed to eat only one before her children, and John, consumed the lot.

On her way to Dona Gracia's, she could see the cemetery on the corner was busy with people. She wondered if someone important had died yesterday for it looked to be a big funeral. But they weren't clustered around one graveside but making their way between graves, small family groups gathering around specific ones. This must also be a time for remembering the dead, she reasoned, then forgot all about it as she was bidden to

183

enter Dona Gracia's home.

She emerged sometime later, reached home, and called her children and Grissel to her. 'We're going somewhere special and I need three clean boys with hands, faces and ears scrubbed, and hair combed. I will be inspecting... and that includes you, Uncle John,' she said as her brother appeared in the doorway. The children shrieked with laughter.

Fifteen minutes later and the boys stood before her in a row – three sturdy lads of varying heights and all looking so like their father it made her heart ache.

'Very good,' she said. 'And Ysabeau and Johannes will come too, for this is something they both will enjoy.'

Off they set in procession into the gathering dusk, Bethia leading, with Abram walking by her side but refusing to take her hand, John on her other side and the older two boys deep in conversation behind with their servants bringing up the rear.

Grissel, Ysabeau, holding her baby, and Johannes stood to the side while Bethia, John and the children sat on stools before a three-sided booth containing a white candlelit screen. The show began with a singer and a tambourine player, while behind them ships, horses with riders, and swaying trees set the scene for the shadow puppets. Then out came Karagoz, who had one arm much longer and thicker than the other, presumably to denote he was the worker whereas Hacivat appeared to be the talker. Bethia could follow little of what was said but, judging by the reaction of the crowd, it was funny and full of double meaning. The boys laughed uproariously at the movement of the shadow puppets and, turning round, Bethia could see Ysabeau, big-eyed and smiling. John did not say much but looked thoughtful. The outing had been a success and she had forgotten her worries, albeit briefly.

Whenever they were out together John created a stir; this

tall Scotsman with the red hair cascading onto his shoulders, the trimmed red beard and his way of acknowledging and remembering those he met with a cheery wave and a big smile. She discovered he too had a name: *Kirmizi Dev*, Red Giant, the street sellers, the boatmen, the waifs of the street would call out when they saw him. One old woman, who Bethia had found nothing but sour-faced, would have John's special cup of hot salep ready for him each morning and refused any payment. John would swallow it with great courtesy and evident pleasure, regularly bringing the seller a gift of honey cakes.

'I don't know how you can drink that stuff,' said Bethia. 'It's so bitter.'

'It does have a most unusual flavour. What *is* it made from?'

'The root of a flower called an orchid, or so Grissel tells me. Do you actually like it?'

'Ach, I've drunk worse and I wouldn't offend the old lady. She looks to have had a hard life.'

Bethia gazed at him. 'You're a good man, John.'

'I guess all Father's whippings were to some benefit then,' he said wryly. 'And I am planning to take some back with me to sell in Scotland. The bitterer the taste the more people will believe it's a remedy.'

Bethia took John's arm as they walked back down the hill, the white walls which encircled the palace rising high to one side. 'Have you decided what else might be useful for trade in Scotland?'

'I've some ideas,' he said. 'The shadow puppets would be new and strange. I've commissioned some to be made and they'll show me how to use them.'

'You'll become a puppeteer?'

'No!' He laughed. 'I'll teach others.'

'You think there's much money to be made from that?'

'There's money all right, but I wouldn't offer it in the streets.'

'Too cold in Scotland,' said Bethia.

'There's that, but I'll make far more providing it as entertainment in the homes of rich merchants and bored noblewomen – and it'll be a useful way to make further connections.'

She nodded appreciatively. Clever John.

'But that's only a sideline. There is a root come from the Americas called black cohosh which is said to help cure infertility.'

Bethia turned her head and gazed up at him. 'Where on earth did you learn about that?'

'I spend my life speaking to people, Bethia. It's what I'm good at. I bought some in Leith recently and sold it on to the apothecaries. Dona Gracia was interested when I mentioned it.'

'You've been meeting with her?'

'Only once, at her request, and we spoke of this and other matters.'

She said nothing. John was grown man and could look out for himself.

'I'll source a regular supply for her and she in return has ordered her suppliers to deliver chasteberry leaves, which I, in turn, will promote as another cure for infertility in Scotland, but this time come from the exotic East.'

And how are you to fund this she wanted to ask but did not. She knew the answer anyway. If he should end up in debt to the Mendes too, so be it.

A few weeks later and John was ready and eager to leave, and urging Bethia to come with him. When he began to discuss the route they might take, Bethia said she was prepared to go if they went via Ancona, where she might manage to do what no one else seemed to, and gain some news of Mainard's whereabouts.

John was dubious but agreed to at least see if he could find a ship going there.

He haunted the quays over the next few days refusing any offers of assistance. Bethia couldn't understand how he hoped to arrange passage without at least a smattering of Turkish.

'I can manage,' he said, 'for many of the captains have French, or indeed are French. But I've failed in my task and cannot find a ship bound for Ancona. It seems the sultan has forbidden all trade there.'

Bethia leapt to her feet and danced around the room. 'It worked. Suleiman enacted what Dona Gracia begged for: a blockade of Ancona.'

'Who would think it, that a woman could sway Suleiman the Magnificent.'

'Hush, John. This may seem a benign city but the sultan will tolerate no disrespect, even spoken behind closed doors. He has many watchers. Indeed, his network of spies is said to be greater and spread more widely than any other king of Europe.'

'But I'm not denigrating Suleiman, only admiring Gracia. And I don't understand why you won't seek her help to arrange passage home.'

'Because I don't think she'd willingly see me leave. Mainard is one of her agents. She'll want me to remain here, and especially as I'm building a good business as *kira* to the seraglio, which she benefits from.'

The door banged open and Abram burst into the room, crying with indignation. 'Uncle John, Uncle John, they say I's too small to ride a horse. But I's not.'

John turned to attend to his nephew. 'You can be as bold a buccaneer as your brothers, if you choose.' He swept the lad up, tossing him in the air until Abram was shrieking with laughter. His brothers rushed to join in, clamouring around John's legs and reaching their arms up to claim their turn.

'Are you truly going to risk everything by lingering here?' John said once Bethia had chased the boys back to Grissel.

Bethia sighed. 'Our whole lives are one long risk. Nowhere and nothing is safe. There are great risks in travel too. We were fortunate to evade a corsair's ship on the way here and nearly lost Samuel-Thomas on the journey to Geneva.'

'So Will told me. But Bethia, soon the winter storms will come and, whatever you decide, I'm leaving the moment I find a ship.'

Bethia went to bed, and in the night it started: a shivering and shaking which she couldn't control. But the next morning she rose and steadied herself. Off she went first to Dona Gracia's for her instructions and goods and thence to the harem.

When she returned home she told John she would not go with him. 'My husband is coming, I can feel it here,' she said, striking her fist against her breast.

John raised his eyebrows. 'I pray you're proved correct.'

He left three days later. She knew it likely she'd never see her wee brother again and wept, but only in the privacy of her own chamber and once he was gone.

Her business was thriving. She could feed her family; she was their provider. There was nothing to be afraid of.

And then finally, word came. Mainard was found.

Part Five

Mainard

1555 to 1556

Chapter Twenty-Five

A Coffin

Mainard's head felt like an empty vessel with a few stones rattling around inside it. He struggled to open his eyes, focusing all his strength on raising his eyelids, but he could not do it. He gave up the effort and drifted away once more.

When he next came to, he could feel hard wooden planks beneath him, his body lifting and falling like a rag doll dragged along by a child. Jacopo had had one which he was most attached to and Mainard removed it, saying a boy of near on five years old should not be playing with dolls, but Jacopo was clutching it to his chest the following day. Someone, Grissel he suspected, had returned it to him.

There was a jolt more severe than all the previous ones and his face banged against something hard, close above. This was not the prison in Ancona. Where was he being taken, and in what? Couldn't think. His eyes flickered open; darkness with sharp beams of light stabbing through the cracks. But the effort to keep them open was too much and they closed on the knowledge he'd likely been given some potion.

There was a terrible screeching and the lid above him came off. He blinked, dazzled by the light, and struggled in the narrow confines to lift his head but soon gave up the effort, letting it fall back. His limbs lay inert as a cripple's. He could hear a noise; it was his own voice groaning. He forced himself to close his mouth.

A face, thin and dirty, appeared above him and a hand wiped Mainard's own face with a damp cloth, cooling and refreshing. He tried to speak but the words wouldn't form in his mouth.

'Don't struggle.'

The face disappeared and a large shadow blocked the sunlight. Mainard's head was gently lifted. He pressed his lips together but they were forced apart and bitter liquid poured down his throat. He coughed as the lid was sealed above him, the hammering loud in his ears.

He came awake with a start and sat up in one smooth movement. He wiggled his jaw from side to side and opened his eyes as wide as he could. Swinging his legs onto the floor, he stood up, swayed then fell back onto the bed. He lay there for a moment gathering his strength to move again. Holding onto the bedpost he hauled himself upright and waited, head hanging, until the dizziness passed. Letting go, he walked to the door, placing each foot down with great concentration. He lifted the latch and the door opened, much to his surprise; this was clearly no prison.

Then Francesco Foscari was before him.

'What are *you* doing here... wherever here is?' said Mainard. 'And more to the point, what am I?'

Foscari grinned. 'That, Master de Lange, is quite a story. Come into the salon and I will explain all.'

Mainard followed Foscari along the passageway, pressing his hand against the wall to keep his balance. They entered the salon and he staggered towards the nearest chair. Dropping into it, he rolled forward over his knees, head dangling close to the floor, swallowing to contain the nausea.

After a few moments he looked up to find Foscari

observing him. 'I feel terrible. What did you give me?'

'Only a potion to make you sleep.'

'It was certainly more than a single potion. I remember it being forced down my throat several times. And it didn't just make me sleep, it made me insensible,' he narrowed his eyes, 'for what I'm assuming was some days.'

Foscari moved towards him and Mainard flinched as the man came closer. If he'd had the strength he would've stood up to fend Foscari off, but his limbs were soft as calf's foot jelly. Foscari squeezed Mainard's shoulder and Mainard felt strangely comforted even though it was certainly Foscari who'd drugged and shut him up in a coffin.

'Where is Johannes?'

Foscari tilted his head to one side. 'Your priorities are strange. Here you sit, confused and unwell from your journey, and yet almost your first concern is a scrawny lad who I understand was once your potboy.'

Mainard shifted in his chair. He didn't have to explain the workings of his household to a man who'd kidnapped him. 'Our servants are loyal.' He paused, hoping it was still true of Johannes. 'And we in turn look after them.'

Foscari sniffed and pursed his lips. 'I don't pretend to understand how a Converso home may function, but be assured your potboy should be safely on his way to Constantinople.'

'And why am I here and not on my way to Constantinople with him?'

'Let me explain.'

Mainard drew his head back at Foscari's tone.

'I have brought you to the home of my brother in Bologna.'

He held up his hand as Mainard opened his mouth to shout *why in the name of God, or the Devil, Bologna.*

'No one will think to look for you here. Nor are they

likely to connect you and I, for no one will have seen us travelling together since you were hidden. The Inquisition was about to take you, there was no time to debate and agree. I had a plan and had to act immediately.'

'But why not take me to Pesaro, or even Venice, where I could get a ship bound for Constantinople?'

'Ah, good question,' said Foscari leaning back, causing his chair to creak most alarmingly.

It was Mainard's turn to hold up his hand. 'Don't tell me. Joseph Nasi is behind it.' He narrowed his eyes and stared at Foscari. 'He had me kidnapped,' he said slowly.

'You could put it like that, but a more accurate description is Don Joseph had you plucked right from under the nose of the Inquisition.' Foscari stroked his head, shiny as ever in the light from the tall windows of this home of a clearly wealthy man. 'He...'

'Yes, yes,' said Mainard. 'He has a task for me which made it expedient for him, but not for me, that I come to Bologna.'

'Not Bologna exactly,' said Foscari, leaning back slowly, while the chair creaked long in response. 'He wants you to go to Frankfurt.'

'What!'

'There's business he has with the Fuggers and you have a sister living in Frankfurt, or so I understand.'

'Never mind my sister. What of my wife and children waiting for me in Constantinople? Is it not enough I stayed behind when any wise man would've left – and all at Nasi's direction.'

Foscari interlocked his fingers and rested them on his belly. His calm demeanour incensed Mainard. 'And how come you're Nasi's errand boy?'

Foscari smiled slowly. 'I will put the insult down to your disoriented state. Don Joseph and I do some business as you know and it's in my interests to satisfy him since he's the richest man of my acquaintance. He's seeking an alliance with another of the richest families in the known world, the Fuggers, and considers you will easily be accepted by them because of your brother-in-law's connections.'

'Hah! Then he knows nothing. I have had no connection nor any correspondence with my brother-in-law since he left me languishing in an Antwerp prison six years ago.' Mainard extended his twisted foot. 'Where I was tortured.'

'But you are in contact with your sister,' said Foscari. It wasn't a question.

Mainard remembered Bethia describing Gracia Mendes as a giant spider sitting in the centre of its web watching and waiting, and controlling all that touched its threads while constantly spinning more to entrap who she could. And he was well and truly caught in the Mendes's web.

He could feel the flush of anger suffusing his face. He'd served them well and didn't deserve to be so manipulated. He wondered if Dona Gracia knew what Nasi was about. Somehow he suspected not. He pressed his palm to his forehead; needed to think without Foscari watching him with those shrewd eyes. He could find his way to a seaport and embark for Constantinople, although he'd have to borrow funds from somewhere as no doubt all that was in the house at Ancona had been seized. If he arrived in Constantinople without discharging the commission Don Joseph had given him, then he'd likely receive little assistance and have to build new trade from scratch, without the Mendes's powerful connections – for Dona Gracia, whatever she thought of Don Joseph's methods, and however she might remonstrate with him in private, would not show any dissension in public, especially now Joseph Nasi was married to her daughter.

He dropped his hands and looked up at Foscari. 'Why Frankfurt when the Fuggers base is Augsburg?'

'Their contacts are spread as wide as the Mendes, indeed probably much wider. No one is as rich as the Fuggers. And in Frankfurt there is the twice-yearly fair which they attend.'

Mainard shook his head helplessly. 'Tell me what it is I have to do.'

And so within a few hours he was on his way, having left a letter with Foscari and extracted a promise the man would make sure it was sent with all possible haste to Bethia in Constantinople.

Chapter Twenty-Six

Schyuder

Mainard journeyed in the company of a group of well-armed, well-stocked and well-guarded merchants. Travel was always perilous but the dangers had increased exponentially with the Pope's vigorous pursuit of heretics in Italy, Philip of Spain's vicious Inquisition in the Low Countries and the Duke of Guise's determined eradication of the rising numbers of Protestants in France. Inevitably, Conversos were getting caught up in the religious turmoil and, along with Jews, would no doubt be used as the whipping boy by all.

The further he travelled north the more he felt tugged to turn around and make a run for his wife and sons. He'd never felt the strength of his attachment so viscerally before. It was as though there was a great cord stretching from his belly and stretching, and stretching. Then he had to laugh at himself, for the umbilical cord was a woman's domain. He would've felt better if he'd had at least some communication from Bethia, but he'd no notion of whether she'd yet arrived safely in Constantinople. His family could be paupers in that vast city for all he knew. He reminded himself that his wife was a resourceful woman, an experienced traveller and the Mendes family would provide support. But still, he would feel more reassured when he received a letter. It was several weeks since he and Foscari had parted, so Bethia should soon know where he was bound, if not why, although she was wise enough to read between the lines.

They passed through Augsburg, the centre of the Fuggers' great mining empire, and again Mainard wondered why he could not simply speak with a Fugger there, deliver the coded message and collect what was required. He was tempted to try and gain access to the Fugger home but knew it was a fool's errand. The richest family in Europe were well guarded and would not allow an itinerant traveller through their door. It was not how things were done. An approach must come through known channels, which it appeared his brother-in-law, the sly fox, was among.

The group he found to travel north with from Augsburg was a smaller party, less well armed and less well guarded. At the forefront of his mind, for now, was his own safety. They went by river for much of the journey, which was quicker but had its own perils – sandbanks, fast water, other barges – and a level of discomfort, crammed in as they were and required to lie down in a line like corpses awaiting burial when passing beneath very low bridges.

And quicker than expected they reached Frankfurt. Mainard showed his credentials and was waved through the gate and into what seemed a compact, inevitably overcrowded and yet attractive town. He'd no trouble in obtaining directions to Schyuder's business in the Buchgasse – Book Lane – how appropriate. Schyuder was a printer still, a small fish in the big pond of Frankfurt. Mainard was surprised he'd removed here from Strasbourg, where there was less competition, for it was said the number of printers in Frankfurt was greater than its rat population.

The man was not to be found in the cramped rooms from which his printing business was run, but Mainard recognised, and was in turn recognised by, the mumbling Dutchman who greeted him when he entered. It seemed Schyuder showed more loyalty to his workers than his relatives, given this fellow, Elrick, had come from Antwerp with him.

Following Elrick's directions he found his way to one of the tall, narrow houses which abounded in Frankfurt, close to the river and around the corner from a church. Obviously Conversos could live near a church here without fear of the Pope's Inquisitor descending to expel them and confiscate their property. But in any case, Schyuder, from the moment he'd adopted a German-sounding name, had discarded his Converso origins – except when it might be of use to him, as with the connection to the Mendes.

His brother-in-law was doing well enough it seemed, although the house was in a narrow street facing into other houses of equal height which allowed little sunlight. The small, dark entrance hall to which he was admitted confirmed his impression of gloominess.

He heard a noise from above. A woman's voice calling, the sound of running feet on wooden boards, a child crying, another laughing, a thump as someone fell, a shout now from the woman, and the distracted servant, small and neat in her white kerchief and capacious apron, who'd let Mainard in, edged past him and went scuttling up the stairs. She reappeared carrying a limp child, and behind her two boys and a girl, all of middle years, thundered down the stairs narrowly avoiding a smaller child who was determinedly descending unaided, face screwed up in concentration.

The children crowded around eyeing him curiously while still managing to knock against one another. At the top of the stairs a well-dressed woman of comfortable size who was either with child or tending towards excessive plumpness, or perhaps both, appeared. Geertruyt, for it was she, looking not much older than when he'd last seen her six years ago, shrieked and came down the stairs in such a rush he feared for her safety.

She flung her arms around him, still crying out. 'Mainard, may the Lord save and keep me. Mainard, is it really you? What are you doing here? Why did I have no notice of your coming? Oh, Mainard, I am so happy to see you.'

After she'd hugged and exclaimed, she released him and stepped back. 'This, children,' she said, looking down at her brood who, wide-eyed, stared back at her, 'is my little brother and your uncle.'

Mainard had always been closer to his younger sister Catarina, finding Geertruyt noisy and overly interfering, but he felt his heart swell at her loving welcome. It was good to be amid family again.

He glanced up to see Schyuder himself descending the stairs. 'Ah, you are come. I had word you might.'

Geertruyt turned to her husband in astonishment. 'You *knew* Mainard was coming and didn't tell me?'

He placed his hand on her arm, a small man next to a taller, younger, well-rounded wife. 'Travel is uncertain, my dear. I didn't want to disappoint. Your brother might've been unavoidably delayed or indeed not come at all.'

She accepted this explanation with a nod then bustled her children back up the stairs, took the limp child from the servant and ordered her to fetch refreshments and, with a glance at her husband, said to Mainard, 'We may have an hour to catch up before you need talk business.'

The tallest child tilted his head and looked up shyly at Mainard as he slid past.

'Pauwels?' said Mainard.

The lad nodded.

'You were a small boy and not the strapping lad you are now when last we met.'

'You used to throw me up in the air. I liked it very much.'

Mainard smiled at his nephew, who grinned back. 'How old are you now… you must be close on seven years.'

'I will be eight very soon.'

'Then I think you're too old to toss in the air now, but perhaps we might spar with a wooden sword, if you have them.'

Pauwels grinned. 'Can we do it now? I can fetch me and my brother's swords. He can watch,' he added, as though conferring a great honour.

'Mainard,' Geertruyt called. He'd forgotten how loud she was.

They didn't have long together before Schyuder appeared in the doorway and beckoned, but Geertruyt managed to say a great deal about her clever and naughty children and her life in Frankfurt – much better sort of people here than those to be found in either Antwerp or Strasbourg – and inquire of Mainard how Bethia and his children were. He noticed she didn't mention the child laying across her lap, and when the servant, having brought refreshments, took him away he didn't stir. There was something odd about the positioning of his limbs, and the legs especially hung inert.

'He's slow to grow,' said Geertruyt, observing Mainard watching, 'but every child is different and soon he'll be running around with his brothers and sisters.'

Mainard wanted to ask *just how many children do you have* but didn't like to admit he'd lost track. If Bethia were here she'd know. He sighed. It was the least among the many reasons he wished his wife was with him.

He rose then and went, most reluctantly, to speak with Schyuder. It seemed there were not one but two tasks required of him. Schyuder opened his mouth to give the details but Mainard interrupted him.

'I didn't know until now you were part of Don Joseph's web of connections?'

Before Schyuder could reply Mainard answered the

question himself. 'But then Gracia Mendes and Joseph Nasi will have spies beyond what I can begin to imagine.'

Schyuder shrugged. 'They've been useful to me on occasion.'

Mainard leaned forward on the stool Schyuder had directed him to while he took the large chair. Even on a low stool Mainard near rose above Schyuder. Yet it was Schyuder who held the power, for the moment.

'You removed from Antwerp hurriedly – and without saying farewell or sending a message.'

'It was best to go quickly.'

'And without warning?'

Schyuder steepled his fingers and repeated Mainard's words. 'And without warning.'

'So you knew I'd been taken.'

'I knew no such thing,' said Schyuder softly. 'I chose for my family's sake to leave.'

'Well your timing was impeccable. I thank God for my good friend Ortelius, without whose assistance I would be languishing in prison still, or more likely dead.'

'You are indeed fortunate to have such a friend.'

Mainard clenched his fists. He wanted to punch Schyuder's self-satisfied face.

Schyuder got up suddenly and walked to stand in front of an etching, likely of Frankfurt, which hung on his wall, chin resting in his hand and with his back to Mainard.

Mainard sat motionless on his stool, waiting.

'Your father was a good man,' Schyuder said quietly. 'I was saddened to hear of his passing.'

Mainard's face softened.

Schyuder turned. 'He helped me greatly when I was imprisoned. I am sorry I was unable to aid you in return.'

Mainard said nothing, still did not believe Schyuder was unaware of his arrest.

'I never repaid the funds he so generously gave to secure my release and would like now to make good the debt.'

Mainard's eyes widened in surprise. This he had not expected.

They discussed terms. Schyuder wanted Mainard to take at least part of the repayment in books. 'For I understand they're much in demand in the Ottomans, especially the Talmud… and the Tefillot.'

Mainard stared at Schyuder and saw the glimmer of a smile spread across his thin face. 'I take it you know about Catarina and her determination to keep a hold of the sacred texts – and the danger she placed us in several times because of it.'

'I have heard all about it, including Geertruyt's views on Katheline changing her name to Catarina.'

'Did my mother write and tell you?' Mainard said, although he found it difficult to believe Mama would be so foolishly indiscrete as to entrust such stories to letters.

Schyuder shook his head. 'One Will Seton visited us in Strasbourg soon after he was banished from Geneva because of your sister's activities. I don't know what he was sadder about, leaving Calvin's presence or parting from Catarina.'

Mainard stretched his leg out to ease his foot, which was swollen more than usual from so much travel. 'Ah well, he has a wife now, a very pretty Frenchwoman, so Catarina is all forgot. We met her when they passed through Ancona recently.'

'A Frenchwoman? First he hankers after a proselytising Converso and then a Catholic?' Schyuder stood up as he spoke and pulled over a heavy chair from the corner, which screeched across the floorboards, leaving white marks.

Mainard was surprised Schyuder should be so careless and rose stiffly to help him, lifting one end and saying, 'Oh no, Cecile is a most committed follower of Calvin.'

'That is as well. It's difficult enough to maintain harmony within a marriage without each party embracing a different faith.' He pointed to the chair, which was now positioned at an angle where they could converse with ease. 'Sit down.'

Mainard sank into the chair and Schyuder picked up the stool and gestured for Mainard to lift his leg. Mainard lowered his foot onto the stool, which Schyuder adjusted until it was sited perfectly. 'I think we need a cushion.' A hand bell was rung and a servant dispatched to fetch one.

'Where were we?' said Schyuder sitting back in his chair and yet again steepling his fingers.

'Books,' said Mainard. And they embarked on a debate about the merits of taking printed works to Constantinople, with Schyuder arguing they would sell extremely well amongst the many Jews and Conversos there, especially as printers were few since Moslems did not permit any of their sacred texts or indeed any written work to be printed.

'And that means, being an enterprising people, Jews will already have set up their own presses to meet demand,' countered Mainard. 'I am certain Dona Gracia will be funding it, as she did in Venice and Ferrara.'

'Yes, but the presses have to be brought from overseas. I understand there are none built there, nor the skills to make them because of the ban on printing Arabic texts.'

'Then I'd be better to take a printing press, and safer too. At least I wouldn't be risking arrest for transporting heretical books.'

'Taking both would be even more lucrative,' said Schyuder, and leaning forward explained how he thought it might be done.

Mainard tried to listen with an open mind but again he was doubting Schyuder's integrity. There was no question he was devoted to his wife, but that did not necessarily extend to his wife's family and, if Mainard was caught crossing Europe with illegal goods, he could not trust Schyuder to exert himself to help him, any more than he'd done the last time.

'This is all very well,' he interrupted, 'but why am I here? What does Joseph Nasi want from me that I must be made to travel in the opposite direction to where I wish, and need, to go?'

Chapter Twenty-Seven

Familism

Schyuder denied any special knowledge of Joseph Nasi's intentions, saying, 'I don't claim to understand the workings of the minds of the Mendes. Perhaps it's more he trusts you to carry out his instructions successfully.'

Mainard snorted. 'Given by now he'll have Bethia and the children under his dominion, he also holds great sway over me.' Yet, as the words fell from his lips, Mainard knew he was being unfair. Don Joseph had never been anything but straight in their dealings in the past but still there felt to be a kind of desperation that had not been there previously. And he *had* once carried off his thirteen-year-old cousin to get his hands on her fortune.

Schyuder echoed his thoughts. 'Dona Gracia most urgently requires at least some of the vast sums owed her to be repaid. The fair here in Frankfurt is soon and we have couriers coming who have bills of exchange which you're to take to Constantinople.'

'Along with books and a printing press!' Mainard snorted. 'I shall be the most laden traveller to cross the Alps since Hannibal and his elephants. And why must I wait for the fair?'

'It's when everyone will be here.'

Mainard tugged on his ear, trying to contain his impatience at the delay.

'People come from far and wide to Frankfurt for this. It's a most remarkable gathering. I know it's frustrating, but there are opportunities for you here.'

Mainard gazed at his small, wiry brother-in-law. There was a kindliness about Schyuder which he'd never noticed before. He sat up; there might be at least one good thing to come from this enforced visit. It was likely his great friend Ortelius, the map seller, would come to Frankfurt. He would write letting Ortelius know he was here but first he must pen a letter to Bethia.

'May I have ink, quill and paper?'

The door opened and the servant announced the meal was ready, while Schyuder was laying the materials out. 'Come, your letter can wait an hour. This is the most important aspect of our day and I think you'll find how we break bread together of interest.'

Mainard, preoccupied with what he would write to his long-suffering wife, wondered what Schyuder was babbling about, but his brother-in-law took his arm most insistently. Containing a sigh, he allowed himself to be led from the chamber.

There was a crowd around the long board when Mainard was ushered in. Schyuder went to the top and directed Mainard to sit next to him. The room, low ceilinged and wood panelled, was lit by a few candles in wall sconces. Yet it felt stuffy and overfull. Mainard, looking around, caught Elrick's eye and wondered what one of Schyuder's workers was doing here.

Elrick dipped his head. 'Good evening to you, Master Mainard. This is my wife,' he indicated the small, dark, toothless woman next to him, 'and my son.' He tapped the shoulder of the youth with the beginnings of a beard hunched on his other side, who flushed.

Mainard nodded in return, trying to mask his confusion both that Elrick and his family would break bread with the Schyuders and that Elrick would address him so directly and without Mainard initiating the conversation. He gazed around and recognised the small, neat servant who'd let him into the house earlier in the day. The door opened and another servant bustled in carrying a platter with slices of beef on it which she leant over and placed among the range of meats already there. Another followed who, judging by the food splatters on her apron and her bright red face, was likely the cook. She took off her apron, flung it into the corner and slid onto the settle with a great sigh.

'Are we all here?' said Schyuder.

'Apart from Annis who is with our boy,' said Geertruyt, nodding at her husband from the other end of the board.

'Then we will begin.' Schyuder looked to Mainard. 'Give me your hand.'

Mainard held out his hand, reluctantly. He did not want to sit holding his brother-in-law's warm, damp hand in his. Elrick's son, squeezed in next to him, in turn held out his slim, pale hand for Mainard to take.

'*Jesus Christ dwells within each of us.*'

Mainard jumped at the loudness of Schyuder's voice and Schyuder gripped his hand more tightly.

'*We can feel the inner light of Christ on our souls. Its strength, its purity, its love.*'

Schyuder paused for a moment, so his audience, or was it congregation, could sense the touch of Christ within.

'*Man and God were united before the Fall but Adam broke our oneness with God. In seeking knowledge of Good and Evil, Adam attended to his own desires and wishes and so God created his son, Jesus Christ, who willingly died on the cross to restore the unity that previously existed between God and Man.*'

Schyuder exhaled and Mainard too let go the breath he hadn't realised he was holding.

'*But man is a pernicious creature and twisted the teachings of Christ to meet his own perverted needs. And so our good*

208

*friend and guide to the wider Family, Henrik Niclaes, has cut
across all confessions, be they Catholic, Protestant, Jew or
Mohammedan, to join and prepare for the New Age where
ceremonies will be meaningless and man will be restored to the
Godhead, and the support and love of our wider family will lead
us along the true path.'*

Mainard opened his eyes wide and gazed around, but
all other eyes were closed, even the smallest child's, and
all faces concentrated on following the words emanating
sonorously from Schyuder's lips – although the smallest
child was shifting in her seat. Schyuder spoke on.
Mainard suspected some of the detail Schyuder was
giving was more than usual. Most probably the family,
workers and servants were already familiar with the
doctrine of Henrik Niclaes, who Mainard had heard of,
for Ortelius had mentioned him in a letter. Mainard did
however consider it would only have been courtesy for
Schyuder to explain, before he pinioned him to his seat,
that the gospel of Niclaes held sway in the household.

Schyuder finished his prayer and Geertruyt dished
the potage into bowls while the cook filled the plates and
passed them along the line. It appeared the entire meal
was served at once, presumably so the servants could join
them in breaking fast. There was silence apart from the
noise of chewing. Mainard grimaced and extracted a
long, dark hair caught amongst his food. Perhaps the
cook should pay less attention to her soul and more to
having her head securely covered.

The family and its adherents ate with keen enjoyment
and soon the plates were empty. Mainard expected
everyone to rise once the meal was over but they did not.
Instead Schyuder asked a question, sat back and waited,
and soon a most spirited debate was underway on how
the light within each person might be consciously
cultivated. Schyuder at one end, fingers forming the
inevitable steeple as he tossed in the odd comment aimed
to challenge the family's thinking, and Geertruyt at the

other, strident in her insistence that Man was entering a New Age, although less certain there was no ascent to Heaven upon death.

Mainard felt something tickling his knee and absentmindedly rubbed it. It came again and he bent to look beneath the board, where he found three children, at least one of whom he was certain was a Schyuder by the roundness of face and stubbiness of nose.

'Had enough of this talk?'

They nodded. 'Pauwels says you're going to teach us sword fighting,' whispered the tallest of the three. 'But I said,' he continued before Mainard could formulate a response, 'you're too old for that.'

Mainard couldn't help but laugh at the challenge from such small spawn. 'I will try my best and hope you'll show tolerance of my advancing years.'

'Good,' said the lad. 'We'll meet you in the yard behind the kitchen.'

Mainard stretched out his hand. 'Let's shake on it, and may the best man, or woman,' he said with a nod to the girl among them, 'win.'

'Where is all this coming from?' Mainard asked Schyuder the following day when they were again closeted in his workroom.

Schyuder repositioned his cap, which had slid over one eye, flicking the tassel to the side, but as soon as he bent even slightly forward the tassel dropped to dangle before the eye once more. He grimaced at Mainard, tugged the offending cap off his head and tossed it on a stool saying, 'It was a gift from Geertruyt and she likes me to wear it.'

And there Schyuder did it again, thought Mainard. Just when he'd determined his brother-in-law was not an honourable man Schyuder displayed unexpected care and sensitivity. Yet still he could never fully trust him, for Schyuder's loyalties were to the family he had sired and only extended beyond them when Schyuder judged it expedient.

'What were you saying?'

'I was wondering how you came to join this new group?'

'Henrik Niclaes, who prefers to be known as HN, is an interesting fellow. He'll likely be here at the fair for he has a new book out.' Schyuder leaned forward, a sheen on his pale face, and Mainard stared back at him. 'He's no fool is HN; has made a very good living as a cloth merchant and now sales of his books will boost his income further.'

'And is HN's,' Mainard couldn't resist emphasising the initials, for it seemed an affectation, 'interpretation of doctrine acceptable?'

'You mean do the authorities consider it to be heretical?'

'Do they?'

'Oh, probably. But it's not so much of an issue here, for he has not so many followers. And I'm certainly not seeking converts ...' His voice trailed away.

'But Niclaes would prefer if you did.'

'Perhaps. But for me it's a private matter within my home – and you know,' he gave a laugh which sounded forced to Mainard, 'a man's home is his castle, as the saying goes.'

Mainard leant forward himself. 'Still, I'm surprised you would get involved in this new sect.'

Schyuder's forehead wrinkled mightily. 'I don't consider Familism, as it's being called, to be a sect. Would you call Calvinism or Lutheranism a sect?'

Mainard had no desire to get drawn into debating what constituted a sect. 'I'm only surprised that you would want to risk a charge of heresy, apostasy or proselytising. God's blood, man, you have a wife and, if I am counting right, five children.'

'Six,' said Schyuder, gazing at the floor. 'We must not

forget our poor crippled Albrecht.'

Mainard heard the sorrow in Schyuder's voice and thought to inquire what was wrong with the child, but Schyuder forestalled him, saying, 'We've expended considerable effort, and expense, in seeking a physician who could treat him or at least give us a diagnosis, but all to no avail. Our child is wasting away before our eyes. It's very hard on Geertruyt.'

'And you,' said Mainard softly.

Schyuder brushed his hand across his eyes.

Mainard thought of his own three boys and felt tearful himself. His brother-in-law sat silent, the question Mainard had earlier posed unanswered. Mainard didn't have the heart to pursue it. He supposed as long as Schyuder's adherence to Familism, or whatever it was called, remained discreet it mattered not. And, if what Ortelius had communicated to him about this group was true, then Niclaes advised his adherents to continue to worship whatever faith predominated locally in public, while privately following his new doctrine. Mainard only hoped Schyuder's servants were to be trusted.

'My servants are loyal,' said Schyuder suddenly.

Mainard blinked, had not realised he was such an open book. He said nothing, simply inclined his head.

They moved on to discuss the Fuggers and what was expected of Mainard, so far as Schyuder was aware. It didn't seem overly burdensome and Mainard felt more than equal to the task of passing on a message and collecting bills of exchange from the Fuggers and delivering them to the Mendes.

'The Fuggers are very cautious,' said Schyuder.

'I should imagine so,' said Mainard. 'You don't get to be so rich otherwise.'

'They'll do business with no one unless they're either known to them or introduced by someone they do know and trust.'

'Yes, yes. I understand now that's why Nasi wanted

212

me here,' said Mainard, impatient to get to his letter writing.

'Good,' said Schyuder. 'For it wouldn't do to hold a grudge.'

'I am not so foolish,' said Mainard, hoping it was true.

Finally Schyuder went and he was left to write his letter to Bethia. He aimed for a pragmatic tone.

I am in Frankfurt to run errands for Don Joseph.

No, that would not do, and made him sound like he was Pauwel's age. He took a fresh sheet:

My dearest wife, I am with Geertruyt and her family for reasons which are complex. I will explain on my return.

He paused there, pen dripping ink onto the board. He picked up the penknife left carelessly open and used it to mend the point, but instead it sheared off. Taking more care, he cut a fresh notch and bent his head to his letter once more.

I miss you more than I can say and will be by your side with all possible haste, indeed would be there now if I could order my comings and goings as I wished. Kiss our sons for me and tell them to be good for their mother.

Mainard gazed down on the page, wished he'd made his writing bigger. It looked such a sparse letter to come from a heart filled with love. He wrote a few more lines about Geertruyt and her children, folded the letter with care, running his fingers along the creases to make them smooth then searched around Schyuder's desk for a stamp and some wax amid a jumble of broken quills and scraps of paper. He thought of the neat order Bethia maintained around all their ledgers and accounts, each

213

paper carefully filed, fresh ink made up regularly, new pen sharpened daily. She wouldn't tolerate such disorder. Christ's tears how he missed her.

Geertruyt's head appeared around the door. 'Are you done, brother? We have some young ones here who are pleading to have their uncle's attention...' she smiled, '...and I too seek your company.' Her smile faded as she saw his face, while Mainard strived to compose his features.

'I am ready,' he said overly heartily. 'Let me at them – or more correctly, let them at me!'

Mainard was a silent watcher as the family, servants and workers broke fast at their daily meal together. The relaxed manner in which aspects of Familism were discussed, readings given from HN's books and passages from the Bible dissected constantly surprised him. Even the older children had something to say and would contribute a thought or voice a question, the answer to which would be treated with great seriousness. He saw how much it built Pauwel's confidence that he was answered respectfully, his questions and occasional fears never dismissed nor laughed at. Elrick's son too spoke up, as though he was a son of the house and not the son of a worker.

There was much good in the readings, but some of what HN had to impart left Mainard with questions, and as many doubts. HN expected the Day of Judgement would soon be upon them, Schyuder repeated almost daily and with great solemnity. Mainard thought of Will Seton relating Servetus's conviction that the world would end in the year of our Lord sixteen hundred. Niclaes, like Servetus, considered it his most solemn task to make the world aware of its imminent ending and furthermore that the House of Israel was to be restored. What did that mean – that Judaism would be in the ascendancy once more? If so, Schyuder skipped over that part in his daily instruction.

And what of HN himself, Mainard wondered. How much trust could be placed on the words of a man who, it was said, had begun to have visions as a child, and did he really want to become an adherent of a faith – could it be even be called a faith – which stated there was no life after death nor any resurrection of the soul? It was a bleak prospect. And what of the claim much of the Bible was metaphorical and should not be taken literally – a statement on its own which could have the speaker tried for heresy. Yet, when they sat around the board together, all sharing food and debating ideas then Mainard felt closer to God than he'd ever done in church.

Chapter Twenty-Eight

The Book Fair

The fair at Frankfurt, held twice yearly in early spring and late summer, was of a size and scale that left Mainard wondering whether he would be able to explore it in the time he had – for he was determined to leave just as soon as his business with the Fugger family was concluded – and more importantly whether he would be able to find Ortelius within this dense busyness. He'd written to his friend but received no reply, although it was entirely possible Ortelius had already left for Frankfurt and passed the letter bearer en route.

The fair was much more than the buying and selling of books, although there was an abundance of them. Mainard initially chose to spend his time amid the booksellers and watched in fascination as a bookbinder removed the large bundles of paper from the barrels in which they were transported for safekeeping, sewed them together, then trimmed them for size before adding the cover. This would be how he would transport any books he took to Constantinople and it looked to be eminently practical.

He wandered amid the bookstalls, watching and noting what was selling. He was curious to learn what new works were likely to be considered heretical by the

Catholic Church, for they would be in demand in the increasing number of places in Europe which were either already Protestant, like Frankfurt and Geneva, or leaning towards it like Lyon, Rouen and even parts of Paris… and Antwerp, if they could ever get out from under Philip of Spain's control. Seeking a gift for Bethia, he found a recently published book called *A Description of the Northern Peoples* by a man with a most northern sounding name of Olaus Magnus. Mainard touched the wooden cover, running his finger over the title tooled in leather on it, *Historia de Gentibus Septentrionalibus*. He perused a few pages and was immediately absorbed by the breadth of subjects it covered, from snowflakes and sea-serpents, to elks and artillery, to watermills and werewolves. He became aware of the seller watching, a scowl beginning to form on his face at the amount of time it was taking Mainard to commit to a purchase. It was an expensive book and he wasn't to be hurried. He carefully turned a few more pages, pausing when he came to an illustration which he bent to study more closely.

'These are not done by woodcuts,' he said, glancing up at the seller.

'No, mein Herr, it's a new means of incorporating drawings into a book. These are engravings.' He pointed an ink-stained finger. 'They're more delicate and give a far greater elegance of line than the woodcuts, which look rough by comparison.'

'Indeed,' said Mainard slowly. He glanced up at the seller. 'But I think I prefer the bluntness of the lines formed from a woodcut. I suppose both could be used depending on what the artist is trying to achieve.'

'I suspect we'll soon find all books have engravings; woodcuts are quite disdained and already I'm having to reduce the price of books with them.'

Mainard pursed his lips and studied the engraving further, Bethia would be interested to see this newer art form. He made his decision and handed over the full price asked, and the seller, face lightening that there was to be no haggling, wrapped the package up most carefully, forming a handle with twine for ease of carry.

Mainard moved on through a narrow alleyway created by the stalls and into an area where they were selling chairs, woven baskets, and iron implements for the fire most beautifully curved and plated in gold. Sellers shouted their wares and prices, buyers stopped to greet acquaintances, while grubby urchins wove their way at speed around all. He came to an area much like the Bourse in Antwerp, where men in tall hats, swords hanging by their sides, stood in groups engaged in deep discussion.

'It's where they set up bills of exchange, agree currency exchange and also pay debts and settle lawsuits,' said Schyuder appearing suddenly at his side.

'Ah,' said Mainard.

'This is where you'll find the Fuggers, but I've learned they're not expected till next Thursday.'

Mainard swallowed a sigh. Six more days at least before he could leave. 'In that case can you direct me to where they sell maps.'

Schyuder grinned. 'Are you planning on taking up your old profession again?'

'Map colourist? No, sadly not. And I'd barely begun, was only just admitted to their guild.'

'The maps and prints are to be found in the area over behind the church. Once you've had a look come back. I've left Elrick in charge of our stall and would appreciate your company. He wants to talk of nothing but HN and his ideas, and, central to our life though they are, it's pleasant to have occasional discourse on other topics.'

Mainard passed through the section of the market devoted to paper and parchment, leather and stamps for book binding, and gold leaf for illustrating. There was a negotiation going on about the purchase of a large stock of paper which was entertaining many, judging by the crowd which was forming in front of the stall, but he didn't stop to listen.

He picked up a print by Lucas Van Leyden. They seemed to be available in abundance at this fair, although Mainard didn't overly care for either the subject matter of cows being milked, or the execution. A fellow pushed in next to him calling out to the stall holder, 'Anything by Dürer?'

The stallholder, engaged in negotiating with another customer, gave a curt shake of his head and the fellow tutted and walked away knocking carelessly against Mainard. Mainard turned ready to swing and had to clench his fists to control himself. He was appalled by the surge of anger – a sign, he supposed, of his frustration at being delayed here.

He moved away in the opposite direction to the man, who was now being belligerent with another stallholder about the lack of Dürer prints at Frankfurt this August. Perhaps he was in a similar situation to Mainard and had a commission to fulfil and a family depending on him.

He came to the area where maps were for sale and in studying them again found his composure. There might be a need for map-makers in Constantinople and he could found his own guild. Of course, he'd only been a map colourist, but still, he could entice a map-maker to come there and support him. He shook his head, he was engaging in a boy's daydream, but then of such dreams a new future could emerge, and one free of the Mendes family.

He returned to the print stalls, finding one selling the work of that fellow Bruegel.

'It's called the *Tower of Babel*,' said the stallholder.

Mainard had a sense of being watched as he studied this lopsided tower cut away to reveal the interior. He glanced up but the stallholder was busy with another customer. He bent to the print once more. It had the look of a sketch of the ruin of the Colosseum which he remembered hanging on Ortelius's wall. And in thinking of his great friend, whom he sorely missed, it was as though he'd conjured him up. Mainard blinked. It was Ortelius, older than when they last met and his hairline further receded, but still with the kind smile.

'A most interesting work and a perfect example from the Old Testament of the perils of miscommunication.' Ortelius grinned at Mainard and bowed. 'Well met, my friend.'

'You received my letter,' said Mainard bowing deeply in return.

Ortelius shook his head. 'You can explain all over a tankard of the excellent Frankish ale. Are you going to buy that print?'

'Perhaps later,' Mainard said, knowing, much as he would like to, he must conserve his funds. God's blood, was this what it was like to be poor! He'd never experienced such restrictions before. This must be how his brother-in-law Will felt all the time.

Once they were seated in a hostelry with their drinks before them, Ortelius, ever sensitive, did not immediately probe as to why Mainard was in Frankfurt. Instead, he returned to the *Tower of Babel*. 'I have that print you know. It's provoked much discussion amid the Family.'

Mainard looked at him, waiting for clarification.

Ortelius stroked his top lip as though considering how or whether to continue.

Mainard leant forward. 'You mentioned Henrik Niclaes in a letter once. Are you a follower?'

Ortelius bent forward and lowered his voice. 'Speak quietly. As ever, any new thinking is to be stamped upon, and HN's ideas are considered dangerous, especially by Lutherans. Curiously, the Catholic authorities seem less troubled by him, although their opinion need not concern us in Protestant Frankfurt.'

'And the Breughel print?'

'Oh, its visuals are a means to engage in thoughtful

discourse, to examine ourselves and whether our prosperity is in support of God, as Calvin states, or is an insult to his Word.'

Mainard rubbed the twin furrows between his eyebrows. He wasn't sure what Ortelius was talking about, but was curious to hear more. He again leant towards Ortelius. 'My sister's husband, with whom I am staying, is a follower of Niclaes, and I've had daily exposure to his thinking since I arrived here.'

Ortelius took a long sup of his ale. 'Have you met the man?'

'Niclaes? No.'

'He's an odd character. Most definite in his ideas. He's here at the fair, for he has a book which Plantin had printed. Plantin sees merit in HN's ideas, but as a group we've moved beyond them.'

'What group?' said Mainard, forgetting to keep his voice low.

'The Family of Love. 'Tis a great name, do you not think? What better way to espouse Christ's true path than by creating a fellowship of loving connection.'

Mainard nodded slowly. It was as though a light was suddenly shining on his muddle of ideas. The very name of the group drew him and, espoused by a man for whom he had nothing but respect, it might finally find his true path to God.

They moved onto discussing the purpose of Mainard's visit before parting company but that evening he went to join Ortelius and his friends, including Plantin. They prayed before they broke fast together, using the same prayer as was spoken at his sister's. Then the discussion began immediately as they ate; a great flow back and forth.

Mainard knew of Christophe Plantin from when he lived in Antwerp, but Plantin had become more established – and richer – since Mainard left the city. There was a solid strength about the man, as though he

221

was certain who he was and where he was going. Ortelius too had changed since last they met when he visited Venice four years ago. He seemed calmer, but then he was fixed on the great work he was collating, which seemed all-encompassing. A faraway look came into Ortelius's eyes when he spoke of it, and Mainard himself could feel this visceral hold it had as words tumbled from Ortelius's mouth.

'It is to be a Theatre of the World. Can you imagine, de Lange, we're gathering together the remarkable maps made of every known continent so we may see in one book how the whole world looks? 'Tis a pity my friend Gerard Mercator is not here, for you would like him. A most learned and erudite man. He's developing a means by which we may scale the maps so as to see the whole world on a single page.'

Before he could say more they were interrupted by Plantin calling them to order. 'Your passion for map-making is not the topic, Ortelius.' He stroked his long nose and said in sonorous voice, 'We are focused on our souls and what becomes of them after death.'

Mainard and Ortelius took the hint and both leant forward to make their contributions to the discussion.

At one point Ortelius rose and returned with the Breughel print he and Mainard had looked at earlier.

'You had this with you?'

'No, no. I went back and purchased it. It's a gift for you, but I thought we might make use of it today to aid our conversation.'

Mainard thanked Ortelius, but he was made uncomfortable by the generous gift and wondered if Ortelius suspected he had financial difficulties. He shifted on his seat and wiped the sweat from his brow with his handkerchief.

'Please excuse me,' he said. 'My family here in Frankfurt will be wondering where I am and I promised my nephew another lesson in wielding sword and staff.'

He smiled. 'And a promise to a child should be kept.'

Plantin nodded, saying, 'Very true, promises made to young lads *must* be kept else how will they grow to be honourable men? I hope you'll join us tomorrow for I have much enjoyed your contribution.'

The other men nodded their agreement and Mainard said he would return the next day. He left feeling better, the sense of oppression weighing less heavily upon him. Once out in the street he realised he'd left Ortelius's gift behind. He would claim it tomorrow – and be more effusive in his thanks.

Chapter Twenty-Nine

Henrik Niclaes

Mainard sat down to write to Bethia again. He reminded himself it would take some months for a letter to reach Constantinople and then for her reply to travel here, by which time he would be long gone, yet the fear for her safety gnawed at him constantly. The letter finished, he pressed it to his lips and gave a silent prayer to God to watch over his wife and sons.

Schyuder frowned when Mainard said he wouldn't join them again that evening. 'Found more congenial company, have you, de Lange?'

'I'm meeting new contacts which may be useful to me should I seek to start a printing business in Constantinople.'

'Ah,' said Schyuder, his face relaxing. 'Then you are wise to further the connection.' And Mainard could see Geertruyt smiling and nodding across the room.

He strolled through the crowded streets past an organ grinder with a shivering monkey on his shoulder and tried not to stare at a man who'd only half a beard, one side of his face luxuriant and the other raw scraped skin – probably a punishment for some transgression – feeling a growing confidence that a printing business in his new city would be far from a foolish idea.

But when he reached the inn where his new friends

had again taken a private room in which to meet, the atmosphere felt oddly strained. Ortelius stepped forward to greet him. 'We've been discussing Philip of Spain's latest purge in the Low Countries.'

Mainard had been too caught up in his own troubles to attend but rumours had been circulating for some time about Philip's determination to root out every last vestige of heresy from his lands, no doubt encouraged by his new wife, Queen Mary of England.

'Charles of Hapsburg seems like a saint by comparison. He was certainly wise enough to leave his financial powerhouse to do its work unimpeded.'

'Such a pity the man chose to abdicate in favour of that Spanish stripling,' said Plantin coming to join them.

'I certainly can't see the attraction in retreating to a monastery in the Spanish mountains,' said Ortelius, and they all laughed.

But it was a forced, awkward kind of laugh without any real mirth.

'Come, de Lange, we've another guest tonight who you will be most interested to meet.' Ortelius swung his arm over Mainard's shoulder and guided him over to where there was a group engaged in intense discussion judging by the way they were all leaning inwards. The group parted and Mainard saw at its centre a small man with a flowing grey beard. He was quite innocuous to look upon, until Mainard caught his eye, and then it was a struggle to look away.

'HN, this is my good friend Mainard de Lange, come from Italy, but who once worked alongside me in Antwerp. Mainard, may I present Henrik Niclaes, founder of the Familists.'

They bowed to one other and Mainard tried to think of something to say but nothing came. After a moment HN continued speaking.

'As I have said many times, the Day of the Last Judgement is imminent. We must turn all our efforts to preparing. I am called by God to herald it, and all who are anxious about their souls should join us. We are the Company of the Elect who might attain a state of union and become *Godded with God.*'

There was much more in this vein, and Mainard, if he hadn't known Ortelius so well, would've thought he'd joined a company of the insane. What did the man mean by *Godded with God*? Christ's bones, he didn't need an association with a madman who seemed to consider he was another son of God and the equal of Jesus Christ.

He saw Plantin had drawn away too, and, as HN shifted his piercing gaze to another acolyte, he felt released to join him. He'd heard nothing but good about Christophe Plantin when he lived in Antwerp: an honest, if astute, businessman who took great care of his family and workers. He hoped people might say the same of him one day, if he could only live somewhere long enough.

Plantin was near as tall as Mainard with a long nose which looked as though it'd been broken at least once. He pressed on his side as though in pain while they spoke together and shrugged ruefully when Mainard inquired if he was well.

'Unfortunately an old war wound, or at least a knifing in the street, which I fear I'll suffer from for the rest of my days.'

Mainard had a vague memory of Plantin being set upon by a group of drunken ruffians one night while he was most decidedly sober and out on an errand. The men had mistaken Plantin for another and stabbed him.

'I'm sorry to learn it pains you still.'

'At least I'm alive.' Plantin smiled, a smile that reached the eyes, and Mainard found himself liking this man more and more. 'What think you of Master Niclaes's ideas?'

Mainard twisted his earlobe. 'They are…' He paused, wanted to say *dangerous*, but uncertain how Plantin would react, settled for 'unusual.'

Plantin laughed, which had HN glance over at them, broad forehead wrinkling.

'What do *you* think?' Mainard leaned in, curious to hear Plantin's thoughts, but Niclaes had broken away from the group and was making his way to them.

'Later,' said Plantin.

HN was a man who liked to hold court, was Mainard's overall impression. He spoke for about an hour, pausing only when the food came and then briefly to give thanks to God. Like a street performer controlling his troupe where all must originate from him and then return to him for the final trick at the end, he brought to the board *Den Spegel der Gherechticheit,* the book he had written and which he was here at the fair to promote.

'*The Glass of Righteousness,*' whispered Ortelius to Mainard as he passed it to him.

'Why has he written it in Low German instead of Latin, which could be read and understood by far more people?'

Ortelius shrugged. 'His followers are local.' He lowered his voice. 'And I fear his Latin is not so good.'

'The Kingdom of God is within you,' intoned HN gazing around the table, those piercing eyes resting on each man in turn. 'We must teach ourselves to despise outward things and give ourselves to things inward. And in this way the Kingdom of God will come to you.'

Mainard was aware of Ortelius nodding in agreement by his side and looked inquiringly at him.

'When HN speaks thus then I remember what it is I appreciate about Familism,' Ortelius said. 'Above all things, it is *inward*. It's about quiet reflection and coming together with your family, both the immediate birth family and the wider family of friends.'

'I suspect my brother-in-law Will would claim that's a description of the faith he has fought for.'

Ortelius nodded slowly. 'I remember him. Tall young man who'd suffered greatly for his cause. But

Protestantism is not so far from Catholicism in that it insists all must be converted to its cause. Familism is not about observance and doctrine tearing our world further apart. Indeed, HN advises we conform to the established church wherever we may be, while cultivating the Christ within and remaining secretly loyal to our convictions.'

'So he would make Nicodemites of us all?'

'I have never understood why the Rabbi Nicodemus was so pilloried for quietly visiting Christ under cover of darkness. For me it's the sign of a wise man.'

Mainard hesitated between shock and laughter, and chose the latter. He clapped Ortelius on the shoulder. 'You are not wrong, my friend.'

Mainard was almost sorry when the Fuggers finally did appear, and chided himself for it. He'd spent several evenings with Ortelius and his friends and had learned much. Already he could envisage sharing their thoughts with his wife and family, and following Schyuder's example but somehow more in depth. They would have an adjunct of the Familists in Constantinople. He felt a great energy at the prospect and an equal relief at a way forward where he and Bethia might share a faith more fully... a faith he could believe in. He'd once been a true Christian but was never able to embrace Catholicism in the same way after he was wrongly taken and tortured as a heretic in Antwerp. And the religion of his ancestors he too felt apart from. In any case, if he renounced Christianity for Judaism he would also have had to renounce his wife – and she him. Their children would be made bastards. He couldn't do it, even if he had ever felt the great pull, which his sister Catarina clearly did, back to Judaism. But here he could create a way of worship and principles for living which would hold his family close and show a true faith in God the Almighty. Even better, in Constantinople it would likely be seen as a form of Christianity, and the sultans tolerated all faiths, while inevitably not judging them equal to Islam.

His meeting with Anton Fugger went well. He discharged the commissions Joseph Nasi had tasked him with and collected at least some of the debt owed to the Mendes family, but inevitably not all.

'There have been unforeseen complications, but I would hope to have the balance to hand within the next six months,' said Fugger in his rough way.

Mainard had expected more courtly dissembling and less directness from this man, dressed in dark robes of finest wool with an impeccably white cambric undershirt, his beard cut and combed so it stood out stiff as a brush and hair cut very short hidden beneath his cap. Schyuder had said the Fuggers took a hit when their mines in Hungary and Austria had ceased production but added that they were heavily involved in the profitable spice trade, controlled the cattle import trade from Hungary and were dipping into South America – as much as Spain would permit – and could not help but show his surprise that he wasn't receiving payment in full. Worried it would be he who was sent to collect the funds in six months' time, he opened his mouth to question further but was forestalled by Fugger, who raised his hand saying, 'And I undertake to have the funds delivered by my agent in Constantinople.' And with this Mainard had to be satisfied.

He'd made his preparations to leave the next day and was sitting a while with Geertruyt when, finally, a letter from Joseph Nasi was delivered. It began simply, if abruptly, enough.

Foscari dead, and we all hope you, being a most resilient fellow, have safely reached Frankfurt. If so, your business must be near done. Do not under any circumstances return to Ancona.

'Christ's tears,' he muttered to himself as he read

about the torture and burnings of any Converso in Ancona the Inquisition could lay their hands upon.

'What is it, Mainard?' said Geertruyt, dropping the mending she was engaged in on her lap, needle stuck precariously on top, and basket overflowing with the torn clothes of small children at her feet.

He shook his head slowly, barely able to believe what he was reading and ashamed he'd been here in Frankfurt leading a pleasant life when such terrible events were taking place in Ancona.

He bent his head again and read on, aware of Geertruyt watching him.

'Well?' she said.

'They burnt an old woman and a man threw himself from the window of his prison in preference to such a fate.' Mainard paused, wondering how the man had managed such a feat. Even when he was moved to the upper levels of the Het Steen in Antwerp there had still been bars on the windows.

'They are burning people in Constantinople?' said Geertruyt, blinking.

'No, I don't believe it's a means of death much favoured by the Turks... at least I hope not.'

'So where are they burning people?'

'Everywhere in Italy it seems, but with most particular attention on Ancona. My poor wife didn't know I'd escaped from there.' He shook his head. 'Foscari was killed before he could send my message to her.'

'So all this time Bethia has thought you in the hands of the Inquisition.' Geertruyt shuddered. 'How terrible for her.'

'For all she knows I am still. Nasi is writing only in hope I'm here. My letters will not have reached them yet.'

Mainard stood up suddenly and walked around the room. He scarce knew what he was doing beyond containing the longing to set out right this very minute for Constantinople. He flung himself back into his seat abruptly, making the chair rock. Geertruyt, for once without the usual coterie of children hanging on her skirts, came to him and stroked his shoulder. His impulse was to twist away, for he was not deserving of such compassion.

'You are a good husband. Bethia is fortunate to have you.'

He did not think his wife fortunate at all. No doubt feeling his shoulder stiffen beneath her hand, Geertruyt ceased her ministrations and returned to her seat.

'I will pray for you, Bethia and your sons,' she said, making the sign of the cross.

Mainard watched in disbelief. His sister's spiritual practices appeared to consist of a great jumbling of the rituals and doctrine of the faiths she'd been exposed to, so she made use of Catholicism, Protestantism and Familism without distinction.

Her children came then in a great rush through the door, followed by the servant carrying the limp Albrecht. He could feel the love of family coming from her as she smiled and listened and bent to answer a question, placing her arm around the child asking. She was a good and content woman, and even a crippled child had done little to dull the certainty of her place, and worth, in this life. There was nothing to deride here and much to respect.

Chapter Thirty

The Book of Friendship

Mainard went to see Ortelius that evening to say farewell, knowing it was unlikely they would ever meet again.

'Stay a few more days and meet Gerald Mercator. I think you would like him. He's a rare and sensitive soul and what he doesn't know about map-making could be written on the head of a pin. It is no wonder he's known as the Ptolemy of our century.'

'You tempt me greatly, good friend, but my wife has been in distress because she's had no word from me for so long. The man I sent letters with was killed and Bethia thought I'd again been taken by the Inquisition… and no Ortelius to help this time.'

'Then you must go with all possible haste, for I would not have your gentle wife left in any further doubt as to your well-being. But before you leave, would you write in my *Book of Friendship?*'

'Of course.'

'I have it at my lodgings.'

They walked briskly through streets emptying as curfew drew near. Once in his chamber, Ortelius slid the book from beneath the mattress, unwrapping it from its cover of green linen.

Mainard watched the tenderness with which Ortelius

placed it before him. He looked up at Ortelius. 'I see the book is...' he wanted to say sacred but amended it '...precious.'

Ortelius pursed his lips, considering. 'As precious to me as my maps.' He reached down and stroked the cover with his fingertips. 'You have sons – have created a family. The contents of this book bring together my Family of Love, my friends.'

Mainard opened the book and turned the fine parchment with great care. He bent his head and quietly read a few of the inscriptions.

Like a green hedge totally interwoven, that which is knotted together is long-lasting.

Lately Spain boasts of a discovered world. That is nothing, Ortelius, compared to your light, because you are working to unite old and new in one map.

Union brings Strength or Power. Thus we must remain united as one, clinging to one another, and driving away partisanship, the origin of all evil, of destructions, of plagues.

This is a wonderful book to have in your possession, to dip into constantly. And to ponder the shared thoughts.'

'It is. And I'm most grateful to my friends for their insightful contributions however disparate our beliefs may sometimes be.'

Mainard could see the glint of a tear in Ortelius's eye as he gazed down upon the book and had to blink them away himself.

Ortelius walked away and sat on the edge of his bed. 'You know HN's initials could also stand for *Homo Novus* – and New Man is how he likes to think of himself. I don't always agree with him and he can be a most obtuse and self-serving character with little tolerance or forgiveness for the foibles of others. And yet... and yet he has ideas which have saved my soul. I commend them to you, for you, de Lange, are in a most invidious position, married as you are to an Old Christian. And I suspect, once amid the large community of Jews in Constantinople, you will come under increasing pressure to revert. The Family of Love is a way forward for you and your family to quietly embrace God without a need to cleave to any one faith.'

Mainard sat very still. He was aware of Ortelius watching him and waiting for a response. 'I have come to the same conclusion,' he said eventually.

He left Frankfurt the next day with the bills of exchange, a small printing press, several heavy kists full of books, the print of the *Tower of Babel*, some gifts for his children and many messages of good wishes from his sister for Bethia. Even the journey, which he'd been most concerned might involve passage through Italian lands with its accompanying dangers, was resolved. Anton Fugger had arranged a passport for him to take a route through France, which, so far, appeared tolerant of Conversos – at least wealthy ones – and then take a ship from Marseille.

He joined a group of men who were travelling fast and they embarked on a ship before the end of September. There would be autumn storms to contend with but nothing as sustained as if he was crossing the Mediterranean in winter. Unusually for the time of year, the problem was light and capricious winds rather than any storms. It took five days to reach Palermo where he was to transfer to another ship, which fortunately had itself been delayed. He never left the quayside, simply being led by the helpful captain from one ship while his goods were transported. Then they were in the Aegean, the wind changeable so they never knew where it would be gusting from next. He'd hoped they might put in at Thessaloniki, where Mama and Catarina were, but the winds were not favourable and captain made straight for the channel which led to the Sea of Marmaris, and by then Mainard was too full of pulsating anxiety to reach Constantinople to much care about anything else.

Finally, this greatest of cities was before him. Even Mainard, with all attention on reaching his family quickly, could not but stare open-mouthed at the confluence of sea meeting land and the vast walled city rising on the hills before him.

'The Bosphorus,' said the captain, come to lean on the railings beside him. 'Which is the channel to the Black Sea and the great crossing between Europe into the wonder and mystery of Asia. He pointed. 'The inlet before us is called the Golden Horn. The sultan once asked Michelangelo to design a bridge to cross here.' He grinned. 'No doubt the boatmen plying back and forth were glad not to have their living destroyed, but it would've been a remarkable sight.' The captain glanced upwards and roared at a sailor scrabbling across the ropes, and Mainard was again left to his own thoughts as they came about to anchor.

Venice, which he'd always considered to be a city of waters, paled in comparison to the sheer scale of the harbours before him. No wonder the Ottomans had besieged the Byzantines with such constancy to possess this place, and were determined to hold onto it judging by the fortifications surrounding the city.

Mainard shielded his face, for the sun sparkling on the gently rippling waves of the densely blue water was so dazzling he was seeing back spots dancing before his eyes. He took a deep breath of the healthy sea air, already with a hint of the foetid tang of the dense populace packed behind the city walls. But still his sense of well-being grew and his hope of finding a place of safety and rest. The more he looked upon Constantinople the stronger his conviction that only good omens were with him for this new life here.

Part Six

Will

1556 to 1562

Chapter Thirty-One

Bereft

God had chosen to take Will's beloved wife and yet spared the child. An Englishwoman, Margaret Locke, whose own child had died soon after birth, already had his daughter installed in her home before Will returned from Dieppe. And he could not look upon the babe without thinking what her life had cost, and without wishing it was she who'd been taken and not Cecile. May God forgive him.

'What shall you name her?' Mistress Locke had said. 'We should have the child baptised as soon as possible.' Her voice trailed away when she saw his expression.

He didn't reply.

Calvin had taken a great interest in the baby and Will found him there one day when he reluctantly came to visit. Calvin held her close, gazing down into the small face with tears in his eyes.

'Such a precious gift from our Lord,' he said, bending to kiss the tiny forehead. He looked up at Will. 'I think you must name her Cecile, in honour of her most devout mother.'

Will allowed it, yet it had the effect of leaving him more rather than less estranged from his daughter.

Knox arrived in Geneva the day after the baptism and Will was glad it had been done without Knox present. He came to see Will immediately he heard of Cecile's death and wept bitterly at Will's great loss. Will had no tears left and no patience for a lachrymose Knox. He tried not to blame him but it was always there; if Knox hadn't dallied in Scotland and Will hadn't been left with the burden of Knox's family, he would have reached Geneva before the baby was born. He knew God had chosen to take Cecile, he knew she would've died whether he was with her or not, but at least he would've seen her one more time and said farewell. He pondered deeply on all Jesus Christ had to say about forgiveness but it was very hard to forgive John Knox – especially when Knox seemed oblivious to any wrong he'd done Will. Instead, after he'd finished weeping, he moved on to commending Geneva.

'In other places, I confess Christ to be truly preached, but in manners and religion, so sincerely reformed, I have seen nowhere better. Geneva is the mirror and model of true religion and piety.'

He had no further need of Will, for he'd brought a new assistant from Scotland, and the English congregation had provided him with a house and a reasonable living. Although, as ever short of funds, Will was glad not to be working closely with Knox. In any case, it soon transpired Calvin desired Will to return to his service, and most specifically to manage the scribing and proofreading of the many tracts which were pouring from his lips. There was a great urgency about it all, as though Calvin sensed he'd much to say and too little time in which to say it.

He asked Will to work with a man newly come to Geneva called Gilby on an English study Bible. 'For my understanding of that language is not sufficient to make my involvement any more than a diversion, slowing down production. And it's most advanced thinking, with each chapter including either an argument or summary or both.'

Will felt his heart lift for the first time since Cecile left him, but once the work was done and he was back to simply correcting proofs, he slumped.

Knox too had a pen which was on fire and used the same printer as Calvin, which Will considered most unfortunate since they were destined to meet more regularly than he cared to.

A year passed and Knox's son was born and most deliberately not named for a saint; he was called Nathaniel – gift of God. Will witnessed the baptism, a weeping Knox before the pulpit, thinking how Knox always shed tears with such ease, and a smiling Elizabeth in attendance. There was no sign of Marjorie, no doubt at home recovering from the birth. Will tried genuinely to felicitate Knox but there was a bitter taste in his mouth that Knox should have both wife and child come through the valley of death unharmed. Then Will was ashamed to have such unchristian thoughts and withdrew further.

However, Knox did invariably have a harried look about him these days, and it wasn't only to do with the controversy his tracts were causing. It seemed domestic harmony was not easily attained for a man used to independence, and, thought Will, no sane man would choose to share a home with a wife and mother-in-law – especially a mother-in-law who'd been disinherited by her own husband, for Richard Bowes had died, and, sending a clear message to his disobedient wife, left a will in which she wasn't mentioned. All Geneva was talking of it, and Will, for all he didn't care for Elizabeth, considered she deserved at least some acknowledgement by Bowes on his deathbed, given she'd birthed fifteen children by him.

Nevertheless, the story of her disinheritance added grist to the mill of Genevan speculation about the relationship between Knox and Elizabeth, and especially of how closely she guarded Knox, jealously restricting other women's access to him. For it seemed Knox must be reserved to answer her doctrinal concerns alone. She was not entirely successful in so doing, but the effort Knox had to make to remove himself from her constant clutching, he complained privately to Will was *maist wearisome*. Will had no desire to be the recipient of such confidences and had felt ashamed of the pleasure it gave him to know all was not perfect harmony in the Knox household.

Marjorie, not to be outdone by her mother, also made her presence felt in Geneva. Emboldened by her husband, she declared the hooped petticoats worn by the many French Protestants living there to be most inappropriately ostentatious for any sober, God-fearing woman to don, since women should dress with quiet modesty. Will, thinking of Renée's court in Ferrara, considered too many words were being wasted on something so insignificant. Then Knox declared:

the stinking pride of women in wearing superfluous apparel must be subdued and most especially their pride and desire to allure.

Almost inevitably Knox's discourse led into his current preoccupation – the regimen of women – and he added:

the garments of women do declare their weakness and inability to execute the office of men and thus they become malicious perverters of the established order.

Knox had already written a tract while in Frankfurt against women rulers, Queen Mary of England specifically, but he further developed his thinking in *The First Blast of the Trumpet against the Monstrous Regiment of Women*. Here his concern went further than the rule of women, and he wrote a note asking Calvin his opinion, posing questions which were verging on sedition and would place him in peril were they to fall into the wrong hands. Of course, Knox was safe enough in Geneva, but he rarely bided there for long, making a couple more trips to Scotland, on which Will was not invited to join him – and didn't care.

'What am I to do with this?' said Calvin waving a letter from Knox. 'He wants to know if a minor can rule by divine right, could a female ruler transfer sovereignty to her husband, but most difficult of all, should the people obey ungodly or idolatrous rulers? I wish he would let go of this preoccupation with women as rulers. 'Tis naught but a distraction. The important thing with any king, queen or regent is what faith they follow and in doing so that they set a good, and pious, example to their people. It's not our task to challenge kingship, be it a king, queen or regency of a minor.' He rattled his fingers on the board. 'I have more pressing work to attend to and cannot spend time pondering the finer nuances of how to express my thoughts without offence. In any case, I have little confidence Knox will take notice, for he's become single-minded upon this issue.'

'Why don't you refer him to Bullinger in Zurich? I'm sure he'll have sound advice to dispense,' said Will.

Calvin's sombre face lightened. 'Excellent suggestion. I will write a few thoughts to Knox then pass this matter on.' He stretched out his fingers, cracking them. 'And what do you have for me next?'

But Knox, it seemed, paid little attention to either Calvin or Bullinger's cautions. When he sent the manuscript of *The First Blast* to Calvin, it was evident that rather than treading delicately, he was stamping across all queenly sensibilities. Calvin, weary of the whole subject, waved it through. 'He knows I cannot well read English. Why is he doing this?'

'John Knox wants John Calvin's approbation for his book in which he claims female rule is against the natural and divine order,' Will responded.

Calvin sighed. 'In this, France agrees with him,

243

having enacted a law where no woman may succeed to the throne however direct the line of succession. But *I* do not agree. There is no divine order which says women cannot rule. God can use women as special providence – look at Mary Magdalene and indeed the Virgin. And I say it again, why is Knox so concerned about this? There are many more vital matters than whether women, born subordinate to men, can ever rule as equals.'

When he left Calvin Will decided to visit his daughter, now nearly eighteen months old, on his way to the rooms he rented close to St Pierre. Margaret Locke said the child was asleep but he could look in on her if he kept quiet. Will gazed down upon the small face. There was a wonderful innocence about a sleeping child, the skin so smoothly pink, the small creases around the closed eyes, the gentle breath.

He should've come earlier and watched how well she was walking now, Margaret Locke, big with child again, told him. Will hoped Margaret would want to keep Cecy, especially once she had her own child. He met her husband on his way out, who suggested Will should be considering alternative arrangements, 'For Margaret will soon have too much to do with her own baby to give Cecy the attention she deserves.'

'You must marry again, for the sake of the child,' said Calvin, after inquiring the next day why Will looked troubled.

Will shook his head; could never replace his Cecile.

Calvin pressed his palms together. 'I can understand. Since my wife died I've never cared to take another.' He paused. 'But then I, sadly, did not have a child to consider.' He paused. 'A reliable servant might suffice.'

Will thought of Grissel. Perhaps he could entice her away from Bethia, although she'd have a long journey to reach Geneva… and she was a Catholic. It would not work.

It was late autumn and the first snows fell, the wind

blowing chill off the mountains and swirling over the broad expanse of lake. Scarves were in evidence again, tightly wrapped around necks and over the top of bonnets to hold them in place, mufflers, fur collars, gloves both leather and knitted, and good wool cloaks – for the well-off at least – were all pulled from the storage chests where they'd been kept well layered with lavender to repel the moths. The deserving poor, although not nearly as well protected against the cold, had shelter and a warm meal once a day. The undeserving poor fended for themselves as best they could on scraps at street corners and, as for the prostitutes, if Geneva had a house of ill repute it was so well hid even its male citizenry couldn't find it.

Will hurried from cold to warmth, back and forth between Calvin's house, his own lodgings, the church where he was again regularly preaching and the house where his daughter was lovingly cared for. Another summer passed and then in November of fifteen hundred and fifty eight news came which eclipsed all else. Will first learned of it when he met Knox in the street, smiling broadly.

'Mary Tudor of England is dead,' Knox said so loudly that two men passing turned to stare.

The excitement amongst the English congregation was palpable. Even more so when it was confirmed the Princess Elizabeth was now queen. All talk was of returning to England, for surely Elizabeth would take her country back to the true faith.

Knox was in high glee, hopeful he himself could return to his congregation in Berwick. 'They are in sore need of me, for they, most wrongly, allowed true worship to slip when Jezebel was on the throne.'

Will, listening, felt a rising anger. It was all very well for Knox, safely in Geneva, to criticise the choices of people who were surrounded by the burning pyres of anyone who made the smallest transgression. And, yes it

245

was true Knox had taken some risks visiting Scotland as frequently as he'd recently done, but Mary of Guise had restrained her bishops – all the evidence showing she was not in favour of such a cruel death however heretical the perpetrator, although Will's heart failed him a little as he thought of Walter Myln who had been burned in St Andrews in March, Archbishop Sharp acting quickly and most determinedly before the regent could stop him.

Myln's final words had been committed to paper and sent to Calvin:

I will not recant the truth. I am corn, not chaff; I will not be blown away with the wind or burst by the flail. I will survive both.

But terrible though it was to burn an eighty-year-old man alive, it was the first such act since Will watched George Wishart die twelve years ago. In comparison to both England and France, Scotland was not so very brutal.

Knox was jubilant for a short time only. It seemed Queen Elizabeth had read, and taken great exception to, *The First Blast of the Trumpet against the Monstrous Regiment of Women*. Word came from her faithful assistant Robert Cecil that one John Knox would not be welcome in England. Will considered it most unfortunate he was with Calvin when Knox appeared, bursting with indignation at such an outrage.

Calvin was unsympathetic. He flapped his own letter in Knox's face saying, 'I have had communication from Foxe. He says your tract was most ill-advised.'

Knox puffed out his cheeks and went red in the face. Before he could speak, Calvin continued.

'There are inevitably questions about Elizabeth's right to succeed, since the doubts about whether her father's marriage to her mother was legitimate circulate still. You will, no doubt, know your Queen of Scots has, encouraged by her uncles, proclaimed herself and her young husband to be king and queen of England. I would advise you to immediately publicly state your support for Elizabeth and then she may permit your return to Berwick. And, since I understand most of your congregation here are preparing to leave, you'll likely want to go with them?'

Although it was presented as a question, Will could see it was more of an instruction. Calvin was not usually so direct.

'I will not write,' Knox said, spittle spraying wide. 'Elizabeth is creating a great confusion between the Roman whore and our good strong faith. I'm told she permits the continued use of both cross and candles. The new queen can be neither a good Protestant nor a resolute papist while she attempts to straddle both worlds.'

Calvin leant forward. 'My dear Knox, I strongly advise you be more measured in speaking of the queen of England.'

When an angry Knox left, spittle still glittering on his beard, Calvin looked to Will. 'I had hoped you would have given me better warning of the language used in this most unfortunate book; an unwise and unnecessary distraction from important work.'

Will began to splutter himself. 'I did tell you he needed to modify his language.'

Calvin raised his eyebrows.

'I most certainly did,' said Will, feeling like a small boy before his dominie.

Calvin was silent for a moment. 'I think we've all learned that when Master Knox gets a head full of bees there's no stopping his agitation until they've swarmed. But most unfortunate he should pour it out onto paper so his views are there for all to see until the Day of Judgement comes.' He smoothed his beard. 'On another matter, I've a suggestion to put to you, Seton.'

Will waited, could feel his heart beating.

'Your French is excellent, almost as though you were born there, and we have great need of preachers in France...'

'I'll go,' said Will.

Calvin nodded slowly. 'I thought you might. And while you are gone on God's essential work, I will watch over your child.'

Chapter Thirty-Two

Rouen 1562

Will had travelled back and forward across France for near on four years now. He'd like to say time had moved quickly but it had not. It crawled, slow as a caterpillar across a cabbage leaf. He performed his duties well enough he knew, or else those in his pastoral care would've sent him on his way. He was punctilious, reliable, took great risks at their behest, but was again dour Will Seton. All the joy from the few years of his marriage to Cecile were swallowed up, gone, so brief he could barely remember them.

The network of Protestant preachers sent by Calvin, who was co-ordinating all from the safe haven of Geneva, was considerable. Of course, Calvin was over fifty and both elderly and sick. He could not be expected to undertake such duties himself, despite being a Frenchman. So wherever Will was called he went.

Calvin was kind enough to write regularly giving him news of wee Cecy, who he took joy in visiting. Will had heard only once from Margaret Locke, who'd defied her husband and insisted on keeping the child, so was especially grateful to receive Calvin's epistles – although there were sometimes gaps between them for Calvin was frequently unwell, troubled as he was by quartan fever. Of course, the letters were also a continuing discussion of important doctrinal matters; Calvin never wrote without that. Will found they ay lifted his spirits, albeit briefly. He poured over them, reading them again and again.

Cecy chatters incessantly, her vocabulary increasing by the day. Margaret Locke tells me the child can speak English almost as well as she can French, although her understanding of Scots needs to await her father's return. Not that I am suggesting you do so any time soon, for you are engaged in vital work and raising a small child is best done by a woman. You could not have a better woman to care for her than Margaret, for she loves Cecy as though she was her own daughter and shows no preference between her and the children she has borne.

And now, enough of the temporal and back to matters spiritual. I am convinced that any gift which God has bestowed is not for the private endowment of said believer but for the common good and the believer should regard himself as the steward of what he possesses. You are that steward in France.

The sense of purpose these words gave Will was palpable. He was in France at Christ's behest, and although he might wish to see his child he must do God's, and Calvin's, work. And he knew, had she lived, it would've been what Cecile wished.

He bent his head back to the letter.

We must always remind our followers that to be outside the church is to be outside Christ and without salvation.

He felt an overwhelming love for John Calvin, for his unadorned and gentle way of ministering to his congregations. Calvin was all about clear exposition,

Knox about oratory. But then Calvin wanted understanding whereas Knox wanted believers.

Will travelled deeper into the interior of France, moving steadily further north and nearer to Montargis, where Renée of France now lived. Duke Ercole had died a few years ago, and her son, now duke, was a staunch Catholic. The duchess had hurriedly left Ferrara and returned to this castle not far from Orleans, which had formed part of her dowry. Once there, she most determinedly, but quietly, reverted to a Protestant life. Word was she didn't overly care for the pastor Calvin had supplied and Will wondered if there might be an opening for him instead. And he wanted to see Renée again, for it was under her benevolent gaze he'd enjoyed the happiest time of his life. But before he reached there, the call went out from the second city of France for Protestants to come to their aid. And so to Rouen Will went instead.

Spread along one bank of the meandering Seine, it was a sizeable city, second only to Paris, or so Will had been told. A well-built and maintained wall encircled the town, on top of which men could be seen patrolling, with the towers of its great cathedral and many churches reaching high above. Descending the hill, Will had a good view of the fortifications and was impressed, and even more so when he passed the fort which overlooked the town and clearly formed part of its defences, and where he could see men at work hauling cannon into position. He also had a good view of the bridge across the Seine, and marvelled at the skill of the engineers who designed it and the masons who fashioned its smooth curves of elegant supporting arches with their great bases sunk into the water. He could see ships anchored in the river and much activity as goods were transferred from them onto barges which would take them onwards through the shallower water to Paris.

Passing through the gates, he was clapped on the shoulder by one of the guards.

'Welcome. Are there any more like you coming?' He called to his fellow. 'Imagine a whole troop of giants like this and what we could achieve.'

Will could not help but smile, although he was by no means certain whether the guard saw him as defending the Protestants or Catholics of the city.

The area immediately before the cathedral was wide, but otherwise, above the mire of each cramped street rose a myriad of houses where every storey bulged out over the one below until the topmost were so far out over the street they looked as though they were leaning against one another. The further Will ventured, the worse the stink rising from privies, cooking and garbage became, trapped as it was beneath the morass of housing where fresh air could not penetrate. Looking up, Will caught only the barest glimpse of dark grey cloud above, then he brought his gaze down to street level and the many hanging signs, some so low he was in danger of skimming the top of his head on them – gilded fleur de lys, carved bunches of grapes larger than any real ones, a dragon with its mouth open ready to swallow the great curves of its tail. Even the smallest houses had bears, elephants or birds painted on their lintels in a great vibrancy of colour.

A light rain began to fall, which suddenly grew heavier and was soon bouncing off the lead roofs. He was startled by a stream of water splashing down on him from above and, dodging out of the way, he looked up to see the leering face of a gargoyle attached to the edge of the roof spouting water from its open mouth. He took shelter in a doorway until the brief storm passed before continuing his exploration.

Now he was amid the streets of artisan shops, with every guild, it seemed, represented. He strolled past bit and spur makers, furriers, nail-makers, saddlers, tailors, chandlers, inkwell-makers, comb-makers, gilders, joiners, bakers, balance makers, cordwainers, hatters and, he was happy to see, a bookseller. Bending to enter through the low door, he was met by the shopkeeper rubbing his hands together.

'How may I help you, young master? You're a visitor to Rouen I think, for I would've remembered if I'd seen you in our streets before – a man of such great height your head must be near brushing the clouds.'

Will smiled politely, as though it was the first time he'd heard such a quip. 'I've just arrived in your fair city.'

'Ah, you and many others. Half of France seems to be making their way here.'

Will gazed around the small shop lined with shelves, all the books facing outward. There was no crucifix attached to the walls, no serene Virgin nor any other sign of popish blather.

The man forestalled him. 'The Protestant half,' he said with a laugh, watching for Will's response.

They had a helpful discussion about Calvin's tracts and how Will could arrange for some to be printed here, which might prove safer than transporting them secretly from Geneva. It was all most fruitful and he emerged from the shop over an hour later with directions from the bookseller to the home of the pastor who was his contact in the town.

Drawing close to the cathedral, he passed a shop where playing cards were made. A reminder that, although Rouen had four Protestant preachers, although there was agreement the Protestant congregations could meet in the *halles* for psalms, prayers and discourse, this was a Catholic city still. Calvin had forbidden the manufacture and playing of cards in Geneva more than ten years ago, at the same time he'd closed all the brothels. A recent letter from brother John told of playing cards being banned in Scotland since the Protestant Reformation there two years ago. Father, John said, had been made most irate, for he'd a considerable stock of them and now would have to find some country, both

Catholic in outlook and where they were not made locally, to offload his supply. Will grinned thinking of John's letters, which were aye entertaining in their naughty humour.

'We're glad to have you,' said Pastor Georges, when Will finally located his house, bowing and then reaching out to shake Will's hand. 'We've had a call out for Protestants to come to Rouen since Wassy.' He shook his head. 'The arrogance of these Guises knows no bounds. Evil men, especially the duke, and right after the edict was issued declaring we were *not* to be persecuted for following the faith. Did you know he massacred at least fifty worshippers including a woman and her child?'

Will shook his head slowly. 'Terrible, terrible.' He paused, not wanting to cause offence by what he was about to say but he needed to know. 'I was told there were reprisals here in Rouen by some *Huguenots*?' It was the first time he'd used the word which he'd increasingly heard being used to refer to French Protestants and it felt most awkward in his mouth. He wasn't entirely sure why they were so named, believed it was something to do with people gathering to worship in houses rather than churches.

Pastor Georges folded his arms, chest thrust out and Will forgot his meandering thoughts. 'The people of Rouen responded to the massacre at Wassy with righteous anger, and let me tell you how. It was entirely reasonable Cardinal de Bourbon should have insults shouted at him... God's wounds, what did he expect? And especially after the Duke of Guise was cheered through the streets of Paris for the terror he inflicted.'

Will nodded, thinking how Catherine de Medici was treading a narrow path allowing the Huguenots some rights to privately practise while holding the Guises at bay.

'Then at Lent, which the Protestant church rightly took no account of, damage was done to the cathedral, but again only insults shouted at the priest leading worship. It was as nothing to the increasing numbers of so-named heretics burned at the stake. And last year, after the procession of Corpus Christi, Protestant houses were attacked because we didn't join in the procession. It was all too easy to identify our homes since we refused to hang a tapestry from our windows for this popish celebration.'

'I've heard much of what you suffered here in the past few years and also how many people you were able to save.' Will remembered celebrating with his previous congregation in a small town near Lyon when word came of the breakouts in Rouen when those wrongly imprisoned for their faith and, even better those about to be immolated in the flames, were rescued.

The pastor sighed. 'Not everyone was fortunate enough to be saved. Poor Pierre Quitard was executed for nothing more than holding a list of all the towns in which leading Huguenots resided. But enough of our misfortunes. You are here and there is plenty of work.'

He directed Will to a house off one of the narrow garbage-strewn alleys with which Rouen abounded. 'A widow and her children live there. Her husband was a baker who was burnt at the stake two months ago. We tried to save him but the authorities have grown cunning. They moved the place of execution from the Vieux Marché to a balcony of the Bailliage, where it has, so far, been impossible to rescue our martyrs from the flames.' He patted Will's arm. 'But I am glad you are come, for we have need of you.'

Chapter Thirty-Three

Killings and Burnings

The widow was still young and pretty, despite having birthed six children, the smallest of whom was a babe in arms. Will would not have considered it appropriate to board there had not Pastor Georges assured him she was most devout and respectable... and her mother lived with her. The widow was too busy calming the fractious baby and trying to release her skirts from the two small children gripping either side to do more than agree terms and show Will to his chamber but the mother was a different matter. Her face, which had been sullen, suddenly came alive with smiles, much nodding and a stream of blethers flowed from her lips. It was with great relief Will shut the chamber door on her, still mouthing platitudes about his comfort, offering to fetch another blanket, asking if he wished to avail himself of their linen laundering services, wondering what time it would suit him to break fast in the morning, and all said in a remarkably shrill voice. Christ's bones how he hated women who twittered.

He tugged his boots off and stretched out diagonally along the bed, hands behind his head and feet dangling off the edge. He could hear the rising wind calling down the chimney and stirring the ash in the empty grate. The window rattled as the wind banged against the opaque

256

glass and his mind drifted back to Scotland. He wondered how Knox was faring. The news from there over the past three years had been remarkable. Knox had already returned when Mary of Guise died, from dropsy. Will had no idea what a death from such an ailment would entail but it was said her mind wandered at the end. The Lords acted swiftly and a parliament was called, and with such a name: a *Reformation Parliament*. They absolutely rejected the authority of the Pope, denied forever transubstantiation and approved a Protestant confession of the faith. So many Lords supported it, it was unstoppable. His country was Protestant. Or as Knox bluntly wrote, *Scotland has shaken off the Roman whore*.

Calvin had written to Will then inquiring if he would return to Scotland now the true faith had prevailed.

Not yet, Will had replied. *Once France follows Scotland then I will go home, but until then I believe God has called me to bide where I am.*

Calvin had responded approving Will's decision and praising him for remaining in peril when he might have retreated to safety. But Will didn't feel worthy of such plaudits – truth be told he felt there was little for him in Scotland, nor anywhere else, without Cecile.

He awoke with a start and sat bolt upright, still fully clothed. There was sunlight filtering through the glass and he could hear the insistent beat of a drum. He must've been tired for he'd slept the whole night through with his clothes on. He flung the casement wide and leant out. The stink from below had him draw back, but not before he'd seen a group of men with angry faces passing the end of the alleyway. He pulled on his boots and leapt down the narrow staircase, through the single room where the fire burnt bright beneath the pot hanging on its tripod and the children played in the bed recess, out into the alleyway and on to the muddy street.

Around the corner a small group of militia appeared led by a drummer and followed by a couple of officers.

Will watched baffled, and he was not the only one as people emerged from their houses, turning to one another to inquire what was happening. They stood arms folded and sullen-faced as the soldiers tried to corral some into following the beat of the drum. The officers waved their swords and shouted, demanding that the Rouennais join the Crown in the fight against the Prince of Condé and the false religion.

The soldiers were headed towards Will at one point. He stood tall and straightened his shoulders, and they retreated. But he was confused. Catherine de Medici, so far as he was aware, had not instigated a fight against Condé. The soldiers were fools to be strutting about in all this arrogance when there were so few of them. The muttering of the crowd grew. A stone was thrown. The officers looked around, startled anyone should dare attack the Crown. It was only then that they seemed to become aware of the numbers of people following close behind. The two men stood their ground, swords pointed, while the drummer, oblivious, marched on with the group of militia huddled close behind him. One officer shouted halt but the soldiers took to their heels as stones rained down upon them.

The crowd roared triumphantly. Will considered there was something remarkably ugly about the gaping, mostly toothless, pink stretched mouths. He stood to the side, watching still, assuming the crowd would let the officers retreat, thinking it was all about frightening them and nothing more. But he hadn't accounted for the anger – perhaps no wonder after so many recent burnings. They went for the men, who vanished in their midst.

It would only be a beating, nasty but usually survivable. A sword flashed in the air and then an agonising scream. Will had not intervened when Cardinal Beaton was murdered all those years ago and, however evil the man, he should've stood trial and been lawfully sentenced to death. Will had vowed then he would not stand by again.

He pushed his way into the throng. One officer lay on the ground while men kicked and stamped on his body, and even the face with the dead open eyes, but the other was on his feet still and fighting for his life.

'Enough,' roared Will. 'It is enough. You have made your point and will gain nothing by killing him too.'

'Death to the false believers,' shrieked a man, but the others had fallen silent, gazing down at the dead man.

'Go,' said Will softly to the surviving officer, who hobbled away, fast as he was able, blood dripping down his face.

A few men went to follow but Will stopped them. The crowd quickly dispersed, leaving the body lying in the street for the sweepers to remove.

Will returned to his lodgings. He sat down on a low stool, elbows braced on knees and head in his hands, pondering how things might unfold in Rouen... not peacefully, if this first morning was anything to go by. The mother bustled around bringing him some weak ale, a plate of bread, roasted eggs and a handful of dried figs. She smiled at him effusively when she caught his eye but otherwise remained silent. Will nodded his thanks, drank the ale in one long gulp and rolled the trencher between the palms of his hands. There was a simmering anger in this city and he sensed it would not be cooled by the death of one officer. And killing did not, could not, serve God's purpose. Christ would never, under any circumstances, have taken the life of another. But it was difficult to see how God's will would be enacted in Rouen, and the rest of France, without it. And God's other creatures, the Catholics, had no compunction about burning every Huguenot from the German Ocean to the Mediterranean Sea.

'You seem troubled, young master,' said the mother, her voice much less shrill than the previous evening.

What was her name? He shook his head at the

proffered jug of ale, aware this was a poor household in which he was being given their best food and he should show restraint so they could all eat and drink.

'I'm wondering if it's possible to make reforms without resorting to violence.' A small fire burned in the nearby grate and Will took the poker in his hand and tapped at a burning log.

'Monsieur Maupin, my late husband, often said it's not easy to decide what's right,' she said simply.

Maupin, that was her name.

'I fear violence is unavoidable.'

Madame Maupin's eyes filled with tears. 'As my poor daughter's husband discovered.'

Will thought he should say some words of comfort but they eluded him. And truly there was no comfort to give in knowing a man died an agonising death.

'The regent may surprise us,' she continued. 'I think she's doing all in her power to rein in such action, but there are the Guises...' Her voice trailed away.

'There are the Guises,' Will echoed.

They looked at one another and Madame Maupin sighed. 'If King Henri was still alive, God bless him, the Guise family would've been kept under control.'

Will stared at her, surprised she should so venerate a Catholic king.

'He came here you know about ten years ago. Oh, it was a magnificent royal entry. Your queen of Scotland was with them, such a pretty child, along with the king's wife, and his mistress.' She fell silent. 'There were Tupinambá Indians brought all the way from Brazil, naked as the day they were born and a great beast leading the way.'

'An elephant?' said Will with a smile. 'I saw the Joyous Entry of the Holy Roman Emperor in Antwerp. Although what I remember most about the day was my nephew made his own grand entry as my sister was delivered of a son.'

260

Madame Maupin laughed. 'Yes, the best entry of all is a safe delivery.'

Will stood up; the pain of losing Cecile never grew any less. 'I must away,' he said abruptly.

The *bailli*, who'd been in Paris when the attack on the recruiting officers took place, returned to Rouen with all possible haste. The leaders among the attackers defended themselves, saying the officers were acting inappropriately as agents of the Guise family in a place not within their dominions. Will learned the *bailli* had not sought to charge the perpetrators and hoped it would be the end of the matter. But then a man heard singing psalms in French by the river was stoned to death by a group of angry Catholics and, in return, a nun was hanged for reasons Will was unable to ascertain.

Walking the streets of the town, he could feel the anger as though it was a physical presence. People loitered far longer than was usual, heads bent close together, whispers rising to an angry clamour. It was like St Andrews after Wishart was burned at the stake, everyone waiting for the explosion to happen.

Will met with his new congregation in a house only a stone's throw from the cathedral. Bible in hand, he spoke to them and, although some of the men had looked askance at his foreignness, they quickly settled, listening attentively and nodding when they agreed with the doctrinal points he made. The group were eager to meet daily and their number grew and soon they were using a hall, since thankfully the most recent edict permitted Huguenots to do so.

Every day something more happened: two men were arrested for standing up in church and refuting what the priest was saying; a flock of geese was painted across the altar in the cathedral, which Will learned was a prize commonly given to the king of liars during street festivities; more statues of saints had their noses sliced off. Then one day a member of his congregation passed Will a broadsheet, chuckling.

Will bent his head to read while the small man blethered at his side.

'Very good, eh? The body of Christ these Catholics eat is nothing more than *a god of paste* and how true it is their plain old wafer is but *chewed up, passed through and shat out.'*

Will handed it back. 'Better we attend to the salvation of our own souls than concerning ourselves with such drivel.'

The man looked surprised but, after a moment, nodded sagely. 'A wise thought, master.'

The Catholics of Rouen responded in kind, over and above the inevitable burnings. They couldn't deface Protestant churches since there were none, but they issued their own broadsheet which Will could not resist glancing at when Madame Maupin appeared clutching one in her hand, face red with indignation.

'They say we are demons and worse...'

Naught but gluttons who know not the meaning of abstinence and must fill their bellies regardless of the suffering Jesus Christ endured and even over Lent. And their priests naught but lechers who give free range to their lasciviousness and are slaves to their carnal desires.

Will put his head in his hands. He was no longer convinced that priests should marry. Cecile would be alive if he'd remained celibate.

He felt Madame Maupin's hand rest gently on his shoulder. 'You are a good man and your wife would've died in childbirth whoever she married. It was God's will.'

Will looked up and smiled sadly but felt comforted by her words.

She took her hand away and bustled over to the fire. 'But now I must make the meal; hungry children must be fed.'

It was fair day, and Will, drifting among the stalls curious to see what they were selling, became aware of a man marching up and down holding a placard. He squinted trying to make sense of the words. *The Ruin of Stinking Mass*. Some vendors cheered, but a rosary bead-maker shouted, 'You Protestant bastards are nothing but demons, lechers and gluttons.'

A crowd was gathering to watch and one man began a psalm in response. Will joined him, singing with powerful voice. Then a group of priests were among them calling for silence.

'You've eaten too long without doing anything,' shouted the man with the placard. 'We're shining a pure light upon the Scriptures.'

The crowd surged forward and, amid the tumult, the priests fled. The crowd now turned their attention to the tents marshalled along the edge of the fair, where the prostitutes plied their trade, and tore them down.

'Rouen is best avoided,' Will heard the rosary maker mutter as he quickly packed his wares.

Many Protestants, emboldened by their successes, grew louder in their protests. The numbers gathering in front of the cathedral to sing psalms, drowning out the service within, were greater every day. Will, made uncomfortable with the energy being put into attack rather than directed inwards towards following God's true path and saving one's own soul, didn't join the throng. Yet it was difficult to avoid them, given the square in front of the cathedral and surrounding streets were now filled by several thousand people whenever a gathering happened. One night the church and convent of St Celestine's was broken into, its valuables stolen, statues defaced, artwork destroyed and any nun caught raped. Will, remembering Bethia's friend Elspeth who'd been sent to a nunnery after an adulterous liaison with an artist, prayed that a Protestant Scotland was treating its former nuns more kindly and that Elspeth was safe. Sickened by the attack on defenceless women, Will preached a sermon during which he barely contained his rage.

But for the Catholics of Rouen all this was a clear message; the balance of power had shifted. Skirting around the city walls to visit a sick member of his flock one wet morning, Will observed a line of carts making their way through the city gate loaded with families and their goods. The wealthy Catholics were leaving.

Chapter Thirty-Four

Under Siege

One day the good people of Rouen awoke to find their city gates firmly closed against all comers and word that a force was on its way to demand their surrender and swift return to Rome, or the city would find itself under attack. A bare twenty-four hours later and men were camped before them although their numbers were small and the inhabitants of the city could still come and go by river.

'Hah!' said Pastor Georges when he found Will upon the ramparts. 'This is a paltry force that will easily be got rid of.'

But Will was not so sure. 'More will likely come and, if my previous experience is anything to go by, we'll soon have every wastrel in France hidden amid true Protestants come to loot under the pretence of rendering assistance, before our besiegers block all ingress. In the meantime we'll become short of supplies and hungry, although…' Will scratched his head '…less so than in St Andrews, for there we were contained within the castle walls whereas Rouen's city walls cover a far greater area. So large an area,' he said thoughtfully, 'I worry how we can defend it.'

But those leading the forces within Rouen had considered this and written to Queen Bess of England, requesting she send soldiers. It was barely a hundred years since the city had rid itself of English sovereignty, during which France's heroine, Jeanne d'Arc, was burned at the stake in this very town. Elizabeth was clearly wary, and who could blame her? Promoting the Protestant cause was one thing, but to send troops in its defence onto foreign soil could be perceived as a declaration of war on another nation. Nevertheless, as summer waned, more mercenaries appeared, said to be funded by England, and Will found it strange to be fighting on the same side as Scotland's traditional enemies.

Will and Calvin had recently corresponded debating what constituted correct action, with Will asking most earnestly for guidance. *Was it ever right to kill in defence of the true faith?* he wrote.

He had once run a man through with his sword but that was to save his sister, and in the same situation he would do it again – although he'd left the sword in Geneva; didn't consider it appropriate for a man of God to carry one.

Calvin wrote a lengthy reply, taking a wider perspective than killing, his concern more about whether legal authority should be overturned.

> *It will help us little in advancing the cause of true faith if all is done through seditious acts. We must, at all times, show respect to the duly constituted authorities. Reform will come through working with them and praying to God to show them the light. The destruction of church property must be discouraged at all times. Judicial permission must be given for any acts of iconoclasm... and this includes taking action to stop executions.*

When he read these lines Will sighed heavily. How would they ever receive judicial permission to stop executions when the judiciary were those who ordered them in the first place? He feared Calvin was taking an overly simplistic view of complex issues.

The letter had concluded that:

respect for the established order is fundamental to meeting the core tenets of our faith and even martyrdom is preferable to any violent protest. We will effect change by steady example and quiet prayer only.

However difficult it might be, Will felt he must endeavour to follow Calvin's guidance.

As the siege deepened, his landlady stayed indoors as far as was possible, but her laundry business was suffering. 'I need the money to feed the children,' she said simply when Will remonstrated with her for going to the river unescorted.

'Then I will be your guard, but I can only spare two hours a day.'

She gratefully assented, and so Will found himself at watch while she scrubbed and rinsed clothing by the river. Soon other washerwomen, learning what time she would be there with her Scottish guardian, joined her, and the place was again full of companionship, banter and the occasional argument.

Dieppe, Le Havre, Bourges and Orleans had all declared for the Protestant cause, which would spread the Crown's forces very thin. Many hoped the peoples of Normandy might now be left in peace to follow the true faith.

Will wished he shared their optimism.

In Rouen, every altar, baptismal font, pew, coffer and any other religious object of Catholic significance that could be prised loose had been destroyed. The elders of the town were furious. A public meeting was called demanding that this wanton destruction end. Will, standing at the back, watched as everyone around him nodded their agreement. It was determined a letter of apology be sent to the Crown, specifically Catherine de Medici, who it was known, while not sympathetic in any way to their cause, was at least prepared to show a degree of tolerance – especially for Rouen, which formed part of her son's jointure.

Will, who'd become friendly with one François Civille, a wealthy merchant who was part of the group formed to draft the letter, had sight of it before it was sent.

This was naught but a spontaneous outbreak led by children, and men who have no more intelligence than children. We are loyal subjects to your great Majesties and do not in any way endorse such Wanton Destruction and attacks upon the Homes of our fellow Catholics. We apologise for the Troubles these acts have caused you and say all we want is to follow our true Faith and worship unhindered with the Permissions of your Majesties. We humbly beseech that you might bring an end to this Siege with all possible haste so we may all move unhindered and work toward the greater Glory of God.

All most appropriate, thought Will, and perhaps it might sway the regent, if only she could control the Guise family, who it was said wanted to take Rouen and thus fill their rich coffers further. He bent his head to the letter once more and flinched when he read the next sentence.

Yet we cannot but be aware this act of iconoclasm should also be considered a demonstration of Divine Displeasure towards the display of Idolatry formerly to be found in our Churches.

The letter ended by again reiterating that the writers were humble servants to the Crown. Will looked at Civille and raised his eyebrows.

'I think this letter might have held more sway if its

next to last paragraph had been dispensed with.'

Civille shrugged. 'We may bow low, but not too low else how will they be clear we are staunch Huguenots still?'

With which sentiment Will, as a staunch Calvinist himself, could not but concur.

The gold plate taken from the churches was retrieved, wherever possible, and melted down to pay for the garrison. It raised what seemed to Will the vast amount of 58,000 livres and yet only provided enough to pay barely two months stipend to the soldiers and mercenaries filling the town. But then they helped themselves to what they could anyway so he need feel no concerns there. And the Crown countered by seizing ships with a rich cache of cloth belonging to the merchants of Rouen which they impounded to help cover their costs in besieging.

It was a relief to learn that the royal army was concentrated at Bourges and the numbers of troops outwith the city walls were rumoured to be no more than three thousand – and had no cannon. The length of the city walls, as Will knew having walked their circumference, was such that far more men, as well as firepower, would be needed to take the city. He began to feel hopeful their besiegers might creep away. However, after his experiences at St Andrews, he warned Civille the Crown troops might try to tunnel their way in.

Civille took him to various points where skin membrane stretched tight across frames with bells attached had been set up. 'Any underground vibration will set the bells off. It would be difficult for them to begin a tunnel anyway without us seeing it and of greater concern is that they will send ships down the river to bombard us.'

It was early autumn now and the rains came; cold, damp, dreary duty for those patrolling the walls. They learned that the royal army had successfully broken the siege at Bourges. This was worrying information, but Civille and others were confident the Crown would ignore Rouen for the time being and move onto Orleans.

'Elizabeth of England is sending reinforcements and we're reliably informed they will be with us any day,' Civille said when Will expressed concern. He clapped Will on the back. 'You worry like an old woman, my friend.'

Movement outwith Rouen had been restricted for some time now, and with so many people shut up together and the street sweepers diverted to soldiering duties, the town soon grew pestilent. Will felt as though he was reliving each disastrous event from the siege at St Andrews Castle, and though he was determined to follow Calvin's instructions and not lift a sword to fight, he could help maintain some order amid the filthy, rat-infested streets.

He persuaded Civille to introduce him at one of the meetings held by those who'd taken on the governing of Rouen, where he proposed any not manning the walls should be pressed into service to shovel the ordure into designated areas from where it would be cleared at night through a gate. Agreement was given, provided Will took charge. He nodded while feeling a flutter of panic. He was after all a stranger in Rouen. But he reckoned without the support of the washerwomen, who, grateful for his help, took up the shovels themselves and made certain no idle fellow refused his turn.

One day there was great disquiet on the streets and Will hurried up onto the ramparts, where the guard, who was familiar with him moving among them, permitted entry. The sun rose on government troops marching and they kept coming and coming in great rows. Soon there was nowhere he could look out from the wall and not see them. The whole outer wall was encircled, and worse, Rouen was cut off from the fort which overlooked the city and controlled access to the south. There were men in the fort but nobody could reach them now, even if any soldiers could be spared. And once their firepower was used up then no more could be got to them.

They'd known of course the army was coming, but so convinced was everyone that the Crown forces would go to Orleans first – it was after all midway between Bourges and Rouen – they'd believed the rumour that only a detachment was being sent on ahead. It was said there were around twenty thousand men in the royal army, but after watching them take two days to arrive, Will put it at nearer thirty thousand. And behind them came horses dragging cannon.

He slipped down behind the wall and rested on his haunches. Too late to flee now, anyhow his conscience would not permit it. He was here to the end but he would not kill. Calvin's words were his now. They must find a way to bring those corrupted by popish wrong-thinking to a true faith without slaughter. God's wounds, he wished he knew what it was.

The commander overseeing their besiegers, Antoine of Navarre, knew what he was about, and as September flowed into October, siege trenches were dug. It was curious Navarre was leading the royalist troops when his brother, the Prince of Condé, was a known Protestant. But Condé was not here in Rouen, no doubt reluctant to openly defy the regent.

The washerwomen could no longer ply their trade. Although the city walls were close to the river and it was impossible for their besiegers to dig trenches or even patrol there safely, they did have some presence on the far side of the river bank, and the last ship which had attempted to dock had been fired upon and sunk.

Will, in between his shovelling duties, spent more time upon the city walls, and the men seemed to welcome his presence, especially when he said a prayer or sang a psalm with them. He was there on a day of bright sunshine, over-warm for mid-October, when a soldier nearby rested his musket on the rampart, lined it up, took aim and fired.

'Think I got the bastard,' he muttered.

His neighbour clapped him on the shoulder. 'Think you did too.'

Out in the desolation before them, behind the barricades and in the trenches, there was much running back and forth, waving of arms and shouting.

'It's clearly causing consternation,' said Will. 'Who do you think you shot?'

'Some fine fellow. Looked to be important in his fancy uniform and trailed by a lot of equally fine fellows.'

Soon word was being passed along that Navarre himself had been shot. Then it was confirmed, Will knew not how, that Antoine of Navarre had been struck in the shoulder. He was alive and it seemed still able to direct operations, for a serious assault was made on the fort. All day Will watched from the city walls, surrounded by other equally helpless watchers, as cannons were hauled up the hill by straining horses and shouting men and turned on the fort. He wondered that an attack was not made from the city to draw away some of the royalist soldiers, and eventually, late in the day, a sortie was sent out... and slaughtered. Only a few men made it back, and it was some small satisfaction that their sharp-shooter on the ramparts managed to hit some of the pursuers.

Darkness fell and Will returned to his lodgings. The women were doing their best to contain themselves but Will could see the strain in their faces, sense the fear like a physical presence, watch the shaking hands as they dished the watery soup into bowls and passed them around.

'Is there any hope?' said Madame Maupin.

Will wanted to reassure but could not, in all honesty, do so. 'Once the fort is taken, very little. But...' he sat straighter on his stool, 'miracles can happen, as Jesus

Christ showed us many times.'

'And surely God is on our side.' It was statement not a question and Will felt no need to reply. His shoulders slumped. God was testing them and they must suffer stoically for their faith.

The next day the walls of the fort were breached and the troops poured in. The royalists could now fire on the city from there. It was only a matter of time before Rouen fell.

Chapter Thirty-Five

Taken

Will wasn't overly troubled about dying, although he would prefer a less painful death than being consumed by flames, fairly slowly, from what he'd observed. He *was* concerned about the ongoing care of his six-year-old daughter. He'd done right to leave her with the Locke family, for men knew nothing about raising a small child, especially a girl. And they would raise her in the Calvinist faith, but still, they were not her kin. He worried what would happen when she came to marry, indeed what would happen, likely much sooner, once Calvin was no longer there to oversee all. He'd written to brother John some months ago requesting his help. John was well aware of the troubles in Rouen, for it had, he complained to Will, been most detrimental to the trade he'd set up supplying herring in return for cloth. Will was surprised trade still flowed almost as freely between France and Scotland since the Reformation. Yet it seemed the auld alliance with France continued, certainly where that was concerned.

John had responded promising he would do all in his power to bring the child to Scotland where she would be raised as a Protestant in a Protestant country and, almost as an afterthought, mentioned he was recently married and his wife would be most honoured to have the care of wee Cecile. Of more concern to John was what Will was doing in Rouen still.

You have already endured most severe punishment from the siege at St Andrews, although you are rarely heard to complain. Do you truly wish to expose yourself to enslavement on a galley again? You are no longer a young man, and 'tis better, as your child grows to womanhood, she have a father's guidance.

Will snorted reading John's epistle. The cheek of him to call Will an old man. John was what?... No more than seven years younger and already into his twenties. In any case, Will considered he was as likely to be shut up in some French prison as worked as a galley slave, although neither was desirable. But whatever God willed he would endure.

Will had then communicated his wishes to both Margaret Locke and Calvin and they had responded confirming Cecy would be released into John Seton's care when he or a proxy appeared in Geneva. He'd been surprised not to receive any protest from Margaret Locke, no expression of desire to keep Cecy with her, and it worried away at him. Perhaps Cecy was become a troublesome child? Nevertheless, Will felt his conscience was clear where his daughter was concerned. If he were to die when the city was overrun then he could happily meet his maker... and his wife.

All able-bodied men were now required to hold the ramparts, even pastors. The captain found him a sword, a twisted rusted-looking thing, and Will turned it this way and that in his hands then looked down into the man's face.

'I am a priest. It's not right I should wield this.'

'Ah well, one swing of your fist will probably be sufficient.' The man studied Will's hands and Will too gazed upon them. 'Although your hands have the whiteness of a scholar. Better to fetch and carry,' he said, and moved off to deal with more demanding matters.

There was activity below as some of the cannon dragged with so much effort up the hill were brought back down by their attackers, horses and men harnessed and all straining to prevent a runaway descent. Loud were the jeers from the watchers on the wall when one cannon broke free, the ropes holding it to horses snapping, and set off with several men, who were roped on, being tossed around like debris on a stormy sea. There was no stopping the cannon and, with the ground dry and hard, for there'd been no rain for several weeks now, it only came to an abrupt halt when it collided with a boulder.

But the entertainment was over and the broken bodies carried away. By the next day their besiegers had all their cannon in position and the attack began in earnest. The smoke, the noise – thumps that shook the ground beneath his feet, thunderous crashes, wood splintering, roared instructions, shouts, cries – went on all day with some respite at night. It was surprising how soon he grew accustomed to the noise, although he found the screams of the women and terrified children deeply distressing.

The firing from the trenches surrounding them was disturbingly effective given the bulwarks of the ramparts. The men had to keep themselves tucked down behind the walls, shooting back as best they could. Will was more at risk than the shooters as he scurried back and forth bringing supplies, and soon his back was aching even more than usual from bending double.

He was sent next to the ramparts above the town main gates where he encountered Civille and his company engaged in a fierce fight. Civille acknowledged his presence with a nod and Will passed him the shot, which he rammed into his arquebus.

'Those popish whores are up to something below,' Civille shouted to Will.

'Take care,' said Will, grabbing the gun which was thrust at him. He gasped as the barrel burnt his hand, quickly shifting to grip the wood.

Civille shoved his head out of a crenellation in the rampart and as quickly drew it back again while the noise of battle intensified. 'I could not see, must look again.'

'Do not stick your head out there, they'll be waiting for you to reappear.'

'I know,' said Civille, and crept further along the wall, hunched down.

But it seemed their attackers had expected this, either that or it was a lucky shot, for when Civille looked out again he was hit. Will rushed to pull him back but was not in time to save the man. Civille toppled forward and slid down the front of the rampart into the ditch below. Will heard the whine of a bullet in his ear as he dropped down. He sat crouched, back against the wall, breathing heavily.

There were shouts of derision from the men around him, and Will rose to glance out briefly once more. Their attackers were retreating to the trenches. He ran down the steps to the gate, insisting he would join the foraging party in the hope of finding Civille.

When they did emerge into the evening shadows it was quickly evident the foragers were more interested in *what* they could retrieve than *who*. Bodies were picked over thoroughly – pockets emptied, and boots, jerkins, indeed any half-decent piece of clothing removed – and then the corpse rolled into the ditch and roughly covered either by soil or excrement from the midden heaps which were piling high around the walls. The stench of putrefying bodies soon had Will swallowing hard in spite of the linen he'd tied over his mouth and nose.

Civille's servant joined him and together they searched, climbing over rubbish and rolling bodies over to check the faces, but without success. They were being called back to the gate when a man working in front of

277

them kicked at the fingers of a poorly buried corpse sticking up through the earth. There was a glint of gold and the man dropped to his knees to investigate. The servant gave a cry and leapt forward.

The scavenger hauled on the dead finger, holding the servant back with his other arm. Will grabbed the man by the shoulders and tossed him to one side. The fellow rose to his feet ready for a fight, but when Will raised his fists in response, he thought better of it and, with a growl, backed away.

Civille's servant was clawing at the earth like a dog digging for a bone and Will knelt to help. A face, clogged with dirt, emerged. The servant raised his hand for Will to stop digging and held his fingers beneath Civille's nostrils.

'I think he breathes still.'

Will opened his mouth to proclaim it a miracle and then chided himself for such popish nonsense. Together he and the servant carried Civille between them as best they could, but after several minutes stumbling over the blasted ground plus the great difference in their respective heights, Will determined it easier to sling the wounded man over his shoulder. He remained insensible and didn't stir even when Will laid him gently down on a bed. Will leant against the chamber wall to catch his breath and watched as the servant tenderly wiped Civille's face clean of blood and dirt. It soon became evident the shot had skimmed his right cheek and shattered his collar bone.

'Master, you have done much to help already,' said Civille's servant, 'but if you could assist me to remove his clothes so I may determine the extent of his injuries I would be most grateful.'

Will, in attempting to remove the ruff from around Civille's neck, lifted his head gently and saw the blood was holding it thick as dried-on porridge to the skin.

'He must have been hit more than once,' said the

servant from the other side of the bed.

Will studied the wound in both neck and cheek. 'I don't think so. Civille was bent over and the bullet has sliced his cheek and down the neck, passing out by the collar bone.'

He left the servant to minister to him, returning daily to check on progress. Civille lay insensible but Will considered it remarkable he'd not succumbed to infection and was still breathing. On the fourth day he was surprised to be met by a more cheerful servant.

'My master is recovering,' he said.

Will bent over Civille, who opened his eyes. 'Seton,' he whispered, 'I thank you.'

Six days after Civille was injured Will himself sustained injury. He was on the ramparts assisting a man who'd likely broken his leg when his world went dark. He knew nothing until he came to, lying on a bed, to find a group of men standing over him. He lay still, feigning insensibility, which was as well, for as they spoke he learned these were the besiegers. Rouen had been taken.

The argument was over what to do with this *pestilential heretic*, and Will realised it was him they were referring to.

'He's a big fellow. Be of use for the galleys,' said a gruff voice.

'Not injured he won't.'

'True, and we have enough to guard as it is. Let's dispose of him now.'

And before Will knew what was happening he was flying through the air in the dark. He landed with a thump, all the breath knocked out of him. The bastards had thrown him out the window!

He lay still on the surprisingly soft heap of earth. A stench worse than the general smells of Rouen assailed him: putrefying bodies. He coughed and coughed then began to laugh and couldn't stop. God truly was watching out for him to provide such a soft landing.

Too weak-headed to stand, he crawled. Some fool had dressed him in a nightshirt in the midst of a battle and he needed to find some clothes. The breeches he took from a corpse barely skimmed his knees but would do for the moment. He crawled further, could see the glint of dark water moving ahead and was grateful to have found the river. He sat on the edge of the bank until he saw the torchlight of a patrol, then slipped in the water, his bare feet touching soft mud and the water level with his chest.

He moved until he was in deep darkness beneath one of the arches of the bridge and pulled himself out onto a pile. If he could find something drifting by to hold onto, the current would carry him towards the sea.

Then he made out the dark shape of a boat drawing closer, passing silently beneath the bridge. It must be fugitives from Rouen, else why quiet and unlit?

'Hello,' he hissed.

'Hush,' came the response.

'I'm Will Seton, the pastor,' he said softly. 'Can you help me?'

There was a mumbled debate with one voice sounding more insistent than the other. The boat had drifted past but they rowed back and drew up by the stanchion.

'Quickly,' a voice hissed.

Will stepped carefully down. The water in the bottom of the boat felt warm on his feet after his immersion in the cold river.

They rowed in silence, a torch lit Rouen fading behind them.

'Thank you,' Will said once they turned the bend in the river.

'One good turn deserves another,' said a gravelly voice.

Will turned to look at the man sitting on the bench behind him. 'Civille, is that you? I am glad to see you've escaped, after all the trouble we took to save you.'

Civille gave a low laugh. 'As am I you. Here, you can have my servant's cloak.'

Will thought to refuse as the servant reluctantly gave it up, but he was shivering uncontrollably. 'Where are we going?'

'Downriver to Le Havre. Where are you headed next?'

'To Scotland,' said Will, surprising himself. 'I will go home to Scotland,' he repeated, through chattering teeth.

Part Seven

Bethia

1562 to 1582

Chapter Thirty-Six

Tiberias

It seemed Dona Gracia had a vision which was consuming her, as if she were being slowly eaten from the inside out. She intended Tiberias should become a place of the Jews. The city would still be within the sultan's empire, of course, but would be controlled by Jews in a way it had not been since the tribes of Israel were scattered.

Mainard didn't think much of Dona Gracia's plans when he told Bethia after Don Joseph and his train of servants had left. 'I do not see how it can be – it's forbidden for Jews to have sovereignty.'

'What do you mean? Are you saying there cannot be a land of the Jews which is ruled by them alone?'

'Not until the Messiah comes.' Mainard twisted his earlobe. 'In any case, Don Joseph tried something similar in Ferrara. Don't you remember? He wanted to purchase an island where Jews might live but his request was denied.'

Bethia shook her head. 'Not really. But surely Dona Gracia will have more success here. Suleiman respects her.'

'Huh!'

'Why do you say that?'

'I'm aware Suleiman was none too pleased when the

lady persuaded him to write to the Pope desiring the Conversos of Ancona be freed, and his request, demand or however it was worded was disregarded. No ruler can easily tolerate such disdain, for it begins to eat away at his power and the perception of him.'

'You're not telling me anything I don't know. I was there, remember. The Grand Turk was furious with her. You could feel it as you walked the corridors. It was fortunate for us in a way, for it's why Dona Gracia sent me alone to the harem, which has made a good living for us.'

Mainard nodded slowly. 'It has indeed, and I am proud of my observant wife who wasn't afraid to seize an opportunity and made sound judgements thereafter.'

Usually, Bethia would've puffed with pride to be so described. Today she clenched her teeth together and said nothing. It was more than five years since Mainard had been restored to her and, when he had at last arrived in Constantinople full of tales about the Frankfurt Book Fair, Ortelius, Schyuder's family and his new adherence to Familism, she was surprised by how angry she'd felt. He'd been roving around Europe having a merry time while she'd been left to navigate the strangeness and peril of a new city with three small boys, to the great detriment of her health and soundness of mind and she could not embrace his return with the joy he clearly expected – and evinced in seeing her. Indeed, his assumption they could slide easily back into a life together had left her angry because it showed he didn't understand the trough of fear and despair she'd lived in with no knowledge of his whereabouts, or if he was alive. Yet, even when she snapped at him, he remained calm, which somehow had made her more furious.

'I understand,' he'd said one day apropos of nothing.

She'd glared at him. 'What do you understand?' Then walked away before he could tell her.

Mainard had followed, catching her arm. She shook

286

his hand off and kept going.

'Bethia,' he'd called, 'please listen.'

She'd hesitated, hearing the note of desperation, but the anger was still there, a tight knot deep in her shrunken belly.

'After I was imprisoned in Antwerp and we eventually found one another again I could not allow myself any weakness. It'd been too hard to survive,' Mainard said.

Bethia remembered it all too well: how Mainard wouldn't let her close; seemed barely able to look at her; and avoided intimacy.

'And it was Dona Gracia who reprimanded me for my coldness. She told me not to squander the love you had for me. She said that she, of all people, knew the value of loyalty and you had shown exceptional loyalty to me. And she was correct.'

Bethia had clamped her teeth together so hard her jaw hurt. 'When you went to Frankfurt you were certainly showing loyalty, but it was to that rat Don Joseph, not to me.'

His lips had narrowed and he said slowly as though explaining to a child, 'Bethia, as you well know, our debts to him were in excess of one thousand scudi.' He glared at her then as suddenly the fight had gone out of him. 'If I'd found myself in Pesaro when Foscari released me from...' he'd snorted, 'the coffin within which I was being oh so carefully transported, then it's entirely possible I would've ignored Don Joseph's directions, got on a ship and come to you. But I was already in Bologna and fearful of the consequences.' He'd sat down suddenly on Papa's big chair, head in his hands.

Bethia had shut the door on the noises of the house going about its business.

'You are right,' he'd said. 'I *could* have taken the funds Foscari gave me to travel to Frankfurt and used them instead to come to Constantinople.'

287

Bethia had thought on the long months without him and the agony of not knowing. If he'd come sooner she would've been spared, but her work in the harem most likely would never have come about, for they would've fallen from favour with the Mendes and been scrabbling to make a living. She'd gazed at the mosaic-patterned walls of this comfortable home in Galata which they'd likely *not* be occupying if Mainard had fled here.

Mainard lifted his head. 'I am truly sorry.'

She'd pulled on the fringe of her shawl, intricately patterned and too bright to wear on the streets of Constantinople. 'You did what you thought was right,' she'd said slowly, then rubbed the top of his head as though he was one of the children, the curls springy beneath her hand.

She became aware of Mainard observing her as she remembered their reunion. Still even those moments of re-connection did not mean there were not times when she found him annoyingly oblivious.

'Have I said aught that displeases you, my love?'

'I feel more patronised than praised. I'm no longer the innocent you enticed away from her home to marry.'

He stiffened. 'I don't remember it required much enticement,' he said, and walked out of the room the picture of injured dignity. But she wanted to speak more of Tiberias and followed him.

'What benefit is there for Suleiman in giving the Jews this place?'

Mainard slung his cloak over his shoulders and tugged his cap over his curly hair. 'We'll speak later,' he said abruptly. 'I must away to oversee the printing of the book the rabbi has written. I know in comparison to the funds you bring in from your business my earnings are small, but it's still worth doing. Just.' And with that he opened the front door and went out, slamming it hard behind him.

Bethia stood staring at the door for several moments

then felt a small hand slide into hers. 'Is Papa angry?' said Abram, gazing up worried-faced at his mother.

Bethia's own anger blew away like a dandelion clock on a windy Scottish day. She smoothed his hair, which immediately sprang back into tight curls, like his father's. 'You know some days when you feel cross and you don't really know why?'

Abram considered carefully, as was his wont, and then slowly nodded.

'Papa is having one of those days. He'll be all better by tomorrow, just like you would be.' And yet as she spoke she felt a small kernel of shame, for really it was she who'd been out of humour.

Abram was silent for a few moments and Bethia waited for the inevitable question. 'Can I make him better?'

'Yes, my sweet. I'm sure you can do something to make Papa feel better.'

Abram nodded solemnly.

'Now let us to our lessons. Your Latin is coming along very well.'

'Then can we play *tavla*?'

'What?'

'You know, with the board and the small stones.'

'Backgammon, you mean.'

'*Tavla* is what Gehveri calls it.'

Then we will call it *tavla* too,' said Bethia with a gaiety she didn't feel, although she was grateful their wealthy Turkish neighbours permitted Gehveri and Abram to play together. Since this seemed likely to be her sons' permanent home then the more connections they had, the better.

In giving Abram permission to *make Papa feel better*, Bethia had not thought to inquire what form this might take. That night, lying with her back to Mainard, who she'd elbowed a few times in a vain attempt to stop him snoring, Bethia eventually fell into restless sleep full of twisting dreams where pigs and demons danced across an unusually glacial Bosphorus. She was awoken by a great shout close to her ear as something heavy landed on top of her. She sat bolt upright to find two small boys leaping around the chamber each covered in a white bed sheet.

'Boys!' roared Mainard sitting up next to her.

The taller of the two ignored him and continued his gyrations; the little one stopped and stood still. 'We're not boys,' hissed Jacopo, 'we're demons. And you must do as we bid else we'll take you to the underworld.'

Mainard fell back against the bolster and let out a sigh.

'Don't be sad, Papa,' said Abram clambering onto the bed to stroke his father's cheek.

'I'm not sad. Only baffled as to why I've been woken for a performance that could perfectly well have happened during daylight hours.'

'It only works in the dark to be demons,' said Jacopo in the reasoned tone of one explaining something to the dim-witted.

'Yes, don't you see, Papa. It had to be very, very dark,' said Abram. 'And you've told us many times you like it when we do our theatre.' He patted his father on the forehead, but Bethia could see by the furrowed brow he was seeking reassurance as much as to reassure.

'It was kind of you to try and cheer Papa up,' she said, 'but perhaps next time not in the middle of the night.'

'But…' said Jacopo, and she raised her hand, which even he could not ignore. 'Go back to your beds, boys, and we'll speak in the morning.'

Abram, after giving his father a final pat on the face, slid off the bed and wandered to the door. 'Mama…' he whispered.

'I am coming to tuck you in, cosy as a bird in its nest.' But before she could move Mainard climbed down from the bed and shepherded the boys from the chamber.

'Are they sleeping now?' she whispered when he slipped back into bed soon after.

'Yes,' said Mainard, reaching out to take her hand.

They lay silently for a moment, but Bethia, wide-awake, decided now might be a time to inquire further about Tiberias and a Jewish homeland.

'It is Dona Gracia's most fervent wish,' said Mainard when she asked why. 'She's old now and fears death without a lasting legacy. And it's also a sacred place of the Jews. Jerusalem, of course, would be preferable, but the Christians would never tolerate that, nor the Arabs for that matter.'

Bethia sighed. 'So much for one city to carry.'

'I've been told the Jews of Jerusalem are treated as little better than stray dogs,' Mainard said softly. 'But many have settled in Tiberias. Don Joseph wants me to go there, as we're shipping wool to them for dyeing and weaving.'

Bethia sat bolt upright in bed and looked down on him in the shaft of moonlight piercing the gap in the shutters. 'Then I will come with you.'

Mainard lay and stroked her back as she sat hunched forward on the bed. 'We'll talk about it more in the morning,' he said soothingly.

'I wish we could be done with the strange demands of the Mendes family.'

'That would be most unwise,' Mainard said. And she knew he was correct, for Don Joseph was now the great friend of Selim, the sultan's eldest living son and most likely successor to the ageing Suleiman.

Mainard left a few weeks later for Safed, without Bethia. She tried to see him off with a strong heart but couldn't help but cling to him. She did not however resort to pleading with him either to refuse Don Joseph's orders or to take her too, and Mainard's relief was evident. He held her close, whispering, 'I rely on your strength, Bethia.'

And all was well really, for he was back within two months with much to say of the development of Tiberias and of its weavers.

'These are learned men in the ways of Judaism. And what is more, none among them is ashamed to go to the well and draw water, or go to the marketplace to buy bread and vegetables.'

'I shall look forward to seeing you take up the bucket and the basket,' said Bethia, much amused.

But Mainard was too focused on the sages of Safed to raise a smile. 'The debate,' he said, walking up and down their small patch of land where he had found her overseeing the gardener, 'is very lively amid the Kabbalists, and they sing the Lord's praises in the fields at sundown after a day's work.'

She felt the fear of his draw to Judaism like a sharp knife slid between her ribs but managed a ghost of a smile, touched by his enthusiasm.

Mainard nodded almost to himself. 'Some say what's happening in Safed is a sign the Messianic Age is imminent.'

Bethia stiffened. 'Our Messiah, Jesus Christ, has been with us for over fifteen hundred years.'

His face wiped off all expression. She couldn't bear that they were at odds and him just home. She swallowed and adopted a lighter, more inquiring tone.

'Why is Dona Gracia seeking a Jewish homeland in Tiberias and not Safed then?'

'Tiberias is an area within Safed that was once populous but is now deserted. Dona Gracia has rightly identified it as having potential, if only the city walls are repaired and vigilant guards provided. And she has persuaded the sultan that he'll gain revenue if it's brought to life once more.'

Bethia nodded slowly. 'So she will become Suleiman's tax farmer for Tiberias.'

'Exactly.'

'And will encourage Jews to live there. So that is what your sister meant in her most recent letter when she talked of moving to the Holy Land?'

'Ah, a letter from Catarina is always entertaining. And how is my mother?' said Mainard moving towards the house.

'Catarina didn't mention her, but she enclosed a note marked for your attention only.'

'Good, good,' said Mainard, but he wasn't attending to her, all focus on getting to the letter. Bethia was certain it contained yet another plea, or demand, for Mainard to go to Venice and retrieve Papa's bones, for Catarina was still determined they should be taken to the Holy Land for burial or, at the very least, be brought to Constantinople. What she continually ignored though was that it was not an easy matter to exhume a body – especially without the Pope's permission.

Bethia followed him inside. She'd a letter from Will, telling of his remarkable escape from yet another siege – what was he thinking to get caught up so again, and this one very terrible, for it was said more than a thousand of Rouen's citizens were slaughtered when the city was taken – but she would tell Mainard of it later. She sat very still watching him read, weary of the dark shadow which lay over her that he would revert to Judaism and take their sons with him.

'The Family is what we cleave to,' he had said many times since his return from Frankfurt.

But the world beyond the family could not be disregarded.

Chapter Thirty-Seven

A Pragmatist

Bethia's business with the Sultanate of Women continued to grow, and Grissel, now Bethia's assistant and relieved from daily kitchen duties, did much of the purchasing at the markets, negotiating loudly in fractured Turkish. The traders loved her, and on the occasions Bethia joined Grissel, she was always entertained as the quips flew fast as any swordplay. She'd been approached many times by a range of men seeking Grissel's hand in marriage but Grissel had refused all offers.

'Do you not want a husband?' Bethia asked.

'And hae some man telling me whit to dae? I dinna think so.' Grissel grinned. ''Tis enough that you gie me orders.'

'Well, I wish any man better luck than I have had in directing you.' Bethia folded her arms. 'Even when you seem at your most meek and obedient you're usually hatching some wild plot.'

'Aye, weel. I'll bide wi' you. Better the devil ye know.'

Bethia shook her head but couldn't help smiling.

'And ye ken the work we do is braw, going to the place where all yon women live…'

'The harem.'

'Aye right. When would the likes o' me, a servant lass from St Andrews born the ither side of the blanket, get tae

294

see sich a place.'

'It is remarkable,' said Bethia. But it was also a rather sinister place.

'No that I wid want tae be shut in there wi' them,' said Grissel echoing her thoughts.

'What about children, Grissel?'

'Weel, I'm certainly no going to hae them withoot the husband. Ma mither was fortunate yer father let her stay on as a servant when she had me.'

Bethia frowned. 'I can remember you as a baby. How old are you?'

Grissel shrugged.

'Younger than me, and Will. You must be about twenty-six years. It's certainly more than time you were wed.'

Grissel's lip wobbled in a way that reminded Bethia of her as a small child. 'Do ye want rid o' me, mistress?'

She slid her arm through Grissel's. Grissel smelled of the perfumes of the hamam, for she'd taken to using the local bath house regularly and was likely the cleanest Scottish servant to be found anywhere.

'Of course I don't want rid of you. You could be married and we'd still work together. There's the man who sells the lace or the apothecary's assistant. Both seem fine men, and they are Greek Christians too.'

'Aye and if I marry ain o' them I will hae to leave you.'

'Naturally you would live with your husband.'

'And then, when you go off to yet anither country, I'd be left behind. The only Scotswoman in Constantinople.'

Bethia laughed. 'I think we're settled here.'

'Aye, that's what ye thocht in Antwerp and Venice. My heart tells me we're no done with journeying yet.' Grissel shook her head emphatically. 'I dinna want a husband and your laddies are as dear to me as ony I micht hae. And I saw you when ye birthed those bairns and it's no a rigour I'd willingly subject myself tae. Ma life is braw. Why would I want to make ony changes?'

'Well, when you put it like that, why indeed.' And Bethia went about her day happy to know she had a contented servant. But she also found her thoughts drifting to who Grissel's father might've been. He was clearly a strapping fellow for Grissel was taller than her, and in some ways looked more like Will and John than she did, certainly in size and colouring. But then Bethia knew she favoured her small dark-haired mother whereas her brothers favoured their tall, once red-headed father. She puzzled over it then shook her own head. Anyway, Grissel's hair was yellow, not red.

Samuel-Thomas was now thirteen years old and growing into a *muckle lad*, as Grissel would have it, and looking likely to be at least the height of his father, if not his uncles. Bethia hoped he would bulk out more, for he was all skinny arms and long legs. She caught Mainard studying him often, a thoughtful expression on his face.

'He'll soon likely grow as broad-shouldered as Will or John – or you for that matter,' she said. But it seemed this was not what was preoccupying him.

'I think our sons should be brought up as Jews. It's perilous for them not to belong, otherwise they're isolated from every group, and faith, in Constantinople,' he said one day.

Bethia dropped the pen, leaving a large blot of ink on her workings. She had thought this was coming, especially after his trip to Tiberias, but prayed her suspicions were ill-founded. 'When you returned from Frankfurt you told us we are *The Family* and sufficient unto ourselves. Our boys belong to us.'

'Our children are too vulnerable otherwise, my love.'

'Not if we return to Venice or even Scotland,' she said hopefully.

He shook his head slowly. 'I've considered the wisdom of Frankfurt, for there, as Familists, we might fit in. But who knows when there'll be another purge of

Conversos or attack on Jews. Even Familists may be eradicated. We're vulnerable on every count. We will not leave Constantinople.'

'But Conversos and Jews could equally be turned on here.'

'They could, but for hundreds of years Jews have lived in Constantinople, in the main unmolested, regardless of which sultan held sway. We're regarded even more favourably than Christians.'

'Why is that?'

Mainard looked sad. 'Because we are without country.' He paused. 'My love, it is the safest option.'

'But you cannot be certain.'

'I know it with as much certainty as I can know anything in this transient life. There's safety in numbers, and wealth. We are protected by the law of *ahl-al-dhimma*. And although we're restricted as to the colours we may wear, should not build new or repair old houses and other petty tyrannies, as you know those restrictions are not enforced among the Sephardi Jews.' He gave a short bark of a laugh. 'We are treated better than the Christians. And we can trade, and travel, freely. It *is* remarkable after the endless limitations of the Christian world.'

Bethia stared down at her hands clenched tight. She wanted to sink to her knees and howl *but they are my sons and you are taking them from me.*

Instead she said, stiffly, 'I didn't think they could become Jews with an Old Christian mother.'

'I've found a rabbi amid the forty-odd synagogues of Constantinople who will accept us.' He frowned. 'Others wouldn't countenance it… Because there were no Jewish witnesses, they said our marriage had no standing. This is why Don Joseph's marriage to La Chica wasn't binding in Jewish Law and he could marry Reyna.'

Bethia sniffed. 'And where were we to find Jewish witnesses in Scotland?'

'I know.' Mainard's face lightened. 'But Rabbi ibn

Habib was himself a Converso and considers special circumstances prevail here which makes the boys conversion permissible.'

Bethia's eyes narrowed. 'And what of you?'

'Naturally I will join them in taking instruction.' He gazed down at the mosaic tiles and rubbed his crippled foot across them. They no longer wore outdoor footwear in the house and Mainard mostly went barefoot, saying his foot pained him less that way. 'I don't suppose you would consider joining us? There are Converso women fleeing here still who receive instruction – not so many as before, for Europe must've near emptied of us. The rabbi says he has a new group starting soon and would be willing to take you, if you came with a true heart.'

He looked at her hopefully but she was too angry to appease him. 'So it was all a lie – the Familists and our discussions around the board and your endless communication with Ortelius, Plantin and others on the subject. What of your signing Ortelius's Book of Friendship?'

'You have misunderstood, Bethia,' he said with such quiet patience she felt a strong desire to scream. 'One does not exclude the other.'

'And has the rabbi confirmed that to be so?'

He didn't meet her eyes then. 'I need not tell him. As you well know, in Familism we quietly go about our business, we are pragmatic and we do not think everyone should be constrained to be of the same voice.' He picked up her hands in his and she let them lie there unresisting, did not return the pressure as he lightly squeezed. 'We are among the Family of Love and that overrides all; our true connection is to one another.'

She drew her hands away. 'And where is Christ Jesus in this? Henrik Niclaes had much to say of him.'

Mainard shook his head. 'HN sees Jesus as symbolic only and, as we've discussed often, our purpose in this world is to become *Godded with God*. I can pursue this equally through the rabbi and Judaism and you may join me, as I have said, or continue to cleave to the Virgin.'

'You won't come to church with me any longer?' Although recently, truth be told, he'd joined her less and less frequently.

'Bethia, I cannot.' He gave a grim laugh. 'My love, do you not understand. As I said, our boys must make their lives here in Constantinople and it's much easier if they turn to the faith of our ancestors.'

'Your ancestors you mean.'

He continued as though she hadn't spoken. 'There are tens of thousands of Jews here; we're a sizeable group, well thought of in the main by the Moslems and, for once, not weak and powerless.

'Why not go the whole way and join Islam? That'll make it even easier.' Her eyes grew large as she saw his expression.

'You considered it! You truly are the pragmatist.'

'If it's pragmatic to do what's best for your family then yes, I am a pragmatist and proud of it. I did consider Islam briefly, but it will not suffice. And,' he placed his hand on his heart, 'this is right. I cannot express to you, my love, how right and true it is that I should join my ancestors. I no longer feel riven.'

'No, perhaps *you* do not. But I do. I will not belong, even amid my own family.'

'That is a difficulty,' he said.

'But a lesser one.'

He sighed. 'Yes.'

She turned from him, staggered as she went through the doorway and then recovered. Retreating to her chamber, she sat on the bed they shared, staring down on the hands resting in her lap. She felt as though Mainard had fed her through the wringer, bit by bit. He'd promised he would continue to share faith with her. He had *promised*. And slowly, year by year he had withdrawn, so impalpably, so, so dishonestly – there was no other word for it – she'd all the time doubted her own perceptions. He had said he would remain a Catholic and he had not. And yet she knew she was being unfair. What else was he to do – he must protect his family – and especially after he had wrongfully been imprisoned as an apostate.

The house was quiet. Grissel who knows where, Johannes out and about on errands, Ysabeau nursing her latest child, the other servants in the kitchen, her sons, who no longer needed her in the same way, at their lessons. Perhaps she could go home to Scotland. If she wrote to brother John he would make arrangements for her to come. She could explain how much easier it was from his end to do so, explain it was a short visit only, to see Father. He was an old man now and there was Mother too, who John said was very wandered these days. But she would be returning to a recently turned Protestant Scotland which did not welcome Catholics any more than Rome welcomed Protestants. She lowered her head into her hands and groaned.

When she lifted it again, standing before her was Abram, her sturdy boy.

'Why are you sad, Mama?'

She drew him to her and whispered in his ear, 'Because my boys grow big so fast.'

He leant into her but only momentarily. Then squirmed away, glancing over his shoulder as he did, making certain this moment of weakness had not been observed by his older brothers, who would tease relentlessly that he was *Mama's baby, Mama's big baby*, usually followed by pretend crying, falling to the floor and kicking their legs in the air.

Grissel appeared in the doorway. 'You're needed in the kitchen for we must be telt how tae cook the ox tongue. The master says only you can do it richt. And he's looking for you because he canna get the figures to add up and he says it's an awfie mess.'

Bethia pushed herself slowly upright while Grissel stood in the doorway watching, hands crossed over her small round belly. She was fairly certain Mainard had sent Grissel – since when did Grissel ever call Mainard *the master*. She wondered what Mainard had said, or maybe Grissel had been listening at the door again. Grissel crossed the floor and took Bethia by the arm in a most familiar and inappropriate way.

'Shall we go to yon wee kirk later?'

Bethia turned and stared her full in the face.

Grissel had the grace to lower her eyes. 'I like it there,' she mumbled. 'The folk are friendly and it's proper, no like the churches all they Greeks go to. I canna make heid nor tail what they're on aboot. It wis guid we found St Benoit's here in Galata, even if it is full o' French folk.'

Bethia allowed herself to be guided from the room. She could feel her spirits lifting, a soft grey cloud rather than a thick black one.

'Ah, there you are,' said Mainard when she came later to the workroom after reminding the cook how to roll the tongue up so it would hold in place, pronouncing the baklava Johannes had bought from a new supplier to be excellent and cuddling his newest daughter while a smiling Ysabeau looked on.

'Yes, here I am,' she said.

Chapter Thirty-Eight

Hebrew Lessons

Bethia could hear the murmur of the boys studying Hebrew, a holy language like Latin and Greek. Will had started to learn it when they were in Geneva and Calvin made use of it. She could learn it too, had always enjoyed study. She lingered outside the door then turned and went into the kitchen to Grissel and her other servants; a woman swaddled by domestic duties, as it should be.

But Bethia was curious, and one day she entered the chamber and sat down at the back, much to the consternation of the boys' tutor.

'Go on,' she said, and Samuel-Thomas nodded his agreement from the front. This seemed to suffice, and on the tutor went while Bethia slid her stool next to Abram, watching what he did.

'I hear you have become a Hebrew scholar,' said Mainard the next morning.

She narrowed her eyes and looked at him. 'I am a student of the language only.'

He threw up his hands, smiling. ''Tis a good thing, I think.'

'And I have learned the Hebrew for prince is *nasi*. No wonder Don Juan Micas became Don Joseph Nasi when he arrived here.'

Mainard winked at her. 'He is man of vast ambition

302

and, given he's the close friend of a prince, may yet achieve high honours. Recently he prevailed upon Suleiman to write to the king of France yet again demanding repayment of the one hundred and fifty thousand scudi owed and when the king did not respond the sultan detained all the French merchants unfortunate enough to find themselves in Levantine ports.'

'Nothing about Don Joseph *Nasi* would surprise me. Now, there is some error in these figures you've given me. Where is the original paper so I may check the quantities?'

Mainard dug it out and nothing more was said of her Hebrew lessons. She went every day and the tutor grew accustomed to her presence although he never engaged her in any discussion. She was tolerated as a silent observer, except when the rabbi came, on which days Mainard requested that she not attend at all.

They still had the family discussions at the evening meal, for Mainard kept his promise, saying he would never stop this time of exchange and sharing – it was too precious. He often read aloud from a book called *The Kuzari*, which Bethia liked to dip into privately as well. The author wrote of the differences between Judaism, Christianity and Islam – and in listening to Mainard read passages from this man Judah Halevi's book, the places where the different paths crossed were also evident. In this way they continued to create their own treasured small family connections where each person's perspective was valued, and never derided, and where no one was afraid to speak up – a true Household of Love. Although Mainard and she counselled their children this must always remain within the family and shouldn't be mentioned outwith their close-knit group. Even Abram, young as he was, understood the dangers of a loose tongue. Familism was something all faiths might turn on.

But Friday night was different. Bethia dimly

remembered it was one of the signs of Marranos and secret Judaisers, whispered about in Antwerp, that they should have a special meal every Friday. Now two meals were prepared on a Friday, one that met Catholic sensibilities and the other the requirements of Judaism. And the food too was blessed by both traditions.

In the beginning it felt strange, but soon it became the way things were done in the de Lange household and no one remarked on it. They avoided visitors on Friday evenings, but it was rare to have any outsider break bread with them anyway. On Saturdays Mainard took the boys to the synagogue and usually on at least one other day during the week. They were gone for a long time but she never asked what they did.

They were invited to a Jewish wedding and Bethia went amid the women, thankful she could speak Ladino and was even learning some Judeo-Greek. It was her first visit to the synagogue and she couldn't believe the noise. For her, church was a place of controlled quiet, the silence broken only by the priest's voice and the mumbled responses from the congregation. Here everyone chattered throughout, except for those moments when, as if by magic, they all seemed to know they must repeat some verse. The rabbi shouted – he had to, to be heard – and the men, wrapped in their prayer shawls with the little caps on their heads, rocked back and forth muttering incessantly. Bethia was baffled how anyone could commune with God amid such noise. But the feasting went on for days, and she danced – oh how good it felt – albeit only with other women. She remembered being chastised for dancing in Geneva and was grateful this religion was more joyous than dour Calvinism. And the women were kind to her.

Mainard came one day saying the date of the boys' circumcision was now agreed. Bethia had known this was happening and had decided she wouldn't think of it, but of course she did, constantly praying for guidance and that Jesus might cast a protective cloak around her boys while drawing some comfort that Christ himself had been circumcised and survived.

'Although normally in Judaism we would hold the *brit milah* soon after birth, in Islam it can take place when boys are older.' He laughed in a way that sounded forced to Bethia. 'And Don Joseph at his advanced age, along with his retainers, as you'll well remember, went through it near on ten years ago and all was well.'

She suspected he was trying to reassure himself as much as her but noticed he was gazing over her shoulder as though he didn't quite want to meet her eyes.

'You're going to do it too.'

Now he looked at her. 'I think I must.'

'Oh Mainard, you're too old.'

'I am not so very ancient,' he said, puffing his chest out and trying to make her smile, but she could not.

'Did not one of Joseph Nasi's men die as a result?'

'No, no. That's not what killed him, the man was sick anyway.'

'And I heard some of them were unable to perform ever again.'

Mainard swallowed. 'Where did you hear that?'

'Women share when we come together at Jewish weddings.'

'I must do this, Bethia,' he said, his voice thick with emotion and perhaps fear.

She shook her head slowly. She was as impotent here as a badly circumcised man. Nevertheless, she spoke to each of the boys privately saying they did not have to do this thing.

'But I want to be the same as all the other boys,' said Samuel.

And even wee Abram was adamant he wouldn't be left out. 'Papa is doing it and my brothers,' he said. 'Please let me too.'

'You do know it will be painful?'

Abram thrust out his chest. 'I'm not scared. We men can bear pain very well.'

She stroked his back. 'I know, my son. And it would also be brave to say you're not going to be circumcised.'

'Mama!' he said, eyes wide with indignation.

She sighed and desisted.

The day of the circumcision came and she hugged all four of her men and bade them farewell from her doorstep as cheerfully as she could, while somehow controlling the shaking.

'Aye well, I hope their pizzles will work after being half chopped aff,' said a loud voice by her side.

'Oh Grissel… they're not half chopped off. It's only some unnecessary skin removed.'

'But yon knife could slip.'

'A flat piece of silver with a slit is used as a shield. The foreskin is pulled up, slid through the slit and cut while the penis is protected beneath the shield,' said Bethia with an authority she didn't feel, despite Mainard having explained the process more than once.

Grissel grunted. 'I'd be gey surprised if they can find their paur wee pizzles, they'll be aw shrunken doon hiding.'

Bethia could see Grissel was fighting tears – which somehow steadied her.

'Come,' she said, sliding her arm through Grissel's. 'Let's go out and buy honey cakes, and then we'll oversee the making of all the boys' favourite foods.'

'Did ye forget, we hae to go to the harem wi' the new perfumes.'

Bethia's shoulders slumped. 'Well reminded, Grissel.'

It was the last place she wanted to be, but when they arrived Nurbanu, knowing of the rite of passage Bethia's men were undertaking – for she extracted every last piece of information she could from Bethia on each visit – had ordered a small celebration of cakes and the cool sherbet drink. There was quiet talk of the merits of the perfumes Bethia had brought, which the women labelled delicate with a hint of orange blossom, a request for some more of the rippling silks come from the East, and the large emerald Selim had recently bestowed on Nurbanu was admired. And Bethia felt as though she was treated with a new respect because she was now part of a special and important group – the mother of circumcised sons.

The boys returned proud despite the discomfort, and she smiled upon them with what she hoped they took as pride, whatever feelings it masked. She giggled with Mainard when he hirpled across the floor and brought him a sleeping draught which she'd had the apothecary make up. She was less sanguine two days later when he told her he must have the bed to himself until he healed for an unexpected tumescence had been agony.

'You're too tempting, my beautiful wife,' he said as she went off to sleep among the boys. It was better she be near them anyway for they needed her those first nights. Jacopo especially seemed to be suffering and bit on his lip to stop the tears, which had Bethia near to howling herself. They would not let her look on the work done to them and even Grissel when she attempted to see *whit was left o' their pizzles* was chased away.

Otherwise she kept to the background while the celebrations went on for several days, arranging all as Mainard directed. At night she stroked the boys' foreheads when they couldn't sleep, murmuring words of love, and said nothing about the path they were going down which was taking them further and further from her.

Chapter Thirty-Nine

Death of Suleiman

Mainard was reading Samuel Usque's *Consolation for the Tribulations of Israel* aloud, hoping his sons would learn more of the language of their forebears, since it was written in Ladino. He translated as he went along with Bethia giving occasional assistance. But their sons were more interested in the tale it told than in absorbing Judeo-Spanish – which they heard in the streets anyway – for Usque described his long journey from Portugal to Ferrara. And it was the frequent asides Usque made commenting on the avaricious rulers of the countries he passed through, who alternated between providing a safe haven for their Jewish subjects, at least the wealthy ones, and persecuting them when a fanatical clergy so directed – and when it was to their advantage – which particularly engaged them. The boys had much to say on the subject and Bethia could see Mainard was delighted they were taking such interest. She herself had grown more and more curious about stories of the Jews now her sons were firmly Jewish. Both Samuel-Thomas and Jacopo had had their bar mitzvah, and Abram's was to be this year – 'and then I will follow the Torah's commandments too,' he'd told her eagerly.

Usque was certainly safer ground than the debate they'd had a few weeks ago on whether the soul perishes

308

at the point of death. Abram, her wee innocent, had mentioned it in his classes and the rabbi was quickly at their door, saying this was a most dangerous path they were treading… how could the immortality of the soul be denied? … even Christians would never do such a thing… and forbidding any further heretical talk.

Bethia watched and added to the discussion when she had a point to make, and her sons listened to her with the same curiosity as when Mainard spoke. But then Johannes interrupted the Usque reading to say Don Joseph had sent a servant to fetch Samuel-Thomas, or Samuel as Bethia must now remember to call him, for he had discarded Thomas like it was a worn old stocking.

'It's easier to be just Samuel,' he'd said when she questioned it.

'But Thomas is the name of my father – your grandfather,' she said sadly.

'You may call me both in the home, if you wish,' he'd replied magnanimously.

Thomas was one of Jesus's disciples… the doubting one, which seems apposite, she wanted to say, but did not.

Jacopo too was now to be Jacob. The rabbi felt it less heathenish and more appropriate. Bethia sniffed when told. 'Let's hope our Jacob will not usurp his brother like the biblical Jacob did.'

'I think we need have no fear of that,' Mainard had responded, sweeping her into his arms and kissing her neck in a most ticklish fashion until she was left quite breathless with laughter.

Don Joseph had only a single daughter, and that after many years of marriage to Reyna, and the child had sadly died. Suddenly, having barely spared her sons a glance, he seemed most taken by them, and especially Samuel.

'It is not to be wondered at,' said Mainard, 'for our eldest is a most engaging young man and wise beyond his years.'

309

It began simply with a message that some curious pieces had come from Persia which he thought Samuel would like to see.

'What curious pieces?' said Bethia, 'and why should Samuel want to see them any more than you, or his brothers, or me for that matter?'

But Samuel looked hopefully at her. 'Please may I go?'

And because he was a good son who cared for his brothers and loved his mama, she allowed it. Soon he was spending time regularly with Don Joseph.

'It will do him no harm to understand more of how Nasi conducts his business,' said Mainard when she expressed her concern.

'He's only fifteen.'

'Near sixteen and more than time to further his education,' said Mainard.

'*We* have been educating him.'

'Yes, yes, my love. But this will expand it.'

She sighed, although she knew Mainard was right.

Then an opportunity came which Don Joseph urged them to take. In the huge complex which was the Topkapi Palace, there was schooling for boys preparing them to work in the vast administration of the empire or to train in the military as a janissary.

'I know about this,' said Bethia when Mainard told her what Don Joseph was suggesting. 'I've seen them when I'm in the palace. They live in huge dormitories. These children are brought from the Christian countries of the empire to serve and have to convert to Islam.' She stood arms akimbo, elbows jutting sharply. 'I even know what it's called – *devshirme* – and I thought Jews were exempt from this tribute.'

'No, no, you have misunderstood. This is for a position in command. Of course, Samuel will have to undertake basic training, but then he'll rise quickly.'

'Well I do not like it.'

But Samuel begged to be allowed to go, and Bethia,

against her better judgement, gave way. Soon he spent most of his time in the palace, sometimes with a sword in his hand and sometimes a pen. He had a beard now, a little on the sparse side, but still he walked out as a man among the Turks, especially as he was near as tall as his father. Occasionally Bethia would catch a glimpse of him on her way to the harem – so young, handsome and full of life that her heart ached.

And two years later, Don Joseph came again to their home, was fed and feted royally, and then told them, in his high fluting voice, how the Grand Turk had seen Samuel and wanted him to travel as part of his entourage on an expedition to Hungary.

'It's a great opportunity,' said Don Joseph.

And Mainard nodded in agreement. 'How did he come to meet our sultan?'

'I took him with me one day.'

'Has he met Prince Selim?'

'Of course.'

Mainard's brow furrowed. Bethia reminded herself to ask later why meeting the sultan's son and heir was any more perilous than being with a man who'd had his eldest son strangled while he watched from behind a curtain. Bethia shook her head, glad yet again to be part of a merchant's family where her eldest would not consider it incumbent upon him to commit fratricide and rid himself of Jacob and Abram when he took up his inheritance.

'Suleiman was much taken with Samuel. He thinks he will make a doughty warrior.'

She watched as Don Joseph, who was dressed with his usual flamboyance, played with the cuff of the sleeve of his robe, pulling it out then tucking it in over and over – and forced herself to turn her eyes away before she was caught staring. Instead, she waited to see what Mainard would do, hoping they could discuss it privately before any decision was made.

'Let me speak with Samuel. I'll not force the lad if he does not want it.'

Don Joseph's eyes widened in surprise that Samuel should be given a choice.

'I would counsel accepting Suleiman's benevolent offer, which few receive... the sultan does not expect refusal when his wishes are made known.'

He left then and Bethia could see by the flush on his face he was not amused. Mainard spoke with Samuel when he was next home and explained what the Grand Turk had offered.

'Yes, I know about it,' he said. 'It's what I've been training for, Papa. Do you know how I would serve him though?'

An astute question, thought Bethia.

'As I understand it, you will be among a group who carry messages.'

Samuel shrugged. 'I will do it.' He straightened his back. ''Tis a good thing and God will smile on me if I serve my sultan. May I be excused now, Papa?'

Mainard nodded and Samuel strode from the room calling for his brothers to hear his news.

Bethia sighed. Mainard took her hands in his, looking down into her face. She could see the individual grey hairs, springy amidst the dulling black of his beard. 'Suleiman is not as Selim,' he said. 'I've heard no rumours he likes boys. Our son will be safe.' He dropped her hands and murmured almost to himself, 'As much as there is ever a place of safety for anyone.'

If Bethia wept quietly in her chamber, she made certain Samuel saw only smiling efficiency, and thought for what she could pack to aid him. She told herself it wasn't much different than the lads coming to the university in her old home of St Andrews who were stuck in often dank and wretched lodgings. But then she learned Samuel *was* travelling into danger for this was a campaign to wrest the fortress of Szeged in Hungary from its count. Quite what Count Nicholas Zrinski had done to offend Suleiman she had no idea. Mainard, when applied to, said it was more likely the fortress was of strategic importance than any specific act by the count.

'And I understand,' said Mainard, 'that Suleiman does not want his legacy to be his failure to take Malta from the Knights of St John last year. He wants a victory. He's been heard to say *only with me do my armies triumph*, for you know he was not there for Malta.'

'Triumph or no, I could wish he'd left our son out of it,' muttered Bethia.

Mainard turned away and she knew privately he wished the same.

They went to the palace gates to watch the great lines of janissaries, colourful as peacocks in their red and yellow short tunics with contrasting leggings, and their tall hats which Samuel had said were called börks and which had a slot for a spoon.

'Is this so they can sup their porridge?' she had said, but Samuel, unamused, had shaken his head impatiently.

'No, it's a sign of brotherhood, the brotherhood of the spoon.'

Bethia had laughed, but when Samuel looked indignant she desisted.

'The janissaries live like monks,' Mainard added, but Bethia remained baffled as to what a spoon had to do with either brotherhood or celibacy.

The men marched past, some with bows over their arms and then those with scimitars and, just when she despaired of seeing Samuel, there he was, proud on his brown horse with the white face which had cost a considerable amount to purchase and equip, an expense which Joseph Nasi failed to mention they would incur when he was urging they accede to the sultan's request – and a rare moment too – for Jews were not generally permitted to ride horses within the city. He was amid a great phalanx of riders tall and straight-backed, all holding the reins with one hand and staring straight ahead. She hoped he saw them out of the corner of his eye and would know his family were there to see him off to war.

There was a gap in the procession and Bethia was easing herself from the crowd when Mainard clutched her arm.

'We cannot leave before the sultan has come,' he whispered urgently. 'Look, I think this must be him now.'

'Where?' said Bethia, looking for a man with a tall turban on a tall horse.

'There,' hissed Mainard.

A single line of men emerged from under the high arch of the gate, long sleeveless tunics over shirts with exquisitely embroidered sleeves and the plume in their börk dyed vivid red, so long it rose high above their head, the end curling so it narrowly avoided skimming the ground. Behind them came a black carriage, and the crowd were encouraged to cheer wildly by the soldiers lining the street. Bethia could indeed see the monstrous turban through the carriage window.

'Can we go now?' she said as the supply carts appeared. She was in truth too stunned to say more. All she could think was *who goes to war in a carriage?*

It was May 1566 when Samuel left and late autumn of the same year when he returned. Bethia felt the pain of missing him every day. He came back as part of the huge escort for the coffin containing Suleiman the Lawgiver, who had died suddenly on the return journey. Work had already begun on his mausoleum, which was to be sited next to that of his beloved wife Roxelana, who'd died eight years previously, and was to be even more magnificent.

Some days later, and Samuel was restored to them, white-faced with tiredness.

'How are you, my son?' asked Mainard, while Bethia

and Grissel fussed around Samuel, removing his stained coat and exclaiming at how thin he was.

'Can we speak in private, Papa?' he said, but Bethia followed them into the workroom determined not to be excluded.

Samuel looked at his mother, hesitated and shrugged. 'Suleiman did not die in Belgrade a few weeks ago, as they're saying. He collapsed and died two months ago in Hungary.'

'During the attack?'

Samuel shook his head wearily. 'The sultan was already ailing. He wasn't even there when the fortress was taken.'

'So his lasting legacy is a victory which was achieved without him,' said Bethia.

'Hush,' said Mainard.

She pressed her fingers to her lips to prevent anything further slipping out.

Mainard turned back to Samuel, placing his arm around his son's shoulders. 'How do you know this?'

'Because I was there when he died.'

Bethia gasped and wrapped her arms around them both. They stood silently for a moment, then Samuel freed himself from his parents' embrace.

'The sultan had told his servants to go, sent everyone else away except his doctor. I was sitting in the corner of the tent polishing his shield. I think he'd forgotten I was there. He dropped like a stone.' Samuel slumped, parodying the sultan's fall. 'The doctor rushed to his side, knelt by him and rested his head on Suleiman's chest. I stood up, could not think what to do. The doctor told me to bring the shield, bade me kneel too and hold it close to the sultan's mouth. I held it for so long my arms were shaking.' He covered his mouth with his hand and mumbled, 'I was so afraid I would drop it on our sultan's face.' He dropped his hand, took a deep breath and went on. 'Eventually I was permitted to lower the shield. The

315

surface was still shining with no misting of breath upon it. Nothing.' Samuel shivered. 'He was dead. The doctor chased me away, told me I must tell no one, and I never saw our sultan again.'

'But how…'

Mainard shook his head at Bethia. 'Have you told anyone of this, my son?'

'No,' said Samuel.

'And, as the doctor directed, you must never do so. We will forget it was ever mentioned. Do *not* speak of it to anyone.'

'You do not need to tell me; the doctor disappeared soon after. They said he'd died unexpectedly.'

Bethia pressed her handkerchief to her mouth. After a moment she stepped forward to wrap her arms around Samuel once more and give him some comfort, but he took a step back. 'I'm not a child, Mama.'

She nodded, lowering her head so he wouldn't see the tears in her eyes. Instead, she sent him off to bathe and change, for he stank, sweaty as any grown man in his stale clothes. Mainard gently shook his head when she turned to him. It was only once they were in bed that night they had a whispered discussion.

'It was to make certain Selim became sultan, wasn't it?' said Bethia.

'Yes. Selim was far away, and the pretence Suleiman was still alive needed to be kept up until Selim could be brought there. It was as well Suleiman was travelling in a carriage – if he'd been on horseback the vizier would've struggled to keep the charade going.'

'He must have putrefied. I'm surprised the stink didn't give the corpse away.'

'The vizier likely had the doctor remove the heart and other organs before he had the doctor killed.'

'So you think the vizier had the doctor murdered.'

'I think it highly likely.'

Bethia thought of Jacob, who'd already declared his

aspiration to become a physician. 'Let's make certain Jacob is never the attending physician to the sultan.'

Mainard blew air out through his lips. 'That would indeed be a dangerous position for our lad, but I think we are safe, for his abiding interest seems to be in treating beggars off the street.'

Bethia thought of the small pack of bandages and herbs Jacob had assembled, creeping out to practise on whoever would let him until he was found out by Grissel and brought home in disgrace. 'God's bones, you could hae caught something very nasty and brought it into our house wi' you,' Grissel had shouted, sending him off to change his clothes while a watching Bethia tried to contain a smile.

'I've been thinking on that. Padua is the place to send our Jacob, for he will learn both anatomy through the dissection they practise in the winter and physick from their herb gardens. Nowhere better than Padua to study medicine.'

'How can it be safe for him to go there?' And especially since he's circumcised, she thought, but didn't say.

'The University of Padua is outwith the Pope's domains. I understand a number of Jews study there, and Jacob will have an advantage over many of them, for he has a clever mother,' he nudged her, 'who made sure he learned Latin.'

Bethia could feel the tears leaking from the side of her eyes and sliding down into her hairline.

Mainard lay on his back, hands behind his head, and spoke to the ceiling. 'I know you will not be eager to let another son go. 'Tis most unfortunate Samuel had to deal with the death of the sultan on his first foray. But Bethia, we cannot hold them. They must all go away from us. The joy is they will always return.'

'But they will be changed.'

Mainard laughed, a low throaty laugh – his voice

oddly raspy like an old man's. 'The whole purpose of them going away is to bring about change.'

'I know, I know. But I feel like I'm losing them.'

He held her then, murmuring in her ear, 'My love, but we cannot keep them children forever.'

'Yes,' she said slowly, her voice growing stronger. 'Our task is to make strong and resourceful men of them, like their father.'

He laughed. 'They need look no further than their mother for strength and purpose.'

She turned to him then, and, for a while, they thought only of each other.

Chapter Forty

Dona Gracia

The guns went off with a suddenness that made both Bethia and Mainard jump. 'Another poor miscreant thrown into the Bosphorus. It's a daily occurrence,' said Mainard.

Bethia shuddered. 'Selim is making his presence felt.'

It had been a summer of the plague, which had carried off many of the poor and a surprising number of the wealthy. A communal day of prayers was organised; animals were butchered and distributed to the needy and prisoners were released. As summer waned the plague retreated, but, just when it finally seemed over, the harvests failed and there was a shortage of bread. People began to mutter that the new sultan was a harbinger of ill omen, and Selim responded with a wave of executions.

Grissel appeared to say there was a message come. Bethia sighed for Mainard was again summoned to the palace by Don Joseph who rarely left Selim's side. The new sultan had made his loyal companion the Duke of Naxos as almost his first act upon succession. Now Duke Joseph controlled the mining of minerals on East Naxos, especially emery, a most useful substance for smoothing nails, and which Bethia regularly took to the harem. Pumice from Santorini was also under his aegis, and again popular. It seemed Selim couldn't do enough for his friend Joseph Nasi.

What this time? she thought wearily as Mainard left. She'd work to do but found it difficult to concentrate as she awaited Mainard's return. There were accounts to prepare for a meeting with Dona Gracia's factor – the lady herself was looking increasingly frail these days. Even her voice, always so strong and decisive, was wavering and weak. Bethia put her hand to her heart; the world would feel a more dangerous place without Dona Gracia, for all that she'd sometimes chafed under the great lady's control.

She wandered around the salon. Samuel, whose presence had no longer been required at the palace after Suleiman's death, and Abram were out overseeing the printing of a new book by Samuel Usque sent from Ferrara. It didn't need both boys, men really, but neither was much interested in the cloth trade and Mainard had yet to determine who would eventually take over which aspect of his business. Her suspicion was that Abram would get his way out of sheer doggedness; Samuel carrying the burden of responsibility as the eldest was ever too eager to please.

She heard the front door open and hurried into the hallway.

'Don Joseph had a proposal,' said Mainard, leading her back to the workroom, for Ysabeau had appeared, the latest baby strapped to her back, to wash the floors.

Bethia waited, arms folded across her stomach. 'Where is he sending you now?'

'What? Nowhere. He has a wife for Samuel.'

Bethia dropped onto a chair with a suddenness that had it rocking. 'But Samuel is too young.'

Mainard grinned. 'I married you when I was not much older. And this is a most advantageous match, an opportunity unlikely to come again.'

'A marriage should be more than an opportunity.'

Mainard rolled his eyes. 'An opportunity is not a bad

320

place to start.'

'Who's the family?'

'They're Conversos recently come to Constantinople from Antwerp. I've heard of them but never met them. She's the eldest daughter and the parents are wealthy.'

'So her family are New Christians?'

Mainard wouldn't meet her eyes.

'But they're converting,' she said slowly.

'Samuel is a Jew and could marry none other than a Jewess.'

Bethia leant forward. 'Do you not see, my husband, how alone I am.'

He came to her then and pulled her into her arms, whispering, 'It matters not what their faith is. Our sons will always love and care for their mother.'

And his words were some small comfort.

In any case, all was thrown in the air the next day when the tidings came: Dona Gracia had died. Bethia surprised herself by how much she wept, and Mainard too looked shaken. 'The end of an era,' he kept muttering.

She dried her eyes, dressed and they went out immediately to Dona Gracia's home.

Bethia walked up the hill, the sun already hot, a few steps behind Mainard in his long robes, a blue short-sleeved coat overlaying a yellow caftan, and the yellow turban which had long since displaced the bonnet with a feather, and all of which denoted his status as a wealthy Jewish merchant. She wiped the sweat from her brow, wishing she was not required to wear black robes, so bakingly hot under the sun, and not certain she should be going in any case. 'Will they want me there?' she called.

Mainard turned to speak to her. 'You worked with her for many years. It would be disrespectful if you did not come.' He walked on, then stopped again. 'Go among the women as soon as we enter.'

She could sense Mainard was by no means confident she, an Old Christian, would be welcomed among former

321

New Christians who'd reverted. But when they reached the house there was already a great throng there, Moslems among them, who had come to mourn the death of this remarkable woman.

She went to whisper her condolences to Dona Gracia's daughter but it was difficult to get near, so surrounded was Reyna by weeping women. It was fourteen years since Bethia had arrived in Constantinople and, were it not for Dona Gracia, she wouldn't have her business as *kira* to the harem. A very good business it turned out to be too, and she felt the tears begin to fall at the prospect of a world without this great lady. And seeing she too wept, the women welcomed her as though she was one of them. Again she thought how much easier and less lonely her life would be if she adopted their faith, of how she would belong instead of always being set apart. Instinctively her hand sought the reassuring touch of the crucifix which she carried in her pocket and her gratitude to Dona Gracia swelled, for she'd been accepting of Bethia's differentness.

She attended one of several services in memory of Dona Gracia Mendes, careful to enter the women's area, watching intently and following whatever those around her did, while listening, as best she could, to the Hebrew.

'Did I understand correctly, that Dona Gracia was of the House of David?' she asked Mainard when they reached the privacy of their home.

'It's said she was the last remnant of the House of David, which is why she was our *ha-gevira*, which means our highest-ranking lady, our queen. And yet…'

He paused, but Bethia, guessing what he was about to say, spoke. 'She was like a man in how she faced down the world.'

Mainard inclined his head in agreement. 'I don't know if you followed but the rabbi said Dona Gracia straightened the path in the wilderness, the path to an awesome God.' He swallowed. 'The rabbi also said, *this lady behaved like the strongest of men and was unlike women who are selfish in their pursuits. Dona Gracia's door was always open to the guest. All heeded her discipline and trembling seized them before her. She was the morning star, the guiding light of her people. Her righteousness will stand forever.'*

'Huh!' said Bethia. 'I would hardly describe women as selfish in their pursuits. We place everyone else's needs before our own.'

'What the rabbi meant is a woman's vision is narrow. Dona Gracia was unusual in seeing beyond the confines of home and family.'

'She certainly was ambitious, and bold. But Mainard, what did it all come to in the end? Tiberias failed and she leaves only Joseph Nasi as her successor, and when Reyna dies her line ends.'

'Don't forget the many Conversos she saved. She ran escape routes for years. They're all her children.'

That evening when the family came together Mainard introduced the subject of what kind of legacy we should leave and there was a spirited discussion. Samuel and Abram were all for doing great deeds, as yet unspecified, while Mainard's main concern was to leave the family secure both in their faith and finances.

It was to be a busy year. First Samuel's wedding, which Jacob returned from Padua in time to attend, and nine months to the day Bethia held her first grandchild in her arms. She'd not expected the rush of love, as fierce as for her own children. Her daughter-in-law was a quiet wee thing who seemed overwhelmed to find herself first a wife and then a mother. Bethia, remembering the lonely days when she was a new wife in Antwerp, tried to draw the girl out but it wasn't easy. Unlike Bethia, Mirella had her family living nearby and spent time at her old home with her sisters. Bethia expected this to change after the baby was born, but before the birth the girl returned home, her mother saying it was better to have her travail aided by her own mother and surrounded by her family.

'But we are her family,' Bethia heard herself saying.

'Yes, yes,' said the mother, a plump woman whose jowly cheeks wobbled whenever she moved or spoke, both of which were constantly. 'But my dearest Mirella needs to be among her birth family when her time comes.'

Bethia opened her mouth to say again *we are her family now*, but before she could get the words out a plump hand was laid on her arm. 'As a mother yourself, you wouldn't deny my *chica* the comfort of her own mother during her time of trouble.'

Bethia stared into the narrowed eyes and knew she'd been bested. She'd tried to make friends with this woman, even using her influence to have the *tevila*, the ritual cleansing before the wedding, in the beautiful pink and grey stone hamam close by the palace and built in memory of the *Hurrem Sultan*. But the bride and her female relatives, while seemingly enjoying special access to this sumptuous bath house, had clustered together leaving Bethia apart.

Samuel, equally gratified and terrified by the prospect of fatherhood and this evidence of his own manhood so soon displayed, would not gainsay his bride when Bethia suggested the child should be born in their home.

'Is this the way of things in Constantinople?' Bethia inquired of Mainard, but he eschewed all knowledge of birthing practices.

After Dona Gracia's death, Bethia had experienced a sense of freedom from being beneath those ever watchful and all-knowing eyes but increasingly she missed her extensive knowledge and sage counsel. Dona Gracia would've advised how to handle this daughter-in-law who spoke only Ladino, seemed to have no interest in anything but giggling with her sisters and evinced no desire to connect with her new mother, casting her eyes upon the ground and reluctantly whispering a response whenever Bethia tried to engage her in conversation. Actually, she realised, it was a relief to have Mirella out of the house.

There was a restlessness now about Bethia, like an itch she couldn't find the source to scratch. She was a forty-year-old grandmother. Surely she should be feeling calmer, serene even. She could settle to nothing and yet was busy as she always preferred to be. Her business at the Sultanate of Women was prospering and she kept the ledgers for Mainard's trading business, although she'd passed over the accounting on the printing business to Abram, who was more than competent and, she observed, seemed to find making the calculations and entering the figures in his careful copperplate as absorbing as she once did. She wandered into the workroom to find him there, could hear him breathing loud as he concentrated. She went closer but it wasn't bad today. Some days he fought for air, and Jacob had instigated regular steamings, which gave Abram a little relief. Yet always there was this rasp as though his body resisted taking in air. She went to her son then and touched him lightly on the shoulder. Wee Abram, grown as tall as his brothers but trying to keep up with them still.

He turned his head and gazed up at her. 'Don Joseph has the monopoly on French wine and gathers all the import duties. 'Tis a pity we cannot use a cheaper source.'

She let her hand drop and drifted away to the window. 'He's still trying to recoup funds from the French. Their king borrowed heavily from Dona Gracia and it was never repaid.'

Abram went still and she knew he was absorbing the information. 'I wonder if there's some way we might assist,' he said, drawing the words out as he spoke.

'You sound like my father, always looking for an advantage.'

'We'd be fools not to,' he mumbled, and bent his head once more to the leather-bound ledger.

There was a rattling on the front door. Bethia waited but Grissel was out, Ysabeau wouldn't hear it and the two new girls seemed afraid of their own shadows. She opened it to find Mirella on the doorstep, baby in arms.

'Can I come back?' Mirella said, eyes downcast.

'Have you come alone, without any servants?'

The girl nodded. 'It was the only way I could escape.'

Bethia threw the door wide. 'Let me take the baby. You look ready for a lie down.'

Mirella handed him over without any sign of reluctance, slid past Bethia and up the stairs to her chamber.

Bethia gazed at her grandson's sleeping face with the tiny curve of a smile upon it. 'And what's going on here, wee man? Will you tell your Nonna all the secrets?'

Mirella's mother appeared early the next morning and said icily she'd come to see her daughter. 'If that was permitted.'

'Just as though I was somehow responsible for Mirella's escape,' Bethia said later to Mainard.

'Do come into the salon and I will call her,' said Bethia, waving to Ysabeau to fetch refreshments.

'Don't trouble yourself,' said Mistress Rojas. 'I can fetch her myself.' She went to push past Bethia, who stood firm.

'It's no trouble at all.' Bethia held her arm out directing Mistress Rojas into the open door of the salon.

Grissel appeared at the kitchen door, curious as ever.

'Please tell the young mistress her mother is here.'

Mistress Rojas blew air out through her lips and reluctantly went into the salon.

Grissel was back almost immediately. 'She doesna want to see her ma,' she said bluntly in Scots.

Bethia turned to Mistress Rojas and said in Ladino. 'She's sleeping and Grissel didn't want to awaken her as

326

she had a most disturbed night.'

Mistress Rojas rose from her seat on the low couch and opened her mouth to speak.

Bethia took her arm gently. 'We all know how tiring the first child is and would want Mirella to have as much rest as possible. I'll send a message as soon as she's ready to receive visitors.'

'I'm not a visitor, I am her mother,' said Mistress Rojas, but there was a note of pleading in her voice. After a moment she pulled her shawl around her and bustled towards the door, refusing the proffered sherbet. 'I've much to do and will return later, if I have time.'

Bethia tapped on the chamber door. She hesitated then whispered, 'Your mother's gone.'

After a moment the door opened slowly and Bethia walked into the darkened chamber. Mirella closed the door and Bethia sat down on the kist at the bottom of the bed. 'What's wrong, Mirella?'

Mirella stood, head hanging.

'Shall I bring Eliyah to you? Ysabeau is likely finished feeding him.' There was some benefit to Ysabeau's fecundity, Bethia reflected. She had enough milk to feed her newest bairn and act as a wet nurse to Eliyah.

Mirella shrugged, a small movement of the shoulders. She was so young.

'Let's go into the garden. It's not too hot yet and the sky is a beautiful blue.' She placed her arm around the girl's shoulders to guide her from the room and felt her stiffen. Bethia dropped her arm, saying, 'Go ahead of me.'

Mirella went, slowly.

She brought the baby to Mirella, who took him reluctantly, but after a few moments held him close gazing down on his wee face. Bethia felt relief wash over her. Over the next few days she tried to speak with Mirella but got nowhere. Mistress Rojas returned and Mirella asked Bethia to stay with her. It was the first request her daughter-in-law had ever made. *Was I ever this difficult?* Bethia wondered, and determined to ask her own mother-in-law, should she see her again – unlikely for Catarina was still producing children. The fourteenth, or was it fifteenth, had recently been born, and Catarina would no doubt be reluctant to relinquish Mama's help, even for a short visit to Constantinople. Bethia sighed. She would have liked at least one more child but Mainard had said the ones they had were sufficient and he would not risk her life in making more. He had promised they'd one day go to Thessaloniki but the timing was never right. She suspected he wanted to avoid a direct confrontation with his sister over retrieving Papa's remains from Venice; the demanding letters had never ceased.

Mirella settled down. Master Rojas attended the circumcision of his grandson but, according to Mainard, said nothing of what had transpired between his wife and daughter. Mistress Rojas, preoccupied with marrying her other four daughters off, visited less and less frequently, which was a relief to all involved. And soon it was evident Mirella was again with child.

Still Bethia was curious what had gone on, and one day, when she was sitting on the floor talking nonsense to her grandson while he kicked his wee legs and waved his wee arms and gurgled back at her, Mirella, who was sitting in a nearby chair watching, started to speak.

'My mother wanted me to return home with Eliyah, you know.'

The girl was half whispering and Bethia went still, keeping her eyes on the baby.

'She said I was being led away from God in this house.'

Bethia blinked but kept her eyes on her grandson.

'She thought if she made me stay with her then Samuel would come to us, and he could be shown the true path in our home and protected from the corrupting influences here.'

328

Bethia bit down on her lip to prevent the words of indignation escaping.

'My mother thinks the family time we have every day is Godless time. She says there is the Bible and the Talmud and the Tefillot and we should discuss only those. She says it's not right we should have opinions and have debate.' Mirella's voice had grown louder and she finished with a near shout of defiance. 'But I like it.'

There was silence in the room; even the baby had stopped his chatter. Bethia was aware Mirella was looking at her, awaiting a response. She kept her head down, uncertain what to say and unwilling to get drawn into directly criticising the girl's mother.

'Did your mother speak to your father on this matter?' She glanced up and Mirella nodded.

'Papa said he wouldn't interfere in another man's home and he forbade Mama to speak to the rabbi. When Mama kept insisting she must, he became very angry.'

'I'm sorry to hear that.'

Mirella tossed her head. 'Oh Papa is often angry with Mama. She can be very provoking.'

Bethia hid a smile.

'Anyway, I've decided I like our way. And *here* is my home.' Mirella rose and picked up Eliyah from the floor. Pausing in the doorway, she turned. 'I wanted you to know, but would request we not speak of it again.'

Bethia stared at her daughter-in-law's retreating back and a smile crept across her face – not so timid after all.

Chapter Forty-One

The Grand Jew

Joseph Nasi had showed little interest in Samuel after he'd returned from Hungary, for which Bethia was profoundly grateful. Instead, when Jacob returned from Padua in the summer of 1570, he sought to further Jacob's career. Invited to a performance of *Esther, the Jewish Queen of Persia*, which Don Joseph was staging in the vast gardens which surrounded his palazzo, Mainard was summoned to his presence.

'He certainly lives up to his new sobriquet of the Grand Jew,' Mainard whispered to Bethia when he rejoined her. 'He was lolling on cushions while the many around him stood, poised to do his smallest bidding.'

''Tis a pity Don Joseph didn't have a son of his own,' said Bethia sharply when they reached the privacy of home and Mainard could speak of his meeting. 'I do *not* care for the way he adopts mine.'

'It's a matter of great sorrow to Don Joseph he's without issue.'

Bethia narrowed her eyes. 'He's predisposed towards men I think, which will not aid him in producing an heir.'

Mainard sucked the air in through his teeth. 'Yes, you may be right, my love. Another one like Ortelius.' He brightened. 'I hear most favourable things about Ortelius's great work, which he has named *Theatrum orbis terrarum.* We do already have such a book of world maps here in Constantinople, made for the sultan, but Ortelius's will be the first to be widely available. I'm eager to see it.'

'In any case,' she said, reverting to what was foremost in her mind, I cannot like it that Don Joseph is now determined to take Jacob under his wing, and especially after what happened to Samuel. Who knows what he might expose our boy to.'

Mainard grinned at her. 'Jacob is a man who likes women… and possibly a little too much.'

Bethia tapped her lower lip. Jacob had a confidence about him unusual in a young man and not helped by the reaction of women towards him. Even Mirella, for all she was devoted to Samuel, could not help but simper when he took her hand, bowed over it and inquired how his good sister did.

She looked up into Mainard's eyes. 'You have told Jacob to take care. And as a physician he must know of the dangers of…' Her voice trailed away.

He took her hands, gazing down into her face. 'Dipping his wick in too many pots. Don't worry, he'll be fully aware of the risks.'

'Mainard!' said Bethia, yet she couldn't help but laugh. She leant her head against his chest. Such moments of connection were all too rare these days. She could hear the newest baby crying and wondered where Mirella was, not to mention all the servants of the house.

'As for Joseph Nasi, he's incorrigible. He goes nowhere now without two janissaries preceding him and a trail of at least twenty servants following, who are all as well dressed as I am. He's even permitted to enter the sultan's presence without his arms being secured.'

'That is indeed showing favour,' said Bethia. She remembered when she and Dona Gracia petitioned Suleiman how tightly their arms were held.

'Samuel says the merchants of Lviv in Ukraine are

331

angry, for Don Joseph has acquired trade privileges for his agents there which is excluding them. And I heard he loaned the king of Poland over one hundred and fifty thousand ducats to acquire the monopoly on their supply of beeswax.'

'He never seems to run out of funds. I've seen the quantities of food he brings to Selim on a Friday, when I've been in the palace.'

'After Moslem prayers but before the Jewish Sabbath,' said Mainard. 'It's said Selim awaits these delicacies eagerly, and even dispenses with his food taster so much does he trust our Grand Jew. They were all ready to go laid out on porcelain brought from China when I was there last Friday and he invited me to sample a few.' Mainard ran his tongue over his lips. 'The goose livers chopped with raisins, and the broad beans cooked in olive oil were beyond exquisite. Oh, and there were aubergines stuffed with onion, garlic and tomato too.' He grinned. 'I plan to visit him every Friday in future.'

'Stop, stop,' said Bethia. 'You're making me hungry.' She frowned. 'But I don't understand. Surely, from his vast kitchens, Selim could provide such a feast himself with ease?'

'I should imagine so. However, Don Joseph controls the trade in spices from the East. The raisins come from his dukedom and he has a finger in the olive oil trade too. This way Selim doesn't have to delve into his pocket to pay for the ingredients and, I suspect, Don Joseph is also eager to keep him well supplied with claret.'

'But why does he want our Jacob?' said Bethia.

'Ah,' said Mainard, 'let me explain. He's given me to understand there are at least twenty Jewish physicians working in the palace and Jacob could become one of them. He says Selim prefers them because he believes they're less likely to slip him poison or cause his death by some other sleight of hand than a physician from amongst his own people.'

Bethia swallowed. 'Will Jacob be safe?'

Mainard gazed at her. 'Don Joseph has assured me Jacob will never be in attendance with Selim alone and, in any case, is likely to be providing services only to lesser members of the court.'

'We cannot refuse, can we?'

'We cannot refuse,' he repeated, and in seeing he was no happier than she, it steadied Bethia. Life was not about choices, unless you were a sultan or a king – and there would no doubt be benefits for them all in Jacob having such a position.

And so Jacob went to the Topkapi Palace, returning home every week for Friday night dinner and Saturday synagogue. He had learned much of physicking while he was in Padua and began to ask Bethia to source the more exotic ingredients for his potions. Nurbanu knew, of course, that Bethia's son was a physician in the palace and soon he was being called upon to deal with ailments within the harem.

'It's most interesting,' he said over dinner one Friday, 'for I must treat them from behind a screen.'

'How can you make a diagnosis?' asked Mainard.

'It *is* easier if you can make an examination,' said Jacob, and his brothers looked at one another and hooted.

Jacob ignored them. 'But you can tell much from intonation and the sound of the voice. And of course they describe their symptoms to me.'

'Nurbanu said you are sought after.'

Samuel and Abram hooted louder.

'She says you have a voice the timbre of which is most soothing and of itself makes the listener feel better.'

Samuel and Abram began speaking to one another in high-pitched voices. Jacob reached out and cuffed the brother next to him while two-year-old Eliyah watched wide-eyed with glee.

In early spring of 1571 the sultan ordered the assembling

of a great fleet. Bethia, curious as any of her neighbours, went with Mainard to gaze upon the galleys and their smaller accompanying vessels, which Mainard said were called galliots, emerging from the nearby arsenal and all gathered in the Golden Horn and beyond. She shaded her eyes against the sun sparkling on the dancing waves and tried to count. There were ships as far as the eye could see out beyond the peninsula, all pressed together in lines, which would require remarkable skill on the part of the mariners to manoeuvre each into place without banging against their neighbour. She gave up when she reached seventy.

'Over two hundred in total,' said Mainard.

'So many galley slaves,' said Bethia, remembering Will's torment.

'They cannot manage in battle without them, Mama,' said Abram, who was standing on her other side.

'And this is all because of the siege in Venetian-held Cyprus?'

'Without a large fleet we're vulnerable to attack from Venice, and Philip of Spain is as ever prowling to expand his territories. A great and unusual alliance between the Doge, the Pope and Spain is being set up against us,' said Mainard.

The capricious breeze, which had been blowing off the land causing the veil from Bethia's headdress to billow around her, changed direction. Her veil was flipped back, streaming out behind, and they were suddenly assailed by the most terrible stench. Bethia held her handkerchief to her face while Mainard hurried them away.

'I've never smelled anything worse,' she said when they reached home, burying her face in a bowl of rose petals. 'Those poor wretches.'

The putrefying stench lingered, catching at the back of the throat, causing people to retch whenever they left their houses, even a full day after the fleet had left.

Jacob was among them wearing his taj, a tall, tapering, conical hat rich red in colour denoting his status as a Jewish physician, and, as Mainard said, all fired up and thinking he'd perform great deeds like some sort of Odysseus. He was eager to serve Ali Pasha, a Turk from a poor family who'd risen through the ranks to become one of the sultan's favoured men – unusual, since the sultan's elite were normally drawn from the ranks of converted Christians captured as children and trained up in the palace.

Of course, Jacob had gone at Don Joseph's instigation. Indeed, the siege against, first Nicosia and now Famagusta, was driven by Joseph Nasi, or so Mainard said, adding, 'Selim doesn't have the stomach for war. You'll notice, unlike Suleiman, he directs all from the safety of his palace.'

Then why does he engage in warfare?'

'Like all kings he must show eagerness for battle. It's necessary both to maintain his position and to keep the janissaries, who are forever hungry for plunder, happy. And although Cyprus will be rich pickings, this is as much to appease Don Joseph. It's near twenty years since he fled Italy and still he's as angry as though it was yesterday. It might've helped if the Venetians had lifted the death penalty against him sooner.'

'His own fault,' muttered Bethia. 'What did he expect after eloping with a thirteen-year-old heiress?'

Bethia felt as though she'd barely slept since Jacob left, and Mainard too lay wakeful by her side, gazing at the ceiling night after night. Word that came was initially positive. The siege of Famagusta had been broken and Cyprus was now under Turkish control. Don Joseph was jubilant when he learned that the Venetians' garrison had surrendered. Bethia hoped Jacob might then return, but it seemed Cyprus needed the Turkish fleet on patrol, especially since rumours were flying that the alliance between the Doge, the Pope and Philip of Spain had remarkably born fruit and resulted in a mighty fleet setting sail into the eastern Mediterranean to take back Cyprus for Venice.

Summer waned and autumn crept in but still Jacob did not return. Surely the season for war is passed, Bethia wondered. But it seemed it was running late this year.

News of the battle, when it came, was disjointed and sporadic. First the rumours were that the Turks had beaten off the alliance; not a victory but not a defeat either. Then word crept around the streets how more than half the Turkish fleet and many, many men, including the great Ali Pasha, had been lost. It was said he'd miscalculated the size and strength of the Christian fleet and engaged in battle precipitously.

'But what of our son?' said Bethia wringing her hands as she paced up and down. 'Why have we had no word?'

But Mainard, head resting in his hands, couldn't tell her. He went each day to glean what information he could from Don Joseph but it soon became apparent the failures at the Battle of Lepanto were being squarely laid at Nasi's door. 'Selim is furious with his favourite and Don Joseph is sticking close as a teasel burr to him, which I'm not sure is entirely wise,' said Mainard.

'Probably fearful one of the many other followers will insinuate themselves into his place should he vacate it, even for an hour,' said Bethia wearily. She didn't care about Don Joseph, as their living was not entirely dependent on him, and, as *kira* to the Sultanate of Women, she had her own connections separate from the Mendes's empire, although as Mainard reminded her, Don Joseph was not a man to gainsay. Yet it did seem he was at risk of eclipse by other favourites, the girlish prettiness of his face now overlaid with a patina of fine lines like a piece of delicate but aged pottery come from China. And there were rumours that not only the sultan held Don Joseph accountable for the disaster of Lepanto, but the Doge of Venice considered him entirely responsible for the troubles in Cyprus. And then word leaked out how he'd promised Turkish support to the Low Countries should they attempt to expel Spain. Mainard had shaken his head when he recounted it to Bethia, saying he couldn't believe the arrogant foolishness of the man to commit such an offer to paper, and the letter subsequently read aloud in the Calvinist Consistory so all would know of it.

'He's reviled from Madrid to Venice and all points between,' said Mainard, after speaking to a ship's captain come from Ancona with a cargo of English cloth, French claret and German copper – for there might be battles fought between the Turks and the Christians but trade must go on, either overtly or covertly.'

'Are they likely to come here and attack us next?

'We're not actually at war with the Christians, only an endless series of skirmishes,' Mainard responded. 'And our alliance with the French is of long standing and has yet to fail, although Don Joseph placed it under strain when he had first Suleiman and then Selim trying to force repayment of the debt owed him.'

'So the Grand Jew is not so grand any more.'

'I fear not, and it worries me, for all Jewry will be tarnished should he fall from favour.'

Chapter Forty-Two

A Moslem

Jacob was gone for near on eight months, and the sombre man who was restored to them was very different from the lad who'd set off adventuring. He was slender still and not so tall as his brothers, but there was a ruggedness about him, a sense of having seen and survived terrible events that even Samuel, travelling with the corpse of Suleiman, had not endured. It was remarkable he'd emerged unscathed from a battle where tens of thousands had died and many more taken prisoner. Bethia couldn't think of how he too might have ended up as a galley slave without shuddering.

'Why was this battle in Lepanto so far from Cyprus?' she asked.

'We'd left there when Famagusta was taken and gone to Corfu,' said Jacob.

'More pillage?' said Mainard.

Jacob gazed at the floor and nodded. 'We would've done better to return to Constantinople from there, but Ali Pasha learned of the huge fleet assembled by the Christian alliance.' Jacob stuck his chest out. 'The eastern Mediterranean is ours; we couldn't be seen to run away.'

As she listened, Bethia felt glad she wasn't a man.

It was the next day before she noticed. He flinched

when his brother went to tap the left side of his face as part of some jest between them, which Bethia could see Jacob was struggling to engage in. She went to him then and lifted his hair. Part of his ear was missing, sliced off cleanly and neatly. She insisted he stand still while she examine it. The cut was angled in such a way that it had not only sliced off most of the ear but shaved the skin behind it.

'A flesh wound only,' said Jacob, twisting away from her.

'The skin is red...' said Bethia. She was about to add, and puckered, but stopped herself.

'I know it's ugly,' Jacob said.

'Yes, very,' said Samuel, although his voice was sad.

Jacob gave a weary smile in return.

'I've not noticed any diminution in your hearing,' said Mainard.

'I've been fortunate in that respect.'

Mainard glanced at Bethia, who gave a slight nod of agreement. He placed his arm around his son's shoulders and led him away. Bethia was waiting when they finally reappeared some time later.

'What did he tell you?'

'About the battle, not much more than we already knew, except the sea, through which he had to swim when he escaped the stricken ship, was red with blood and thick with bodies and parts thereof. And he saw Ali Pasha killed. He seems to have had a great affection for his commander, who I've learned was a brave, generous and virtuous man.' He tugged on his own ear. 'Do you want me to tell you what happened?'

Bethia hesitated but she was curious.

He saw the Spanish behead Ali Pasha and then stick the head on a pole. Jacob said it felt as though Ali Pasha was watching him as he swam away.'

Bethia shook her head slowly at the barbarism of men.

'But the Turks did some terrible things too. Jacob says the Venetians surrendered at Famagusta, after a promise they could go free as long as they left Cyprus.' He paused and Bethia could see him swallowing now. 'Although we took the city, we'd lost as many as fifty thousand men in the siege and it was claimed a group of Hajj pilgrims had been slaughtered by the Venetians. Mustafa Pasha was so angry he dishonoured the agreement, imprisoned the Venetians and had their commander flayed alive. They displayed the flayed corpse on Mustafa Pasha's galley along with the heads of the other Venetian commanders.'

'What I don't understand,' said Bethia, trying to banish the image from her mind, 'is why the Turks lost, and lost so badly by all accounts. It was a huge force which left here. Was the Christian fleet very much bigger?'

'It certainly had some large ships, including the Venetian galleasses,' said Mainard slowly. 'Perhaps Jacob can tell us.'

But when applied to, Jacob shook his head. 'I saw only what was happening from the galley I was on. The Christians did seem to have greater firepower but...' he swung his arm, '...we had thousands of fighting men. If we'd been able to get close to their ships then our janissaries would've easily overcome them. He paused. 'Our ship did ram the prow of the *Real*, which was their flagship, and with such force we sliced into them as far as the third rowing bench. We could've bested them but another Spanish galley came and so we were overpowered.'

He hung his head, and Mainard went to place his arm around his son's shoulders but Jacob stepped away.

'Thanks be to the Blessed Virgin, you escaped.'

Jacob looked at her oddly.

'And whatever holy gods of the Jews there are too,' she amended, knowing even as she spoke what she was saying was foolish. 'I know, I know there's only one God,' she said quickly.

Jacob sat down on a stool, his back resting against the wall, and gazed at both his parents. 'I didn't so much as escape but was sliced by a sword and flung into the water. When I came to I was able to swim to another galley, which is why I'm still with you. Everyone else on board our flagship perished.' He touched his damaged ear lightly. 'Ali Pasha was a very great man and a holy one too. They called him *Müezzinzade*, both for his strong faith and because he was the son of a muezzin. His family were poor you know.'

'He did have a wondrous voice; I heard him from the harem. When he made the call of the muezzin we all went silent to listen. To hear it was like having the sun emerge after days of rain and the women loved it,' said Bethia.

Jacob nodded slowly. 'I am glad you feel thus for I have something to tell you.'

She waited, all her senses alert, for she knew something momentous was coming.

'I am converting to Islam. For it is the true faith.'

Bethia dropped onto the nearest stool and Mainard's mouth fell open.

'Say something,' said Jacob.

She looked to Mainard, who'd suddenly become a haggard old man, grey-faced and shoulders drooping as though the burden he carried was crushing him.

'You have already made this decision?' he said hoarsely.

'Yes. I spent much time with Ali Pasha and he guided me.' Jacob placed his hand on his heart. 'And I know it is the true path.'

Mainard, normally slow to anger, looked suddenly enraged, face flushing and the large vein on his forehead bulging. She rose and touched him lightly on the arm but he ignored her, glaring eyes fixed on Jacob.

'This displeases you,' said Jacob calmly.

'Absolutely not. I am delighted to know that my son,

who committed to his previous faith, who became a bar mitzvah and thus a son of the commandments, can now drop Judaism like a worn-out garment and don something new instead.'

'I am sorry to disappoint, Papa,' Jacob tapped his chest, 'but I feel the Prophet here in my heart and know it's the true and godly path for me.'

He spoke gently, even compassionately, yet there was an underlying steeliness to his tone and Bethia knew he wouldn't yield. Since he was a small child, once Jacob decided what he wanted, he went at it in a most singular fashion and could rarely be redirected.

Mainard turned from his son and left the room, bowed like a weary old man.

'You've broken your father's heart,' said Bethia.

Jacob swallowed. 'It's best I go.'

'Yes,' she said. Then she could not help but smile grimly. 'Give him a few days to recover from this cannonball you've sent rolling among us and then return. A broken heart can mend, especially when it belongs to a father who loves you.'

Mainard, usually so resilient, did indeed seem broken. The next day he went to the palace, where Jacob had resumed his work as a physician, and sought out his son.

'I do not understand,' he said on his return. 'He refuses to discuss it or give me any explanation and just keeps repeating *it is the true and godly path*.'

Bethia, unusually, was sitting without any work before her. She leant back in Papa's chair, smoothing the carved wooden arms and feeling the strength of it beneath her hands.

'How could he, a Jew, become a Moslem?' said Mainard spreading his hands wide.

'You were a Christian who became a Jew.'

'Bethia, that is very different. My parents were forced to convert, forced to baptise me, and all I did was return to the faith of my ancestors. I do not understand how he could worship in the synagogue for all these years and then turn away from a faith he freely entered into.'

Bethia shook her head slowly.

'What?' said Mainard loudly.

'He was baptised and brought up a Christian until you had them circumcised. You talk of his bar mitzvah yet he could just as easily have had his confirmation, where he would also have taken a vow to follow the Commandments.'

'And what does that have to do with him converting to Islam?'

'What did you expect, Mainard, when you brought Familism into our home? Our sons think that faith is something they can discuss and choose.' She let go of the arms of the chair and leant forward. 'Since the moment Will questioned the Catholic Church and espoused Protestantism twenty-five years ago it has felt as though our whole family has been caught in a strong current trying to grasp at rocks and branches to save ourselves as we're hurtled along. And now Jacob, who, outside his work, seemed to care for naught but bedding women, even kept a mistress if the rumours are true, has returned from war cleaving to Islam. God's blood, we have Jews, Catholics and Protestants in this family, why not a Moslem – and perhaps when Eliyah's a man he may become a Hindoo.'

Mainard stared at her then burst out laughing.

Bethia nodded, went to the workroom and wrote a short note which she told Johannes to see was delivered to Jacob with all possible speed. Then she went to oversee the dinner. But Grissel was before her, instructing the new servant in fractured Turkish. At least the lamb on the spit should be acceptable to Jacob, and of course they never ate pork now. All their meat was kosher, which would meet the rules of halal as far as she was aware.

'You'll need to discover what Jacob's dietary

requirements are,' she said to Grissel, 'for he's a Moslem now.'

Grissel's eyes near burst out her head. 'Wheesht! So it's true. May Christ help and save us.'

'I think Jacob will be looking to Mohammed for that.'

Grissel drew her head back, her mouth a narrow line. There was a pile of dry linen brought in from the line lying in a basket and she began to fold it. 'It's a' jist different pathways to God,' she said after a moment, her usual briskness restored. 'Though five times a day on his knees, it's a lot.' She stopped mid fold. 'He willnae hae to get his balls chopped off like they big men in the women's palace?'

'The eunuchs? I think not. If it was a requirement I fear the Moslem people would die out.'

'Aye, I suppose.'

Bethia could feel a smile creeping across her face. She caught Grissel's eye and they giggled.

That evening when the family again came together, all had much to say and questions to ask Jacob of his decision; even Mirella had an opinion. Yet Bethia could see the discussion came from a place of love and was comforted. Her family would endure.

Chapter Forty-Three

A New Sultan

By the time Mirella had given birth to four children in five years, Bethia spoke to Mainard.

'Have you not told our son the way to avoid successive pregnancies? The girl is not much more than twenty and will be worn out before her time.'

Mainard raised his hands. 'I *have* told him how we prevented further children and I've also pointed out to him the costs involved in supplying dowries for his daughters and livings for his sons. He is fortunate indeed Jacob has followed the path he has and I need only support him and Abram.'

'But did you explain it fully?'

'I did, much to our mutual embarrassment, and I've discussed it with him since. It seems he struggles with the way of Onan and is by no means certain it's appropriate within the laws of Judaism. He says that Onan was greedy and selfish.'

'How could it be selfish to spare your wife constant pregnancies when you already have many children? Surely it's selfless?'

'I believe Onan's sin was his refusal to sire a son on behalf of his brother.'

Bethia rolled her eyes. 'I think we're wandering onto dangerous ground here.'

'Well, I don't know what else I can do. As his father I've advised him, but he is a grown man.'

'I'm sure there must be something in Jewish law about obedience to your father,' Bethia muttered.

'I must refer him to it then, before we're completely overrun with children,' Mainard said, nudging her, and she could not help but smile.

After the birth of the fifth child it was Mirella herself who laid down terms. One morning Bethia noticed her son was disgruntled. He appeared in the workroom and wandered over to the window, which he flung wide, setting aflutter the papers Bethia had neatly piled by her side while she calculated the profit from recent purchases for the women of the harem.

She contained the sigh, weighed the papers down with a heavy glass bowl brought from Venice and most beautiful in the richness of its shade of blue colouring, and tucked the most recent letter from Will beneath them. He'd written saying how bereft he was that John Knox had recently died, and now he was without either of his mentors as Calvin was long gone to join his Maker. The letter continued with more happy news of his beloved daughter and it was a joy to read how devoted and proud a father he'd become.

She rose and went to her son. 'What's wrong?'

He shrugged and didn't speak. She'd guessed anyway for Grissel had told how Mirella had left the marital bed and was sleeping amid her children. 'And I dinna blame the lassie one bit,' she'd added.

'Perhaps you should follow Papa's advice in the matter of avoiding further pregnancies,' Bethia said quietly.

Samuel's head shot up and he glared at her. 'Is there nothing he doesn't share with you?'

'Not much, my son.'

'Well I hope he's keeping Jacob equally well informed.'

Jacob had married one of Ali Pasha's daughters, the granddaughter of a sultan, for Ali Pasha's wife had been Suleiman's daughter. Inevitably Don Joseph had created the connection, saying, 'Since your son has chosen to follow the Moslem faith then you may as well make an alliance which could not otherwise come about.' The rabbi had been less phlegmatic, castigating Mainard for allowing Jacob to drift from Judaism so easily in the first place and using the marriage as yet another opportunity to berate him. Mainard listened patiently, accepted the criticism, which he seemed to consider fair by what he repeated of it to Bethia, and then let things take their course.

'The wider our web of connections in Constantinople, the safer we are,' he said.

'We are become like Dona Gracia, our tentacles reaching everywhere,' said Bethia.

'I only wish it were so, but not even Don Joseph is as subtle as she was.'

'He must be as rich by now?'

'Perhaps, but he's only in the ascendancy because of Selim. When the sultan is gone then Joseph Nasi will be lucky to survive with his life, never mind his fortune, intact.'

Bethia swallowed. What would happen to her business as *kira* when Nurbanu was gone? She must find a way to make it secure.

And Jacob seemed content. He'd set up home close to the palace and regularly crossed the Bosphorus to see them, although he avoided Friday night dinner. His wife didn't join him, rarely leaving the confines of their home and then only heavily veiled. Bethia visited and was always welcomed graciously but there was an abyss of life and experience she found difficult to bridge, despite the effort they both made. But, on the years when Lent and Ramadan overlapped, Bethia felt a shared connection with her son and his family, although their path was the harder.

'I dinna ken why ye wouldna eat or drink all day,' said Grissel, and Bethia tried to explain how it was an act of piety undertaken to remember the month on which the Holy Koran was revealed to Mohammed.

'Jacob says it's a time to seek forgiveness for sins, be mindful of God and, in denying yourself, learn how desperate it is to be without sufficient food and water. You become a kinder person as a consequence.'

'Aye weel, each tae his own.'

Bethia went quietly to kneel before the image of the Virgin which decorated the wall of the small chamber off her bedroom. She prayed especially for Geertruyt in faraway Frankfurt. Mainard had recently received news of Schyuder's death. Geertruyt's eldest son Pauwels was already running the business but it would be a bitter blow to lose a most beloved husband and something Bethia could not bear to contemplate.

One day word came that Mainard's sister and her family were coming to Constantinople. 'They're amongst those being resettled in Cyprus,' said Mainard. 'The sultan has determined we need a large presence on the island to make certain it remains within Turkish hands.'

'Does Catarina want to move to Cyprus?'

'I doubt it. They've been settled in Thessaloniki for more than twenty years and have a good business there. But most of the Greek Jews now in Constantinople were once moved here from Salonika by order of a previous sultan. It's not uncommon for sultans to so decide; there's even a special word in Turkish for these forcible moves of people – *sürgün*.'

'Is that why the Greek Jews dislike the Sephardim?' Bethia shuddered, remembering her sojourn in the overcrowded area on the other side of the Golden Horn before Dona Gracia had her plucked out and brought to Galata.

'Neither group seem to care much for the other,' said Mainard sagely. 'The Romaniotes think we are above ourselves, not helped when Dona Gracia was given permission by Suleiman to wear Venetian dress. And why would they be happy they have to don a yellow hat whereas it isn't enforced for us?'

'Dona Gracia was furious when their rabbis withdrew support for the blockade of Ancona. She said they were quick enough to come to her for funds when they wanted help with a soup kitchen or to build a synagogue, but the moment she sought assistance for our people they looked the other way.'

'I'm glad to hear you refer to the Jews of Spain and Portugal as *our* people.'

'You are a Sephardi Jew, my sons are Sephardi Jews – apart from Jacob – and my grandchildren. I may be a Catholic but I've worked as tirelessly as any that we might be established in Constantinople.' She paused; it sounded strange but it was true.

Mainard gazed out the window into the garden where Samuel's children were playing a game which involved much running and screaming. 'If Dona Gracia were still alive we could probably have asked her to intercede on behalf of Catarina's family...' He turned and looked at her. 'I wonder if you might beg assistance from the sultana?'

Bethia stared at him then bent her head and rubbed at the ink stain on the knuckle of her middle finger. 'Nurbanu might be amenable,' she said slowly. 'I must take her a special gift, and then I will ask if she can render Catarina assistance.'

She prepared carefully for the visit. Mirella accompanied her, for Bethia was training her daughter-in-law in the duties of *kira* to the harem – a most sought after role. Mirella was young, which the concubines liked, and had begun teaching them how to embroider – any new pastime to while away the long hours was welcomed.

Nurbanu listened to Bethia's request, head tilted gracefully, then gave a nod and gentle wave of the hand to one of her many subordinates. Bethia knew what Nurbanu commanded, as the sultan's wife, would be enacted.

It was all done with surprising speed and soon they received a letter from Catarina confirming that the order for her family to leave Thessaloniki had been rescinded. *Please give my thanks to Bethia for her intervention*, Catarina wrote, but then followed it up with yet another request, or more correctly demand, for Mainard to fetch Papa's bones from Venice.

It is not right he should be left so far from us in a place where we were not treated kindly. He must be taken to where the Messiah will arise. It's the very least we can do for our beloved Papa and it is Mama's most fervent wish.

'Why don't we do what my aunt requests?' said Abram, who'd overheard Mainard reading the letter aloud. 'It's not so difficult to go to Tiberias.'

Mainard sighed. 'It's not the taking of him to Tiberias but the fetching of his bones from Venice which poses the challenge.'

It was a bitterly cold winter. The mist sat across the Golden Horn for weeks, and each time she had to cross it Bethia held her crucifix tight in her hand convinced she was moving through the spirit world. The cold had resulted in a considerable demand for sable within the harem, which she had sourced through Don Joseph and which he sold to her at such a high price she barely made a profit. Then the Bosporus and Golden Horn froze over and Bethia had never experienced such cold, but the women of the seraglio and especially Nurbanu must not be kept waiting. A terrified Bethia was carried across the ice to the palace on a sedan chair.

The kitchens of Topkapi went up in flames one night and they could see the blaze from Galata: a great yellow-red ball rising high in the sky like the fires of hell reaching for heaven. The destruction was considerable, and passing through the palace a few days later, Bethia could feel the residual heat and see wisps of smoke rising from the blackened remains. And then suddenly Nurbanu was no longer the sultan's wife. She was the *Valide Sultan*, widow of Selim II and mother to his successor, for her grossly fat husband, who his janissaries had called *the ox*, was dead. He'd been in power for only eight years, dying after a drunken fall in his bathing pool.

'Joseph Nasi bears some responsibility for that,' said Bethia.

'Perhaps,' said Mainard. 'But, although Suleiman was abstemious and followed the tenets of Islam faithfully, I believe Selim would've drunk alcohol to excess whether it was supplied by Don Joseph or no.'

It was 1574 and yet some things did not change. Murad III began his reign in traditional fashion by having his five younger brothers strangled.

'It's the Turkish way, to prevent a tussle and civil war,' said Mainard, but he looked as sick as Bethia felt.

'They were only children, one a mere babe in arms,' she whispered. 'It is said the mother killed herself after he was torn away from her.' She curled her fingers, could feel the nails digging into her palms. 'The harem has never felt a safe place but now the fear pulses through it. I wish I'd never taken Mirella there.'

Mainard shook his head slowly. 'It is good Mirella is *kira* to Safiye, especially now Murad has married her... and most especially since Joseph Nasi's star has fallen.'

And indeed Don Joseph had removed to Belvedere with Reyna, where it seemed he would live out the remainder of his days in a small – for a member of the

351

Mendes's dynasty – house. He was fortunate not to have followed the fate of Murad's brothers but had gone quietly and quickly, and that, along with a sizeable gift to Murad's coffers and the support of Nurbanu, had been sufficient to save him.

'I wonder how he'll stand it,' said Abram one night at dinner. 'I fear he'll be bored if he's not conniving at something.'

There'd been laughter among the family, but Jacob came one day saying he'd heard a disquieting tale about Joseph Nasi. 'It's said he's been writing to a man in his employ – the brother of a Jew who returned to Spain and reconverted to Christianity. In the letter Nasi claims he was forced to become a Jew because of *unexpected events in his life*.'

'I don't believe it,' Mainard spluttered.

'My source is convinced it's true and says Nasi is seeking safe conduct for himself, his household and, of course, his possessions to return to Spain.'

'Who's telling you this? It sounds to be a vicious rumour set running to discredit him.'

'I was told in confidence, Papa. I am telling you only because it would be advisable to distance yourself further from Don Joseph.'

Bethia, knowing Jacob had been called as a physician to the Venetian envoy, for she learned more about her son's activities through whispers in the harem than he ever revealed himself, suspected that may have been the source. The Venetians knew everything!

Jacob stared at both of his brothers in turn. 'You mustn't share this with anyone. I know you, especially Samuel, do business with Nasi's agents. Take care, for if the sultan should learn of this, all who are connected with him will be in peril.'

'I'll take care,' said Samuel. He looked to his father. 'We should consider where else we may source wine, in particular.'

Mainard shook his head slowly. 'Not so easy. For all he doesn't have the power he once did, he still has some reach – and managed to retain the monopoly on importing wine.' He looked to Jacob. 'What's he offering the king of Spain?'

'His services. Having been right-hand man to a sultan, he's now seeking a similar role with a king. In return he asks for a pardon for his apostasy, protection from the Inquisition and a pledge that Philip will adjudicate any disputes which may arise from his previous business dealings.'

'We will be careful,' Samuel said.

Joseph Nasi's attempt to return to Spain came to naught, as Mainard commented after they went to sit shiva in his memory, for he survived Selim by only few years. Abram continued a connection with his wife, Reyna, who ran a printing business, and Bethia visited her occasionally, as much in memory of Dona Gracia who she still missed.

'It is sad to see such power so diminished,' said Mainard one day when she was recounting her most recent visit to Reyna. 'The fortune which Dona Gracia and Don Joseph together amassed, once greater than that controlled by many kings, has now slipped away through unpaid debts, bribes, dishonest agents and equally dishonest monarchs. But such is the way of the world.'

Bethia tutted. 'I care naught for Don Joseph's legacy, but Dona Gracia was a good woman and I dislike it that her story is so closely tied with his, for he tarnished it by his actions at the end.'

With which Mainard could not but concur.

Chapter Forty-Four

Papa's Bones

Another bitter winter, and so cold the Golden Horn again froze over. The smoke hung heavy in the still air from countless fires, barely keeping the cold at bay, and which were, as Bethia well knew from her brief sojourn in the crowded Jewish quarters, carelessly tended. Not one but several blazes swept uncontrollably through the city. Mainard and she were amongst many Galatan inhabitants to contribute towards shelter and soup kitchens for those made destitute.

Then finally, thankfully, the piercing cold retreated and the warm sun returned. And Mainard determined Samuel and Abram would go to Venice.

'Samuel barely remembers the city and Abram not all,' he said when Bethia remonstrated. And we need to form new connections, for many of those I once knew have died. Better our sons go than I.'

'But is it safe for them to go now they are Jews?'

'Bethia, many Jews live in Venice, or have you forgot the ghetto?'

She made no more objection, relieved Mainard had no intention of going himself. He'd grown grey and stooped, and often seemed weary.

'Ortelius writes that Henrik Niclaes has died,' he said one

evening as they sat quietly, and, unusually, alone together. 'I'm sad to hear it, but I understand he'd become increasingly odd and antagonised many of his followers.'

'No wonder. From what we heard he'd confused himself with Christ and thought he was God's representative on earth. What is the expression you sometimes use and he was so fond of?

'*Godded with God*, but I don't believe he considered that to be the same as being a reincarnation of Christ.'

'Ortelius is back in Antwerp then?' said Bethia, for she didn't want to set Mainard off on the principles of Familism. The discussions they had regularly over dinner were sufficient.

'Oh yes. He returned a couple of years ago. Surely I told you?'

'You probably did. I find it shocking he ran away and left his sister to deal with the Spanish soldiers.'

'I don't believe he ever expected the attack on Antwerp to unfold in the way it did. The Spanish Fury of 1576 will be long remembered as an act of unparalleled savagery. You know they now say more than eight thousand men, women and children died.'

Bethia shook her head, thinking of their old home in what was once, but no longer, the richest city of the known world. She wondered about their neighbours, who'd scorned them as Marranos. It was a long time ago and she prayed they'd escaped the cruel deaths the Spanish had inflicted; it was said the burnings had gone on for days.

'Ortelius says there's a man in London talking of writing a play about Joseph Nasi. It's to be called *The Jew of Malta*, though Ortelius doubts it'll be a sympathetic celebration of Don Joseph's life – Christians do love to demonise Jews.'

'Why *of Malta*? It should be of Naxos since he was its duke.'

'I don't think Don Joseph was ever in Naxos, or Malta for that matter.'

'The Jew of Venice then, for the Jew of Constantinople is overlong.'

He laughed. Bethia smiled back and then she too was laughing. It felt good.

Mainard's face grew solemn. 'It's strange to think he's no longer with us. Sometimes I miss him.'

'And Mama much more.' Bethia had surprised herself by how bitterly she'd wept when the news came of Mama's death, for it was many years since she'd last seen her, but she'd loved her gentle mother-in-law. She sighed. Mama's passing, peacefully in her sleep, had resulted in renewed calls from Catarina that Papa's bones be retrieved.

Grissel appeared carrying Mirella's youngest, a small, smiling cherub of a babe which had been born despite Samuel's claim he'd been following the way of Onan conscientiously. 'When will yon laddies be back from Venice?'

'Two weeks isn't long enough to sail to Venice, do business and return, Grissel,' said Mainard.

Grissel sighed. 'I dinna ken what ye were thinking to send them so far awa.'

'Grissel!' said Bethia, although she entirely concurred with the sentiment.

Samuel and Abram returned within three months. Bethia felt as though she'd spent the whole time they were gone with her teeth clenched so tight her jaw permanently ached. The relief when they strode through the door, the air of confidence about them palpable, was indescribable.

'My boys,' she said, and reached her arms out to wrap one around each.

'How was the journey?' said Mainard, rubbing his hands together. 'Did you accomplish everything we agreed?'

She watched him: the unnatural joviality, the restlessness. She narrowed her eyes, observing her husband and sons.

'Yes, everything was accomplished,' said Samuel, and Abram nodded like one of the yellow spring flowers in her garden blowing in the wind.

'Papa's bones,' she said slowly.

All three looked to her. Mainard went to place a restraining hand on Abram's arm, but he wasn't quick enough.

'Yes, we got them,' he said, voice full of triumph.

She was aware of her head moving slowly, up and down. 'And what are you going to do with them now?' she asked, although she already guessed the answer.

Mainard didn't respond, and Samuel, giving Abram a warning look, started up a discussion about the beauty of Venice.

Soon Samuel went off to be with his children, who'd been waiting to claim their father, and Abram too departed saying he would visit Jacob and apprise him of their good news. Out of the corner of her eye she could see Mainard give a slight shake of the head at him. As the door closed behind the solid figure of her youngest son, Bethia looked pointedly at Mainard but he wouldn't meet her eyes.

'You are going to send the boys to Tiberias with Papa's remains,' she said.

'I am,' he said, his voice rasping even more than usual.

'Then make it soon. Papa needs a resting place. And thanks be to the Blessed Virgin that finally Catarina's letters can end,' said Bethia, spreading out the new silk come from China which she and her daughter-in-law would take to the Sultanate of Women tomorrow and warily watch the endless dance of power between Nurbanu and Safiye. She glanced up at Mainard to find him looking at her, tenderly. 'It's strange to think I've now lived in Constantinople longer than anywhere.'

'And I suspect liked it the least,' said Mainard.

Bethia paused for a moment as she carefully folded the silk. 'It's not comfortable to be a minority, always apart, always different, a curiosity. And yet to run my own business has afforded great satisfaction.'

'You could also have run your own business if you'd accepted marriage to Gilbert of Clatto and stayed in Scotland.'

Bethia snorted. 'I doubt it. His family would've considered his marriage to the daughter of a merchant a step down enough, without me engaging in trade.'

'So you've thought of it?'

'Of what?'

'Of how your life would've been had you accepted Clatto's offer.'

She inclined her head and looked at him quizzically. 'And have you not considered how much easier your life would've been if you'd married the Conversa your parents had chosen for you? You would've comfortably reverted to Judaism the moment you arrived in Constantinople.'

He smiled. 'Perhaps not *the moment*.'

'You might even have done so in Ancona and been taken as an apostate when that evil Pope did his round-up.'

He enfolded her in his arms, nuzzling against her neck. 'Then it's as well I had the wisdom to marry you,' he whispered.

He came to her a few weeks later saying he wanted to travel with Samuel and Abram to Tiberias.

'But you've already been there.'

'It is right I should accompany Papa to his final resting place.'

She held his arms tight, looking earnestly up into his face. 'Please don't go, Mainard. I have a bad feeling,' she let go of his arms and crossed her hands over her heart, 'here, about this journey.'

'I've done it before, my love. It's nothing.'

The plans were made and the bones to be taken with all reverence to the east as part of fulfilling God's plan for an Israelite by birth to be returned to the land which was the beating heart of his people – regardless that he'd lived virtually his entire life as a New Christian.

Bethia touched her jaw tenderly. It had only just recovered from her sons' last journey. 'I want to come with you,' she said.

But Mainard shook his head. 'Let us go alone, my love. It's for the men of the family to do.' He held her, resting his chin on the top of her head. 'We'll go and return within three weeks, if the winds are favourable.'

She said nothing, for she was swallowing hard, intent on holding back the tears. He let go, touched her face gently, then limped away.

'Mainard,' she called, 'the sooner you leave, the sooner you'll return.' It cost her dear to say it but she was glad she had when he smiled – a warm smile which reached his eyes. However much easier her life might've been if she had stayed in Scotland and married Gilbert Logie, that pulse of love was still there when she looked upon her husband of over thirty-three years.

They were gone for more than the anticipated three weeks but it was only after a month Bethia became agitated. Sleep was always difficult for her to come by, but now it evaded her altogether and she managed only short naps full of spectres and twisted creatures reaching out to take her.

The last night was different, for Mainard came to her in a dream. He didn't speak, only held out his hands, his face serene. She tried to go to him but the way was blocked. She woke up then, dressed and went to sit in Papa's tall chair.

And here it was her sons found her, waiting. All three of them stood before her, for Samuel and Abram had fetched Jacob. Samuel knelt and took her hands but he did not need to speak, for she already knew.

Mainard was gone.

Epilogue

Five years later…

Bethia was a most fortunate woman, she knew. For a widow to be so cherished by her family, to be loved by her children, daughters-in-law and grandchildren, what more could anyone ask – except for the impossible of course – the return of her husband.

And then one day Samuel and Mirella came to speak with her. There was a barely contained excitement about them.

'We've decided to send Eliyah abroad for his studies. There's benefit in having one among the family able to understand more widely the countries we have trade with and to make new connections. We thought to send him to Padua, like Jacob.'

'That sounds to be an excellent plan, and Jacob can prepare him,' said Bethia, wondering why they were coming to her in all this formality to convey such information. And it was odd they would seek her approval, for Samuel was his own man.

Samuel turned to his wife. 'But then Mirella had an idea.'

Bethia waited.

'There are universities in Scotland. We thought he could go there,' said Mirella.

Bethia placed her hands over her heart. 'Yes! And his uncles will welcome him. Oh my dears, yes!'

Samuel and Mirella glanced at one another.

'Mama,' said Samuel, 'would you like to go with him?'

* * *

Glossary

ahint	behind
althegether	altogether
ane	own, as in my own child
awfie	extremely
ay, aywis	always
bairn	a baby, a child
birling	whirling, spinning
blethering, blethers	gossiping, talking nonsense, inconsequential chatter
canny	careful, shrewd
cheeky	insolent, naughty
clout	to hit; also a cloth
dinna	don't
dinna fash yerself	don't worry
dither	to be indecisive
dour	pessimistic, humourless
drookit	soaking wet
fair awa wi' himself	pleased with himself

frae	from, as in away from home
gey	very
gie	give
guid	good
hae	have
heid	head
hirpling	limping, hobbling
ken	know, as in 'you know'
kent	known
ma	my
maun	must
micht	might, also power, force
nae	no
naething	nothing
ony	any
ower	too, over; as in overmuch
paur	poor
sair	sore
telt	told
thrashing	a beating, a whipping

twa	two
wasnie	wasn't
wheen	a lot
wheesht	be quiet
whit	what
wi	with
wid	would
yer	your
yon	that, over there

Please leave a review

If you enjoyed this book please take a moment to share your thoughts in a review. Just a rating and/or a few words are perfect on Amazon, Goodreads or a bookshop website.

Reader reviews help sell more books and keep your favourite authors in business!

You'll find a couple of stories free to download on my website, www.vehmasters.com, which gives more glimpses into the Seton family's life.

I send out a monthly newsletter giving insights into research and my writing with the occasional free gift which I'd be honoured if you subscribed to, again via the website www.vehmasters.com

And if you'd like to read more about The Seton Family, the final book in series will be published in November 2024.

Acknowledgements

I'd like to say a big thank you to my friends and family for their ongoing support and encouragement. And readers and bloggers, thank you for your kind reviews, and especially for inquiring when this next in series would be out... and pre-ordering it too.

Richard Sheehan thanks for the confidence your impeccable editing inspires and Margaret Skea thanks too for your advice on the story arc and plot lines. My wonderful friend Esther Mendelssohn was again an early reader and challenged me to make some very necessary improvements.

To my beta readers humble thanks for their great suggestions – Lynette Johnston, Justin Newland, Zoe Masters, Sue Palmer, Mike Masters – and Sandra Greig who, thankfully, invariably picks up on aspects I've lost track of.

I'd like to very gratefully acknowledge the resources I'm able to access through the National Library of Scotland, including their wonderful maps, and also the help I've received from other national libraries who are invariably tolerant of the inquiries I make – always in English. I've used lots and lots of sources but special mention must go to two wonderful books about the remarkable Dona Gracia Mendes: *The Woman who Defied Kings* by Andree Aelion Brooks and *The Long Journey of Gracia Mendes* by Marianna Birnbaum.

Hugest thanks of all, as ever, go to Mike for all his love, support and help... including doing the cover, images, typesetting and formatting once again.

Historical Note

The history of the era in which The Seton Chronicles is set is so remarkable as to need little embellishment. I write almost to explain to myself how ordinary people of the times survived and made sense of it all. I aim to follow events as faithfully as I can however on occasion there are some wonderful nuggets which require a slight flexing of dates. Pieter Breughel's *Tower of Babel* was indeed used as a vehicle for discussion by the Familists but not until after 1563, when it was painted. I have also inferred Dona Gracia died a few years earlier than she actually did. Christopher Marlowe's play *The Jew of Malta* is thought to have been inspired by Don Joseph Nasi, who became quite notorious throughout Europe, however it wasn't written until 1589 and I mention Marlowe at work on it several years earlier than that.

* * *

Let me know if you do spot any glaring inaccuracies, or want to chat about my books. I love a good blether with readers.

You'll find me at www.vehmasters.com.

The Castilians is Book
One of the Seton
Chronicles

The Conversos is Book
Two of the Seton
Chronicles

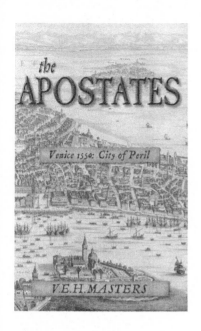

The Apostates is Book
Three of the Seton
Chronicles

Made in the USA
Las Vegas, NV
19 February 2024

85973997R00225